Footprints

Footprints

Edited by
Jay Lake and Eric T. Reynolds

HADLEY
RILLE
BOOKS

Front cover photograph NASA, as17-140-21497, Apollo 17 rover excursion.
Back cover painting copyright © Eric T. Reynolds.
Cover design © Hadley Rille Books.

ISBN-13 978-0-9819243-9-7

Published by
Hadley Rille Books
Attn: Eric T. Reynolds
PO Box 25466
Overland Park, KS 66225
USA
www.hadleyrillebooks.com
contact@hadleyrillebooks.com

to those who paved the way
to those who supported them
and to those who left the footprints

Contents

Introduction

Paleontologists often find fossilized trails or footsteps of creatures long extinct such as those left by dinosaurs and other animals. Hominid footprints have been found, including a remarkable set discovered by Mary Leakey in Laetoli, Tanzania, from over three and a half million years ago, and the recently discovered footprints in Kenya a million and a half years old. We can tell much about the creatures who left them including their gait, weight, how fast they were walking, whether they were upright, and many other characteristics.

When studying those ancient human footprints we have an advantage in formulating hypotheses about the creatures who created them. Being of Earth, we share a significant amount of DNA, and can make certain assumptions.

On July 20, 1969, Neil Armstrong and Buzz Aldrin left the first footprints in soil beyond Earth. If far-future visitors from the stars descend to the Moon long after humanity has vanished, what would they make of the bootprints left by twelve Apollo astronauts? Since the Moon has no atmosphere and very little seismic activity the footprints will be as fresh as the day they were made. Some of the decaying equipment left scattered about might also hold clues to our origins. And several astronauts left a memento or two. But the visitors would have little to go on to get a picture of what humans were like physically, much less our culture and technology, without very careful consideration.

In this anthology we present twenty-one scenarios where far future aliens speculate about the footprints and other evidence left by the astronauts. For some visitors, their discovery figures into their folklore. For others, it's a threat to their core beliefs. But as you will see, just like footprints of Earth, their discoveries can have profound affects on their culture.

Jay Lake
Portland, OR

Eric T. Reynolds
Overland Park, KS

Working the Moon Circuit
by James Van Pelt

The problem with running full reality skin shell rentals is that everyone wants to try the vices. You'd think with so many other ways to get the experience of visiting remote archeological sites that booting into a rental wouldn't hold much attraction, but there are kinds for every kind, as they say, so we keep a stock of fully functioning skin shells. It's supposed to make the experience more "authentic," whatever that means, but the real draw, as I said, is the vice.

As one of the curators, I'm booted into a shell semi-permanently, of course. Hands, face, feet, hair, teeth: the whole package. When I'm not interpreting the data the ancients left behind, I run tours and help customers orient themselves to the new equipment. Bipedal locomotion, for example, takes some time to master, and binocular vision with the eyes on top the organism can also be confusing. Why the feet have to be so far from the sensing organs is beyond me, but that's the way this species worked. No wonder there aren't any of them around any more.

So, I took the first tour of the day down to the observation deck. What I wanted were questions about how the ancients who left their mark on the airless surface traveled, how they achieved so much in metallurgy and physics without the benefit of groupmeld or infinitely researchable infoquarries. What I wanted were questions about their thinking, about their spirits, and if I thought remnants of the dead lingered, but tourists never asked interesting questions. They came to see the remnants and to abuse the skin shells, and then they left. None of them stayed long enough to learn who I was, and I didn't care about them. It's lonely work.

These ancients were first-tier primitives, discovering everything on their own, scrambling out of an impressive gravity well in canisters designed to carry the conditions their unmalleable bodies could tolerate. A truly impressive achievement, and although they have long since disappeared, they

15

left footprints in the dust, and their machines mark the possibilities of persistent sentience.

Instead, the dilettantes spent a desultory hour touching each other, stumbling into walls, mangling the language, and occasionally shrieking just to see how much volume the vocal chords could manage. Hard to believe these were the masters of the universe. One, though, a dark-haired woman who had been coming to the lectures for weeks, hearing the same presentations over and over, stood almost comatose on the edge. As always, she caught my attention with stillness. The first time I saw her, I thought that the port hadn't taken and the body was unoccupied, but she had moved away from a loud man who pulled at his lip, then laughed when it slapped against his teeth.

Ignoring tourist boorishness is easy, though. Except for the dark-haired woman who evidently had decided to be a permanent resident, they come and go. The gallery remains, like the footprints themselves.

I like the set up. In the morning, the perfectly clear floor hangs an inch above the airless surface, exactly duplicating the impressions in the dust, so the customers can study the several million-year old footprints up close. A couple hours later, the observation area is drawn thirty feet up to give a panorama. The ancient landing vessel rests on its four feet, surrounded by the detritus of the expedition. I explain what each piece is for customers who want the full experience of wearing the skin shells. Instead of shooting the info straight into their storage centers, I tell how the main ship they see is just a landing stage, that the primitive explorers detached a second vessel to blast their way back to a meeting with orbiting transport, where the explorers abandoned the second ship to go home.

This took some explaining, and most of the tourists would port the facts later, once they figured out that "listening" to information, and then trying to process the audible signals was an incredibly tedious way to learn anything.

But they wanted the experience. At least that's what they said.

The vices, though, caught most of their attention. Some drugs, for example, altered the shell's perceptions in interesting ways. Eating, for others, entertained them for hours, particularly spicy foods or sweets. Part of my job involved purging the skin shells of the unnecessary calories and then exercising them remotely to maintain muscle tone after the tenants evacuated. And, naturally, most of the tourists grew interested in sexual possibilities. Since I had been wearing my skin shell for several years, and had become comfortable in it, tourists often approached me for help.

One of the women shells caught me after the morning tour, a red-haired model, a bit shorter than me. I had, while becoming acquainted with my skin shell in the first months, experimented with its sexual possibilities quite often. This red-haired one hadn't been a favorite. They all feel slightly different, although, who is animating the skin is more interesting than the skin itself. As stimulating as sex in these shells can be, the personality interaction makes the encounter.

Red Hair said, "I'm only here for a few days, and the rest of my tour group is clumsy in this form, but I hear that procreation activities can be quite pleasant if you're with someone who knows what they are doing. I have an hour before the next presentation. Would you mind helping?"

See what I mean?

I begged off without explaining to her that if she wanted real authenticity in her skin shell that she should wear the clothes we provided instead of running around the center naked.

After I'd given the second tour of the day, the overview, where I talked to the group about human explorations, and the short, sad history of their species, I went to the observation deck alone. All we had for information about the old explorers came from their space probes and the scattering of landing sites we'd found on what had been their home planet's moon, but we were able to extract quite a bit about them, including their genetic information which we used to create the shells. Of course, it helped that they were aware enough of space's preserving qualities to include information about themselves in their probes, but we also could deduce quite a bit by their tracks. They're eagerness to send records about themselves into the unknown puzzled me for a long time. No other long-dead species whose remnants litter the surface of airless orbs attached plaques or audio records or visual images of themselves. It's almost as if they knew they couldn't last. The urgency that pushed them to explore also cut them short. Their energy turned in, turned on them, ending their brief history before it properly started.

The supporting frame for the center gave us flexibility. Two beautiful arches crossed above the landing site from which the viewing deck dangled, allowing me to position the observatory wherever I liked. I moved to the spot directly over the landing craft. With the sun near the horizon, the ancient mess of footprints around the craft stood in sharp relief. Every part of their expedition was written in the dust. We had reconstructed their entire stay: which footprints were first, which explorer made each print,

17

where they went and what they uncovered. They didn't wander far and they missed more than they found. Evidently they hoped to discover water on their moon, but they went around one of the many craters with ice at the bottom. From where I stood, I could see a line of tracks that bypassed the site. They wondered if they were alone in the universe, but, improbably enough, they just missed finding a mining facility that a much older space-faring species had left, invisible from above, but obvious from the surface. The ridge that hid the evidence from them cast its long shadow almost to the lander's feet.

A voice startled me.

"Do you think," said the dark-haired tourist who I thought was inanimate earlier, "that their civilization was doomed because they lived on a double planet?" I hadn't heard her come into the room. She had never spoken before.

Like many of the tourists, she didn't wear shoes. Many of them *say* they want an authentic experience, but they won't play the part. Her hands were clasped behind her back as she studied the lander below. "I mean, what other species grew up with a monstrosity of a moon like this in their sky? Do you think they felt how it tugged them around?"

She didn't look at me as she waited for an answer.

"They wouldn't sense the gravity. It would just be a part of what they knew." I wondered why she had been silent for so long and why she decided to speak now.

"But it would be huge in their sky. Look at the planet itself." She glanced up. The home world, its features obscured by the opaque atmosphere, half in the sun and half dark, hovered above. "When they lived on the surface, the air was clear, you said. Wouldn't they see the moon? Wouldn't they fear that it would crush them?"

"The moon wouldn't be as large to them as the planet is to us, but it's true they would see it. Maybe having a goal so visible drew them into space. It might have caused them to develop technologies before they could handle them."

She let her gaze wander across the landscape. As I said, the personality behind the shell was more interesting than the shell. Whoever animated this one had layers. "I would be afraid. As I slept, I would feel the moon, bigger than anything in the night. It would be bright, wouldn't it, like another sun?"

"Maybe, I don't know. I haven't seen the moon from a distance."

She sat on the floor so that she could see the landing site between her spread legs, a surprisingly graceful move for a tourist, but then I remembered she'd had weeks more practice than the rest of them. In fact, after me, she would be the most experienced person at the observatory in her skin shell. She pressed her hands against the smooth surface. "Were they a species that made myths? Did they have explanations for their moon, before they began exploring space, I mean? Many species worshipped their sun when they were young. Maybe they worshipped their sun *and* their moon, or maybe some of them believed in the god of one but not the other. There could have been wars. What if they came to the moon because they hoped to find a god, and when they didn't they had no reason to live?"

I wanted suddenly to sit beside her. My normal presentation didn't cover this material. They were the questions I thought about. "We know some about them, but not what you are asking. The artifacts don't tell us everything."

Two more tourists came into the room, two of the male shells. One held the other's arm. "We were experimenting with durability," said the first, supporting the weight of the other's arm in his hands.

"The digits break," said the second. "And they hurt! It still hurts! Must be a flaw in the design. If the system is damaged, you should get the signal and then be able to turn it off. I'm very uncomfortable!"

"He's never had an endoskeleton. I told him the little things could snap, but he put them in the door anyway," said the first one apologetically.

Two of the man's fingers were bent backwards unnaturally. The knuckles were swollen and purple.

I thought that I was lucky he hadn't destroyed the shell entirely. On the last tour, a tourist entered an airlock without protection and opened it. When I talked to the angry guest remotely an hour later to explain that he'd lost his damage deposit, he complained that he shouldn't be responsible for a unit too fragile for a change in environmental conditions. He also complained about the pain. "I was so distracted that I almost stayed with it until it expired. I'll have to have the experience wiped. Very traumatic," he said bitterly.

I said to the man with the broken fingers, "We can load you into an undamaged shell."

"Good," he said. "I'm going to try the other gender. I understand the experience is different."

They left, headed for the decanter center where he would transfer his consciousness to an empty shell.

The woman on the floor laughed, an utterance tourists didn't handle well. "I talked to him earlier. He was mad because they wouldn't rent him two shells at the same time so he could have sex with himself. I'll bet he didn't break his fingers in a door."

I shook my head, a gesture I'd seen in one of the historical records. I realized she wouldn't know what it meant. "What a waste. You'd think he could get whatever weird simulated interactions with himself he wanted, without renting real shells."

She leaned forward, almost folding herself in half on the floor. "I can always tell when it's a simulation."

Thirty feet below, every pebble cast a long shadow. Shadows filled the footprints too, shallow as they were. She was right. If this were a simulation, I'd feel the falseness of the information. My senses would bump against the experience. Tech folks called it "perceptional dissonance," the distance between what the simulation is feeding to your consciousness and what your sensory organs are not telling you. Most beings don't notice the dissonance, or they don't care, but, for purists, the real experience is worth the tiny improvement.

"I was here yesterday, before the tour." She pressed the side of her face against the floor. It would be cool and smooth. "I thought I saw something move next to the lander. That's why I decided to talk to you."

My skin prickled, a reaction I'd never felt in this body. "What do you mean?"

"I thought I saw someone in a space suit. Its head was encased. The image only lasted a second." She sat up, then stood, running her hands up and down her arms. "These shells send so much information. When I touch myself, why do I feel it both with my hand and my skin? It's redundant. I took a shower my first day; I thought I would fall unconscious with the overload. There were so many sensations, touch, taste, feel, sound, sight. How could these creatures think with their bodies signaling them about everything?"

I'd forgotten what my training days in the shell had been like. Most of the tourists reveled in the sensations, not that these bodies were the most sensitive in the universe. Few rivaled them though.

"Sleep scares me," she said, "even when I'm tired. In sleep, the shell sends me signals. Strange images. Emotions."

"Dreams."

"I know. The orientation mentioned them, but experiencing them is different."

I wondered if it was possible that she was new to body porting. Veteran tourists didn't comment on this level of being in the shells, and veterans wouldn't stay in the same shell for an extended period. Other shells provided as many or more variations, although none of them combined them like these did. "If you go back to your room, I can send you a drug that will tone down the sensory system. You can build to full engagement gradually."

"No, I'm getting used to it. I do think I'll go to my room to rest, though. Turning down the light and shutting away sounds helps. They even have a sense of smell! What a vivid world these creatures lived in."

I nodded. Most tourists noticed the shell's limitations. No overmeld capabilities. No tie to universal data. Faulty memory. Odd mental connectivity issues that sometimes strung thoughts together in a peculiar fashion. Physiologically induced emotions. Dreams.

"I have more questions, if you have a moment." She looked at me for the first time. "But I'm tired. Could you come to my room?"

Normally I would say no. This could be another blatant foray into sex. I surprised myself. "Yes, if I have time."

When she left, I moved the observatory back to the surface level. The floor reshaped itself to take on the terrain's contours, wrapping around the artifacts so they could be inspected up close without actually touching them. I knelt at the lander's feet to reexamine the ancient explorers' markings on the ground. Nothing had changed. Whatever the dark-haired woman had seen was in her imagination, but I'd seen movement too on the airless surface once, from the corner of my eye, when I glanced away, the flag that stood next to the lander shifted as if a hand was placing it there. The impression was so strong that I checked the playback. I saw my own reaction to the movement—I flinched—but the flag hadn't moved. Another time I saw a figure.

Some of the information they'd included on their probes mentioned religion. Clearly they believed in an afterlife. As desperately as they flung their machines into the sky (the period where they could escape their planet was vanishingly short), I wondered if they were trying to reach their heaven. Maybe the dark-haired tourist was right about them.

I stood nearly on the dust, in an alien shell, surrounded by warm and nourishing air on the surface of an airless moon. Every seam, every curve in the metal, each crease in the crumpled foil they used to protect the vessel stood in sharp detail in the setting sun. I put my hand on the form-fitting floor that wrapped the lander, only an inch from the actual artifact. What had these beings hoped to find so far from home? Had they been satisfied to reach this inhospitable place?

I put my foot over one of the creased impressions left in the dust, and then stepped into each print for twenty paces so that I retraced the path one explorer took so long ago.

Nothing appeared. No suited figure. I remember the one I saw, its features hidden behind a metallic sheen of faceplate. It had hopped and skipped from the lander to a small solar array, and then vanished. Like the apparition the dark-haired woman had seen, it left no tracks. It might have retraced old footsteps too, as I just did.

A leg that supported our resort stood in the distance, cutting a shadow across the sun. Above me, the bulk of the guest rooms and the rest of the facility blocked the starry sky.

Without making a decision, I found myself at the dark-haired woman's room. She didn't speak when she let me in.

"You said you had questions." I sat on the edge of her bed. The room had no other furniture. Part of a loaf of bread rested on the shelf by the door. We had no idea what the ancients' food actually tasted like, but we had pictures, descriptions and a good sense of what the shells needed to maintain strength and health. All part of the experience.

She sat next to me. Most tourists don't wash the shells often enough, and their bodies take on a stench. She smelled of the shower's cleansing solutions. "Have you done this long?"

"Here?" I said. "Several years. The research is interesting."

"And none of them are left? They never escaped this sun?"

"There's no evidence they did. Their planet is tectonically active. All remnants of them and what happened to them has long since been buried. The atmosphere isn't even the same."

She turned to me, put her fingers on my arm and squeezed. "They did so much with so little."

I shrugged, another gesture she wouldn't understand. "Species come and go. For all I know, the species of my original shell is gone too."

"You're very old, aren't you?"

It was an unexpected question, but how she said it revealed her. "You're not," I stated.

"I'm a reconstitute. Who I was broke down—the data corrupted--they said. Sometimes it happens, and out of what was left they made me."

"How long ago?"

"Twenty years, conscious. There have been several rebuild sessions over time, and they stored me for a while."

"I've never met someone who was young."

"There's a lot to see." I realized she meant there was a lot *for her* to see, not that there was a lot to see of her.

She turned her back to me. "My skin is irritated. Can you scratch it?" She pulled her shirt off. "Be gentle. It's all too intense."

I brushed my fingernails lightly over her back at the shoulder blades.

"Lower, please."

When I hit the spot she tensed and made a non-speaking sound.

"Is that better?"

"Yes, but please don't stop."

I traced circles and zig zags on her skin from the tops of her shoulders to her lower back, redoing the patterns again and again, gradually increasing the pressure. Soon her skin reddened, and I switched from scratching to kneading the muscles.

"That's good. Can we switch places?"

I nodded. "Yes." Was she interested in trying the sexual possibilities after all? If so, I had never seen this slower approach. The idea didn't seem as repellent as it had earlier. I couldn't tell if my change of attitude was mine or the shell's, whose physical response showed her attentions had provoked it.

"Can you take your shirt off too?"

She mimicked the actions I'd done to her, barely touching my skin as she circled my shoulder blades or paralleled my backbone from neck to waist. I'd ignored the shell's possibilities for a long time. It's true that you can get used to anything, but as I sat on her bed, no longer thinking about shepherding tourists or the difficulties of putting together a coherent story about an eons-dead civilization, I became aware again of the shell's sensory powers. Beside her clean scent, I smelled the bread on the shelf, and the slight chemical tinge that was in the observatory's air, always. The pervasive but dim light emanating from the walls killed shadows, a welcome change from the starkness of the light on the moon's surface. My hands rested on

23

my thighs in the soft light. I thought about the oddness of my fingers' design, but also the cleverness of how they could manipulate tools, their adaptability. And I could hear her breathing, and the sound she made when she shifted behind me, even the whisper her fingernails made against my skin.

Mostly I felt.

I've had sex in these shells, and there's much to recommend the experience, but the action is short, short compared to what the dark-haired woman was doing to my back. She leaned forward, placed her forearms on me, rubbing the skin with her skin, pressing against the muscles, sending signals to me of movement, friction, pressure and warmth.

I made a sound like the one she'd made earlier. For the moment, my universe closed to become focused and small.

The ancients truly were primitives to have so many senses tuned so high. Their lives must have been dangerous and brutal. Why have sensitive spots on their backs, which they would never feel something with, unless they were constantly expecting danger? But if the sense of touch everywhere was to preserve them, why did being touched there feel so good?

I moaned again.

"I can't groupmeld," she said. Her hands stopped.

"How is that possible?"

"Limitations in the adaptability of my reconstruct, evidently. I don't miss it, really. I've never known what it is like." She scratched the small of my back with short, gentle motions. "I thought you might like to know in case you wanted to find me there."

Her touch floated from spot to spot. My entire back tingled from her ministrations. I said, "I haven't done a groupmeld for a long time, but it's a comfort to know I can when I'm ready," which wasn't true. I hadn't integrated my consciousness with the infoquarry since I'd taken over this skin shell, and I didn't want to. It was the tourists, I think, mistreating the shells, ignoring the import of the artifacts, bumping against anything that would bump back while they were here. They could be in the groupmeld too, adding or taking what they wanted from everyone else. Plus, a groupmeld disoriented me, made me lose a bit of self, at least for a while. Many of the friends I'd had long ago went in and never came out, joining the overmind. The last time I'd melded, I'd sensed for an instant a friend's familiar thought, like a ghost, but it flittered away, and I couldn't find it again.

She said, "Sometimes when I get to know someone, they ask to meet me in the groupmeld. I just wanted you to know I couldn't. I only know what I know, and nothing else, and you can never know me."

I thought about the lander sitting on the lunar surface and the tracks around it. The ancients left evidence, but I could not talk to them. Being in their bodies wasn't the same as the groupmeld. I'd never know them either.

She kissed my back, her breath hot and moist. "The skin has a taste," she said.

I stood. "There are other visitors I should attend to. Will you be at the afternoon session? We'll do a discussion of the ethics of archeological tourism."

"I know. I've heard it before. Can you come back later?" She sat on the bed with her legs crossed, her shirt on the floor, her face turned toward me, a visual echo of the extinct who'd been here before.

"I have many duties."

Back on the observation deck, the changeless tableau waited. Since the moon revolved very slowly in relation to the sun, the shadows were nearly the same as when I'd left. I accessed the recordings from the last couple of days, examining them closely for the dark-haired woman. She had come to the deck alone yesterday. The image of her walking slowly to the center of the room captured her grace. Truly, she moved like she'd been born in the shell and not recently taken it on. She stopped, dropped to her knees, stared at the lander as if she'd seen something surprising then shook her head and rubbed her eyes. The recording captured nothing on the Moon's surface, though. The moon and abandoned equipment were the same as they had been for millions of years. Either her apparition was imagination, or it couldn't be recorded with our instruments.

She didn't come to the late presentation. The tourists listened as well as any group of them ever did, which meant barely at all. A few in the front of the group looked attentive, but the rest giggled and coughed and touched themselves during my chat. I suppose if they extended their stay, the skin shell's novelty would wear off. The red-head who had propositioned me earlier was there, wearing clothes this time, but the pants were on backwards and unzipped. A woman next to her kept mumbling in her ear while I talked, and I realized it was the body we'd given the tourist who'd broken his fingers.

The deck was close to the ground again, so the lander stood taller than my head, as did the flag. I liked this time of day best, when the observatory didn't cast a shadow on the artifacts. The group stood to the side so we didn't put our shadows on the lander either.

"We have catalogued the numerous sites for your perusal, including site 423 with the dead explorers in the capsule. If you have signed up for the transport option, a shuttle will take you physically to our observatory there, or you may prefer to transfer directly into their flesh units. I suggest you take the real-time journey, though. We have replicated several of their vessels to give you a more authentic recreation of their technology. You will pass over numerous interesting and historical points on the way."

As I talked, the dark-haired girl joined the group. At the same time, a figure moved in the background, beyond the observatory's confines. Startled, I kept the presentation going. I'd spoken it so many times before that the speech required no attention on my part.

A bulky figure shuffled toward one of the experiments, kicking up dust that sprayed straight away from its feet and fell in perfect parabolas. The equipment on its back made it top heavy, and looked as if it might tip it over at any point. The suit was white with dark gloves. Tubes dangled from the front, feeding into the huge pack on its back, and on its shoulder was a patch that matched the pattern of the flag by the lander.

The dark-haired woman followed my gaze so that she saw the apparition too. Two of the tourists looked behind them, and then chatted with each other. They had seen nothing. Only the dark-haired woman and myself could see the vision.

"It's just litter," said the red-haired woman. The woman next to her, who had now wrapped her arm around her waist, said, "They were children, weren't they? They never escaped their sun. Their consciousnesses were shipwrecked within them."

The space suited figure straightened from its task and gazed at the planet overhead. I tried to imagine what their home looked like when the atmosphere was clear and they could see all the way to the surface. There must have been visible bodies of water. Analysis indicated over half the planet may have been covered, and there could have been water vapor clouds too. What did it look like when their sun caught the water and reflected back like a jewel on fire?

For the longest time, the figure in the space suit looked up without moving, and then it vanished. The dark-haired woman was crying. Although the ancient records mentioned physical manifestations of emotions, I'd never seen a skin shell cry.

"We're having a going away party in the cafeteria," said the red-haired woman. "The shells are alcohol sensitive."

I waited until the tourists had left. The dark-haired woman stayed behind too.

She came close to where I stood, next to the lander. "Do you think we made the skin shells so well that we can see the spirits of their dead? Are we seeing ghosts?"

"I don't know. Maybe. They were a strange people who started a long trip they couldn't finish."

From my point of view, I could see most of the footprints they'd left, the scattering of equipment and tools, the lone flag duplicating the patch on the suited figure's arm, but beyond the jumble of marks in the dust, the Moon's surface was trackless. They'd only begun. They didn't have groupmeld or the infoquarry. They couldn't know any experience other than their own, each one of them, alone in themselves, working together to get so far.

The Moon's gray surface was sobering and hopeful. Much could be accomplished by the isolated working together.

"How long will you stay?" I asked.

"If you don't mind, a long time, I think."

I took a deep breath. Even breathing produced sensations in the ancients' shape. "I don't mind."

"I have to decide what to do with my life."

Her voice sounded like it had come to belong to her. Unlike the tourists, she wasn't borrowing it anymore. She was becoming herself in this shell, and I would never know more about her than she could share through the imperfections of speech and the limited (but intense!) senses of the skin shells.

And that seemed enough.

Snowball
by Alastair Mayer

The exploration ship *LifeSeeker* came out of warp again just inside the inner edge of the Oort Cloud. It paused a while, scanning, then made a few short warp jumps in different directions, extending the standard scan to locate planets by their parallax. The crew noted a bright planet within the star's habitable zone—the distance at which water could, though perhaps not would, exist in liquid form—and jumped *LifeSeeker* as close to it as they dared before continuing in under normalspace thrusters.

"Leader," the Astronomer caught the captain's attention, "this planet has a large moon, but the planet itself is ice-covered. I don't think this could be the origin." He referred to the robotic probe they'd discovered drifting away from this star, inactive but still thermally bright against the cosmic background.

Leader's brow crest flattened in consternation as he considered this. Not the origin? He hated coincidences. "From analysis of cosmic ray damage, you said the probe hadn't been adrift in interstellar space long enough to have come from any other system."

"Yes, Leader. And it was only four percent of the distance to the next nearest star, which is in a very different direction." Astronomer paused. It was unlikely, but—"Perhaps another starfaring race left it?"

"We haven't found any other starfarers yet, or even seen signs. The technology is too primitive, too." Leader made his decision. "Plot course for their moon, and begin an orbital survey on arrival." They could check out the planet itself later; the moon would be easier. Any species who could send a robot out of its solar system could put robots on their moon.

They had indeed. The orbital scans turned up many probable landing or impact sites, locations on the surface showing refined metals and radial dust patterns of low-velocity impact. A hand's worth showed unusual radiation signatures.

"Summary report?" the captain asked the assembled group of science department heads.

"Telescopic analysis shows six sites with structures significantly larger than at any of the others, five of these have nuclear sources in close proximity, all of them have outlying smaller structures or equipment. They are all on the side of the moon facing the planet."

"Interesting. Structures?"

"Octagonal platforms apparently supported on four legs, approxmately three bodylengths wide. We located a number of smaller, three-legged structures, one of them near an octagon. We also found several other structures, metal debris from impacts, and possible wheeled vehicles or robots."

"Any signs of activity or possible hazard?"

"None we could detect. No electromagnetic or gravitic emissions beyond normal background, except for the radiation sources noted earlier, and they are low level."

"Very well. Where is the octagonal platform that is near a three-legged structure?"

Cartographer brought up a hologram of the moon, made a gesture that caused a number of points on the surface to light in a variety of colors, and pointed to a close pair of lights near the equator, some distance south of a pronounced crater with bright rays. "Here, Leader."

"Ah, nearly at the closest point to the planet. Excellent. We'll land there and deploy survey teams to the other sites. I also want a preliminary survey of the planet. Have a science team take the longboat to do an orbital survey."

"Yes, sir. Will they land?"

"Depending on what the survey shows, yes. But no landings without further discussion, and they must stay alert for any signs of activity, organic or robotic."

November 19, 1969 -- Apollo 12 Lunar Module Intrepid, *descending toward the lunar surface.*

Pete Conrad focused on flying the LM; they were now just four hundred feet above the surface. He'd taken manual control at seven hundred and quickly killed most of their descent speed. He wanted to get close to Surveyor Crater and look around some before kicking up dust. He thought his ground track was a bit too far south. "I've got to get over to the right."

At his side, Alan Bean watched the instruments. "You're at 330 feet, coming down at four feet per second."

"Yeah." He adjusted the controls. This wasn't quite like flying a helicopter; the lower gravity meant the engine didn't use much thrust to balance their weight, which meant he had to tilt the spacecraft a lot more to get the same effective sideways or back-and-forth thrust from it.

"You've got eleven percent fuel. Loads of gas, 300 feet, coming down at five."

"Check."

Bean glanced away from the instruments, looking out the window. "Oh! Look at that crater; right where it's supposed to be! Hey, you're beautiful."

Conrad spared a glance in that direction. That bright object near the rim of the crater, was that Surveyor? But he was still too far north and east.

Bean checked the instruments again. "Ten percent fuel. 257 feet, coming down at five; 240 coming down at five." The LM tilted again as Conrad adjusted course. "Hey, you're really maneuvering around."

"Yeah." He killed the rate of descent, keeping the craft pitched over to reduce their horizontal speed: he didn't want to overshoot the landing area. There was a spot, between Surveyor Crater and Head Crater. He needed to angle over to it.

"Come on down, Pete."

"Okay."

"Ten percent fuel. 200 feet; coming down at three. You need to come on down." Bean sounded a little nervous, like a passenger trying to press an imaginary brake pedal in a car.

"Okay." Conrad straightened the LM, descending again toward the spot he'd picked out. To the left he could now clearly make out Surveyor III sitting on the gentle slope of the crater where it had landed two-and-a-half years earlier. He focused on the landing; they were getting close.

Bean was intent on the instruments. "190 feet. Come on down. 180 feet; nine percent fuel. You're looking good. Going to get some dust before long." In fact Conrad could already see some. "130 feet; 124 feet, Pete. 120 feet, coming down at six. You got nine percent," the number flipped over, "eight percent. You're looking okay. Ninety-six feet, coming down at six feet per second. Slow down the descent rate!"

Conrad goosed the control, the exhaust kicked up more surface dust.

"Eighty feet. Eighty feet, coming down at four. You're looking good.

Seventy feet; looking real good. Sixty-three feet. Sixty feet, coming down at three."

The dust grew thicker outside Conrad's window. The films of Neil's landing, *Apollo 11*, hadn't shown it this bad.

"Fifty feet, coming down; watch for the dust." Bean focused on the displays, not the view out the window. He hadn't seen the dust yet.

"Yeah." Conrad's answer had a wry note.

"Forty-six feet."

A voice from Ground Control came over the radio. "Low level." That was a fuel warning. Both astronauts glanced at the annunciator panel, the "DES QTY", descent quantity, lamp was lit. Less than two minutes of fuel left.

"Okay." Bean started a countdown clock. At twenty seconds of fuel left, they'd have to make the decision to either land or abort, jettisoning the descent stage and rocketing back to orbit. He looked back at the display. "Forty-two feet, coming down at two. Forty, coming down at two. Looking good; watch the dust."

Out the window, Conrad could no longer see the horizon nor indeed much of the ground, so much dust sprayed out from under the LM. He looked over at the "eight-ball," leveling the spacecraft. But now he couldn't tell if he was drifting sideways or backwards—if he landed with too much horizontal speed, the landing gear could buckle. Even if the LM didn't crash, a bad angle would make it impossible to launch back to orbit. He looked out the window again, managing to see some rocks through the dust that let him judge his speed. He looked back at the eight-ball again to level the ship.

"Thirty-two, thirty-one, thirty feet. Coming down at two, Pete; you got plenty of gas, plenty of gas, babe. Hang in there."

The voice from Houston came again. "Thirty seconds remaining."

"Eighteen feet, coming down at two. He's got it made! Come on in there."

From the side and rear landing legs thin metal probes projected down a few feet below the pads. They touched the surface, buckled. On the LM's instrument panel, a blue, circular light lit up.

Bean saw it immediately. "Contact Light!"

Conrad cut the descent engine, and the *Intrepid* dropped the last few feet to the surface.

*   *   *

LifeSeeker, near Surveyor Crater

The *LifeSeeker* was the third spacecraft to land at that spot in the Ocean of Storms. The octagonal platform stood stark near the edge of a gently sloping crater, on whose slope a smaller spacecraft sat on three splayed legs. The *LifeSeeker* survey crew kept a respectful distance, not wishing to disturb the footprints that encircled the octagon and led to the tripod and beyond. A technician suited up and took a gravsled over the site, pausing to take detailed images and scans of the platform, the scattered equipment, and what seemed to be scientific instrument packages, cabled together and in turn connected to a dish antenna pointed up at the planet overhead. The radiation they'd detected came from one of the packages in the instrument cluster, a vertical cylinder with fins radiating from it. A power source.

"Retrieve the power unit; perhaps we can determine the age from the isotopes," the captain directed. The instruments were long dead. It wouldn't matter.

Other survey teams spread out over the moon in their scoutboats. They found similar instrument packages and dish antennae at five of the sites; a sixth had a simpler experiment suite. Near three of the former they found wheeled vehicles with footprints leading to and from, and wheel tracks leading away in several directions. They followed the tracks and found areas where footprints reappeared, where the surface had been disturbed.

"They must have used the vehicles to cover more distance, then stopped to make detailed studies. Exploring or prospecting." One of the Scouts reported back.

At two other places on the moon they found another kind of wheeled vehicle, apparently entirely robotic, and traced the tracks of each back to landing vehicles.

In many places they found debris, scraps of metal and plastic film and fiber and circuits, smashed and scattered when the original craft had hit the surface. They sampled them for later analysis.

LifeSeeker's Longboat, near the planet

The scout team orbited an almost featureless world. In their careful approach to the planet they'd noted several artificial satellites, some in an equatorial orbit nearly synchronous with the planet's rotation, others in lower, highly inclined orbits. Nobody would deploy so many and such varied satellites around the snowball below them. But they detected no other signs of intelligent life; the satellites' power and maneuvering systems were long dead; the planet's surface almost covered in glaciers. Near the equator there were stretches of open water, and elsewhere in the ice large cracks had repeatedly formed and refrozen. Perhaps an ocean beneath.

"How could intelligent life develop on such a frozen world?" Pilot said.

"Maybe it froze later," Planetologist replied. "This planet is near the outer edge of its sun's habitable zone, near freezing on average. If the sun's output dropped slightly, or the concentration of greenhouse gases fell off too much, or if heavy clouds or dust high in the atmosphere blocked the sunlight, that might tilt the balance."

Climatologist picked up the explanation. "Once the ice covered enough of the planet, the albedo would be so high, it would reflect so much sunlight back into space as to cause a runaway feedback cycle and the planet would freeze over. It happened on our homeworld a billion years ago."

"How did it ever thaw out?"

"Our sun warmed as it aged, volcanic activity increased greenhouse gases in the atmosphere, microorganisms on the surface of the ice reduced reflectivity."

"Could that happen here?"

"Possibly. It depends what caused it, what the long term activity of this sun is like, how much tectonic activity there is. Let's ask for permission to land and see what we can determine from ice cores and penetrating radar."

LifeSeeker, near Surveyor Crater

"Physics team, do you have an analysis of the radioactive fuel yet?"

"Partially, Leader. It is primarily uranium-234 oxide, with a significant fraction of plutonium-238 and a scattering of other isotopes, probably decay products. But of more significance is the plutonium. The 238 isotope has a relatively short half-life, about ninety-five years—eighty-eight revolutions of this planet around its sun—and it emits helium nuclei."

"So a useful isotope for a crude power source, then."

"Yes, the generator assembly contained thermocouples, for turning the heat of decay into electricity. There were similar designs on the probe we found outside this system. But there's something else. The half life, and the fact that we detected so much plutonium with the uranium, means this couldn't be very old, no more than a few millennia, possibly less. I'll have a more definite number when we've finished the quantitative analysis."

Leader's brow crest bristled in mild surprise. Such a short time? "Get me the number; it might help us figure out what happened."

* * *

LifeSeeker's longboat, orbiting the planet

The planetary survey team had part of the answer. The first hints had come from a close examination of some of the orbiting satellites.

"This is odd—look at the density of microcraters on the surface of this one," Planetologist said.

"It's probably been up here a long time." Pilot said.

"No, it doesn't correlate with the cosmic ray exposure. It's almost like it ran into a cloud of something."

"That could happen, debris from another satellite perhaps, exploded or hit by a meteoroid."

"I'm going to do a trace element analysis on this surface, see if I can determine what hit it, or what it hit."

"It didn't hit satellite debris" Planetologist announced definitively.

"What's your data?" asked Climatologist.

"I'm finding traces of silicates, carbonates, and even chlorides, not what you'd expect from another satellite."

"Salt?"

"Yes, and the silicates and carbonates could be from sea bottom mud. I think a large impactor, an asteroid or comet, must have hit this planet's ocean. The blast would have kicked up the sea floor, the salt would be left when the water boiled away."

"And this satellite flew through the cloud?" asked Pilot.

"I don't have a better explanation."

Pilot just wiggled his brow crest, a shrug.

"I'd like to see what we find with our core sampling and deep radar," said Climatologist.

"The density of this planet is high enough that the oceans can't be very deep, just a skin on the surface. Even a modest asteroid or small comet could hit bottom."

LifeSeeker, near Surveyor Crater

The octagonal platforms and the surrounding areas proved the most interesting. All had numerous and overlapping impressions in the dust, oval with several ridges through them. At each octagon, near the base of the ladder-like leg, they found curious, stiff fabric bags, L-shaped, with a hard surface along the bottom of each. The shape and ridges of this surface matched the impressions in the dust.

"If these were monuments, I'd say these bags were some kind of offering," said the Studier of Ancient Peoples. "The numerical significance is interesting."

"How?" asked the Engineer, who had been examining one of the instruments they'd recovered.

"The platforms have eight sides. We found four of these objects at each site, and two of the large rectangular boxes. Two, four, eight. See the progression?"

"And the wheeled vehicles: four wheels, two fabric platforms," said another.

Engineer's brow crest flattened. "Most of our wheeled vehicles have four wheels, it's a convenient number by the laws of physics, not numerology. And many have two seats, for a driver and observer or navigator."

"And the octagons?"

"Again, a convenient shape. Four legs for a landing craft makes sense, better load distribution than three, lighter than five. At this level of technology"—chemical propulsion—"weight would be critical."

"The four baskets?"

"Not baskets, bags. Footbags—they left footprints!"

"But why leave the footbags?"

"I can think of two good reasons," said Engineer. "They are incredibly dusty, they wouldn't want to bring that inside their ascent vehicle." Analysis of the blasted upper surfaces of the octagons had made it apparent that an upper component had rocketed itself away, presumably returning the visitors home. "And again, the weight. The large box structures, and other debris we found scattered around the base, all probably excess weight jettisoned before launch."

"What do you suppose they looked like?"

"No way of knowing for sure. Probably bipedal, if those were footbags, two explorers per lander, given two seats in the vehicle."

"The footprints look consistent with two legs, and there are no tail drag prints," said Studier of Ancient Peoples.

"I don't think those vehicle seats would work with tails."

"They could have had tail stubs, or thin tails they kept down a suit leg."

"And we have no idea how many upper limbs they had, or heads, or what sensory organ clusters."

"We may eventually determine some of that by analyzing their tools.

They'd be designed to be easy to use by beings with a given configuration of manipulatory appendages and sense organs. We can run computer models."

August 2, 1971, the Apollo 15 landing site near Hadley Rille

Jim Irwin and Dave Scott were near the end of their third and last excursion on the Moon's surface in nearly as many days. The official timeline had them transferring their samples to the Lunar Module, and parking the rover a short distance away and aligning the antenna. Their personal, unofficial timeline had one more task.

Scott was behind the rover, out of sight of the TV camera, when he heard Joe Allen, the CapCom, back on Earth.

"Jim, how are you doing?"

"Oh, fine, Joe," Irwin answered. "Transferred a few bags up to the porch."

"Sounds good." Allen's reply came back.

Dave opened a bag and carefully removed a small plaque and a polished metal figurine. The crew had planned this in advance, a memorial to astronauts and cosmonauts who had died in the furtherance of space exploration.

Irwin's voice came over the radio again. "We have about three more bags to transfer up."

Allen's response came a few seconds later. "Super." There was a long pause. "And, Dave, you might want to check TV Remote."

He was busy setting up the memorial. "Okay, Joe. Just a sec." Bending down against the pressure of his suit, he placed the plaque standing up on edge, pushed down into the soil a bit to hold it. Then he laid the figurine—a stylized astronaut—face down on the lunar dust in front of the plaque. He looked at the names on the list, he'd known many of them. Authorized or not, this was right. Some of these guys never got to go.

Scott rose, the suit's pressure almost pushing him up. He started to ready the Hasselblad camera to photograph the memorial.

Allen's voice came again over his headset. "Dave, give me a call on your present activity."

"Oh, just cleaning up the back of the Rover, here, a little, Joe." Scott answered. He quickly took a couple of pictures.

"Oh, okay." A pause. If that had sounded as weak to Allen as it had to Scott, he didn't mention it. "And, Dave, we do not have our TV yet. You might want to check TV Remote."

"Okay, Joe."

*　*　*

LifeSeeker, near Surveyor Crater

"Just a moment," Studier of Ancient Peoples said, entering some commands to bring up an image on the display over the table. "Look at this: we found it near site five. It doesn't seem to be a tool."

The display showed a metal object lying on the lunar dust, smooth-surfaced and showing little detail, roughly rectangular with a narrow wedge cut out of one end, splitting the object for nearly half its length. A smaller, rounded rectangle protruded from one side just beyond the slot, and the end had a small rounded projection centered on it; the sides of the object, and the projection on the end, were straighter, forming a right angle to the top surface. Near this object stood a larger, thin flat metal plate with row of markings on it. The patterns of markings were similar to markings they'd seen on other equipment, probably a written language of some kind.

"Do you suppose this could be a model of one of them, like a doll or effigy? If it were stood up on the two ends of this bifurcation. . ."

"That would put the smaller knob on top—a convenient spot for a visual sensory cluster. But it has no manipulative appendages, no arms or tentacles."

"It's stylized, or perhaps they extrude from the body."

"In a space suit?" he inclined his head no.

LifeSeeker's longboat, on the planet

Radar analysis of the planet from orbit had revealed an important clue. The outlines of landmasses under the ice bore a resemblance to the odd shapes that had been inscribed in circles on the plaques found on the legs of several of the octagons. Those circles must have been representations of the beings' home planet. The shapes were only an approximate match, which caused some confusion until Climatologist reminded them to account for a drop in the ocean levels as ice accumulated on land. Adjusting for that, the match was nearly exact. More evidence that the moon explorers had come from this planet, and it had frozen over since.

The longboat settled on its landing gear on a smooth plain of ice, near the original shoreline in the equatorial zone.

"Are you sure we're on the landward side of the original ocean level?" Planetologist asked Pilot. "We want what would have been dry land when the glaciation started, not ocean sediments."

"If your estimates are correct, then so is our position. But I can move further inland if you wish."

"That won't be necessary." Planetologist turned to help Drill Technician with his suit. Once sealed up, they airlocked out onto the icy surface and prepared to set up the equipment a few hands of arms away from the ship.

A strong wind whistled down the icefield from the interior of the continent, picking up flakes of snow and ice, making the air sparkle sometimes under the nearly cloudless sky.

"This is frustrating," said Drill Technician, fumbling with the coupling to the laser head in his suit-gloved hands.

"You could take your gloves off, the air is technically breathable," replied Planetologist.

"No thank you, I prefer my skin unfrozen, and I haven't had feathers since childhood." As with most of his species, the downy feathers which helped maintain body heat in infants had molted as he grew. "All right," he said, snapping the last component in place, "we are ready to begin."

They stepped back to a safe distance and fired the drill. As the laser beam bit down into the ice, a plume of steam jetted out of the hole, freezing out as an icy cloud a few bodylengths above them. After a short while, the plume started blowing smoke and dust fragments and it hit bottom. The laser cut off.

"How does the data look?" As the beam had been burning its way through the ice, sensitive instruments had been staring down its length and observing the plume. Variations in composition were analyzed. A complete stratigraphy of the borehole had already been recorded before the laser shut off.

"Very good," Planetologist answered, pulling data from the drill's computer to his helmet's screen display. "Look, we have banding, probably seasonal variations." He touched some controls, running another analysis. "A count of 729 cycles, 729 of this planet's years."

"How many of ours?"

"About 787, but that's not allowing for whatever has worn off the top or melted out from the bottom, of course."

"On to the next location," said Drill Technician resignedly. He began packing up the gear.

February 6, 1971 - Apollo 14 landing site, Fra Mauro Base
Al Shepard and Ed Mitchell were near the end of their second and last

walk on the Moon. As they discussed which pieces of equipment would be returned, and which would remain behind to save launch weight, Al picked up the handle of the rake-like contingency sample scoop, pulled a small metal object from a large pocket on the outside of his suit, and began assembling them.

Mitchell was gathering film magazines together; there was one he didn't think had been used. He called down to the CapCom in Houston. "Fred, magazine KK has never been used, is that right?"

"Stand by."

Alan took the opportunity, and stepped in front of the TV camera, holding up the modified tool. "Houston, while you're looking that up, you might recognize the handle of what I have in my hand. It just so happens to have a genuine six iron on the bottom of it." He held something up in his other hand. "In my left hand, I have a little white pellet, familiar to millions of Americans. I'll drop it down." The small ball dropped slowly to the dusty surface. He raised the makeshift club in his right hand, as best as the pressurized suit would allow. "The suit is so stiff, I can't do this with two hands, but I'm going to try a little sand-trap shot here."

The first swing struck the lunar soil short of the ball. Mitchell, looking on, said in an amused tone "You got more dirt than ball that time."

Shepard grinned to himself. First golf swing on the Moon, and just dirt. "Here we go again," he said, and swung. This time he connected, barely, and ball went off at an angle a few feet.

Fred Haise's voice came over the radio. "Looks like you sliced it, Al."

But Shepard was getting the hang of it now. He stepped up to the ball again. "Here we go. Straight as a die; one more." The swing connected and the ball went off at a low angle, hard to see against the bright lunar surface. Twenty yards? He had one more ball, he could do better. He dropped the ball and stepped over to it. This was it. He reached back, twisting and raising his arm as much as the suit would allow, and swung. The impact felt solid. The ball soared, a tiny white speck fading into the distance. He grinned. "Miles and miles and miles."

LifeSeeker, near Surveyor Crater

The Leader summoned his department heads together in the upper deck briefing room for an analysis of what they'd found, the snowball planet shining in half-phase through the overhead window.

"Physics? Your analysis of the radioactive fuel?" That would give the most definitive dating.

"The composition is consistent with the sample being originally nearly pure plutonium-238 oxide approximately 10.4 half-lives ago," said Physist, "decaying primarily to uranium-234 oxide."

"10.4 half-lives, making it?"

"About 988 years, or 915 of this planet's years old."

"Nearly a thousand then," the Leader's voice trailed off, thoughtful. "They were landing on their moon when we were inventing steam engines." He pondered this. What were the odds of the civilizations of two different stars developing the same technology almost simultaneously? No, that was premature, he knew little about their overall technology, nor how long it took them to get to this point. "What else?"

Physicist showed images of a flat, square slab, its surface an array of hundreds of circles. He zoomed the image to reveal them as clear solid— sapphire, quartz, diamond, it wasn't obvious which—with the back surface of each cut to a perfect cube corner. "These are retro-reflectors. They will return a light beam back in the same direction from which it came."

"Oriented to face the planet?" said Leader

"Exactly. We believe their function was either to provide some way to precisely fix the position of the landing site, or perhaps to allow extremely accurate measurements of the planet-moon distance. Either way you would need a beam of coherent light to reduce dispersion."

"A laser?"

"Precisely."

"So, they had lasers, nuclear reactors, chemical rockets—surely nuclear rockets couldn't be far behind. What else?"

"We disassembled some of the instrumentation," he gestured to a side table where various pieces of retrieved equipment, objects and samples were arrayed. "It's electronic, at a relatively primitive state, but they had semiconductor technology and what we examined was structured in a way that shows they understood the underlying concepts, even if their fabrication techniques were crude."

"Implications?"

"They had lasers, semiconductors and controlled nuclear reactions. But we found no evidence of gravitics—oh there's what was a crude gravimeter, essentially weights on springs, but nothing comparable to their electronics."

"Still, whatever took them out must have happened quickly, almost as soon as they developed space travel." Leader didn't like the implications, it was too coincidental. Was there some outside force involved?

41

The Planetologist spoke up. "No, Leader. Our surveys of the ice don't agree with that."

"Oh?"

"We cored down to rock surface, and counted seasonal layers. On average there were only 730, plus or minus a few. 730 revolutions of this planet, around 788 of our years. The glaciation happened nearly 200 years after the moon exploration."

"Perhaps it stopped snowing a while back."

Climatologist joined in. "No, the planet isn't completely frozen over. There are areas near the equator where there's open water, enough to allow precipitation, although much less than when this started. We also ran climate models—tricky, since we don't know the exact starting conditions. The pictures on the plaques helped, giving us an idea of the sea level then, which lowered with the growth of the glaciers."

Another member of the planetary survey team spoke up. "We also found some satellites in high orbit which don't seem to be as old as what was left here on the moon. We don't know the exact cosmic ray flux here over the years, but the orbits were high enough that the planet's magnetic field wouldn't shield them much. The exposure rate would be similar to the rate here. We found satellites of different ages, some as old as the lunar gear, validating our method, and some as young as the probable onset of glaciation. Nothing more recent."

"And the glaciation? What caused it?"

"Impact winter," said Planetologist. "Things must have been near the tipping point, but a large meteor struck and threw up a huge cloud of debris, probably also starting global fires and raising intense smoke. That would block the sun, cooling the planet. Huge amounts of vaporized water would form clouds doing the same, and where the water fell as snow the ice would build up. If the initial impact is sufficiently catastrophic, even a technological civilization, at least at the level we've seen, couldn't cope."

"But that was two hundred years later. They had nuclear power. Space travel. They must have known how to build nuclear rockets. They had lasers. They were bold enough to send six vehicles and however many robots to this moon, and sent robots beyond their system. Look at where we are," he gestured to indicate the landing site, "they could do pinpoint landings!" Leader stood up and started pacing. "And they had two hundred years to improve their technology before the asteroid hit. We were starting to build *starships* by then! How does a spacefaring society let itself get wiped out by an asteroid?"

"Perhaps. . ."

"Yes?"

"Perhaps they weren't really spacefaring. If this was a stunt, a single expedition?"

"So much effort? And then throw it away? But they had the technology. Six landings, they had the desire. They had the knowledge—they must have known of the dangers of asteroids, all they had to do is look up at the craters on this moon to see that. What sane species develops a capability and then ignores it?" The captain's brow crest rippled with agitation.

Nobody had an answer. The Leader paced, pausing by the sample table, looking vainly at the artifacts for an answer, but there was none.

A small white sphere caught his eye. He picked it up, examining it. The surface of the white sphere was covered with small dimples, like little craters. Part of the white plastic covering was discolored, almost tanned, probably from the solar wind.

"What's this?"

"We're not sure, sir. We found it some distance from octagon three, the one with the two-wheeled cart. It was a chance find, there were no footprints or tracks leading up to it."

"Curious." He held the ball out at arm's length, then looked out the topside window at the planet overhead, itself a white sphere. In his hand, the small dimpled ball looked the same size as the planet, and nearly as white.

His brow crest flattened. He shook his head and dropped the ball back on the table. He hated coincidences.

The Shifting Sands
by J. Michael Shell

Though I do not explore in an official capacity, I have always acknowledged my duty and debt to the Silicate Sentient Cabal. Unfortunately, I have never encountered anything worth adding to the data banks of our Great League. To my utmost joy, that has changed. I now send this account in hopes that it will facilitate a better understanding of ourselves and our place in the universe. I am also, in deliberate haste, on my way back to the Chrystal Homeworld with the incredible find I am about to describe. If I am correct in my assumptions, the Ancestral Sands will surely shift in elation.

Again, I am not an official scout of the Cabal. My ship is tiny, and my self-funded equipment minimal in both quantity and quality. Still, my hunger to explore dominates my purpose, and has led me to a tiny system in an outlying arm of a modest, class-four galaxy. It was an indication of radiation on my old, Glassflow Five ray/wave scanner—still an expensive piece of equipment for an independent explorer—that led me to the fourth planet of a backwater system crowned by a small, yellow, type-G star. Sure enough, that bluish world scanned out to be saturated with enhanced, device-released radiation. Apparently, some silly, semi-intelligent sentient species had exterminated themselves. Though this sort of thing rarely shows up in the data banks, it is not unheard of. I would not, of course, have troubled the data sorters with this bit of information had I not decided to put down on the single, tiny satellite orbiting this dead world.

It was luck, if you will, or perhaps the Ancestral Sands shifted to direct me. Either way, the system's little star sent a shaft of its luminosity to spark off a shiny, metallic object sitting in a crater of this pocked and desolate moon. Apparently, the now extinct inhabitants of the dead, blue world had managed to mount an expedition to this place, which begs the question— why didn't they expend their energies toward the highly profitable enterprise of travel, rather than self-annihilation? But that is a question for the philosophers—I, in my very limited capacity, am a creature of science.

There were very few artifacts on that barren surface. Still, my humble vessel (a modified Exoglass Tourcraft) has a tiny cargo bay, so I was only able to retrieve about half the relics I found there. But my most important, awe-inspiring find fits neatly in the raised cup of my high appendage.

When I found it, apart and far away from all the other relics, I immediately had high hopes (and the stone in my breast pumped harder). Perfectly spherical, dimpled as the face of a newborn, it was white as the Virgin Sands and marked with a name. Immediately, I returned to *The Granule* (my affectionate name for the vessel I pilot) in hopes that my practically-ancient, virtually obsolete Glassflow Illumiverse scanning analyzer could confirm my suspicions.

If you are familiar with the old Illumiverse model scanning computers, you know I had some time to kill before I received my report. During that time, I occupied myself at the linguistics analysis computer (another desperately old Glassflow model), trying to decipher a piece of cuneiform text I'd found. For all my effort, I discovered only that the self-destroyed inhabitants of the blue world were called the *Mankinds*, and that they had apparently mounted their expedition to this satellite in hopes of mining something called "peace." I saw no indication of mining activity, however, and must assume that their search for "peace" was a dismal failure.

Finally, the Illumiverse chirped and I felt my fluid gel and quiver in anticipation. The hard-data analysis determined that my tiny sphere had an outer surface comprised of some sort of resinous composite—very tough, very thin, very much a *shell*! Beneath this shell was an encircling, cushioning layer of highly elastic fibers, obviously there to protect the inner core—and, yes, I dare say it; *the yolk*!

The yolk, my friends (oh praise the Ancestral Sands) is gel/fluid and silicate! If—and here I venture totally beyond the bounds of my knowledge and experience—if a way could be found to *incubate*, we may actually be able to return to the universe a lost brother of the Great League of Silicates.

*   *   *

This report will predate my arrival on the Chrystal Homeworld by some months, but I travel with all haste to present you with my prize, my *jewel*—the last of the terminated *Mankinds*. Hopefully, if incubation can be accomplished, we can one day call him by his intended name. Though hard to pronounce, I'm sure we will all be eager to welcome "Titleist" to the Silicate Sentient Cabal!

Sailors in a Sea of Suns
by Brenda Cooper

The room breathed, the ears of its bluish-white walls tuned to the same frequencies as its inhabitants. The two deep-ochre beings with large darker-brown faceted eyes curled close together on the floor. The adult breathed in long and slow, then let out air splashed with spices and light, damping the faint traces of fear pheromones hanging in the rounded spaces in the room. The child, smaller by half, reached one arm up and trailed the point of a claw across its parent's forehead. The child's reward was to be curled more closely into the adult's many arms and to hear the words it longed for, thin and soft as an exhale, from the adult's mouth. "Now it is story time."

The child shrugged deeper into the adult and put two of its own small arms on the bigger one's bracing arms and replied, "Tell me about the sunships?"

The adult stiffened a little, "I will tell you of a sunship and two of its people. This is a day for you to hear about Tuk and Haxh."

"Again? It's such a sad story." The child's nether feet drummed just softer than pain against the adult's thick brown abdomen.

"There is a sunship. Besides, it is a teaching story for you."

"I don't like it that Tuk dies."

"I will die one day."

The child hesitated, and then it repeated the adult's words, sounding content. "I will die one day."

"My parent said that children inflict pain more ruthlessly than enemies."

"What do you mean?"

The adult held the child more closely. "You will find out."

"Tell me the story."

The room waited.

The adult hesitated, breathing out a thicker mix of comforting scent, which was taken in by the walls and the child. It waited until all three beings breathed in unison, even though one was a child and one was . . . it had a guess. Maybe. The adult didn't know, for sure. It only knew they lived inside it, and it felt like captivity. It's memories had fuzzed with time.

Well, the story was a deep distraction. Its own parent had told it, and had learned it from its parent. The adult began, its voice soft and sure. "Tuk and Haxh had been flying survey duty through space inside of their sunship, Kli'ang'in, for so long that Haxh was halfway to becoming an adult and had never been outside. Indeed, Haxh knew only the company of the two others, the ship and the parent, and all of the things they had taught Haxh. But everything else it knew might as well have been made up."

The child tapped its feet once again. "You're leaving part of the story out."

The adult flexed two arms and then relaxed them; a tender warning to the child. "They did slow down once. Perhaps I forgot that part, since it does not really matter. They circled a frozen world for three turns, but Tuk chose not to land. Any life there must lie dormant under a sea of ice, and while the sunship was strong, it was not strong in the way of burrowing under ice. Besides, in that early year, Haxh was too young to have adventures—just like you. It did not yet know how to sift information for truth."

The child tapped again, using all eight feet, and then it said, "And they sailed away on the light of the sun."

"Yes, Kli'ang'in used the light of the sun of the frozen world to speed back up, and after that, they sailed by many suns with either newborn planets or no planets. Even in a ship that sails as well as Kli'ang'in, space is far and wide, and it is long between stars. In those many years, Tuk became older and more brittle, and it began to hurt it to walk. So Tuk worked twice as hard as ever at exercises and lessons, at writing up the samples in the hold, at everything. Tuk did it all with Haxh by its side, the two of them together almost all of the time. Tuk felt afraid to die before Haxh had landed and tasted air and light and learned enough to become its own person. Haxh felt Tuk's fear, and it wove deep into Haxh's heart and made it feel heavy and sad."

This is how they flew the last leg, sad and sad.

Tuk worked hard to make the years pass, but it was not enough. They held each other, and they sang stories to each other, and they helped each other with exercises. Whenever it could, Tuk told the teaching stories it knew to Haxh. It even made up stories, and designed hunting games so that

Haxh could search through the ship using clues to find artifacts that were part of Tuk's stories. They cleaned and cared for the inside of the sunship that cared for them. Together, they watched the clear shimmer of the sunsails, nearly invisible between stars.

No matter what entertainment Tuk dreamed up for its child, Haxh slept more, and moved less. Haxh's color paled: its carapace faded to tan, and its legs became nearly transparent, just the grasping claws and walking claws staying dark. Haxh's eyes sagged and began to drip clear liquid, the way Tuk had seen its parent's eyes do right before death. Because Haxh was a child and not a parent, Haxh's damp and diseased eyes disturbed Tuk like sand under its carapace, like something it could not fix but needed to.

Haxh had been cheated. Tuk had led a grand life. Tuk's parent had also lived a life not cut short. Together, the two of them had explored a planet of caves and beautiful stones and carpets of living beings that moved all together across the paths between the stones, eating air and cleaning the bones of their world. They had found another planet full of furry beings who flew between trees and over water, eating the trees while the trees, occasionally, ate them. The trees and the furry beasts had all lived with joy and abandon, and died with brief flashes of anger at the futility of it all. Tuk's first landing had been on a water planet, where they could photograph and study schools of jelly-bodied beings so small and clear they could barely see them between the sea-floor and the glittering surface. Tuk had gathered all those memories when it was younger than Haxh.

And Haxh had seen nothing except Tuk, and Tuk's artifacts, and the inside of a sunship.

One day like any other, Kli'ang'in spoke.

Now, this is very rare. Sunships care for their charges, and obey those who care for them, for they are all one and the same. They take travelers between stars, and they look, like we do, for other life. But they are content to read the play of starlight, to watch for objects in the vacuum of raw space, and to fix their vast shimmery sails. They dream. A stream of wordless knowledge flowed always between Kli'ang'in and Tuk, but only about the routines of the day: shared facts that are not a conversation. So when Kli'ang'in spoke, Tuk and Haxh shivered and stared at each other. They were in the same room, and the walls themselves vibrated with voice. "I slow. A sun with eight planets is a year-of-slowing in front of us. The third planet may have water."

51

Tuk marveled. It had never heard Kli'ang'in speak so far from a destination, so it must know how slow and old Tuk had become, how thin and uninterested Haxh had grown. If its passengers die, the sunship would perish, too.

"Thank you," Tuk said.

Kli'ang'in did not reply.

Haxh placed an arm on Tuk's back, and said a single word. "Finally."

Tuk's hopes had been broken before. Even the ice planet had been almost enough to do it. "Take care, Haxh. It may be nothing."

"If it is nothing, Kli'ang'in would not have spoken."

"We must get strong," Tuk said.

And sure enough, Haxh returned to its exercises, and the two of them held each other again from time to time, and took comfort in the hope that this new place would have life.

In time, Kli'ang'in's great sails spread as wide and thin as they could, furling at the edges, belling out as they caught rich solar wind, the edges fluttering lightly.

Tuk and Haxh watched out the window of the eyes of Kli'ang'in. The yellow of the fertile sun gave an orange glow to the sails, reminding Haxh and Tuk of how large Kli'ang'in could be. If the sunship were to land on one of the methane ice planets farthest from the sun, its great sails would cover it all, leaving some edges to flap in the light before they tore off and flew away from the system.

Tuk watched the light in the sails for so long that Haxh brought it food and water. "It is beautiful," Haxh told Tuk, "but don't we need to exercise and stay strong?"

Tuk had told Haxh that forever. *Discipline*, its own parent had said, is how you live. *If you stop doing what you must every boring day after every boring day, you will die.* Tuk had said this to Haxh over and over, but now it said, "I may never see the light of a sun stop us again."

Haxh stayed with it and they did not exercise that day.

Kli'ang'in picked a place between the third and fourth planets. The third planet was frosted with ice over almost half its surface, and the rest was blue water and a tapestry of land: Green of plants, ribbons of thin blue rivers, whites and grays of clouds. Life had to exist there. Tuk's heart sang with it as it recorded notes and took images, and told the data stores deep in the sunship's center to compare this place to all the data it had from all the other sunships when last Kli'ang'in had been home, seven seasons of adult and alone and child ago.

The fourth planet had only the smallest bits of ice. The rest of it was land: folded canyons, pushed up mountains, flat plains scoured and filled with red dust and wind. But it had a touch of atmosphere, so there was hope there, too. Tuk asked Kli'ang'in to search them both for life. The familiar hope of all new places lightened Tuk's body so its front legs floated near its head when it walked the soft round hallways of the sunship.

Kli'ang'in sent bits of itself down to the surfaces of both planets.

Tuk and Haxh waited.

Time passed.

Bits of the sunship returned, gathered back one by one and fed their data to the data stores.

No record of this star existed inside the annals of the sunships or even the lists of legends the explorers brought back as stories. "This means they have never made life that traveled," Tuk told Haxh.

"How do you know?"

"If any of their generations of life could sail between the suns like us, we would have heard of them."

Haxh fell silent for a while, carapace pulsing in and out with breath, scenting the air with disbelief. "We cannot know everything. The universe is big."

An understatement. "To travel like us is rare. To die young is the fate of almost all life." The air did not change or signal acceptance, so Tuk turned the subject. "Let us look."

The fourth planet had life. Small life, barely-there life. Life that would amount only to life. It would not go to the stars. It took less than one percent of the surface of its world's land; it would be a footnote in a catalogue. But it would be that. The sunship bits missed little. They also found a few pieces of dead metal machines remained in a rock crevice sheltered from the dust and the wind by the wall of a crater. The piece of the sunship which found them did not dare touch them for fear they would crumble to nothing. It took pictures and measurements.

Haxh pulsed perplexity. "Does that mean somebody found this place?"

"I don't know." Tuk watched the bits of sunship data again and again, but added nothing. It breathed out confusion and the way it carried its legs reminded Haxh of sadness. In an effort to cheer its parent up, Haxh suggested, "Let's look at the third planet."

It had been frozen pole to pole, many times. It was thawing now, warming, giving birth to life. Liquid water ran and pooled and tumbled across its surface. Green and gold and yellow filled many places between mountains, and small black beings scuttled through the bright foliage in groups of hundreds. Here and there, some of the beings flew. Nothing, of course, resembled Tuk or Haxh or Kli'ang'in, but some of the beings reminded Tuk of the planet of the trees and furry things. "What is the symbiosis level?" Tuk asked the data stores. When they replied, "Seventy percent," Tuk glowed happy, clapping the front two legs together.

"And we are?" Tuk asked its child.

"Ninety percent."

"And this means?" How much had the child learned?

"That if this life is to grow like us, it will have to be helped."

Tuk felt proud. "Like we were. But what else does it mean?"

Haxh took longer to answer this time, struggling to remember its lessons. "It means they can be helped. They can join us and our others. Because they cooperate."

"Very good."

Haxh was not done. "We will bring back a possible new life to our world. We will be able to take Kli'ang'in home to see some of the other sunships."

"If our studies show our guesses to be truth."

Haxh shifted its weight to its back four legs and looked out of the eyes of the sunship, watching the white and blue planet below it. "Have you ever found a system with life on two planets before?"

"I have found life on five. But life that can join us is rarer. I have only found that here."

"So my first place is a special place?"

"Yes. Perhaps you are more lucky than I thought."

Haxh glowed.

Tuk continued, speaking matter of factly. "And I will be lucky to die here."

"I am not ready to be alone."

The adult cringed at the scent of Haxh's angry breath. "I was not either. But If I was not alone first, I would not have you."

Haxh fell silent for a long time before asking, "What is life usually?"

"Stupid," Tuk said. "It competes itself to death or it starves itself or it poisons itself or its home." Tuk scented the air with sadness. "Or it is simply unlucky. In its time between death and birth, my own parent found a planet that had been killed. Its life had made some of the most beautiful mountains ever seen, sculpting them with fire and the work of countless hands. But the random movement of rocks destroyed it. An asteroid struck shortly before my parent arrived, and it killed all living things on the planet."

Bits of sunship went out and back and out and back and out and back, and Haxh grew impatient and Tuk grew more weary and more tired, in spite of its excitement. Death stalked it from the inside out, although it tried to hide that death from Haxh.

A year passed. Then two. Tuk grew even weaker, and tried to send Haxh to the planet without it. Haxh refused.

They built a catalog, took a hundred virtual flights, and gathered so much data they filled half the spare data storage inside of Kil'ang'in. They cleaned and cared for the inside of the sunship which cared for them.

One day, Haxh stared through the eyes of Kli'ang'in, as if it could see the life on the third planet from here. "We have verified the life below us matches our hopes. I am ready to land."

"Very well," Tuk said. It spoke to Kli'ang'in out loud, so Haxh could hear. "Where should we start?"

Kli'ang'in spoke in both of their heads for the first time, its voice so loud Haxh jumped and shook before settling back on six legs and cocking its head sideways, listening. "I have found much life on the planet. I could take you to waterfalls full of leaping fish who eat the sun like I do, or to a desert full of creeping brown that eats the sun and turns it to water. Or I could take you to something that could not have been made by any of this life."

A mystery. Haxh clasped its hands and settled its weight back. "I want that."

"It is on the moon," Kli'ang'in said. And then it spoke aloud again. "And Tuk can go there. It is a simple enough place for me to protect its landing."

Hope filled Haxh, even though it had not spent a spare thought on the barren moon. "Can you go there?"

Tuk's front legs rose with joy and its body jerked once in fear. "I can."

Kli'ang'in detached two bits of itself and slithered like new skin over Tuk and Haxh. Haxh did not move until it breathed in the new skin and recognized the smell of Kli'ang'in, the warm embrace of the sunship now covering all of its body: legs, and head, and carapace and hope and love for Tuk and the sunship all covered and now together. Tuk stepped through the wall of Kli'ang'in and some of the thin material spread to become sails fifty times its height. Haxh followed. As they flew from the sunship to the moon, the light of the system's star made their wings yellow-gold, glittering in the damp places that carried the clear blood of Kli'ang'in.

The white of the moon's surface matched the stars, the round edges sharp against the blackness of sky, monochrome compared to the bright winged beings approaching it. Round dark blotches highlighted craters and rocks and shadows.

As their sunship-wrapped feet touched the plain surface, the sails folded back into them, thickening the protective cover around their bodies ever so slightly. Dust rose slowly up to their lower knees, then settled back. Silence surrounded them. The ground was marked by small rocks and dents, and further off, larger ones.

The sunship broke the silence inside them both. "Walk north and west. Be careful. Tell me what you see."

Suddenly cold, Haxh asked, "You have seen this?"

"Of course." The rare gift of sunship warmth caressed Haxh's skin, and it felt all right again.

There was nothing to see except the ground, so they looked there. Haxh saw first. It stopped and stared, then levered itself slowly down near the surface, careful of the fragile sunship suit that kept it alive. Ovals, with stripes across the narrow sides, dents in the ground. The shapes were longer than two of Haxh's feet. The voice in Haxh's head whispered. "Look at the ground where you have walked."

The same. Haxh sized.

As if Kli'ang'in had heard Haxh's unspoken thought, it said, "Not from your people. I gave you that shape on your feet, so would know this was a footstep."

Tuk could no longer bend as well as Haxh, but it held its body as close to the ground as possible and looked. It stepped back, carefully, then lay down in the dust, settling into thinking posture. Haxh settled so close to it the skin of the sunship merged, so they sat together in a bubble, adult and child.

Haxh waited until Tuk uncurled a bit, and raised its head. Even though it had been sitting still in thinking posture, it had grown paler and its eyes so weak its child wondered if Tuk could speak. But it did. "Someone was here before. Surely one of us, observing. There is no other reason to go to this moon. No bounty, no life."

Haxh had been thinking, too. "No life here, ever?"

Tuk breathed out certainty so strong it reminded Haxh of the way Tuk controlled it when it was small. Haxh manufactured the gentlest antidote it could, one that would not hurt its dying parent. Then it disagreed with Tuk for the first time ever. "But life changes always. You have said that."

"Not here on this moon. Life never arose here; there are no beginning substances for it."

Tuk would die soon, and should have hope that its last discovery would bring honor and knowledge home. Haxh stared at the white and white-green-blue planet floating in space above it. "Perhaps it came from there. The planet is rich in life."

"Nothing down there can fly so high. Not for centuries, and not without help."

Haxh hated that answer.

Tuk's eyes closed.

The sunship skin let out a small scent of condolence and of agreement all at once, an off combination. Haxh felt it respond inside of it, the sunship's silent voice saying, "I believe you are right. Come home."

Kli'ang'in had spoken directly to Haxh.

Tuk must be unable to speak.

Haxh would be alone soon.

It sat and pondered the footsteps on the moon for a long time, it and its parent enclosed in the embrace of sunship skin, its parent's breathing slowing, and slowing. The constant presence of Kli'ang'in provided a small comfort as Haxh examined the idea of becoming alone for a long time before it, too, had a child. Did the footprints mean there was no choice, and it had to keep going? That this life could not, after all, become enough to join it and the others? Or did the footprints mean others had beaten the three of them here, as Tuk's last thoughts said? After all, there had been the bit of twisted metal on the fourth planet. It had an origin.

Tuk's breathing stopped.

Haxh left Tuk behind, for the dry cold on the airless moon might preserve Tuk's body there beside the footsteps their sunship had found. Haxh was so saddened, so alone, it never landed on the third planet. Instead, it flew back on the bright gold sunsails of Kli'ang'in, the two of them searching for someplace happier to study. So this is the end of the story of how Haxh grew up, and the choices it made.

*   *   *

The child breathed out sadness. "I do not like it that Tuk dies."

The adult held it close, choosing not to taint the air with soothing smells. The child must grow up sometime. "But Tuk must die for its child to go on and find its destiny."

"Haxh never went back, did it? And it did not go home. What would have been the point?"

The child was gaining in ability. "There was no reason for it to go home. Whether the steps came from the third planet or someplace else. Do you understand why?"

"If they came from there, then the life on that planet wasn't ready. If it was prepared to live in harmony, it would not fly to such a barren place. And if the sun had been found, then the data was already returned in a different sunship."

"Or the ships of another life."

"You like to scare me. There are no ships of other lives. We have never seen them."

The room continued listening and hoping.

The adult and child remained silent for a long time, the child's legs bouncing a bit from time to time, showing that it thought about the story.

The room contemplated whether or not to blow out the scent of sleep.

The child's legs twitched one more time, and it raised one claw to the adult's face. "I think Haxh should have gone back with the information. It should have taken pictures of the footsteps."

The child had never reacted this way to the story before. The adult asked, "Why?"

The room paid attention.

The child didn't hesitate anymore, but plowed forward fast, its words and scents pouring one on the other so it was hard to follow. "Life changes. Most life dies young. The moon they went to had no air, so the footsteps might not have been young. The life they found might have been the kind of life that can join us."

The adult glanced around the room. It sipped sustenance from the air, sweet and stronger than usual. Not laced with sleep scents like it expected.

The child sat up in its adult's arms, and then pulled away so they stood side by side, not touching.

"Very good Haxh," the room said, its voice sweet and deep. The bluish-white walls grew clear in four spots, one on each side of the room, if a not-so-square room could be said to have sides.

The adult and the child shivered. They looked out of the eyes of the room, and saw stars. They glowed like clear hard points of light in two directions, but through the other two eyes of the room, the faint mist of sunship sails made the stars shimmer.

They cleaned and cared for the inside of the sunship which cared for them. They flew toward the third planet of a small sun.

In All Things Divine
by Jody Sherry

My first thought upon seeing the alien spacecraft was that a massacre had occurred at its feet. Dismembered pieces of some kind of spacesuit lay jumbled at chaotic angles, brilliantly white in the fierce light of the foreign sun. Cautiously I stuck my walking staff in the hollow of one piece, dreading that the remains of its wearer were still inside. But thankfully it was empty, and I let it fall lazily back to the dust of the moon's surface.

The dust I was already familiar with: a sticky, grey powder that clung to my own spacesuit, refusing to be brushed away. Spreading my lower arms wide, I knelt down to inspect the other pieces. The pattern on the bottom of four of them matched the many footprints that traversed the site. Those were boots, then, despite the strange right angle at the end. There were also two large boxes with multiple fittings that bore an emblem composed of alternating bars of red and white. I pulled at the raised edge on the box covering, which came loose with some effort. Inside were gas tanks and gauges: a life-support system. I wondered if some sort of madness had afflicted these aliens that they had abandoned all of their protective gear.

Leaving the spacesuit pieces, I rose to examine the ship. It didn't look complete; it was really only a platform sitting on four spindly metal legs. The same emblem found on the life-support tanks was also on the top of the ship. I turned toward the blue and white planet hanging just over the horizon, and wondered what the emblem signified. Nothing now, since our scout ships had found no evidence of active civilization on the planet's surface. But in whatever past, the emblem could have been the symbol of a people, perhaps even of that entire world. They would have been proud of their accomplishment, thinking themselves special, or perhaps blessed to have reached this satellite of their homeworld.

Even though I was alone, my chromatophores shrunk under the thin skin of my spacesuit, and I looked away, ashamed. I am a servant of Zeth, and I should not entertain such unholy thoughts. Some day my lack of complete devotion will be exposed, and there will be no more gazing at foreign worlds for me. The astonishing sight of the great methane falls of Larid, the ethereal beauty of the auroral lights of Nisku, the peculiarly strong gravity of Canso that challenged my muscles' ability to carry me; those memories will be all I have left if I am dismissed from the Corps. To be confined for the rest of my days to the monotony of my homeworld is unthinkable.

I grabbed one of the empty boots and tossed it under a leg of the spacecraft. I will not have that fate. I will not be denied the glory of the stars. Even this moon, which is not extraordinary at all, sings to me in a way that I can't explain. I dropped my staff and reached for the two life-support packs, lifting them easily in the low gravity. After stashing them under the craft, I collected the remaining pieces of spacesuit and piled them with the others. The crew of the reclamation ship will thank me for my neatness when they arrive.

Unfortunately these aliens hadn't been tidy at all. There'd been no massacre at the spacecraft; the boots and other spacesuit components had simply been discarded, along with dozens and dozens of other items. Not as bad as the triple moons surrounding Gennes, though. Nothing could be as bad as that, what with debris and artifacts scattered from one pole to the other. That mission had occupied the whole of the reclamation fleet for nearly an entire solar cycle, and at the end there'd still been fears that evidence had been missed. But no task was too great to preserve the faith of the followers of Zeth.

Moving away from the spacecraft, I plucked a tall stake from the lunar surface. It had been buried only a few centimeters, and had a thin metal sheet attached to it. I could not discern its function, and laid it with the other equipment. Turning back to the silvered soil, I had to adjust the polarization of my helmet visor. The contrast between light and dark was so vivid here that it affected my depth perception and my ability to see objects on the ground.

Spreading out from the spacecraft in a well-defined arc were small tools of several types, probably sample collectors. Every site we've cleansed has evidence of excavation. Every traveler wants to take home a souvenir. There were also electronic devices, their buttons too tiny for my fingers. The remains of a pulley system. Empty containers that had held who knows what. And several bags that appeared to contain waste material. I vibrated in distaste. The things I've handled in Zeth's name. All of these things I tossed into the pile, congratulating myself for the accuracy of my low gravity lob.

I moved away from the spacecraft and stepped on something smooth: a banner lying flat against the soil. The upper face had been bleached white by radiation, but when I picked it up I saw the other side wore the now familiar striped emblem. A depression in the ground at the end of the staff told me the banner had once been upright. I held it that way for a moment before adding it to the heap under the spacecraft.

Satisfied that this zone was cleansed of artifacts, I looked beyond the immediate circle of the spacecraft. Rocking my weight between one leg and then the other, I bounded over to the nearest piece of equipment. Set low to the ground, the artifact was packed with an array of tubes. I angled my helmet to look into it and was momentarily blinded by flashes of light from the device. I stepped back, wondering how I'd missed the glow of illumination, but from the side the artifact was dark. Cautiously extending my head again, I saw the light was reflected, not generated. I turned again to the blue planet, wondering who had waited for a signal on the other end.

Our exploration teams had found only beasts on the planet surface, just as they always did. The ships of the Jurian people have traveled to hundreds of worlds, and not a one of them supported sentient life at the time we arrived. Not even on a planet from which we received a radio transmission, such as this one, was the sender ever in evidence. That I am surprised each time, nay even a little disappointed, is my greatest sin. If I were a true believer, I would see each empty system as further proof that space flight is a gift from Zeth to the Jurians, a privilege reserved to us alone. The primitive attempts these other civilizations have made to usurp the power reserved for the followers of Zeth has been punished by their destruction, just as is promised in the Tayit.

Returning to my task, I maneuvered the reflective device up off the surface, and carried it the short distance to the next large artifact. That one was composed of two black panels interlaced with metallic strips running the length of the device, and at one end there was something like a transmitter dish. The panels oriented toward the sun, like some kind of solar powered battery, but their size said they were either thoroughly inefficient or unbelievably powerful. Like the mirrored object, this device appeared to be tuned to return information to the planet. I could understand why these objects had been left behind, but not the legion of other items which seemed to have been simply thrown away.

As I hefted the first artifact on top of the second, I noticed that a trail of footprints led away from the site. I clacked my mouthparts in annoyance.

It would take an extra trip with the Cheno resurfacer to eliminate those tracks. I latched onto the solar panels with my lower hands and pulled both pieces of equipment, using my upper hands to steady the load. Once back at the spacecraft, I secured both objects underneath its platform.

When I rolled my head out from underneath the craft, I noticed a small plaque affixed to one landing strut. The characters were indecipherable, but it seemed reasonable the engraved image of a planet represented the one now halfway up the black sky. A notation or commemorative of some sort. The Jurians don't leave special tokens on our expeditions; quite the opposite, we leave nothing at all. But this short jump between the planet and its satellite had apparently held great significance for the aliens.

I stepped back from the spacecraft, looking for any other markers. There were none, but I did recognize that the strut bearing the plaque had rungs, unlike the other legs of the ship. I climbed this built-in ladder, noting grey moon dust along the top of each step. A footprint matching the ones in the soil stamped the platform at the top. I pulled myself the rest of the way up, and balanced on the ledge. From here I could see burn marks on the interior frame of the space craft, and disruptions in the metal of the platform. It looked as though another section of the spacecraft had detached and lifted off from this one.

I rubbed my upper hands over my arms as I pondered why that would have been necessary. Though the casual discarding of the multitude of objects below could be ascribed to wastefulness, leaving an entire section of spacecraft seemed more than that, as if the aliens had worried about weight and their ability to lift off from the moon. But in this low gravity, the weight of the items was insignificant. Could their technology really have been so primitive that even a piece of spacesuit might have held them back?

I couldn't imagine traveling through space in a vehicle so untrustworthy. My first mission had been terrifying enough, even with the knowledge that the ship was tenth generation Jurian technology with a perfect safety record. Even though I'd hungered so ravenously to go to space that I'd feigned an undying devotion to Zeth to get there. But when the ship's air lock slid open and I stepped out onto that alien plain for the first time, all rational thought left me. The sky was the wrong color, the gravity perceptively too strong, the flora entirely unfamiliar. Panic seized me, and I tried to run back into the ship, causing my experienced crewmates to look at me in amusement. Embarrassed, I willed myself to turn around and follow them, my mind focusing only on the boots ahead of me. At some point my panic disappeared, and I began to appreciate the beauty of the indigo sky and the contorted forms of the life around me. When the mission was complete and it was time for us to leave, I felt unexpectedly wistful, and I knew I'd say or do anything to keep myself in the Cleansing Corps.

Had the alien astronauts felt the same, simultaneously terrified and mesmerized as they stood atop this platform, gazing down on their barren domain? And at some point, had the stark beauty of the grey and black landscape won them over until they, too, were sad to go home? And while I had stepped back into a proven vehicle, they apparently hadn't had that luxury. From the platform, the debris pattern became obvious: the spacefarers had tossed belongings out of the ship and hoped they could get home.

With that kind of bravery, it was a shame to erase their accomplishment.

I banished that thought and glanced at my suit controls. My breathing tanks were half empty, and I had no more time for contemplation. Besides, the reclamation ship would be here soon and its crew would expect that this site was readied for them. I jumped down in a controlled glide, tucking myself low as I landed to minimize the rebound of momentum. Amidst a cloud of dust, I stood and walked to the Cheno resurfacer. Switching it on, I guided it over the collection of footprints near the spacecraft. Its vibrating bristles agitated the thin soil, giving the lunar surface the appearance of unsullied ground.

I next followed the trail of footprints to the area where I'd found the collection of banners and small tools. Using a technique refined by experience, I scoured the area free of offensive evidence. Zeth's will would be done. I looped back toward the spacecraft, scanning the ground for any errant prints. Once back at the ship, I paid particular attention to the discard zone, eliminating not only the footprints, but the impact marks of thrown equipment. With the central camp finished, I headed toward the section where the larger pieces of equipment had stood.

I was almost there when my helmet comm chimed. I blinked to answer it, and then my superior's voice echoed in my auditory openings. "Is the cleansing complete?"

"Almost," I replied, kicking up the speed of the Cheno even as I answered.

"The reclamation ship will be at your site in thirty minutes. Prepare to depart," my superior clicked. "By the grace of Zeth."

I lowered my head automatically. "By the grace of Zeth."

The helmet comm went dead and I continued on. This set of objects had been the farthest from the spacecraft, and the trail was probably twice as long as the other paths. I was already fretting about the time involved when I caught sight of another string of footprints leading away from the site. It was the detour I'd seen when I'd hauled the equipment away, but I'd forgotten it until now. I clacked my irritation and then settled back to work.

As I steered the Cheno over the trail, I was thankful there was only one narrow line of tracks. The path went for a considerable distance, however, without any discernable destination. The ground began to slope upwards, and I raised the Cheno to accommodate the change. With some effort, I crested the rim of a large crater, and saw that the footprints ended there. The alien had walked all this way just to see a crater? There was a double crater right next to the spacecraft. The surface of the moon was pockmarked with thousands of craters. Hundreds of thousands of craters. And yet the alien had ventured far from camp just to see this one.

There was no logic to that action. It would have been a waste of time and air. But as I stared out at the serenely empty crater, divided by shadows so sharp they were surgically precise, I was afraid I understood.

The transport arrived before the reclamation ship. The small craft had barely settled on the surface when a ladder extended from within its belly. I climbed the rungs, then stepped off into the air lock and activated the control to withdraw the ladder. When pressure was attained, the door to the cabin slid open, and I walked forward, twisting off my helmet as I went. I sniffed the cabin air to ascertain who had been sent to retrieve me. Agent Vel.

Vel was a reasonable fellow, not so intense with his displays of devotion, not like the bulk of the Cleansing Corps who made me feel so uncomfortable. Passing through the staging area, I set my helmet down and unshouldered my air tanks before continuing on to the cockpit. Vel was in the pilot's seat, his four hands a blur of motion as he activated the controls to lift the ship and fly onward to the next site. He was tall for a Jurian, his limbs that skeleton thin that the females like.

"Agent Kwet, has the work of Zeth been done?" Vel said, still facing the viewscreen.

I slid into the copilot's seat. "The work of Zeth is always done."

"That is the truth, brother," Vel said, his skin blooming blue in relaxation now that we'd fulfilled the formality of greeting. "It's job security."

I studied Vel for a moment, trying to gauge the irreverence of his statement. Sometimes I wondered if Vel hadn't joined the Corps for the same reason I had, but other times I worried that he was an emissary of the Holy Council sent to test the faith of Corpsmen. "Yes," I finally answered, then changed the subject for safety. "What have you found on your assignment?"

"I've been flying reconnaissance the whole shift," Vel said. "Picking you up was the first time I touched the surface."

"Sorry to hear that," I said. In my mind, surveillance duty was barely a notch above flying the reclamation ships.

"All service to Zeth is a privilege," Vel said. "Besides, doesn't look like I missed much down there."

I almost protested that each world had its own beauty, but I kept my mouth parts still.

Vel continued. "I did document thirty crash sites, though. Thirty! Can you believe that? No wonder they never got any further than this moon—they didn't know how to land."

I didn't think an emissary of the Holy Council would say anything that outrageous. A true believer knew these aliens never went further than this moon because spaceflight was reserved only for Zeth's Chosen People. I decided to take a risk. "Why do you think they kept trying?"

"Because it was there. Because they looked at it every night," Vel said, but then he appeared to reconsider his answer, because his chromataphores shrunk visibly. "But who knows why heathens do what they do."

I clicked sympathetically. I wanted to tell Vel that was exactly why I had joined the Corps, because as a child I'd stared at the five moons of Jurias, dreaming that I would visit them some day. Several cycles later I'd learned that of course I could visit; the moons had been settled for eons. And then in youth camp I'd stood on the outermost moon and dreamt that I would visit the stars. I'd found that was possible, too, so long as I pledged myself to the theocracy and became a servant of Zeth. But Vel smelled nervous now, was probably afraid *I* was sent by the Council, so I let the sentiment drop. "Have you seen the next site?"

"No, but the comm chatter I've overheard says it's similar to the one you just finished. Maybe larger," Vel said. He glanced at the instruments. "We're almost there."

"Then I should grab a fresh airpack," I said, easing myself up from the copilot's seat. "The sooner we're done, the sooner Zeth glows, eh?"

"Exactly. And the sooner we go home."

I hummed in agreement, even though that particular thought had never occurred to me.

Vel was wrong. This second site wasn't a little bit larger, it was much larger. Except for the detour to the crater, the first site had huddled around the spacecraft, all the equipment situated a tentative distance away from that central point. Here the encampment sprawled over the gently rolling terrain, the larger artifacts scattered rather than clustered. Some objects I recognized immediately: the spare framework of the discarded section of the spacecraft, the multi-mirrored instrument, the squat device covered with solar panels. I bounded over to the ship, and quickly found a metal plaque affixed to one leg, just as with the other spacecraft. A few strides away stood the remains of a banner, tattered and bleached like the first, but still upright. Radiation had robbed it of any color or pattern, but I was sure that it once bore the barred emblem common at the previous landing.

But even with those similarities, this site felt different. The widely-spaced equipment, as well as the footprints that casually crisscrossed the soil, bespoke of a comfort and a confidence with the lunar environment. A later mission, perhaps, reflecting knowledge gained and lessons learned.

I suddenly wondered why the aliens hadn't progressed further than these few primitive attempts. Why hadn't they colonized this moon, or any of the outlying planets in this system? My skin grew hot even as I asked the question. I should *know* that it was the will of Zeth that the aliens progressed no further. I should *know*. But I couldn't rid myself of a lingering sense of sadness that said the real reason there was no colony here was the same reason the blue planet was empty of them now. War or famine or self destruction of some kind was the real culprit, not punishment from Zeth.

Just before I applied to the Corps, I came across a manifesto on the Node that said the priests have it all wrong. The writer claimed the theocracy has concealed the earliest records of Jurian exploration, the ones that said that we actually went to space to search for life and other sentient races. But when centuries followed without finding a single living civilization, though plenty of dead ones, the priests began to whisper that it was the will of Zeth that no other spacefarers were found. Eventually the whisper became the proclamation that spaceflight was a sacred gift to the Jurians from Zeth, and the priests rose to power on the popularity of that belief. The theocracy discounts this all, and has tried to find the heretic who spreads this ill message, but they never have. After I made my application, I paid a good sum to have the evidence of my sin purged from my computer's memory, but of course it still resides in mine.

As an agent of the Corps, it's my duty to prove the priests correct. That's why I'm here, to remove the offensive evidence of transgressions against Zeth, and to reassure the peoples of Jurias of our place in the galaxy. It's a noble task. I should feel honored. In some ways I do, but there's always that creep of disappointment each time we come upon another dead civilization. Zeth forgive me.

I've cleansed more than two dozen worlds, and the official way to process a site is permanently ingrained in my mind. Artifacts first, equipment second, physical evidence last. I grabbed the shredded banner by its staff and pulled it from the thin soil, using it to start the familiar pile under the spacecraft. The work of Zeth must be done, and there was no sense in mourning this vanished race.

After collecting the small tools from the site, I loped over to the nearest piece of equipment. Some distance beyond that was an artifact that hadn't been at the previous site: a platform that sat on wheels. I'd noticed it when I first arrived, especially its large size. As I moved closer to the vehicle, I realized it was no trick of perspective; the platform *was* about as long as the spacecraft. By regulation I should have left it for the reclamation ship; it was far too big for me to move alone. But I ignored protocol and went over to it anyway.

Standing next to the platform, I could see it had two seats with an apparent control stick between them. It reminded me of nothing more than a farmer's tok cart back home. I buzzed to myself, amazed once again that these aliens seemed so unprepared for space travel. First they came in a craft so underpowered that they had to discard half of their belongings to make it back, and then they rode in a vehicle that looked like it should be pulled by a pair of tok. I would never travel in a technology so primitive.

I clenched my arms together. Of course I would. I would have been side by side with them.

I climbed into one of the vehicle's seats and looked up into the blackness of the sky. The star patterns were completely unfamiliar, and that sight gave me a thrill, as it always does. I may not have risked my physical safety like those astronauts did, but I've silenced my conscience to stay in the Corps. Whatever it's taken, I've done it. Will continue to do it. For the miracle of gazing into a foreign sky.

On a whim, I tried to bring the vehicle to life, but its controls wouldn't answer. Like its makers, the cart was long dead. Conscious of my air reserve and of my superior's temper, I slid out of the seat to resume my duties. The larger pieces of equipment were far enough apart that I collected them in two groups, one under the spacecraft and one under the surface vehicle. Once that task was complete, I powered up the Cheno and began the process of restoring the soil to its original state.

By the time I'd finished the area leading from the craft to the vehicle, I knew I'd never be able to cleanse this site by hand. The wheel marks from the vehicle extended farther than I could see. I blinked on my helmet comm and waited for the reply.

"Yes, Agent Kwet?"

"This site will require the Litak," I clicked in my most formal tone. "The tracks are quite extensive."

"All your other tasks are completed, then?"

"Yes," I said, thinking I'd better make one more sweep for artifacts.

"The Litak resurfacer is currently in use. Continue your work until the transport ship arrives. By the grace of Zeth."

I bowed my head. "Of course. By the grace of Zeth."

My helmet comm went silent, and I powered on the Cheno again. The Litak would take care of the site in a tenth of the time, but hand work was still the best way to ensure no detail remained. When the glow of ship's lights brightened the horizon, I turned and headed back toward the alien landing craft to wait for my crew mates to appear. I was almost to the ship when a glint of white against the grey soil caught my eye. I stilled the Cheno and reached for the object.

It was a rectangular sheet, thin and flexible. The side facing me was blank, but when I turned it over I dropped it as if stung. On the other side was an image of four aliens, pink and puffy, and clustered close together. Two of them were significantly smaller than the others, as if they were immature. I retrieved the sheet and stared at the picture, dumbfounded.

We seldom come across images of aliens on the worlds we cleanse. With their societies vanished and their technology foreign, we're never able to retrieve their stored records. At least not in the time span of a site cleansing, and the theocracy has no interest in our bringing such information home. On occasion we'll find non-electronic images, usually statues or engravings in what look like public places. This image seemed much more informal, and out of place amidst the debris of a scientific expedition.

The light from the approaching ship changed from diffuse to a defined beam as the ship closed in. It was time to throw the picture in the pile of artifacts, so that it could be crushed in the bowels of the reclamation ship and jettisoned into space. Instead I clutched the image tighter.

The picture had no writing, no insignia, no seal of authority. It was not an official marker like the ones affixed to each spacecraft, nor a symbolic emblem like the one stamped on so many of the artifacts. It might be an image of one of the astronauts, or of others important to him, but it was personal, certainly. It had not been left in the name of their government, or even for the sake of science, but for himself. Because the journey meant something to him.

On Jurias, the punishment for possession of an alien artifact is quite severe. The ship was beginning its descent, and if I held the picture any longer, I risked the pilot seeing it in my hand. I knelt as if adjusting the Cheno and let the image slide back to the ground. I smoothed grey moon dust over it until it blended in with the surface. The Litak would skip over an item this small.

It cannot matter to the astronaut who left the picture that I returned the image to its home, because he and his people are long gone. But just as he left it as proof that he'd traveled to this moon, I left it as proof that I am not the only one who finds the miracle in standing on a foreign world. I think he would understand my childhood dreams and why I will never leave the Corps. I think he would forgive my sins, even if Zeth cannot.

Because we both reached for the glory of the stars.

Dust in the Stellar Wind
by C. E. Grayson

Kimiani, my dearest Vashnt-tat-mari,

The disappointment on your face when I left the council chambers, once again denied permission to enter with you into the Vashnt, thus kept from enjoying the full expression of our love, pains me even now. I can only suppose that those rumors about the specimen I unearthed, and which was destroyed and replaced in transit with that laughable fake, had something to do with their decision. I could not prove the veracity of what I found on Tinamon Vek, but please, believe me when I tell you that not even I would try to pass off a Tel'mondeth costume and a pile of rotted toll-da guts as a real Xu-nam corpse. My relationship with the costumer, and his inexplicable testimony, has nothing to do with anything that happened. It is my hope that, in my absence, you have not listened to the words of Toban—whose name I loathe even in the writing and whom I am ashamed to name my Vashnt-cos—and that you still believe that my quest has been in your name, and so I would not suffer to let it be sullied by such approbations. I would do nothing to ruin the ecstasy we will feel that day when, hand in hand in hand, we enter together through the portals into the Vashnt.

Since that day, since the door of the Vashnt cavern was shut to us once again, I have made certain other discoveries which, it is my hope, will help me to locate the actual homeworld of these strange creatures. A collector, a purveyor of found items, obtained for me a scrap written in their strange language, a scrap of some thin substance he says he found on Tinamon Vek, and which, he claims, was part of a larger piece that covered the golden disk, a piece of which formed my first discovery those many cycles ago.

This is why I left so suddenly. It was not, as Toban has no doubt tried to covince you, to escape prosecution for my supposed fraud. I do not know this man who claims he paid me for the specimen, and whose money I supposedly promised to refund. My Vashnt-cos Geboor, who has served me so faithfully these past few cycles, accompanies me. I cannot tell you exactly where I am going, for I do not want interlopers to make the discovery ahead of me. Nor do I want those authorities who believe Toban's lies to intercept me, and allow the shields of a penitent to come between us again. . .

When I return, my love, it will be as one triumphant. For how can the council deny me entrance when I have found the Xu-nam homeworld, and all the treasures it must contain? And the two of us will enter into the Vashnt, know the pleasures there, and afterword raise our brood in the wealth my discoveries will, no doubt, provide us.

Your devoted Vashnt-ti-moor,

Jooben.

Beloved,

Geboor and I spent a week on Tinamon Vek waiting for the arrival of our source. Abandoned there with no means of transport, I assuaged myself by thoughts of you, and by wandering that vast marketplace, examining the trinkets there. Would that I had had the funds still in my pocket, dearest, because there was a pendant in one of the little wayside shops, like a drop of black frost with a golden star buried within. I held it in my hands and lifted it to hang there before my eye, and for a moment I felt as if it allowed me to stare into yours. I meant to purchase it for you, but since I was afraid of explaining my purpose on Tinamon Vek to the merchant, I was unable to convince him to extend me the credit. The bruises on my face, a result of my attempts to negotiate, and to circumvent the need for further negotiation, attest to the strength of my efforts to obtain for you this treasure.

One day soon I will return there, purchase the merchant's entire inventory, and then cast him loose upon the star-winds. By that time I will be able to afford all the fine things that you deserve, my love.

Geboor supplemented our income by performing his usual tricks for crowds that gathered to watch him. His air-weaving delighted the children, even if his stories made no sense to them. I stayed back with the crowd and encouraged them to drop bits and crits into the loom-case by his feet. I tried not to stare too long at the Vashnt-marin making Telemon Vok a stop along their pilgrimage to the Vashnt, though, once again, I was allowed no respite from my longing for you.

After that wence, which lasted a full ten days, such is the cycle of Tinamon Vek's journey around its world, I received word from the child I had paid to be my lookout, that our collector had arrived. I met him in his hollow near the docks, and I must tell you, when I first entered his place of business, I began to despair. I do not know how to explain the kind of place I expected to find. He claimed that he was a trained archeologist, and that he had once worked for the institute on the homeworld, but he displayed no credentials in his place of business, and I must admit that my cursory attempts to locate his service records had returned no results. I had assumed his name had been changed since then, but as I looked upon the nest of dust and broken carvings piled amidst collected stones and paintings which, I could hope, were not his own work, for if they were, they were the work of a madman, I knew that he must have fabricated his past, or if he hadn't, that he was very different now than he was then.

But all that mattered was that his find was legitimate. Had I come all this way for a fraud, or worse yet, in service to an old one's delusion?

He begged me to leave Geboor in what he termed his antechamber, and to follow him into his inner sanctum. Geboor remained behind without complaint, having become entranced in a string-game hanging from the ceiling. I was certain I would find him, upon my return, having braided himself into the structure of the thing, at which point I would have to cut him free. I can only imagine the reaction of my host if that became necessary, but I left him regardless, following this withered and berobed old one back into the deep parts of his cavern.

I felt some relief to find this inner chamber much more neatly organized than the outer, and began to come to the realization that the outer clutter was the mask behind which hid the true face of his work. Here were carefully catalogued shelves, items packed in translucent boxes with numbers written on the outside, and in the center, a console with which he could access a meticulously kept library. He was at that console as I stood at the door, watching him. Since bringing me inside, he had ignored me, standing as he was, staring down as the sigils scrolled across that plate of glass.

Finally, he said, "Oh, yes. I have it." And then moved to a shelf that hung on the back wall. I followed him, wondering if I was going to have any apology for how long he'd kept me waiting, both in these moments before, and in the wence I'd spent. But in the manner of true genius, there was no apology, no acknowledgment of my impatient struggle. He simply drew a box from the shelf and pressed it open. The lid popped free with a hiss, and I was glad to know the item had been so well protected and preserved.

At first, what I saw was a grave disappointment. It was just a scrap, a rubbing really, color on the paper, lines spreading out from the center, fourteen of them, but they had etches along them, and I could not tell if these belonged to the original or if they had been made as part of the rubbing.

"This is what you wanted." It was a statement from the old man, though it would have been more appropriately phrased as a question.

"Do you know what it is?" I asked him.

"It is worth the price," was all the reply he would give me.

We had negotiated well in advance what price I would pay, and I gave him the crits, and placed the scrap in my coat. Before I turned to collect Geboor and go back to our lodgings to determine what we should do next, the old man asked me, "You know how to read this?"

I looked at the strange lines, and then back at him. The beginnings of an approach had begun to form in my mind, but it was not yet complete. I wish I could tell you, my beloved, that I had a flash of inspiration that made everything clear, but I cannot lie to you. I simply said I did not yet know, but thought that I could reason it out.

"A professor at the Bedned school, she can read it, perhaps," the old man said. "Niarii Togusen. She offered to buy it, but you . . . you beat her price. She may read it for you."

The Bedned school . . . could I really go back there?

I accepted this advice with a nod, but told him nothing of my plans. I began to wonder, did he know exactly what he had found, or was it just one scrap among many? I asked him to show me what else he'd found from this same location, but he told me that this was all there was. I did not mention to him my search for the Xu-nam homeworld for fear I would inadvertently give away the value of this find, and that he would call in his hired goons to take it from me, and demand some higher ransom. I had already given him everything I had and could afford no additional fee. Let him believe this was simply some ancient piece of trash and I just an eccentric collector.

I collected Geboor from the antechamber. He was sitting in the middle of the floor staring upward at a painting that ringed the ceiling, his eye lost in the swirls and curling patterns there. I think if I had left him, he would still be there, tracing the lines with his gaze. The artwork reminded me of those scrawlings left behind by the meditants who form your ancestry, my love, and I left with Geboor, before such thoughts could overwhelm me.

Geboor's earnings provided just enough for a one-way passage to Bedned, so that is where we go next, and I am on that transport now as I send to you this message. What I will find there, I do not know. This is a place to which I wished never to return, for you know what happened to me there, the shame I endured. But if this academic truly knows how to read this scrap, which I believe may be a map, it is worth any endurance.

As ever, your devoted one,

Jooben

Dearest,

How can I convey to you my feelings at arriving here on Bedned, and setting my feet once again on the soil that has come to mean so much, both good and bad, to my life? It was here I developed my love for the history of this vast space we all travel through, and all the creatures in it. It was here Professor Bansh introduced me to his working model of a synthoid Xu-nam specimen, the very thing that earned him his dismissal. And it was from here that I was cast out before the end of my second year because of Toban's lies. Toban, who has so long stalked me, turning my every accomplishment into a failure. Making of all my earnest hopes and dreams nothing but the dust he would shake from his shoe.

But I cannot despise the place entirely, for not only did I find my life's work here, but I also found you. It was here I first laid my sight on you, standing in the window of your apartment, brushing out your long, plaited knot in the burning moonlight. I only wish that I had not waited those months ... maybe then ... maybe then everything would have been different for us.

Geboor and I arrived on Bedned with not a single crit left to us, starving since we'd had no money for provisions the last few terns of the voyage. Geboor's antics in the port's green, frequented as it was mostly by students and others connected to the school, earned us only a few crits, barely enough to purchase the single meal we split between us. But we were here, and getting closer to our goal. I only hoped that this academe would be able to read the scrap, as the old collector promised. I had no assurance, as my messages to her had gone unreturned, though many do get lost in transit through Bedned's antiquated communications system, I am told. I wanted to go immediately to the school to find her and show her the scrap, but it was almost full night and I did not think we would find her there at that hour. I was also concerned about her reaction upon seeing the artifact. She had tried to procure it for herself, would her bitterness at losing out cause her to turn us away, or, worse yet, attempt to steal it or destroy it? It was important that I proceed in exactly the right way.

C. E. Grayson

Geboor and I found lodging in a hostel that would allow us to work in exchange for beds. While Geboor cleaned the vestibule and helped tend the hostel's garden stock, I formulated my plan. From my research en route, I knew that Niarii Togusen had been a junior instructor in nav studies at the school for many cycles, and had recently been risen to the rank of Devotee. How she had endured so long failing the tests for rising yet still remaining in her place, I do not know. I found no record of her ever being allowed into the Vashnt, which caused me to wonder anew at her aptitude, if not her sanity. Was this just another eccentric, one in a long line, whom I'd have to rise above to finish my quest? Would she be of any help to me, or had I come all this way for nothing?

I did not sleep that night, my fears getting the best of me. Thoughts of you finally brought me to calm and solace just before Geboor rudely woke me as he (having had no trouble with sleep at all, since all of the planning and figuring was left to me) rose to clean our bedspace and help prepare the morning meal of which all would partake at the hostel's communal table.

After the meal, we walked across the main plaza of Bedned proper. You remember what this was like in the morning, the crimson dust spraying through the air, lighting on the buildings and forming threads that twisted and danced on their way toward the amber sea. Geboor coughed his way through the town. Since this was his first visit he'd not yet acclimated, and we'd no funds to procure for him a mask. I tried to walk a bit away from him, embarrassed at the wracking noises his lungs made as he walked. It was obvious that one of the pair of us did not belong, and I felt it more useful to avoid notice. Let Professor Togusen have no warning of our arrival. When we appeared, she would have no choice but to help us. I wanted to give her no opportunity to hide herself.

I had never been to the sector of the school that housed the Navistat program, since my own area of study had been speculative historiography, and I had been driven from Bedned long before I had the opportunity to take any of my broader interest requirements. It was strange to me that someone interested in the Xu-nam (if indeed she was, though I could think of no other reason for her to have bid on this scrap) would be a scholar in this course. But perhaps she was a hobbyist, in which case it might be even easier than I had hoped to convince her to help me.

Having had the foresight to check her schedule, I found it strange upon entering the assigned hall to find only three students there. Two of them sat together, slumped against the back wall in an impression of slumber, while one was in the front, leaning forward to stare at the instructor, who stood with her back to her students, furiously tapping at the space above her head, bringing up glowing white sigils and star maps that charted a projected course through the black of space in what seemed very much like a random order.

After a span of watching this, I began to understand why the course was so sparsely attended, and wondered why it was even being offered at all. Of course, Geboor and I went unnoticed, even though we blocked the light that came in through the open door. Even if Geboor had set himself afire again, we might not have drawn her attention. So we waited for the class to end. I sat against the back wall in imitation of the sleeping couple, while Geboor wandered, his attention fixated upon, no doubt, the beautiful starlight that filled the display space.

At last it was time for the class to end, an occasion that was marked by the sudden waking of the slumberers, and the flash to black of the star display. Even at its end, I had no idea what students were meant to learn from such a presentation. Neither did the rearward students, as they left without comment, seemingly having recorded no notes. The student in the front took a little more time to pack away his things and say goodbye to the professor. How like Toban, this one was, so obsequious and mewling, out for any advantage no matter how slight. Togusen shooed this one away with a wave of her hand, giving him no word of goodbye. This obvious disdain strengthened my hope that she could be an ally.

"You and your Vashnt-tat-mari may register for my class at the central office," she said, turning around again to tend to some display. "As you can see, there is still room."

My anger flashed at her unholy jest, but I refrained from castigating her. I merely said, "This is my cos."

"How proud you must be," she said, but she was looking at Geboor when she said it, and I found this disconcerting.

"I have not come to be instructed," I continued. "But I would like your expertise on a matter. I was told that you could help me."

"Help you?" She turned around and regarded me more seriously now, and looked at me like she expected trouble. "If you are a debt collector, you will get nothing from me today. My position here pays me based on the number of students in my classes, and as you can see, I do not have many."

Then perhaps your profession does not suit you, I wanted to say. You know my wit, my love, and how difficult it sometimes is to suppress. But I needed her to want to help me, so I showed the self-restraint you have so often asked me to display. "I am not a debt collector," I said. "Like I told you, I am in need of your expertise."

"May I ask what payment you would provide? As you may have guessed, I cannot afford to offer my services for free."

Though I should have anticipated this, I had not. "I think you may wish to help even if the only reward is the satiation of your own curiosity." I was duly proud of this retort. "You and I bid on the same item offered by a collector on Telemon Vok. I won the auction, but have brought the item to you now."

Her stare betrayed no emotion. If she was surprised, or envious, or curious at all about what I had said, it did not show on her face. All she said was, "If you are offering it for sale at a higher price, you may already have guessed that is not possible. I lost the support of my financiers even before the end of that auction. I have no crits even to pay the amount at which the collector opened the bidding."

"I simply hoped you'd look at the item for me and help me to read it. Perhaps we could even work together on the project." I was tempted for a moment to tell her of my quest, but I hesitated. There was no use having her think me a lunatic, as so many have. It was possible that she could be one to recognize my genius, but if not . . . I wanted to leave her no fuel with which to light the fire of her calumny.

"You have it with you?"

"Yes."

She reached out her hand without a word spent for courtesy.

How could she have expected me to hand over my treasure? I simply stared at her for a span, and said, with all the authority my actual possession of the thing afforded me, "Let me show it to you."

She smiled a satisfied smile and dropped her hand, so I brought it out and held it up in front of my chest. I could see the longing in her face as she stared at it, the tension there in her translucent green rims.

She bid me follow her to the center of the room, where she air-keyed open the display that had hovered there earlier, eliciting a delighted yelp from Geboor. This one was different than what had been displayed before, focused as it was on one piece of the spiral arm. Lines appeared between the stars, lines etched with hash marks I took to be some sort of distance marker. More stars popped into the air around these, connected themselves to those extant with more glowing lines. All the lines converged in at the middle until, finally, a new light appeared in the center of the cluster.

"I lacked but two coordinates," she said. "I needed seven I could be certain of to validate my theory."

"Your theory?" I asked.

"I think this is a map to the Xu-nam homeworld. That's what you're looking for, isn't it?"

I choked down the wail of victory ululating itself up into my throat; she couldn't know how desperately I needed this information or she would make me pay for it, I knew. She was a practical academe in need of funds herself. I did admit that this was my theory as well. She closed the display and pressed down on the data link, pulling the information into the lattice around her middle finger.

"Thank you, you may go now," she said, and made a move toward the narrow door in the basin of the room.

"But you haven't told me," I said, anger causing my neck-quills to rise.

"You've helped me a great deal," she said. "The old one wouldn't let me have a good look, which was all I needed, and that was why my backers abandoned me. But now . . . I can get them back. I can finally make the journey. . ."

"But . . . but I brought this to you. The journey . . . the find is mine to make. I paid for this. . ."

She studied me for long moments and finally said she would see if we could, perhaps, come to some arrangement. After giving her the name of the hostel that housed us, I allowed her to leave.

So now we are there, waiting for her message. I still do not understand the turn of events which led to this reversal, but I will not allow myself to despair. I do know that the place exists, and can be found. That is more than I could be absolutely certain of before coming here to Bedned. And if this treacherous academe will not help me, there must be others here who will. Our fortune, my love, is within my reach. Know that and live in hope.

Jooben.

Dearest,

Rest assured, my love, that I see through the ruse you found it necessary to enact in your message. I know that Toban, if he did not write the message himself, forced you to deny our love and put in the public record that you requested I contact you no further. But I am

81

undeterred. Especially now, as our time together in the Vashnt has never been nearer.

For after a few days of waiting and fearing the worst, and being asked to do the most vile of tasks in order to earn our keep at the hostel, a message did finally arrive from Togusen. It seems that her backers had come through with enough funding to provide a small ship for the purpose of discovering the Xu-nam homeworld, but not enough to hire a crew, save one assistant, who, she told us, worked for the largest of her backers and who, let us be clear, appeared to be traveling with her not to provide assistance, but to make sure the investment was not allowed to be squandered. Since Geboor has some small experience as a pilot, he was asked to come along as well. I was the final piece of her crew, as she will be in need of my vast expertise in the study of the Xu-nam, just in case our discovery of the homeworld indeed finds some of them still living there. This is, of course, our fervent hope.

So we are now en route, following the course Togusen has plotted out over her many years of study, years that rival those that my beloved mentor spent. We have spent long hours in conversation, and I find Niarii Togusen to be of surprising intellect, perhaps even equaling my own, and a worthy companion on this quest. Fear not, beloved, that I will not be tempted to replace you in the Vashnt, for though we may be comrades, there is nothing about her that would lend itself to such a trade. Her mane are not long and braided, as are yours, but blunt cut at the source, forming a ridge of black tufts atop her head that was the style twenty cycles ago, when Togusen was young. For while she might not now be in her post-Vashnt cycles, she is near, and may be almost as old as Professor Bashn himself, I think, though it is hard to tell for those who have made their lives on dusty Bedned.

The fourth member of our crew is a little no-vashn, shorter than any of the rest of us. He dresses simply in grey trousers and shirt, and his mane has been shaved down to the point that it appears it never existed. This may be true. I have heard that some no-vashn suffer from such a condition.

He is silent, sparing no word for me or for Togusen. I'd thought him mute, but have observed him in quiet conversations with Geboor while the two of them sit together, guiding our little ship. I wonder what good he will be to whomever hired him as Togusen's caretaker, but perhaps he has been fitted with a recording device. Just in case, I've made sure to have no conversations in his range.

I do not know how long it will take for this message to reach you, as we are soon to pass the most distant of the relays. I will write and send more as we make our way, but I do not know if any will be sent before we return to known space.

Until then, know I love you.

Jooben

Beloved One,

Niari Togusen and I have spent long spans, spans upon spans, in truth, reconciling what we know of the Xu-nam, the flesh they wore, the air they breathed, the dusting of fur on their skins, the screeching, mewling noises they are rumored to have made (this last being merely conjecture and, perhaps, the most easily discarded of these theories) with what we have found.

Togusen assures me that there could have been no error in her calculations. Her navistat program has been refined after cycles upon cycles of research. Of course, her panicked face betrays her own lack of confidence in her figures.

For we cannot possibly have found the Xu-nam homeworld. We have, in fact, found a world, but this . . . it is the third world from its star, which fits the legends well enough, but it is dense and clouded, surfaced in scalding heat, and atmosphere at once liquid and afire. This could be the home of no living creature ever known to have existed.

Have we come to the wrong place, or have we so misunderstood the Xu-nam that this could, indeed, be their homeworld?

Our little craft is equipped with two automated probes that Togusen has all but admitted to having borrowed without permission from the Bedned School. We sent the first of these into the world's cloud-cover. It ceased transmitting almost as soon as we lost sight of it.

Our disappointment and shame are not the only dangers, however. Our quiet friend—for he calls himself a friend even though he has shown himself to be anything but—has reminded us that he needs return to Bedned with only the ship and what treasures we manage to find. If there is to be no bounty, as his employer was promised, he is instructed to return to Bedned without Niarii Togusen and without, as he himself has decided, me.

But all is not yet lost. This world has a satellite, a large one. Perhaps this will provide the answers we seek. Perhaps it is even the homeworld itself. We will see, as it is our next, and perhaps final, stop.

C. E. Grayson

*   *   *

To the one with whom I will enter the Vashnt so very, very soon,

How to describe to you the joy that inflames my rim at the turn our fortunes have taken? Even Geboor seems to understand how completely our understanding of the spiral arm and our place in it has changed; the discovery will bear my name. And Niarii Togusen's as well. Toban's false claims and my recent shames will be forgotten.

And the pleasures we will know . . . it has been a long time, my love, and you have been so, so patient, and now. . . But I am getting ahead of the story, I know, so be patient with me for a span more and you will understand.

This world is rocky and airless, so we know that it itself cannot be the ancient Xu-nam homeworld I so hoped it was. But it is not empty. It is littered with pieces of scattered machinery, devices of a make we have never before seen. They are pieced-together, inelegant, like the models Geboor made when we were children together. There is no way to tell how they operated or, indeed, what their purpose was. But they are here, and that is the important thing. We could see many of them on our flyover, but have had no chance to examine most of them. Some of them even bear colors and sigils, pictures that look hauntingly like those that are said to be recorded in those old fragments found those hundreds of cycles ago.

But as fascinating as these machines are, I have found something else even more breathtaking and, I hope, fortune-making.

We donned our suits and walked on the world. There is very low gravity, so it was necessary to increase the mass in our boots and then to find a way to hop as we made our way along the dust and the rock. There was a spot upon which a mast was planted, and upon this mast was a hanging piece of some fabric, of the same colors we had seen before. And more than this marker, there were, scattered around, depressions, stamped places, oblong and ridged with lines, that could be nothing else than actual footprints left by the ancient Xu-nam. This was a nest of Xu-nam, what else could it be? And what it could tell us about them is remarkable.

The footprints were placed in what looked like a side-by-side leaping pattern, much like the ones we were leaving behind us. They walked here, and left behind for us the proof.

While I have promised Togusen that we will share all discovery credit

84

and rights to this world, I have plans to file the naming as soon as we are within reach of the relays. This world's name? I will declare it Kimiani. Yes, my love, this world will bear your name in a testament to the reason for my drive, for the reason it was found at all. There could be no more fitting tribute to one such as you.

Our silent friend, whose name, Geboor tells me, is Duriq, has spent his time, with Geboor's help, cataloguing the devices within walking distance, logging the substances that make up the machines, inventorying them for their value in raw material crits. There could be no more short-sighted way of evaluating this discovery, but in material alone, he says, the voyage has managed to pay for itself, if just barely, which I take to mean that his threats toward myself and Togusen will not be carried out.

As if they would have been anyway. Duriq is simply a low-level functionary for a much larger organization. I do not think he could actually have hurt us.

But always in these considerations, I return my eye to the footprints, the actual marks the Xu-nam made on the universe, and I get lost in contemplation of the new mysteries we have to solve.

Undoubtedly, they walked here. This could not have been a permanent settlement, yet it is what we found when we followed the stellar coordinates they left for us. Why here? And why did it take so long for us to finally find it?

And if they could make these machines, these unfathomable constructs, where are they now? Are they hiding from us among the stars? How can we convince them they have nothing to fear from us?

I do not know if I will find the answer to these questions in my lifetime. I hope, my love, that when I return with my impressions of these marks, and what pieces of these machines we can fit inside our tiny craft, and after we spend our time in the Vashnt, that we together sail the stars in our own ship, and raise our brood among them, searching for these strange, beautiful creatures who remain so elusive. And that we will meet them, one day, face to face.

Your beloved genius,
Jooben.

Kimiani Nu-tellen,
The task you charged me with is done. I include this coded image as

proof. Jooben Con-huddell's unwelcome attentions will no more trouble you. The payment you promised should now be transferred to my account so that trouble from no other source will come to you.

Duriq Ba-rundin

Worms In the Dirt
by Gene Stewart

Long before the Moon's pocked face blushed from Sol's ambitions of a red giant stage, and longer still before it faded without ceremony into darkness as it finally drifted out of its orbit to fall into the depths of space, it received twelve kisses from some of Earth's one-time occupants. Each kiss left marks the strangeness of which would unsettle the Cosmos itself.

Staring coldly, Luna watched humanoid primate life collapse and flicker into extinction on Earth after only a brief run. Having once been touched by that species, perhaps the man in the Moon mourned them a little, even though the dinosaurs had existed so much longer.

There being no sky-aware eyes left on Earth by then, such metaphorical empathy would have gone unnoticed. Perhaps all emotions are wasted in this way, unmarked and gone in an instant. As unstable climate on Earth danced with time, life forms flourished and faded. Man gave way to cockroaches, and they to bacteria, and so on. Over billions of years even lower life forms, exhausted from using the same ploys for so long simply to survive, began to let go.

Consciousness, sentience, and finally even motility turned itself off.

Eventually the Moon, farther from its host due to a widening orbit, but still loyal to her once-gravid captor, witnessed Mother, Gaia, or, more dismissively, mere Earth, become a cold, dead, watery planet slowly freezing, as old life often does, slowly evaporating itself to mimic her brother, Mars, in stoic, stolid death.

A lifeless place herself, Luna now waltzed with a distant, uncaring suitor, dead Gaia. A dance of the dead kept time with a bloating sun. As the Moon continued her one-faced circle around poor Earth, faithful to what had become a grave, even the oceans stilled at last, caught in ice or siphoned by thirsty space.

Still those marks remained, those dozen sets of kisses. Footprints, the traces of a moon-buggy's bouncy wheels, and scratches from strange creatures wrapped in bright white suits, their faces purest gold, lingered. Those marks, through time's games, became the only hint that Earth and Moon had once kissed, and the imprints of those few shy kisses remained a secret for age upon age.

Finally, a flicker found them.

Not one of the mysterious moon lights, which were mindless geologic anomalies themselves observed by the humanoid primates that had touched the Moon an even dozen times. This flicker danced with awareness and came from far away. It was sentient energy, a being linked to a collective of such sparks across interstellar distances on a cosmic scale.

This collective of bright awareness, which spanned the galaxy, was alerted to these strange marks on this dusty satellite world by a blip of energy, a spark of communication, sent out to explore for life. And now that those marks, considered evidence of life, were found, excitement built, like static, toward discharge and celebration, for life was precious and rare.

Attention swarmed the Moon.

A ripple of curiosity went through the Flow of energy that spanned the Universe as a single mind.

As to the marks, some were distinct and self-contained. Some formed lines pressed into the ancient, powdery dust. These looped into each other and covered quite an area. Others, more discrete, looked more like the tentative touches of physical beings. These marks were contained in smaller areas, yet offered no sign where they had come from.

Looking up, the energy quiver saw only the host planet over the horizon. Seen by other sensory arrays, the quiver of energy would be a glimmer of static with motes of dust dancing in it, or a flicker of light too quick to pinpoint as it darted node to node. It quivered with variable energy fluxes.

The spark rippling on Luna's surface, studying the marks by absorbing visual spectra, understood they might not mean intelligence. Natural processes sufficed to create intricate designs, sometimes. Still, these had no business being there. Where they had come from was not immediately obvious, and not easily deduced. Nor were they, in any way simple to parse, patterned. They appeared to be entirely random, yet with an underlying purpose to them.

As more of the Cosmic energy being focused on the marks, an effort to decode them began. This happened beyond the spark's immediate awareness. Local attention was preserved, even as Universal thought was applied. Does the eye know the mind's thoughts about what is seen through it?

In positive mode just then, the quiver of static on Luna could be thought of as male. To use such matter-bound references only approximated things. Negative receptors were female, in such a scheme. Positive males leaped to receptive females along nodes, where energy sparks collected, then clustered.

Each collective was a harmonic part of a cluster. Each cluster could disperse or swarm, as need be. Dispersed, they could span a galaxy. Concentrated, they might dance in a single storm on a single planet, over a single valley on a single continent.

The clusters, when they resonated, formed, on a Universal scale, the Flow, an energy being equivalent to the Cosmic mind. It had taken billions of years to emerge as a coherent whole, and now explored its domain with curiosity and eagerness for signs of other sentient life forms.

Sentience mattered, matter did not. Energy could dance on nodes of data as easily as it condensed on a matrix of molecules.

Hovering over the strange marks, the quiver of static in positive mode, he, saw similarities and differences between these and other marks found elsewhere on other planets. Being mostly apart from the Flow, he did not clutter his pattern with this data. Swirls of data could distract him. Instead he let it flow through him to a larger thought process.

His link to the Flow as a whole would draw him into his collective if need be. It would save him from possible discharge, for example, should he stray near a grounding of any sort.

It was not as if he were alone the way the matter-bound found themselves. He thought about the flesh-burdened pityingly.

He had observed such random beings, some sentient, most ruminant, on other worlds. They seemed so ungainly, and utterly trapped within their organic sludge shells.

What a horrific existence to try to imagine. He resonated sorrow for their plight. So isolated were they, so kept condensed on one small particulate, that they seemed almost to be outgrowths of their planets. Like slime mold or mildew or moss on rocks.

So kept in place, such beings.

Placement, specific locality, was for matter, not energy, as the Flow well understood. Static meant to the Flow loss of freedom. Static was drain and possible full discharge. And discharge was numbness, blindness, and negation. Only the leap enlivened and empowered. Crossing gaps node to node meant living.

Aside from the hide-bound sentients, he had seen, too, their intricately marked places. Such a strange concept, place. He had seen many, some inhabited. Places worked by life or other forces into convoluted hollows, with an infinite scatter of details, and gathered objects, resonated in his collective memory.

Some matter-bound, flesh-bound life forms marked their places with a wild abandon. As if, he thought, they'd been driven mad by having to be only there for an entire existence. Never knowing the joy of spanning the Universe, they spanned place instead.

How limiting.

Worse, most never even inhabited their world of matter fully. They kept instead to small corners, or isolated levels. Land dwellers never inhabiting sky or water, and so on. Worse yet, some stayed within only a tiny fraction of a given category of molecular prison.

Amazing, appalling, and so sad.

This place, though, cracked and cratered stone that it was, dusty and forgotten, should not have offered such marks of mad inhabitancy. It lacked air, water, and other components needed by the majority of flesh-bound life forms.

It also lacked moderate temperatures, fertile soil, and changeable seasons of energy fluctuation and absorption.

That the marks were there at all, with no sign of origin, was a puzzle worthy of a swarm.

He looked again at the host planet. This ancient, dusty satellite would have been named by any sentience on the host. That a scant few had called it The Moon or Luna was information long since lost to the grind of time.

That the host planet, that small pale dot, had once been called by a scant few of its denizens Mother, Gaia, and later, more insultingly, mere Earth, had been unknown for tens of millions of revolutions around the bloated red star, itself once called Sol, its system Solar.

No sentience had known such things since extinction long since claimed all life forms on the once watery world.

He knew of the water once so plentiful there, and had already seen, and reported, its lack of life. He had ridden and explored the second planet from the bloated red star for a period of a thousand of its revolutions.

During this brief exploration, and since coming to the dustier satellite, he had noticed the red star's continued expansion and pulsing. It puffed as it breathed out a cascade of energies. It pushed itself toward a fast expansion, what was once called the red giant stage. The Flow knew this as cascading toward return. It meant a run toward the leap into pure energy.

It would happen soon, in Cosmic terms. Hence the need for such hasty exploration. The Flow sought signs of sentience that might benefit from the Flow's nature of being. Energy-based minds, life forms using glow and fade, brightness and light, either directly, as the Flow did, or indirectly, as did many organic life forms.

Already his collective had helped three species leap into pure energy patterns. Their thoughts had been sweet and innocent and welcome as any infant's cry of life. Free from matter's domination, they had become vital, active, and important aspects of the Flow, attuning perfectly to Universal Chime.

Chime, as measured in harmonic resonance, was what the matter-bound sentience forms tended to call Time, their perception being so limited and linear.

As his swarm darted among the markers he had left, node to node, analyzing the strange marks, a thought arose: Explorers.

Had flesh-bound explorers, matter-tied sentient beings, come to this dust once in physical form to leave such random marks?

Some of the marks were round and flat, with holes in the center. Others were ovals, crossed on their short axis by lines. Still others seemed almost scaly, lines with marks across them, going on in crisscrossed loops yet open-ended.

In the crimson glow of the bloated star, the marks in the dust seemed to ripple with a kind of taunt, or dare. They teased the Flow's logic and challenged its overarching view of things.

Could these be physical touches, left on purpose?

It seemed impossible to contemplate, given the obvious lack of pattern in the marks. A huge effort began, engaging first the swarm, then the galactic cluster, and finally beyond to the Cosmic scale. It focused on trying to decipher, decode, and interpret the underlying patterns of these marks.

Surely if a group of sentients from the watery planet—where else could such have come from?—encased in and bound to matter, had made the supreme effort to cross even so small a gap of physical space separating the host planet from its satellite, solely to mark this near-eternal dust, they would have considered carefully what message to leave, what communication to pattern in the marks they made. They must have known such marks would remain undisturbed for the duration of the dusty stone place.

Tens of millions of years, perhaps billions, such marks would last. Surely the message thus traced in such long-term dust must be monumental.

To make such an epic journey, unheard-of by the Flow in all its Chimed existence, only to leave random marks, was so appallingly shortsighted and stupid as to be unbelievable, even of the matter-bound bioplasmic beings.

After all, any marks would last far beyond any species. Such marks would be a chance to say something across a gap of space-time so profound as to be almost unimaginable by any individual, non-collective mind.

And soon the nearby red star would shout its passion and cry out its urgency to become pure energy, birthing a new warmth into the Flow of binding sentience. Such a brightening toward cascade, such a return to the Flow, marked celebrations that lasted galactic life cycles and left signs in nebulae and resonance in Chime that even the Flow might consider permanent.

Not to be able to participate in such a joyous celebration, even in absentia via a coherent message, after making the effort to send a gift of marks, was beyond contemplation to the Flow's impeccable dynamic logic. What kind of sentience would squander a chance to join the collective Cosmic memory with a cheery and brave hello from extinction's deep pit of flesh-time?

Such a notion was too far-fetched.

And so his swarm and soon several galactic clusters flickered and jittered, focused on the lunar shadows, their energies arced across black Lunar sky with intricate laced patterns that evolved more complicatedly than any DNA strand. They desperately tried to extract a message, even a name, from those marks in the dust found by one of its explorer sparks.

A spark, be it noted, who had been involved with three sentient leaps into the Flow so far.

Yet, as more of the Cosmic awareness squinted at the marks, it became more apparent that no message existed in them, and no sense of identity, either. No pattern was found, and certainly no intelligence.

Random, came the conclusion. Over and over came the damnation, at ever higher levels of awareness.

And so the puzzle deepened: Why would any species expend such incredible effort, and call in such monumental luck, and accomplish something the Flow had never seen before by crossing the gap between planets, simply to offer gibberish to posterity?

Was nonsense a contribution to the eternal discourse?

Was it intended as an insouciant criticism of sentience?

Had this been a species bound in flesh, so defiant, so crazed by incarceration in matter and the illusion of existential isolation and intellectual aloneness, that it spent itself in giving a version of the Cosmic raspberries, a universal finger, to coherent thought everywhere and always?

Were these marks anarchy? A stand against rationality itself?

A chill rippled through the Flow.

The spark who had found the marks, hero of three successful explorations, diminished his positive resonance accordingly, alarmed by the notion now coursing through the nodes: Sabotage?

Was this a booby-trap?

Had the Flow finally found a cognizant enemy? Was it an enemy that had planned far beyond its own existence in order to plant a seed of irrationality that would, if ever found by pure thought, cause a systemic collapse of reason and logic? Was the Flow even then irreparably harmed? Were incremental flaws stitching through the system at the speed of thought, leaving damage in their wake and multiplying exponentially?

Was a madness bomb about to explode? Would it break apart the Universe-spanning Flow?

Could mere matter accomplish the destruction of energy, even from a hiding place in physical extinction?

Thoughts swirled like whirlwinds of sparks through the Flow, all focused on what the tantalizing marks in the dust might mean. Were they encoded with a message, or was their existence alone communication enough?

And when all factors were brought to bear, the marks became linked with the nearby star's looming red giant stage in the Flow's thoughts. Could this be a warning of sorts? Was this insignificant star, located on a galactic fringe, a carrier somehow of madness? Would disorder radiate from it as it leapt the gap from matter to pure energy? Might it not, in a way never seen before, never experienced, bring a disturbance into the Flow? And could such a fluctuation not lead, through amplitude and swell, surge and growth, to bigger and bigger eddies of illogic? Did this red giant coming so soon portend, somehow, an onslaught against pure thought?

The Flow calculated and churned, already rippling anxiety and strain in its more local clusters. A sector chimed in with the opinion that any risk was too great to tolerate. If total destruction of the Flow's balance and harmonic resonance were at risk, then the swell to red giant must be stopped somehow, if possible. No matter how tiny the threat of annihilation, the delicacy of Cosmic Mind must be maintained and defended at all costs, even the cost of aborting an energy form's birth.

This new idea cascaded through the Flow with galvanic intensity. It rang with force to unsettle long-standing discussions that had existed for hundreds of thousands, even millions, of local orbits. As factored by the untold trillions of satellites going around uncounted billions of stars, an amazing kind of clock-time might be arrived at.

If every planet and planetoid in the Cosmos were taken into account, and each orbit measured against all the others, timed by start and finish in its circling around its local star, and an average arrived at, then that would become Cosmic Time.

And by that reckoning, there was little time left to debate this unbelievable quandary, arisen from a tiny fleck of dusty rock orbiting a dead planet, itself looping around a bloated, pregnant star. A decision had to be reached, and quickly, if any efforts were to be made, any steps taken toward perhaps, for the first time in Cosmic Mind, stopping the birth of another energy burst as a star shed a spent shell.

A sense of crisis permeated the Flow.

Discoverer, as the energy spark which had first noticed the marks in the dust was now thought of in the Flow, felt the pressure waves of concern pulsing from the universe around him. He did not, despite his positive charge, jump any gaps to such negative ideas. Fear, being a new sensation, merely intrigued him. He sensed its destructiveness but savored, in ways not evident at such a low level of thought, its energy, its alluring power.

Struggles slashed through the Flow now, as Discoverer flickered from one dust mark to another, studying the marks anew, trying desperately to find a coherent and provable notion in them. He wondered if they might not be not communication at all but artifact, incidental to communication, and began seeking clues around each mark. Perhaps these marks had been made in the process of making other marks, now faded.

Dust here, rocks there, slopes and plateaux, all of it added up to apparently random emptiness, the pathetic scratchings of unintelligent

94

beings. And yet, to have made it across the gap from Earth to its Moon contradicted such a dim, grim view of such beings.

And that was when he realized what needed to be done. He flashed a thought into his cluster. It was a question about time left, and a request for permission, and a statement about his willingness to risk himself. Although the ascent of his squawk and the descent of Cosmic Mind's answer took only a few nanoseconds of Cosmic Time, he felt suspense and frustration, impatience and eagerness. All this experienced as electrical tension and pulses of charge and discharge.

His answer came hesitant and bleak, with a touch of despair and a hint of desperation, as if no better alternative could be found to a bad suggestion. Cosmic Mind revered all life, all pure energy beings, all sentience, and all thought, and risking even a miniscule spark such as Marks Discoverer was not something usually done, or sanctioned. This time, however, given the unusual nature of the situation, permission came, along with warnings parental and avuncular. A waft of general concern followed the granting of freedom to pursue his idea.

Yes, he could explore the Earth again, more thoroughly this time, with an idea of what to look for. He would search for marks similar to what he'd found, and cross-reference any context, hoping it would reveal further clues to meaning and interpretation. And he would be pulled out without warning or notice if the burgeoning red giant showed signs of instability or began flaring or heaving out new pure energy sentience.

This seemed fair enough, a deal brokered for balance.

He blipped up and out from Luna, an arc of negatives channeling him across the gap between satellite and planet. To him it seemed but a blink or three, a restful period during which the connection to the Flow was at its ebb for him, a muted drone in the background of his own humming, buzzing thoughts. At the same time, he knew the Flow remained aware of him, his position, and his mission. Being part of the Flow meant always having awareness showered upon you, and never being isolated or alone, which was considered the ultimate punishment short of total discharge.

A shower of other sparks also rained down upon Earth again, the Flow having decided many inspections stood a better chance of quicker success than a single wandering glance. An invasion of sorts came to Earth once more, mirroring the panspermia that had brought life to a still-molten lump untold millions of orbits ago. This time it brought sentience and intelligence without bothering with viral spirals of DNA or protoplasmic clumping of molecules to form ever more complex matrices for the energy to dance within. Free from form, this invasion caressed like a whisper of starlight, and explored more gently than a glimmer of deep space's hush.

Coming down on a scape illuminated by the huge red star hanging low in the sky, Marks Discoverer arced over rubble-strewn valleys clogged with churned boulders and ragged spume from pyroclastic flows. Dark stains marred the rocks as if acid had fallen once from skies long since gone from blue backscatter to star-speckled black airlessness.

Moving along ridges comprised of blades as stiff and brittle as spines broken by carnivores half the size of river deltas. Sharpened by ice particles howling on a constant wind, the blades of obsidian were honed in places to a single molecule. They would slice hairs into fourths lengthwise, eighths perhaps, were there any hirsute mammals left to contribute to the experiment.

Shimmering along each edge like light refracted from eons-distant explosions, Marks Discoverer left no trace and found no more dust; the wind was too strong there. Not even pebbles or small stones could remain for long in such a blast, and the cold, the ice, leeching all liquids long since from the atmosphere, left only static, which crackled dangerously around him as he moved.

He came to a steep slope downward and leaped from the knife sharp ridge to slide into shadow and shelter. At once the wind's sound deepened from shrill keening to a resonant moan. It was as if that part of the continent, trapped and now squeezed mercilessly by ocean-sized blocks of dark, grit-filled ice, mourned itself. Under it, the planet's core cooled and solidified like an old heart even as the wind played a wavering tone across the hollow socket like a mocking dirge. And at the base of the slope he came upon a hole, a sink, a cave, at the bottom of which lay filtered dust captured as it was swept ever eastward toward what had once been a bountiful inland plain of prairies and forests. Only dust was left of such things now.

Examining the dust, hoping for marks, Marks Discoverer understood that the top layers, and probably many others down to bedrock level, were too young to have taken the impressions of even the lowest form of life. No prints here, no marks at all made by life. Only the random swirls and eddies of dead matter blown without cause or effect by mindless winds.

Rising from the cave, Marks Discoverer moved quickly now, blinking from place to place, seeking any kind of evidence of geological violence. Crevasses in snow- and ice-cracked rocks, leaving rifts in the ground no longer worsened by cycles of melt and freeze, there being insufficient thermal energy from the dying solar matter in the sky.

Moving inland, toward the harsh and hardened plains now sheets of scoured rock, rippling like water caught mid-flow by stellar disapproval, frozen in place by shame.

As he worked, flitting to any tiny bump or ripple, examining all marks for signs of life, he knew uncountable others did the same around him, all of them comparing nature's work to those squiggles and imprints on the Lunar surface, and finding no matches. The Moon marks stood unique.

And even as the scouring of Earth continued, other energies, linked and enhanced, made powerful beyond precedent, flexed into the swollen sun, making changes, linking some atoms, breaking others, and channeling a flow of material once known as the asteroid belt and Oort cloud to fall now at incalculable rates into the sun, gaining it material. It was not much, perishingly little compared to its size, but slowly it became enough to tip things over slightly.

With a quiver felt throughout the solar system, like a jostling in the dark, the dying sun gasped a bit more life and became again, for awhile, stable. It would last now a few more millennia, while an even more ambitious plan unfolded.

Meanwhile, Marks Discoverer looked further and came to what had once been mountains, now nubs and sunken pits, worn down by time and their own mass. He found here other crevasses, other ways down and in, and followed to find cavern systems. All was ice, until he'd gone deep enough that residual warmth from the core allowed small trickles of melt water to move, to gather, and to contemplate eternity.

These, using the energy, little though it was, of the thermal vents maintained, to his surprise, a pocket universe of teeming microbial life.

Life, if not yet sentient.

As he shouted his find in a blip of warning, of joy, he realized there was more here. He sensed movement. He felt a tiny resonance of something more than motility, a quantum more than mere Brownian motion. Moving deeper into the sunless, windless cavern, he opened his senses to the emanations of mind, however marginal, however provisional.

As he did this, the plan evolved around him, without his knowledge. Sol's growing burst of pure energy, normally released naturally by transition, was being removed gently, little by little, even as the mass jettisoned and abandoned by the joyous newborn purity was conserved, to be used for phase two.

This involved moving the energy-drained matter into the heart of a stillborn sun, one of the gas giants in the system, once known by some of the inhabitants of Earth as Jupiter, or Zeus, and giving it a burst from the Flow, a jolt of energy that sparked into life a new sun, creating a new system that, with much chaos and the loss of another of the dead planets, organized itself around this brand new star.

Earth, guided as softly as a cradle is rocked, took up a position in relation to Zeus quite similar to the distance it had once kept from the dying star, Sol. Even its Moon was brought along, set spinning anew, to provide tides to churn the primordial ooze. Now that Discoverer had once more been able to find life where none had been thought to exist, it was time for Earth to warm again, its seas once more to flow.

In the cavern, Marks Discoverer came to a place where dust lay, brought from the surface so far above, and perhaps ground, too, from surrounding rocks by geological forces that ceased long ago. This place allowed melt water and overflow from the underground tidal pool to trickle into dust, creating warm mud.

Marks Discoverer allowed his awareness to touch theirs, and said hello in his way, and received their slow and linear greeting in exchange. He then raised his pitch and let the other sparks know where to look, and what to listen for, and it was not long before many reports of worms were crossing the universe in a chorus of triumphant celebration. The hunch had paid off. Unheard-of measures had come to fruition.

All was joy in the pure energy realm.

In that nutrient-rich mud, nosing and flopping, eating, growing, and reproducing, he found a sentient life form that would once have been called worms. Lowliest of the low, these worms had survived by keeping their heads down. They existed now, with feeble brains flickering tiny worm-thoughts, in the warm womb of an otherwise dead mother.

But like the gods made up by the cetaceans, simians, and primates of once-upon-a-time Earth, this cold dead mother would warm again, and her flowers would blossom, and her air would be refreshed, and her water would flow, and her myriad life forms would once again arise, reborn and resurrected under the lightning-started glow of her new sun, Zeus.

For the first time ever, the Flow, the Cosmic Mind, had moved matter and arranged things to favor, even coddle, life, the rarity it cherished most of all. And so myths came to be true, in a way.

* * *

98

And so the footprints and other marks left so thoughtlessly by our twelve astronauts in the Lunar regolith inadvertently saved the Earth from its once-certain destruction, and its new masters, worms in the dirt, our descendants and in truth our brothers in unawareness, were left safely wiggling and, yes, evolving. What new wonders would they find when first they glimpsed the sky?

The Celestial Sea
by Cliff Winnig

They fell like silver rain out of the black sky. Hundreds, then thousands, then tens of thousands—the droplets impacted softly on the grey surface. They spread, flowing like quicksilver across the barren landscape. When they met one another, they merged into puddles and rivulets.

In a widening circle they tasted the dust, examined impact craters, and studied the dimensions of rocks. The large moon was tidally locked to the planet it circled, and the explorers had landed on the outward-facing side. For this phase they remained spread out, moving slowly towards the inner hemisphere.

Tiny machines formed these puddles of the celestial sea, individually quite unintelligent. But they knew how to map and record, how to share information. Each one carried parts of larger programs within itself, to be assembled as needed on an ad hoc basis.

They ran the first such program when a small puddle crossed a row of regular grooves, followed by a thin indentation and a second row of grooves. The puddle crept a bit further, found that the odd markings didn't resume, and returned to the two rows with their central indentation. It spread itself thin, covering the full width of the feature. It flowed first one way, then the other, along the grooves' path for more than sixty meters in each direction.

Being just one of many small puddles, it contained relatively few of the tiny machines—some 640 million—but the simple algorithms available to it determined that the feature had an 86% chance of being artificial.

So the puddle called to its nearest neighbors, which by then were each over three kilometers away. Five puddles answered the call. On arrival they merged into a single pool, one with greater intelligence, a larger catalog of known natural features, and a fair-sized library of analytical tools.

Using all these resources, the pool determined the tracks, if that was indeed what they were, were more than 99% likely to be artificial.

This result triggered a major restructuring. All parts of the celestial sea exploring the lunar surface began converging on that spot.

Time passed. The machines arrived.

The resulting pond churned, then coalesced around two rising columns. They began shaping themselves into a pair of beings, gradually growing harder, forming sharp-spiked armor reminiscent of chitin. Each one resembled the biological creatures who had once learned to make smaller and smaller machines. Three-meter tall, multi-eyed, bipedal insectoids, they had four arms ending in hands with paired opposable thumbs. Translucent wings hung off their backs, merely ornamental in what was essentially a vacuum. Their creator-ancestors had evolved on a planet of warm seas and lush jungles. Kilometer-tall trees broke the surface of the water to form elaborate interconnected structures. Here, in a landscape as different from that world as could be imagined, the machine-formed beings carried the memory of home like a lantern in the night.

Wari and Valra, famous poets and scientists, examined the landscape around them. As major currents in the celestial sea, the pair had instances treading on planets and moons, or orbiting stars all over this part of the galaxy. For more than ten thousand years the celestial sea had been spreading, out from a star somewhat closer to the galactic core. In that time, the sea had explored a rough sphere four thousand light years in radius. Nothing artificial had ever been detected.

Until now.

Wari and Valra looked at the tracks. Something had traveled along the surface of this moon. Something with wheels. It could have come from anywhere, but nonetheless they looked towards the ghostly white planet floating near the horizon.

They could access the combined memories of their component machines, all that they'd learned thus far about the system. The moon had not always been so far from the planet, yet it had been tidally locked for much of its history, they'd calculated. The planet would have been in the same position in the sky, if larger, when whatever it was had rolled across the plain.

"It might still be extrasolar in origin," Wari said. His natural voice wouldn't have carried, so he sent his speech by focused beam.

"Yes, but we saw nothing like it on the outer side," said Valra.

"True. Any preference of direction?"

"Towards the planet."

"If you like."

* * *

The object came into sight some distance away, but they wanted to examine it closely before drawing any definite conclusions. They had walked beside the tracks for just under two kilometers.

"Looks like a lander," Valra said as they neared it. "Very basic. Notice the two pairs of ramps. It only carried one roving unit, but its design provided for two exits. That means they didn't have much control over where it landed."

"'Front door and back door. I lie on the floor, my fate riven.'" Wari quoted himself, from a lament an instance of him had written six thousand years before.

"This thing didn't just lie around," said Valra. "It made tracks."

"Back the way we came, then?"

"That would be my suggestion."

They walked around the lander. Other than its silver color, it barely resembled the machines of which they themselves were composed. Over three meters across, roughly circular, the device squatted alone on the timeless surface. How long had it been there?

"One thing is clear," Wari said. "This antenna could not have communicated much past the planet."

"Although it could have talked to a satellite with more range," said Valra.

Wari clicked his mandibles at his partner. Though silent here, the gesture still conveyed his amusement. "I thought you favored the planet-once-held-life theory." He indicated the sphere, covered now in the clouds of a runaway greenhouse effect.

"I still do, but I'm keeping my mind open. 'Sunrise through the canopy—I see silhouettes of my mother, my queen.'"

"Unless I miss my guess," said Wari, "this lander predates the oldest queendom by millions, perhaps billions of years."

They found the rover after more than ten kilometers of tracks. It sat round-bodied, with its central section hinged shut, like a sleeping sentinel. It sported two rows of four grooved wheels and a small ninth wheel in the middle. A kind of odometer, Valra suggested.

"Do you suppose it was smart enough to explore on its own?" she asked.

"Might have been remotely operated," said Wari. "Although with a few seconds' delay if they used your planetary base rather than an orbiter, depending on how wide the moon's orbit was back then."

Valra walked around the rover, examining it. After getting a consenting gesture from Wari, she approached the device and carefully touched it, as she'd done with the lander after their visual inspection. She released a million or so of her component machines, which crawled over the surface of the vehicle, mapping, examining, probing. When they'd finished their work, they flowed down to the lunar surface and across the dusty plain to merge with her left foot.

"Definitely radio-controlled," she said.

Wari looked out over the grey desert. "I wonder what they thought of this place. Did they have poets and artists of their own, or were they all just about geology and physics?"

"We may never know," Valra said, tilting her head playfully. "Unless we find more of their probes."

"You think they might have launched other missions?"

"Why not? We're still near the edge of the inner hemisphere. If this probe came from the planet—back when it could support life—and if the moon were tidally locked even then, would they not have wanted to explore the surface they'd been staring at all their lives?"

"Maybe," said Wari. "If they happened to think like you."

Valra clicked her mandibles, laughing at herself really. "Who can say how they thought? They were aliens."

As if to prove Valra's point, the next object they found had no purpose at all, near as they could determine.

A small white spheroid, it rested alone near the moon's equator on the planet-facing side. It had regular dimples on its surface, corresponding to an icosahedral pattern, and a series of glyphs printed on one spot.

Wari picked it up, looking at it. His wide-spectrum vision gave him no further insight, so he popped it into his mouth for his component machines to examine.

"Hard outer layer over an inner core that seems once to have been quite flexible. It had a fair bit of bounce." He spat it out again and gingerly returned it where he'd found it. He'd already memorized its coordinates.

"Perhaps some sort of religious artifact?" Valra suggested doubtfully. "A stylized representation of this moon?"

"It had a lot of bounce for an icon," Wari said.

"Maybe they fired it from a cannon? Could they have fought a war on the lunar surface?"

"No traces of any propellant, though a few iron atoms are still adhering to one side. You know, I think something whacked it here with a metal limb. Perhaps a more advanced version of the rover we found."

Valra snapped her fingers in confusion. "Why would they make a robot do that? If they came from the planet, wouldn't they need to lift whatever they sent up the gravity well?"

"They would. Ballistics test, then?"

"I could see that, but why use a dimpled white sphere? Dimples only make it more aerodynamic if there's air. This ball couldn't have been designed for lunar use."

"That's it!" Wari shouted "It's a ball, like the practice payloads for our ancestors' children."

"A children's carrying game? On their moon? What kind of species are we dealing with here?"

"One that liked making its robots practice children's games."

"You know what this means, though, don't you?" Valra asked, becoming serious.

"It means that probably the lander, the rover, and the sphere did come from the planet above us."

"Which means we now have enough information to send upstream."

"I know. Before we call them, though, let's at least take a quick look around here. Perhaps we can find whatever hit this thing out here."

"All right," said Valra. "A quick look around. Any longer, and you know we'll get flak from the inquisitor."

A short while later, they found the lander where it sat, some three hundred meters away. It had been partly obscured by a low ridge. The area around it held several other artifacts, including another of the small white spheres.

They found grooved tracks and many, many footprints. It didn't take long for them to figure out the mass and size of the bipedal probes that had used this lander, based on the depth and shape of the footprints.

"They walked like us," Wari said, his voice full of wonder.

"This must represent a much later mission," said Valra. "These robots had to be a lot more sophisticated than the rover."

"Agreed. But not so commonplace that they weren't valued." He indicated the golden-and-silver object before them. "Judging by the depth of the lander's footprints, this isn't all the mass that touched down here. These robots also took off again."

"A sample-return mission."

"Almost certainly," said Wari. "But a robot-return mission as well."

"I hope they didn't wind up standing forever in some gallery as a reward for their service."

Wari clicked his mandibles. "That doesn't seem too likely to me. Probably they sent them on a lecture tour."

"Or on goodwill missions to other regions of the planet," said Valra, getting into the spirit of it.

"Perhaps they suffered an even worse fate," whispered Wari conspiratorially.

"The queen's loyal government!" they shouted together gleefully.

That thought, however, brought with it the inevitable followup: the royal inquisitor. They had waited long enough, too long maybe. They would have to call one in.

As it happened, a sufficient amount of the celestial sea was available in-system to reconstitute an inquisitor. While the sea had sent a bit of itself to the inner solar system, most of its local mass swarmed around the mini-systems of the fifth and sixth planets, the largest two gas giants. One particular moon of the fifth world had occupied the majority of that interest. Beneath kilometers of ice they had found a fascinating and diverse ecosystem in an ocean warmed by geothermal activity, itself born of huge tidal forces. As always, they had failed to find evidence of sentient life, past or present, but chromosomal analysis had been conducted on the DNA-like cores of the aliens' cells. Macroscopic evolution had clearly been going on there for six hundred million years.

So when the call came from the third planet's moon, a large part of the local sea devoted itself to forming a royal advisory council. This far from the core of the celestial sea, even a one-way message to the queen would take thousands of years, but instances of appropriate advisors and ministers could always be constructed. These officials found a locked priority tag related to artifacts found near the third planet, so they decided to send down an instance of a black inquisitor.

Wari and Valra had been expecting a white one, or perhaps at worst a red. When His Scrutiny, Glor the Black Royal Inquisitor rained onto the landing site, the two scientist poets stared in utter shock.

It took Glor barely a minute to assemble his body. He looked much like the others, his appearance based on the same species theirs had been, but his subspecies was taller—nearly four meters in height—with more eyes and longer spikes on his digits. Also, true to his rank, the light-sucking machines that formed him appeared quite black, even to Wari and Valra's wide-spectrum vision. He stood nearly invisible against the blackness of space. Only when he crossed in front of some feature could they get a real sense of his presence.

He obliged them by walking to the lander and squatting down by the closest footprints. He seemed to be doing a great number of calculations, for he stood there almost two seconds before rising and turning to address the pair.

"How long did you wait before calling me?" he asked.

Wari and Valra glanced at each other, but they didn't dare beam anything between them.

"Not long," said Wari. "As soon as we found this second landing site, we called. One site indicated a probe, but a second one, here, suggested the planet above as the origin point."

The inquisitor did not even glance up at their mention of the planet. "Didn't you think that the *first* evidence of sentient life warranted a call?"

"We wanted to provide as much information as possible," said Valra. Her excuse sounded weak, even to herself.

Glor stalked towards them, nodding his head in anger. "You wanted to play around with your aliens awhile first. Did you think I wouldn't have the resources to quickly obtain the information you've uncovered? I swear I don't know why they keep sending you two!"

Valra shrank a bit under his onslaught, but Wari held his ground. "Because we're very good at what we do," he said quietly.

"Until you find anything of import!" shouted Glor, looming over the two of them. "Then you don't follow protocol!"

"You," said Wari, "were called."

For a moment it seemed as if Glor would strike him, but instead he turned and examined the plaque attached to the side of the landing module. It had glyphs similar to the ones on the white sphere, some squiggles, and two circles with dark splotches.

"What do you make of these?" Glor asked, pointing to the circles.

"No idea," said Wari.

"Could represent their homeworld," said Valra. "Views from space, of the northern and southern hemispheres perhaps."

Glor straightened and looked down at her, crossing both pairs of arms in front of his chest. "Very insightful. All right. I'm going to show you two something that even the councilors who called me into being here know nothing about. I want you tell me what you make of it."

Glor beamed them images, tagged with their source: a diffuse net of low-intelligence machine clusters, the vanguard of the celestial sea. In deep space, several light years from this moon and its planet, the sea had found a small artificial probe. Measurements showed it to be about three meters across, not counting some protruding limbs, most of that the diameter of its antenna dish. The cameras zoomed in, and simultaneously the data grew richer, as the observing pools merged and grew smarter.

They focused on a golden plaque. It showed a drawing, with two connected circles on the top left, a starburst beneath them, and an abstract image of the probe to the right. Of particular interest were two beings depicted standing in front of the probe. If they were to scale, they stood less than two meters tall: roughly the same size as the robots that had made the footsteps. They had slightly different heights and body shapes, no doubt representing subspecies with different functions. Each had only one pair of arms, with one thumb and four fingers. It was hard to tell with such a simple drawing, but their chitin seemed oddly flexible, as if they were soft-bodied, possibly even endoskeletal.

Below the other images, the plaque showed ten circles of different sizes. A smaller version of the probe was shown leaving the seventh one from the right.

Valra understood immediately. "The circles on the bottom. They're the side view of a solar system. The big circle on the left would be the sun; the other nine would be planets, though nothing is to scale in terms of size or distance."

She looked up at Glor and pointed to the silver plaque before them. "So you agree with me on this plaque. The circles could be maps of the lander's homeworld."

This time Glor did raise his face to the dirty white sphere. Wari and Valra followed his gaze.

"The dark and light areas could represent seas and land," said Wari. "Though we'll never be able to tell now if that world is the origin. Any seas there might once have been have long since boiled away."

"But it has to be," said Valra. "Look in your mind's eye at the golden plaque. The probe came from the third-closest planet. The system has one sun, four small planets, and four gas giants. Perhaps the rings on the sixth planet were really prominent back when they launched it."

"What about the ninth planet?" asked Glor quietly. They all knew that the system they were exploring had eight major worlds, not counting the spherical rocks in the Kuiper belt and the largest objects in the Oort cloud. But the golden map showed only one world past the gas giants, where there should be between eighteen and twenty-six, depending on what one counted.

"Maybe it got thrown out of the system," suggested Wari, touching his head with all four hands in a gesture of confusion. "Or perhaps the one circle represented all the planets in their Kuiper Belt." Yet he failed even to convince himself.

"There has to be *some* explanation," said Valra. "It's not as if a civilization that could design and launch an interstellar probe wouldn't know how many planets were in its own solar system."

"True," said Glor. Let me show you something else. He beamed them more of the datastream, which showed the sea's analysis of the two circles and the starburst pattern. The circles represented the transition of hydrogen atoms, with a vertical line indicating "true" beneath them. That had proven to be the key. The pattern was revealed as a map of pulsars, locating the solar system of the probe's origin. The sea had calculated the steady change in pulsar frequencies, finding that considerable time had elapsed since the probe's launch. The final analysis had been conclusive: the system in the center was the one they were in, shown in the distant past.

Enough time had passed that the planet's crust had renewed itself completely, but the moon had remained much more primordial.

"If you already knew that the third planet once held intelligent life, why send so little of the celestial sea to investigate its moon?" asked Valra. "We should have had at least twenty or thirty currents represented here, not just Wari and me."

Glor looked back at them, and they saw him clicking his mandibles. In a black inquisitor, the effect was chilling. "No doubt we would have, if the local councilors knew about that probe."

Wari and Valra absorbed this information. "Nobody knows but you?"

"Just me, the other black inquisitors in this section of space, and the encrypted courier stream on its way to the queen. We won't tell anyone until we know Her Majesty's will on this matter. After all, this is the first intelligent species we have ever encountered—I can assure you of that—and now you have uncovered more of their artifacts."

109

Valra looked back at the plaque on the lander, but Wari stared at the inquisitor. "You didn't tell anyone."

"That's right."

"But you told us."

"You yourself said that you are good at what you do. Your insights will be included in my update to Her Majesty."

"You're not going to let us merge with our currents, are you?"

Valra looked up in horror, first at Wari, then Glor, then back to Wari. "What?"

Glor clicked his mandibles again. "You know, I admire the way your mind leaps insightfully to the correct conclusions," he said. "I have not often encountered your currents in the past, at least not that my local instance remembers, but I now know why the celestial sea includes you in our vanguard."

"You can't do that to us!" shouted Valra. "That's murder!"

"No," said Glor. "Just eminent domain."

"We can still be of use," said Wari. Valra looked at him nervously. "Leave us here to continue uncovering their artifacts. We can. . ." Here he hesitated, but after a pause he bravely continued. "We can represent the celestial sea in isolation until Her Majesty's decision on this matter reaches our part of the sea."

"But Wari," said Valra. "That will take at least *eight thousand years*."

Wari turned towards her, gazing into her eyes. "We'd have each other, and anyone else that His Scrutiny saw fit to spare. It's better than having these instances terminated, without letting our thoughts and memories flow back into our currents."

"But it's so long."

"Yet," interrupted Glor. "Time now is short. Unlike you, I don't hesitate before making my reports upstream. I shall summon more of the sea to this moon, but no additional currents. The three of us will explore and catalog; then I shall make my report. Now, tell me: if you were the species depicted in the plaque, where else would you send an expedition?"

Over the next few lunar days, Wari and Valra submerged their fears of death or exile and dove deeply into artifact hunting. As they found site after site, they speculated endlessly about the moon's first explorers. Glor encouraged this mindset, periodically feeding them tiny bits of analyses to which only he had access.

The trio found three rovers clearly designed to be piloted by the bipedal robots. After they discovered the second one, Wari put forth the radical theory that the bipedal robots might really have been the biological species themselves, wearing protective gear.

"But that's just crazy," said Valra. "Why risk currents from their own species? At the biological stage, all their currents would have only one instance each."

"Yes but imagine what it must have been like to be such an instance," said Wari. "You'd be mortal, certain that one day you would die, with no chance to flow into a greater current. That would probably make them take risks."

Glor listened silently to the debate.

"I'll admit the rest of this technology is pretty primitive by comparison," said Valra. "But I still say they could've had walking robots."

"Judging from what we've seen, they weren't a species given to waiting until things could be done safely, or efficiently. Besides, they brought the two white spheres. Religious objects or children's toys, they likely had only marginal use in any real science."

Eventually, they found all the artifacts and put forth every theory that Wari and Valra could think of. During that time, Glor sent an encrypted stream to the queen at the start of each lunar night. More and more, Wari and Valra's thoughts turned with dread to their own fates.

"I thank you," said Glor, after finishing his final report to the queen. "You have been of great service to the celestial sea. Also, I have come to enjoy working with you, I admit. I shall have to seek out instances of your currents on future occasions."

"We're more concerned with our present instances," said Wari, taking hold of one of Valra's lower hands with his own.

"Yes," said Glor. "I quite understand. I have communicated with the sea around the fifth planet, and they have sent me an up-to-date template for each of your currents. The machines now in orbit have a complete set. I shall use them to find the deltas between your templates and your local instances."

"You're going to preserve us?" asked Valra.

Glor actually looked away, towards the rocky horizon. "Part of you. I can't spare enough memory for all the deltas, nor risk keeping much of what you know distributed in unencrypted form. Surely you understand." He looked back at them. "I do, however, have access to some very sophisticated parsing algorithms. Your present personalities, though shaped by events and discoveries you will no longer remember, will be preserved and allowed to flow back into your currents."

"But we could still stay here!" said Wari.

Glor crossed his upper arms in front of his chest. "For more than eight thousand years? After such a time, do you think that whatever pitiful beings you had become would be able to flow into your currents? No, mine is the better solution."

"But you mustn't!" said Valra. "We...."

Then she spoke no more, for Glor had sent an override signal to the machines that constituted both of their bodies. They could beam no further speech, even locally, nor could they move.

Silently the pair watched more of the sea rain down from orbit. The resulting puddles crawled over them, interfaced with their minds, and recorded what Glor instructed them to.

Wari and Valra had been holding hands, however. They could talk without beaming, and before their bodies were invaded and dissolved, they had quite a lengthy conversation between themselves.

After he dissolved the pair, Glor sent his final communiqué to the councilors around the fifth planet. Then he dissolved himself, flowing back into a formless pool, his mind and body held distributed in encrypted blocks of data in each machine that had made up his local instance.

Most of the machines launched themselves back into orbit. A skeleton crew—largely made up of machines that had, briefly, been Wari and Valra—remained to do the slow drudgery of going over the entire surface, making sure nothing remained uncatalogued.

Some of those machines carried within themselves pieces of a new program, a Trojan horse really, placed there by Wari and Valra before their minds were invaded, recorded, and dissolved. Over the next few hundred years, that program would periodically appear and run. It diverted machines from their original paths, taking them to a spot not far from the last resting place of a certain white ball, one that had once flown mile and miles.

There, on a flat area of rock, the tiny puddles formed tinier streams, slowly carving glyphs of the celestial sea's poetic language. With time, "The

Ballad of the Lost World" appeared in the inner hemisphere of the moon, facing the lifeless planet that had once sent out bits of itself, questing for its smaller sibling.

> On wheels and legs,
> In fragile metal boxes,
> In delicate, fleshy bodies,
> We came.
>
> We rolled; we walked; we jumped.
> We left the arms of our queen and mother,
> And flowed into the stars.
> We passed.
> But we left behind our mark.

Another's Treasure
by Eric Choi

Asan had never seen so many scribes.

The chamber was filled to capacity. All of the seating had long been taken, forcing those arriving late to stand along the far wall. The murmur of the scribes conversing amongst themselves echoed through the chamber. Recorders flashed incessantly, and Asan was forced to cover hir eyes.

Cas, the moderator, glanced at hir timepiece and turned to Asan. "Are you ready to begin, Learned Asan?"

Asan gestured hir assent.

Cas spoke into the amplifier. "I ask now for the attention of all. We are ready to commence the session."

The scribes abruptly fell silent, but periodic recorder flashes continued.

"Greetings to all," said Asan. "I am humbled by the attendance of so many at this session, although perhaps not surprised. Mass interest in the alien artifacts on the natural satellite of Mongollon continues to be intense, and your presence here is a reflection of that interest.

"It has been but a few short cycles since the artifacts were discovered, and much remains a mystery. Progress, however slow, does continue nevertheless, and it is with great excitement that I announce a major new discovery that, it is hoped, will not only advance our understanding of the artifacts but perhaps also illuminate the creators themselves—the lost race that made the artifacts so long ago."

Asan turned to Cas. "I ask now for the first projection."

The desolation was magnificent.

Site 6 was on a broad, level plain, pockmarked with small craters and scattered with rocks and pebbles of every variety. The plain was bounded on one side by a number of large craters and on the other by a line of jagged boulders. There was little variation in color, the hues spanning only the range from light tan to ashen gray. Above was the blackness of space.

Jaax did not think it was a hostile scene. Somehow, it did not look like a place where an unprotected being would perish almost instantly. On the contrary, it seemed almost inviting.

In the distance, Jaax could see ridges, but with no buildings, vegetation or other features normally used to judge size and distance it was difficult to determine their height. The lack of atmosphere gave an unreal clarity to the view, better than the clearest day on Rathje.

Six major artifact sites, and evidence of alien remnants at dozens of other locations, had been detected by orbital surveys. Of the six major sites, this was the last to be explored by a surface survey team. Jaax had been told the other sites were in much more impressive locations. Site 5, for example, was found at the base of a mountain range, while Site 3 was discovered in the floor of a valley. It did not matter, for Jaax was not here for the scenery.

Jaax was here for the artifacts.

As one of Learned Asan's senior understudies, Jaax had accompanied hir mentor on several excavations, but this was hir first off-world survey. That hir scroll learning would be based upon the mass known Mongollon artifacts was a great honor alone. But if Jaax could document one big find, study something that had not been discovered before—"the nugget," as it was called—all the most prestigious post-scroll institutes would be hirs to choose.

Except for the challenging environment, necessitating the use of suits, the survey could well have been on Rathje. Jaax had participated in many, and regardless of whether they were on- or off-world the ways were similar. The area was carefully marked off in grids, and each understudy was assigned to a specific sub-area, working small tools to uncover artifacts with deliberate care. Recorders documented everything.

By area, Site 6 was the smallest of the major alien remnants on the Mongollon satellite, and it was the last to be explored. It had in common many of the same artifacts found at the other sites. Most prominent of these was a large, eight-sided structure covered with a crumbling dark foil, held above the surface by four supports. Immediately about these structures were strewn numerous smaller objects, whose number and description sometimes differed from site to site. Some of the objects were covered with a fibrous silica cloth, in a sickly hue of yellow that testified their great age. Other objects were made of metallic or silicate materials and appeared intact. Regardless of composition, the purpose of many of the objects had yet to be determined.

The other artifact found at all the sites was a metallic pole and crossbar planted into the surface, with fragments of a polymer substance scatted on the ground beneath. This artifact could also be found at Site 6, but lying on the ground rather than upright. Here, the polymer material, though brittle and bleached white from an unimaginable number of cycles of ultraviolet exposure and covered with the thinnest coating of dust, was revealed to originally have been in the form of a rectangular sheet.

And always, on the ground, were the tracks: elongated ovals with horizontal ridges along the short axis, imprints with only the slightest erosion, sprinkled with the barest dust.

An excited voice called out through the loop. "I have found something!"

Jaax recognized the voice as that of Riso, one of the junior understudies. Riso's location blinked on hir visor, and Jaax turned in that direction.

Riso was pointing to a sealed bag that appeared to be of the same fibrous silica material that covered some of the surface objects. The bag seemed sizeable, probably large enough to hold a Rathjean foundling of median age. Jaax had seen images of similar bags found at the other sites, but to hir knowledge this was the first completely intact.

Excited chatter filled the loop. Jaax's team had discovered the nugget.

Learned Ase was neither an archaeologist nor an anthropologist, so it came as a surprise when Learned Asan asked hir to conduct an analysis. The sample, Asan told Ase cryptically, was not of this world. Hir curiosity piqued, Ase immediately agreed.

Ase placed a tiny amount of the grayish-brown material from Site 6 into a sterile tube and filled it with fluid. The tube was placed into an electromagnetic chamber and bombarded briefly with radiation. Following the exposure, the tube was taken out of the chamber and a quantity of reagent and primer added. The combined mixture was then placed into a thermocycler that heated and held the sample at various temperatures.

After the thermal treatment, the sample tube was again removed, and the matrix materials, molecular markers and buffer compounds were added. The tube was then inserted into the analysis apparatus, and the device was activated.

Within moments, a sequence of dark and light horizontal bands began to form in projection. Ase gasped in surprise. Though not of this world, the pattern was still familiar.

*   *   *

The projection of the Mongollon satellite rotated silently before the scribes, with the locations of the alien artifacts marked upon the grayish orb.

"To date, the archaeological consensus is that the alien artifacts on the satellite of Mongollon are most probably middens," said Asan. "Or, to use more common language, piles of refuse. In general, the presence of such middens is indicative of a nomadic society."

"How do we know the aliens were nomadic?" a scribed asked.

"Material culture study," Asan replied. "In material culture study, it is a given axiomatic that the behavior of a civilization is reflected in its artifacts. Consider our own chronology, when our earliest nomadic ancestors disposed of refuse simply by leaving it where it fell. This method of disposal was adequate because nomadic hunter-gatherers frequently abandoned grounds to follow game. It is ironic, but chronology has shown that the path to civilization begins when a sufficiently sophisticated social order is developed to make possible the proper disposal of refuse."

Another scribe asked, "Are you suggesting the aliens were not civilized?"

Asan paused for a moment before answering. "If by that you imply they were not advanced, then I would disagree. The artifacts dumped in the middens show evidence of some sophistication in learnings of materials science and even basic electromechanics. Atomic signs have even been found at some sites. So, it is thoroughly incorrect to assume a nomadic civilization any less intelligent than a static one."

"At the least, it would appear these aliens were very wasteful," the scribed continued.

"Perhaps," said Asan, "but we should not judge them too harshly. For an archaeologist such as myself, ancient refuse mounds like those on the Mongollon satellite are in truth the happiest of finds. Consider for a moment the reason our own distant past seems misty and dim is precisely because our earliest ancestors left so little refuse behind. An appreciation of their accomplishments became possible only after they began making stone tools, the debris from the production of which, along with the discarded tools themselves, are now probed with sophisticated apparatus and displayed in museums not as refuse, but as artifacts. And so it is for the aliens."

There were many more questions, but Cas intervened. "The time grows short. We must allow Learned Asan to come to the most important announcement of the session."

"Yes," said Asan. "I ask for the next projection."

The image of the Mongollon satellite dissipated, and in its place another appeared. Before the audience now floated a square pouch of indeterminate size, with a pronounced bulge hinting at some sort of mass within.

"A survey team lead by Jaax, one of my senior understudies, recovered four of these objects at Site 6," Asan explained. "They were found encapsulated within a larger bag that also contained other objects of uncertain nature. Similar bags and inner pouches have been found at the other five major sites, but this bag at Site 6 is the only one completely intact."

The projection of the pouch rotated, revealing the other side of the object. Upon this surface was a set of symbols, presumably in the language of the Mongollon aliens, the glyphs still surprisingly legible despite the countless cycles:

DEFECATION COLLECTION DEVICE
MFG BY NEB AEROSPACE INC.
P/N NALG00820975091-5449
S/N 1106
DATE OF MFG—03/27/1968

"The pouch consists of an inner and outer lining," Asan continued. "Bound within the inner was this material."

A hard, grayish-brown blob appeared in projection.

"This unusual substance is biological in nature, and thanks to my colleague Learned Ase, we believe that we have made a significant advancement that will lead to a greater understanding of the lost race whose artifacts we now ponder.

"From this biological material, we have successfully extracted genetic molecules."

The chamber erupted in excited chatter. Cas called for order, then indicated permission for a scribe to query.

"Are you certain these genetic molecules are those of the lost alien race?" asked the scribe.

"Indeed, quite certain," said Asan confidently.

Another scribe queried, "Learned Asan, you spoke that similar pouches were found at the other sites. Why was genetic material never extracted from those?"

"There are two reasons," Asan said. "In the first, only those at Site 6 were found completely intact, in all three instances of the outer bag as well as both layers of the inside pouch. Even intact, three of the four pouches from Site 6 were contaminated with some manner of chemical residue, as were all the pouches from the other sites. It was only this singular pouch, what my understudy Jaax has called hir 'nugget', that not only were the seals unbreached but also the biological material within was uncontaminated."

The scribe wished to continue, but Cas intervened. "There is time only for an additional query. Opportunity must be given to another." Cas indicated the final scribe.

"Learned Asan, with this genetic material, would it . . . perhaps, would it be possible to somehow . . . recreate this lost race?"

Asan made a gesture of amusement. "I am archaeologist, not biologist, so I can hardly be of authority to speak of this. Such a thing would be difficult in the extreme, for the genetic material would likely be degraded and unusable. Thus, my first reaction is to say . . . you indeed enjoy too much the works of fantastic fiction."

The scribe accepted the words in good humor. "To you thanks, Learned Asan."

"And to you all, thanks," Cas announced. "The session is now concluded."

With deliberate care, the indigenous nucleus was removed from the oocyte. In its place was inserted the alien strand, delivered into the enucleated host by vector. A chemical and then an electroshock were applied, inducing the alien strand and the oocyte cytoplasm to fuse. Finally, the entity was placed within the warm shell of the cultivation apparatus, there to be provided the requisite nutrition and stimulation.

Under Learned Ase's watchful gaze, an embryonic foundling began to grow and divide.

Re-Creation
by David L. Clements

"It's good godlight tonight," said Meredith the caravan master as he walked up to our fire.

We looked at the haze of stars all around the sky, the star streams arcing above and, just rising in the east, the blue glare of the Core. Around this, the center of the great merged galaxy, we could see the filaments of the gods, and further to the north the rippling waves of godlight.

"What's the godlight saying?" I asked.

"There are some who can read godlight, but not me. Maybe one day you'll learn," said Meredith, smiling at me.

Our little company of students was traveling to the city to study the gods. Tonight was the last night of our journey, and Meredith was making his final rounds of the caravan, bidding farewell to his fellow travelers. Elsewhere in the camp there was laughter and music, and we'd all join in with the festivities later, but our group had come to save the time the Core rose to look at the godlight and for conversation.

"I have one final story for you all," said Meredith as he sat beside us. "Something an old godlearner told me many years ago."

"What's the story about, Master?" I asked, unable to hold in my curiosity.

"It might not be something your teacher would want you to hear." He glanced across the fire to Percival, our tutor, then passed a flask of liquor to him. "Which is why I've kept it to the end, when it would be rude for him to interrupt. It's a story about where we came from, and about how the gods can make mistakes."

A wry grin crossed Percival's face as he took a swig. "I think they all know how we were remade by the gods," he said, passing back the flask.

"But do they know why?" said Meredith, settling down and resting his back against a tree. "Two hundred million years ago, or so, two spiral galaxies collided. That collision made all that you can see in the sky—the

121

Core, the starswarm and maybe the gods themselves. Not long after that, when the great galaxy was young and the star streams were bright, the gods had a problem. The collision had produced all sorts of debris. Not just the star streams we can see today, but bits of old star systems, planets and moons, stripped away from their parent stars and flung into space. Some of these traveled very fast, and, being chunks of rock, were hard to find. Imagine what one of those might do if it hit us, or, gods preserve us, the Core?"

He paused to look at us one at a time. "So the gods made machines, and sent them out to look for these rocks and destroy them. But that wasn't all. The gods wanted to know where they themselves came from and what had happened in the spiral galaxies in the fifteen billion years before they collided. So the machines were divided into a part that wanted to destroy, a part that wanted to look for history and a captain to take decisions. And sometimes the machines fought."

Sirami the destroyer found it first, a large spherical rock traveling through empty space at a dangerously high speed. This was just the kind of thing it was seeking to destroy, but it had to rouse the others before getting to work. Soon the usual debate was in progress.

"A quick and effective termination is required needing just a few thousand years." This was the destroyer's case before the Captain.

"We must at least characterize it, get some idea where it came from, what it's made of. If it proves boringly normal then I agree with Sirami. But we have to know," said Lahai, the investigator.

It was a familiar script to both entities, the opening round of a dance they had done many times and they knew the Captain's answer would favour Lahai.

They scattered scouting systems across the object's spherical surface, trying to determine its makeup and history.

A few years of effort produced some results. The object's surface was rock melted at high temperatures from being too close to its parent star, and then frozen to solidity by the cold blackness between the stars.

"The lack of impact craters indicates the surface is young compared to its formation," said Lahai delivering the initial report. "Abundance ratios show it formed about seven billion years before the current epoch in one of the progenitor galaxies."

"So the chances for life of any kind are low?" asked the Captain.

"So we can destroy it and move on," commented Sirami.

"Probably... But... There are some anomolies," said Lahai.

"There are always anomalies," muttered Sirami.

Lahai ignored the provocation. "Core drilling to fifteen kilometers depth finds different layers of rock. The outer layer is basaltic - essentially the raw stuff of planets dominated by nonvolatiles. But further down we have marble - calcium carbonate rocks."

Sirami didn't see the importance.

"Such rocks can be produced by life in a water and oxygen rich environment."

"Any evidence for this?" asked the Captain.

"The heat and pressure that processed the rocks to marble would have destroyed any further evidence. But..."

"Yes?"

"There are other anomalies. Things missing that should be there—too little uranium-238—and too much in the form of light elements like lithium and beryllium."

"Do you know what you're suggesting?" said Sirami, unable to keep the scorn from its voice.

"I'm not suggesting anything. I'm merely presenting evidence," countered Lahai. "Your conclusions are your own. All I am asking for, Captain, is more time to investigate."

"What do you need?"

"To dig deeper and in more places, and time enough for neutrino tomography to get a better idea of the interior."

"That will take centuries!" protested Sirami.

"Little enough time in the scheme of things," said the Captain. "Lahai—you may proceed."

While Lahai's machines mined the surface layers for raw materials for the neutrino detectors, Sirami used those same materials to construct the detonation system that would destroy the object. The material was gradually lofted to orbit by strings of space elevators constructed along its equator.

The space around the wandering globe gradually filled with artifacts of high technology. Further out were the bulking masses of neutrino detectors, calmly collecting a trickle of events from the weakly interacting background. Neutrinos easily passed through the object and just about everything else, but slight perturbations in the flux could, given enough time and data, build up a picture of whatever lay below the surface layers. Closer in, they built Sirami's compact globes of gravity guns, the spinning black holes lying at their cores gradually storing power for the inevitable destruction of their target, delivering enough energy to boil the entire sphere into space, its component parts expanding at such speed they could never recombine.

Centuries after construction began, the Captain called a meeting to discuss results.

"The basic system is complete," reported Sirami, "but we need time for testing and to amass sufficient power to ensure our mission is completed."

The Captain acknowledged the report, then moved on to Lahai. "What does the tomography tell us?"

"We have something most unusual," said Lahai. "Unprecedented. It calls into question all we and the gods think about intelligence."

"What are you making up now?" said Sirami.

"Look at the results." Lahai made the provisional output from the neutrino system available to them.

"A stratified geology overlaying older, denser rocks produced in the object's formation," concluded the Captain. "I see nothing odd here."

"You need to work at higher resolution," Lahai indicated. "Look here, and here, and these others here."

There were six anomalies in total. At each one there was an inclusion of some kind just at the boundary between the sedimentary and ancient rocks. As best they could tell the inclusions were spheres of much lower density material.

"They're just bubbles," said Sirami. "This has gone on long enough. Another five centuries and we can destroy this place and move on."

"We need more data. These inclusions appear to be perfect spheres. That's evidence of artificial construction!"

"Continue to gather data . . . for now," said the Captain. "But our primary mission is to eliminate this dangerous object and we all have to work towards that goal."

Lahai indicated reluctant assent. Then it said, "There is another thing. Something Sirami should have known, given how much time it spends studying the evaporation of planetary bodies."

"What is that?" asked Sirami.

"The sedimentary rocks found in the deep drilling all have their formation mediated by liquid water. This body is too small for liquid water to survive for long. UV from the parent star would split the water vapor molecules, and the hydrogen would then escape."

"Maybe it was orbiting a dim star," countered Sirami.

"Then the water would be frozen. The only natural form for this object is covered in ice or dry. The long wet phase necessary for sedimentary rocks must have been sustained artificially."

The Captain allowed more extensive digging, better neutrino scans and more detailed examination of the tailings from the excavations. Soon the first signs of life emerged - fossils from the sedimentary rocks far beneath the melted surface layers, creatures with calcium carbonate skeletons turned to rock by millions of years spent underground.

"Life, yes, but where is your claimed intelligence?" asked Sirami as investigations went on beneath the waiting gravity guns.

"You can't find intelligence in a fossil. We need signs of artifacts, culture, history. They don't survive as easily as fossils. The only hint is the possible use of uranium fission and hydrogen fusion for power. But we need more."

"You're asking to dig down to those spherical inclusions?"

"Yes," said Lahai. "They're the only clear signs of an artificial nature we have."

"But intelligent life from mere atoms is impossible. We've known that for ages. This is a waste of time! We should complete our work and move on."

"The environment here was artificial. The presence of water on something so small clearly shows that, and the duration of that presence - millions of years at least - means there was a concerted effort to keep it wet, probably using volatiles shipped from elsewhere in its parent system. Intelligence was involved even if it wasn't the creatures fossilized. That's what we must find."

The Captain pondered the issue.

"We can't take this long on every rock we find, or there will be disastrous impacts in the Core." Sirami indicated its approval of this position. "But this does seem an unusual example, stranger than anything we've uncovered before. The digging should continue, and aim at retrieving one of these possibly artificial spheres. But the gravity systems must be completed and tested so we can eliminate this hazard as soon as possible."

* * *

A shaft was started directly above the sphere closest to the surface. Neutrino tomography was now showing the objects as five hundred meter diameter spheres with some internal structure - the lower halves far denser than the upper, and a narrow dense shell separating them from the surrounding sedimentary rock.

As the shaft drilled deeper into the object's surface they found more complex fossils amid signs of more complicated geology, veins and deposits rich in certain metals or other rare substances. This confirmed results from the tomography of varying rock densities, but there was no reason why the veins and deposits should be in one place rather than another. The object was too small to have any active tectonic processes that would force minerals into the sedimentary strata. The obvious conclusion was that the deposits were in specific locations for some reason, maybe left there on purpose or abandoned when they were no longer needed. Sirami, of course, didn't agree and instead argued the metals came from asteroid impacts.

Then there was the first accident. The ground trembled around the drilling complex and the shaft itself cracked. Drilling halted while they made repairs and conducted investigations. They soon found the quake had originated far below the surface.

"Seismometers are imprecise," reported Lahai, "but all indications are that the quake was very close to the sphere we were drilling towards."

The Captain was surprised by this report. "This object is far too old for natural quakes."

"There might be tidal stresses left over from close encounters with other bodies. When it was torn from its parent system there could have been any number of these. And there may have been other encounters as it traveled here. The drilling could have triggered such a long-dormant instability," said Sirami.

"No," said Lahai. "This can't be natural."

"Are you suggesting these spheres might be dangerous?"

"I don't know what I'm suggesting. We need to examine records from all our systems to find out what happened. But it's clear that the sphere we were drilling to has been destroyed, crushed during the quake. We need to start another shaft."

"This is just more pointless delay," protested Sirami. "The spheres are unstable, whatever they are. We're not going to reach them so we might as well give up."

"This isn't delaying your activities," the Captian told Sirami, "the gravity guns still need calibration and to fully charge. We'll try another shaft while investigating the cause of this collapse."

But before the new shaft had reached below the basalt layer there was another quake, and a second sphere destroyed, quickly followed by a third.

"This meeting is most irregular," said the Captain.

"We need to meet without Sirami," replied Lahai. "Three spheres have now been destroyed in these mysterious quakes. I suspect Sirami is behind them but I don't have the authority for a full investigation."

"That is a serious charge. It would mean Sirami is operating outside its normal parameters. Why would that happen?"

"Maybe there are extra parameters we don't know about. Consider - it's axiomatic among some of the gods that intelligent life only became possible after the galactic collision, that it can only arise spontaneously in giant magnetic structures. The nanomachines we use and are made from are just artificial constructs. We now have possible evidence of planet-based intelligence arising billions of years before the collision. That would unsettle some and strengthen others."

The Captain paused, considering the suggestion. "Aren't you operating outside your own parameters as well, in questioning the motivations of Sirami?"

"Yes - which is why I know what Sirami might be capable of. The gravity guns aren't fully powered, but they can already do damage."

"The system logs show nothing at the times the spheres were destroyed."

"Logs can be faked. I've modified some of the neutrino systems to search for gravity waves. If this is deliberate then we'll know when the next sphere is attacked. And I've made other preparations as well. As Captain you needed to be informed of this."

"This sounds worryingly as if you've been acting independently, without authorization."

"Yes - but that will only become important if Sirami has been doing the same."

The Captain exuded unhappiness.

The next attack was mere days later, but this time Lahai was ready. Several of the neutrino arrays had grown long interferometer arms which allowed them to detect scattered gravity waves. There was a constant background of these from the gravity gun platforms as they spun up the black holes inside them, but any shift towards a release of the stored energy would be clear.

And it was.

A number of the orbiting weapons platforms started to produce a delicate coherent stream of gravity waves. The output wasn't strong - it was near the limit of what Lahai's sensors could detect - but the waves from different platforms interfered with each other to produce powerful effects at one location only. Instead of the planet pulverizing blasts the systems were designed for, this attack, like the ones before, would destroy only a small region - the fourth sphere.

Lahai's counter-systems kicked in at the same time the Captain was informed of the attack. Small black holes recently added to other neutrino stations tuned into the attacking waves, matching them in frequency but shifted in phase. They weren't enough to stop the attack, but could put it off course.

Rock shattered, crushed to huge density by the gravity waves, then expanded again with explosive force as the attack stopped. It was another quake but it had struck hundreds of kilometers from the targeted sphere, leaving it unharmed.

"What is the meaning of this?" demanded Sirami.

"We might ask you the same," said the Captain.

"Lahai has been producing and deploying weapons systems. That is my preserve."

"And you have been destroying artifacts," said Lahai.

"There are no artifacts," said Sirami dismissively. "I've been preserving our mission by making sure we are not needlessly delayed."

"How do you know there are no artifacts?" asked the Captain.

"Because there cannot be. There was no intelligence before the Core."

"Not everyone agrees," said Lahai. "That is why I'm here - to understand history before the great collision."

"History yes, primitive life, yes - but making up stories of impossible intelligence isn't history."

"You believe so strongly that you don't want to look?" asked Lahai.

"There is no need when the gods have spoken."

"They don't all agree," said the Captain.

"The important ones do, the ones who built me. Who am I to go against them?"

"But the gods can be wrong. They know that, and so should you," said Lahai.

They could not dissuade Sirami. The Captain decided to box it, to return it to the dormant state they had during interstellar travel until Lahai's investigations were completed.

The drilling resumed. After many years had passed they reached one of the spheres and began to understand.

It was a shell of diamond, protecting whatever was inside from almost any outside pressure. Within the shell was a preserved piece of the object before water ran on its surface, before it had an atmosphere of its own. A light aerogel filled the space that would once have been vacuum, holding items in place in the half of the sphere not filled by dark grey regolith and subsurface basalt. The sphere was clearly an artificial construct and as such a marvel in its own right. But inside, on the surface of the rocks, preserved since the day it had arrived, was a marvel of even greater proportions.

At the center of the sphere stood a square platform on four feet made from base metals, scalded by heat on its upper surface. It had mysterious markings similar to other items scattered nearby—equipment whose purpose was clear, such as a reflector array, but other things were more puzzling. And then there were the tracks. Evidence that something had walked here on what, at the time, would have been an environment completely inhospitable to biological life. Most puzzling of all were the items with symbols on them, which they assumed contained some important message to those, like Lahai and the gods, who came after.

They had found what Sirami and most of the gods had thought impossible - evidence that intelligence had existed before the galaxy collision, before the Core.

Lahai's mission changed from scouting to the detailed gathering of information and material. The object's destruction became a secondary goal, only to be completed once every last shred of information had been gleaned.

The entire object was peeled. Over thousands of years they removed the melted basaltic outer layers, then sifted the sedimentary layers grain by grain, molecule by molecule, for information about the object's inhabitants.

A picture slowly emerged. The creatures living there were carbon-based, breathed oxygen, had genetics based on a complex bi-helical organic molecule. Fragments of this molecule were gradually collected from fossils and other residues for later investigation. The object had once been the moon of the home planet of these creatures and had been the goal of their first faltering steps into the universe. The moon had later been transformed into a habitable environment used for millions of years—long enough for sedimentary geology to cover the signs of earlier activity and to turn skeletons into fossils. But before they had been forgotten and buried beneath layers of future geology, the spheres had been preserved, protected against almost any eventuality at the earliest stage of the object's transformation to habitability.

Finally, when the last molecules had been examined and nothing else remained to be gleaned from the spheres or the object by their teams of nanorobotic archaeologists, Lahai and the Captain woke Sirami.

Much time had passed and they were now well inside their home galaxy, nearing the Core whose protection was their primary task.

Sirmai immediately took this information in, realizing the implications. "I was that wrong?"

"Yes," said Lahai. "Not that we blame you for what you did. You were programmed for it, just as I was programmed to try to stop you."

"And now?"

"The job hasn't changed, I've merely delayed it. This moon has to be destroyed before it becomes a threat to the Core, and that is your task."

Sirami indicated assent. "The systems are ready? We can leave?"

"Yes," said the Captain. "Though we will be returning to the Core with all the information we've obtained rather than continuing."

"Very well," said Sirami. And, without further delay, it fired the gravity guns.

The moon's surface, already ground and sifted into **dust** by the archeological study, boiled. Shafts of dust lofted to the sky, accelerated far beyond escape velocity and scattered in all directions. Slowly at first, and then with greater speed as the remaining mass became less, the moon boiled into space, becoming a manageable cloud of scattered dust rather than a dangerous high velocity mass headed into the Core.

And with this destruction two of the three remaining spheres were also destroyed, albeit after their contents were examined and recorded at the submolecular level.

One sphere, the first they had retrieved, remained, pushing their mass budget to the limit as they carried it back to the Core.

*   *   *

130

"When they came back to the Core the gods were astounded," said Meredith. "They wanted to know more about the moon's inhabitants and what the symbols found in the sphere meant. But, try as they might, there was no way to decipher them. Eventually someone proposed a plan almost insane in its boldness. They would remake the inhabitants, in the belief that they'd know what the symbols meant.

"And to remake the inhabitants they would have to remake their world. All the fragments of genetic material recovered from the moon, all the records of fossils and other material, were put together, and they made their best guess at what that world, our world, was like.

"And that's why we're here. We are those recreated inhabitants, brought back to life and consciousness, reborn four billion years later, when the stars in the sky are older and the galaxy we would have called home no longer exists."

"And what did the symbols say?" I asked.

"Well," replied Meredith, sighing, "that's the problem. The gods, in their infinite wisdom, assumed that an understanding of these symbols was written in our genetics, so that when we were reborn we'd be able to read them right away. Gods, apparently, are born like that. But not us. When the first human was born, they asked him but didn't get an intelligible answer— he was too young after all. But they persisted, they made more of us, they made us a home, looked after us. We made our own languages, our own writing, but still we can't read the symbols they found.

"And that is the lesson here. The gods make mistakes. Sometimes they're bad mistakes, as when Sirami nearly destroyed our moon too early, and sometimes good ones, like bringing us back to life. But, they do make mistakes."

Meredith stood, stretching.

"What do the symbols look like?" I asked.

"You can see them for yourself tomorrow - the last sphere is on display in the city," said Percival, "but this is what they look like."

He handed me some paper on which were scrawled incomprehensible shapes that came from a time older than the gods themselves:

Here Men From The Planet Earth First Set Foot Upon the Moon, July 1969 A.D. We Came in Peace For All Mankind.

Artifacts
by Heather McDougal

The object was thin and square, with small white edges. On it was an image of an alien family: two large beings and two small. Their faces were odd, but in a fairly familiar mold, like many of the races she'd studied. Dze was fairly certain they had common ancestors with her own. She looked up at the half-dark sky dominated by the large and dirty planet overhead, the knifelike horizon balanced by the steady clarity and random sprinkling of the stars: so many apparent messages in their random distribution—the ancients had read all kinds of things into their groupings and spacings.

Among them, she could see the Explorer ships, waiting. She shivered. It was cold, here in the long, long twilight. Not like home. The thought made her wince, thinking of Captain Fve and his ultimatum.

A ship had been hovering next to the Dwelling when she had skimmed in from the empty, airless plains, its swirling shape parked buoyantly above the Dwelling. Not the usual ship, it seemed. Its delicate wings were furled, and it exuded steam gently from various elegantly-designed apertures. The metal was stamped with a thousand florettes, and bow and stern were adorned with spiralling crests. It was a masterful bit of engineering: each rivet carefully crafted in gleaming brass, every vent scientifically sculpted. Somebody higher up, then, showing off. Dze put her carpet away and headed thoughtfully into the Dwelling.

In the brightness and warm color within, a darkish person with a resplendent waistcoat dandled an elegant navigational instrument as he reclined on the lounge. Nearby, Kke had pulled up one of the dining-couches and was offering the person a flute of wine.

"It's only aether-made, I'm afraid," Kke was saying as Dze entered, "We don't get much from Home, here." He turned a gleaming eye toward her. "Ah! My colleague. Archaeologist Dze, let me introduce Captain Fve, of the Company ship *Forsworn*."

"How do you do," Dze said, bowing. "A very fine ship for such an isolated spot."

"Ah! So nice to meet you, Archaeologist Dze. Petrographer Kke has been telling me about the deadly boring artifacts you've been finding. Not a terribly bright race, eh?" He leered, twirling the device between arched fingers. The wine he ignored, for the moment.

"Tell me, how would the Crown feel about this site?" He went on. "Not worthy of a preservation order, wouldn't you say?"

"Well," Dze said carefully, keeping her face calm. "It would depend on so many factors. I might, for example, seek some coverage under the "primitive" designation. We don't often see this much evidence of intelligence without design. There might be something we could learn about it—perhaps, for example, it was a slave culture, with some artifacts being made under duress, or without personal input."

The Captain burst into laughter. "Wonderful! Wonderful. Shipbuilders using mindless workers to build ships by the dozens! Alien races making endless boring objects!" He shook his head and twinkled at her. "I love the way you pure-science people think! Such fancy! But tell me, Archaeologist, what are the chances that the Crown will, in fact, give you that coverage? I've got ten Explorers out there, wanting to bring these items, ugly and crude as they are, to make available to Collectors back home. It's all I can do to keep them from coming and taking the things."

Dze stood still, feeling nonplussed. She hated being rushed.

Captain Fve took a sip of the wine and made a face. "Pfaugh! Awful stuff, don't know how you can stand it. In any case, I suggest you contact your Crown agent as soon as possible—perhaps even now. Without that preservation order. . ." he shrugged. "It is unlikely we could stop them, anyway; at the moment they are delaying as a courtesy to me, but you have no guards, here, as you did on Hou7."

"Captain—sir," Dze said. "Can you talk to them? There's something missing here, and I need time to understand what it is. It could be of great importance—" She paused, thinking furiously, "—which could possibly increase the value of the artifacts. Something new in their physics, for example."

"Something new?"

"I'm not certain what I mean by that, yet. Perhaps another view of science?"

The Captain raised his eyebrows at Kke. "Hark to her! Another view of science, she says. Of great importance! Is learning about ugliness as important as the precious minerals we can extract? I would ask you to think on that. I'll speak to the Explorers, but your time is limited: even artifacts as aberrant as these can fetch a good price. Or, perhaps, *especially* artifacts as aberrant as these. Another view of science, indeed! They are in such shocking taste, people want to keep them in special rooms to make their friends swoon. Collectors are sitting up in their seats right now, I can tell you."

Kke, who had been politely silent until now, turned to Dze and said, "I think Archaeologist Dze understands what you mean, sir. You will," he said, turning to Dze, "speak with your agent right away, will you not? Best not left too long."

He turned to nod at the Captain. "But let's not speak of it anymore. May I offer you some of this delicious nut-curd? I make it myself. I'm very careful about ingredients, let me assure you." He glanced at Dze as he handed the container to the Captain, and looked pointedly at the communications-room. Sighing, Dze went.

In the near-dark of the little room, she had a moment lost in the futility of her position, wondering how she would get the agent to understand. This did not improve when she heard the agent's sharp tongue on the other end of the connection. She must have been napping between calls, Dze thought to herself. It was extraordinary how lazy some of the agents were, considering the importance of their job.

When Dze asked to speak to the higher-up, the agent went away for a few minutes, and Dze sat in the gloom wondering how to describe what she'd seen, the mystery of these odd people. Outside the door, she could hear Kke and Captain Fve laughing. She imagined them discussing the inevitable arrival of the Explorers, who would dismantle all the bits and pieces left by the people who had come here—Ghastlies, Kke called them, for the bizarre awfulness of their artifacts.

"Terribly sorry," said the sharp voice, "But Her Excellency is indisposed at the moment. If you would be so kind as to check the Home time when you call again, you may have better luck."

Dze looked quickly at the Home clock, mounted nearby for just this reason. *Crooked! It's the middle of the night there*, she thought, startled, then irritated at Kke for pushing her.

"My humblest apologies," she began, but the agent had already cut her off.

Kke looked up when she came in. "No luck?" he asked sympathetically, and she knew he knew the Home time, had known it when he made the suggestion. She felt herself heating up.

To allay her annoyance, she went to the food area and fetched a flute. "I'll have some of that wine, if there is any left," she said. Kke looked at her quizzically: it was rare for her to drink wine in the middle of the day.

The Captain, however, was ready to leave. "I must go," he said. "Communiqués and so on to see to. Call me about that issue we spoke of," he said meaningly to Kke. Then he looked at Dze. "Absolutely charming to meet you, Archaeologist," he said and swept out the door, the glittering crystal fringe of his sleeve making a soft "shcack" sound as it struck the doorframe.

The susurration of the ship was heard as it raised itself upwards once again toward the aether. Clouds of steam gushed beyond the window: the engines thrummed a little, and it was gone.

Dze rounded on Kke. "You did that deliberately," she said, baring her teeth.

Kke drew back distastefully. "How do you mean?" he drawled, offended. "I didn't invite him here."

"Not the Captain, you fool - calling the agent. You deliberately sent me to call when it was clearly after hours. What was that all about? So you could discuss that 'issue' the Captain hinted at?"

"I don't know what you're speaking of," he said. "The Captain and I have an old acquaintance, and have much to discuss of mutual friends. That's all, on my honor," he said, fingers spread in surrender.

Dze shrugged, and went toward the doorway of the Dwelling. "I don't interfere with your rock collecting," she said. "I expect the same courtesy from you." And, ignoring any further words she swept out, trailed by a strange sense of lost opportunity, like a bad but indefinable odor.

It was then that she'd found the mysterious tracks.

Irritated with Kke, she had skimmed off to the North, ignoring the dull landscape around her. She first saw the tracks as an unbroken line, going onward toward the northwestern horizon, changing the tension in the dull landscape by the way they bisected the plain on a diagonal. She followed, her carpet skimming above the twin lines, disturbing nothing.

The tracks went on and on, into territory not scheduled for exploration for another three years, at least. The monotony was extraordinary: the landscape held no vertical elements, nor horizontal—just the same bland coloring and that same sharp cut between black aether and plain, dead dust. Without atmosphere there was no distance, no sense even of the sublime enormity of it. She found herself nearly dozing off a few times, each time she starting awake, to find the twin lines in the dust were there undiminished, and the plains, with their barely rising and falling bowls, their dull dust and rocky fragments, looking much the same as ever.

In the distance something rose against the dark aether, breaking the perfect line of the horizon. Dze sat up and watched as it slowly grew: vertical striations in dark and light, marching off to either side. Mountains.

She had heard of the mountains ringing the plain where they were stationed, but in the weeks since she had arrived had only seen the seemingly endless horizontals of the terrain. Now they came nearer, terribly welcome, their broken organic forms wonderfully distinct and speaking of breakage, of ancient impact. As she skimmed closer they loomed, cutting the low planet in half. Their grey was different: rather than the grey of ennui that pervaded the plains, this was a denser, deeper grey, redolent of age and mineral strength.

The tracks crossed a great, flat, unmarked place, and rose against the far side, up a lower, clear place in the jutting sharpness of the mountains. They crawled crosswise several times, then topped the rocky grey lip of the crest— and disappeared. Beyond, the high plain began again on a level with the mountains, rings and dips marking its distances like the little spheres in her Cabinet back at the Dwelling.

Dze had stood on her carpet and wondered. Where could the thing have gone? How, in all this dreary vastness, could a wheeled vehicle simply vanish? The crumbling cliffs along the edge of the bowl remained obdurately dull and lifeless as she switched back and forth over them, searching.

Chimes sounded, probably Kke calling her. Sure enough, his voice came, small and flutelike. "Come back soon, your carpet is getting low on everything. The warning is pinging at me."

"Right," she answered him, briefly. One more pass at the place—rocky and unmarked—where the vehicle had ceased to be, and she followed the long, colorless trail home.

Now, standing outside the Dwelling in the planet-light these seven days later, she thought again about the disappearing tracks. If there was a door, why weren't there more marks all around it? Why, if the vehicle had gone inside somewhere, wasn't there evidence of it having used the same route before?

Tossing a stone, Dze watched it arc gracefully and settle in the dust with a little puff, like the little birds in the desert on Hou7 where she had found the domed city, two years ago.

That had been bad, but she had been able to get full coverage as a class 5 Ruin, so at least it had stopped the scavengers before too much of it was destroyed.

This, though, this was different.

Clearly, no one had ever lived here. The things that lay eternally preserved on these airless plains were artifacts of beings from somewhere else, probably from the planet that hung, oily and ruined, in the aether above. Beings like the ones in the image on the square in her hand. She looked at the image again: they stretched their mouths, these beings, and showed their teeth. One of them wore an angry-looking red garment. Yet, curiously, she felt no enmity—neither of these things, she thought, were a sign of aggression for them.

Turning, she walked back inside the Dwelling through the ornate doorway, which had been carefully carved and colored to look like rare Bora wood. Inside, Kke sprawled on the lounge, sampling frozen fruit from a bowl and ignoring her. The curve of his slender fingers echoed the slender, curved legs of the lounge.

Dze went to the Cabinet and opened the door, setting the flat object on a shelf inside so that it stood leaning against a grey metal box. She stood back and surveyed her Collection: the box and family portrait, several mechanisms made of silvery metal, a long metal pole with a flat paddle on one end and a cracked covering on the other end. In front of this was a metal plate clearly designed as a communiqué, showing two outlines of the lost beings, standing stiffly on their odd feet. There were the language-markings down the side of the plate. As a communiqué, she thought, it lacked all sense of nuance, relying on hard, bold lines and childlike simplicity, as if its creators were idiots aping the communiqués of their betters. The metal, however, had been worked with great skill to be smooth and clean and perfectly rectangular. It was very puzzling.

On the top shelf was a row of small white spheres with carefully dented surfaces. The dents were too regular to have come from rough usage, so they must have a designed purpose, Dze thought. Simplistic markings on their sides implied a maker's mark, though even these were as uninflected as a baby's picture-book.

Kke just thought the objects were ugly. "Why do you keep those things?" he said, not for the first time. "They're garbage, left over from ugly tourists. There's no archaeology here, only nasty ghosts. . . .And garbage," he repeated.

Dze shook her head, as she always did. "No," she said. "I don't think so. Those metal shapes, they're bad aesthetics, true, but the people who made them were clearly intelligent—scientific enough to get here, at least. I think they were left behind for a reason."

She thought again of the mystery of the disappearing tracks. As soon as she could, she would go back. There must be a door, she decided: a door in the rock, perhaps, or some kind of hidden structure. Things on this moon didn't just disappear; they left marks. Everywhere.

Kke shrugged, and went on eating. "Someone else got them here," he said. "They couldn't possibly have understood how to do it themselves. The shapes they used look like intelligence, but the lack of aesthetic understanding—it's impossible. No one could have got here on such half-science!"

This was an old argument, and Dze sighed. "You know why I'm here," she said, moving one of the spheres a little on its shelf.

"Right." He rolled his eyes. "Geology keeps the Crown afloat. So what have they got against practical application?"

"You know they're perfectly happy for you to find trinos-rock or bezel and enrich their coffers," she began, but Kke cut her off.

"Fanciful thinking about dead Ghastlies doesn't enrich anyone but the Collectors. Why not simply let them have it all?"

"Because there may be some important information in their relics that can help us—with practical applications as well as theoretical. You know all this, Kke."

Kke gave a short bark of derisive laughter. "It doesn't matter, though," he drawled. "The Company's miners will be here soon. I found trinos in the fourth douzant, did I tell you? Should be enough there to begin operations quite soon."

"No," said Dze absently, touching the smooth surface of the metal plate, the outline of the odd beings inscribed there. On the shelf beneath, a variety of interesting rocks sat, organized by a system known only to her. She had been collecting them since she came, to balance and beautify the Collection.

Closing the gold-and-white carved doors of the Cabinet, she turned toward the kitchen. "You know," she said, "you shouldn't be eating more than half of those fruit. I think you've already eaten twice your share for the week."

Kke snickered. "Sorry. You never eat them, and I like them."

"But I'm saving them so I can eat them later, when food gets low."

"Psh. It's not fair to torture me like that." Kke sat up, the fringe on his embroidered waistcoat swaying. "I've got to go out to the eighth douzant with the lamps, looking for glow-stone—sorry, kedrite to you. My Reader indicates something in that direction," he said, and stalked off toward the carpet-house, leaving Dze feeling—as usual—awkward and uncultured. A few minutes later, Dze saw him skim out on his carpet, a much cleaner one than hers, and head eastward much too fast for the shuddering lamps stacked behind him. Soon he was lost to view.

He'll break the lamps, she thought to herself.

Later, as she stood in the midmonth half-light, looking at another freakishly plain remnant of the previous visitors, she tried to imagine their civilization. Was everything in their lives this hard and smooth and unadorned? She touched the markings on the side of the large metal husk that lay like an empty sea-mollusk, its meaningless curve lying open to the stars. How was it that they had been civilized enough to travel the aether, yet so infantile in their design-sense?

The shell, as she had begun to call this type of remnant, held no answers, its shadow sharp against the cold dust. Dze got on her dusty carpet and sped onward into the douzant, keeping a sharp eye on the landscape and on her Reader, looking for material evidence as well as relying on her visuals. Above her, the planet hung luminous, swirling brown and white with the occasional bluish tinge, looming over the deserted plain like a bloated, peering face. The explorer ships seemed to be in orbit elsewhere, for the moment. She was entering the sixth douzant, a section neither she nor Kke had yet explored.

The carpet drifted down a long shallow slope, dusty and sad-looking in the grim, clear light. She was beginning to feel cold, and adjusted her heating-element to give out more warmth. How dull their own world must have been to make these beings want to come here! Skimming along through the windless landscape, she tried to imagine their lives, their desire to build shiny soulless craft to travel to dead places.

Below her, two long lines intersected the endless featurelessness she was traversing: another trail, bisecting the blankness.

This trail was different than the one she had found three days ago. The tracks were textured differently; delicate patterns interlaced to form a pleasing latticework in the grey dust. It seemed to have stopped many times; there were holes and scuffed places now and then along its trail, as if it had been scratching at the dust and testing what lay beneath it.

In which direction did the object lay, then? She scanned in both directions with her Reader set to several levels of mineral element, and found, somewhere to the West, a largish metal object. She glanced at the sky, expecting Explorers, but there was nothing. So turning her carpet, she headed toward the object, over the lip of another shallow bowl. Some distance beyond, standing alone on the flat ground under the vast dome of aether, a machine stood. A *real* machine, one that seemed understandable, glinting gold in the planet's light: a thing glowing with some awkward portion of immature beauty. Four small wheels clung to each side of the round brassy body, shaped like a bath or a curving soup-dish. A lid arced shallowly above it; a rim ran around the edge. It looked like nothing so much as a pretty cook-pot. Stepping off the carpet, Dze moved carefully toward it.

Its arms were raised threateningly, tipped in odd tools; eyes surrounded it on all sides; yet it did not move. Frozen, it was aged beyond the life of its owners. It was sweetly constructed, despite the clumsiness that plagued all wheeled constructions: the translucent mesh of the wheels and the curving crisscross ridges on its top shone with elegant simplicity, speaking some truth approximating a bulky version of Axn's Effervescent Solidity. She could see its workings, finely-tuned and sturdy. It held the beginnings of intelligence and design—of real science.

Dze walked back to the carpet, looking again at the thing as she stooped to reach into the sac for her Eye.

She scanned it with transparency on, turning the Eye's tempo dial. Slowly, the internal view coalesced: a hollow space full of workings, and among them a small box, where once something important had been housed. The dial went on around, the little box beginning to glow and show a warmth: a little flickering heart. She peered through the visual hole she'd made between Then and Now. A piece of Shining Matter had once resided here, at a guess, before it lost itself. She stared at the small blueness of it and wondered what hands had set it there to warm their creation, and how long ago it had ceased to do so. It was rare for anyone but archaeologists to have access to a long-term static object such as this, and even for them it was difficult to get such a clear image of an object's Past. Most things moved, between their Thens and their Nows, and it was often difficult to really Look well at what they had once been. So she stared at the small glow, feeling blessed by its tiny life and warmth, wondering at the blue color that flickered outward like a kind hand extended.

Perhaps Kke would know something about this Shining Matter; it wasn't her area of knowledge. She resolved to ask him about it later.

The machine held an array of glittering reflectors, clearly for sending, or repeating, signals. So it *was* from the nearby world. Dze glanced up at the planet, above, wishing it was possible to go see it; but the Company's Readers had pronounced it poisonous, unvisitable. The Ghastlies had died of their ugliness, then.

Walking around the thing again, she was again struck by its muted granule of aesthetic sensibility, as if whatever slaves had built it had been allowing their intelligence to peep through. It was difficult to understand what the motivations of the overlords might have been. And why was this one object different?

For the first time since she had arrived, Dze felt a trickle of joy: there was a remnant here after all with some of the intelligence of beauty, however small and hidden. On the way back to the Dwelling, the carpet swooped with her elation, veering and accelerating with little appearance of speed: no wind whipped at her, no dust was raised. Only the pressure of acceleration, and, as she topped each rise, a sensation of lightness.

"I found something today," Dze heard herself saying, as they reclined by their table. They were on the last course, the cold meat and berry-sauce, deliciously in contrast to the heat of the Dwelling. She immediately wanted to slap herself for speaking, but Kke wasn't interested anyway.

"Mm. More garbage," he said, picking up the bread and mopping at sauce. His appetite was voracious, but he concentrated on eating with his best manners.

Dze wished that, for once, he would dispense with manners and relax a little. But Kke was one of those people for whom to use manners was to differentiate himself from savagery, and so he carried them into every exotic locale. His clothes were always clean and cared-for, his carpet always mended and brushed, his movements always graceful and precise. She waited, quieting herself.

"The Company ship will be here in three weeks with the miners," Kke said, plucking morsels from his plate with correct fingers and popping them into his mouth. "They are pleased with my trinos finds. I haven't found much kedrite, but I think there's more further along. . . . I'll ask them to bring more fruit, shall I?"

He watched ironically as she struggled to swallow and answer graciously. "Yes, please. Since you love it so, ask for extra rations."

He raised his brow at her, and took a sip of his wine, the same stuff the Captain had spurned but which they were used to by now. Just as the carved Cabinet and the dainty lounge were all aether-made, rather than proper quality stuff made from organic materials, so was everything that they lived with, moonside. All copies, but they were made with care and served the two of them well, keeping their laboratory as close as it could be to state-of-the-art patterns.

Kke lay back, satiated for the moment. "There was a message from Captain Fve asking you to call him," he said, smirking. "He says that the Explorers grow more impatient. There's only that garbage out there as evidence that anything went on here—when will you give up and let it go? You know the miners won't be able to land without your work-order from the Crown." Even though he smirked, there was an uncertainty to his movements.

Dze listened to his remonstrances with only half an ear. Outside, in the distance, she had seen the beginnings of progress, and she had an intuition that the mysterious tracks from the week before would lead her to some further discovery, but now was not the time to discuss it. There must still be a few days before she need answer the Captain.

Dze sipped her wine and smirked back. Manners, manners.

The horizon seemed brighter, following the monotonous trail. Very soon, the hot part of the month would begin, the transformation from half-light to direct sunlight always shocking. The trip seemed quicker this time: she must be getting to know the way. The dim landscape showed itself subtler than she had been able to apprehend when she first came. She was beginning to see in it delicate variations: lavenders and blues, and delicate crusty textures to the sand, all so subtle and faint they were like parts of her imagination. The harsh light of the sun would be back soon, but now, in the softer light of the planet, it seemed she moved through the muted landscape of dreams.

Arriving at the spot where the tracks disappeared, she hovered a while, looking carefully. Sure enough, it seemed that though there were no tracks, the ground had in fact been disturbed slightly, in a large hourglass shape—where each half spread from slope and plateau. The growing light showed it much more clearly than the last time she had come.

Something caught her eye and she turned, searching the heavens. Sure enough, there was a small ship, hovering close to the horizon. It was no longer in orbit; the Explorers had lost patience. She didn't know if they had seen her yet.

Dropping the carpet into the dust, she quickly lay flat on it, watching them. The ship didn't move. A couple of twinkling lights trailed upwards from the surface—probably already stealing something. She'd never been that far West, and was surprised when she felt a pang, watching the lights: another set of artifacts she would never see, another piece of the Ghastlies' culture and history.

She swore softly, squirming around to get her Eye out. Sure enough, it showed two freight carpets moving upwards, burdened with two or three large objects. The ship above it was undecorated except for its riveted patterns and the ubiquitous vent-design. The builder had given it a slender silhouette, clearly in the interests of speed and difficulty in being seen.

Dze lowered the Eye, wondering if it were possible to get a Freeze order at this time of Home-night. She switched the Eye down two notches, imagining her explanation to the agent and feeling the coldness of the ground under her. It seemed she would have to wait another few hours, long enough for the agent's superior to rise and dress. Lying back on the chilly carpet, she stared up at the sharp star-filled aether, wondering why she felt so strongly about preserving these strange and graceless bits of a lost civilization. It was as if the people who made these things had been deliberately forgetting some part of themselves or their science. She couldn't believe they were as stupid as they appeared.

I wonder what they're taking? she thought after a while, and switched the Eye to Look inside the ship. It was too far away; the things in its hold were undifferentiated lumps, even with the Eye on full.

There was a flash along the lower part of the Eye's Looker, and something about its color made her glance downwards.

Below her, under the rock, was a hollow space. And, as she Looked, she saw machinery in the space.

Carefully, she swept her head from side to side. A passage of some sort. The machinery was connected both to the rock and to a box within which lay a dynamic mechanism. She could see that the dynamic part was alive, its essence unconnected, awaiting the signal to reconnect. At which point the machinery would move the rock she was lying on: a door, it seemed.

Glancing again at the distant Explorer ship and then around the rest of the landscape, Dze considered her options. Undoubtedly there were Explorers eager to watch her every move, to follow her to the prize artifacts. She Looked at the mechanism again: only the dull passage, leading somewhere. Beyond a certain point the rock was too thick, and so the Eye, meant to be a precision instrument rather than a strong one, could no longer see.

It was clear that the dynamic element would need inducing.

Focusing the exciter field on the Eye, she Looked into the space below, at the small box where the dynamic essences were housed. The hair on her arms began to move, and the air in the Eye's view seemed to shimmer. She could feel her scalp stirring, and then the piece of rock shuddered and began to move.

As it opened she saw the cunning construction, uneven edges perfectly concealing its doorness. Inside, the little passage was bare but for a small wheeled vehicle - probably one whose tracks she had followed. At the far end of the space was another door with a large circular knob next to it.

Dze came through kneeling on the carpet and peering over the edge for footprints, but the floor was hard, unmarked stone, slightly worn near the entranceway. Something must have been set near the entrance to sense her arrival, for the rock closed again suddenly behind her, darkening the room for a moment before lights came on in the ceiling.

It was a strange, harsh space, so clearly designed with no aesthetic considerations that Dze shivered. It was strange being surrounded by a space where the laws of Nature were being almost brutally ignored, the edges and corners of the cube so sharp and clear that they scratched across her sensibilities like fingernails on slate. Tensely, she looked at the vehicle, a small thing designed for light transport, with large articulated wheel rims and a strange brushy contraption on the back. Dze looked closer and came to the conclusion that it was a stealth vehicle, designed to brush away its own tracks as it went. They had no non-aether flight, then, if they were so thoroughly bound to this moon's surface.

Still on the carpet, taking care not to move close to anything and disturb it, she went to the smaller door at the other end. The large knob next to it glowed slightly, as if in invitation. Gingerly, she tried twisting it, then levering it, and finally, pressing it.

This last produced an extraordinary result: unseen vents sighed and gushed a fog into the room. She pulled out her Reader to check: the gases weren't poisonous, nor did they Shine, but were warm, with traces of water vapor.

After a moment, the door clicked open, and she went through.

Inside, there were several skinlike clothes hanging along a wall, with hard round head-pieces placed on a shelf above. Dze examined them curiously. Bright and bland, like all the other artifacts. On a low shelf a little further along, several strangely-shaped vessels lay, their wide mouths showing signs of biological residue. They were more interesting than the suits: they came in different shapes and colors, and lacked the aura of blankness that permeated the other things. More than this, they looked worn, as if they had been used. Dze pulled herself away from a fascinated examination of them and continued skimming along the narrow corridor to where it bent sharply and began a short descent to another passage—and stopped in surprise.

On the wall ahead of her was a communiqué of incredible visual style and form, unlike many of the ones she'd seen in other sites. She approached it with a feeling like awe, looking at the swirls and glimmering points, the complex areas of color, the layered depths.

It was made of many, many layers of the same kind of flat material the family-image, back in her Cabinet, had been printed on. In the center of it, made by staining and daubing the material, stood one of the Ghastlies—but it was not ghastly at all: its skin was brownish-pink and it wore very complex aesthetic objects on its arms, ears, and face. And, oddly, it had six more arms than the other images she'd seen. It was riding on a striped creature and seemed very strong: its eyes looked out from the communiqué, all-knowing and calm.

It was definitely an artifact of the Ghastlies—the image was unmistakable. And yet it showed all the culture and learning of a fully civilized, fully realized society. Dze gazed and gazed, as if this single communiqué could tell her everything she needed to know. Why would this single greatest example of a civilization's knowledge and integrity be here, under the surface? Why did none of this meaning, this knowledge, show in any of the articles outside?

The emotion of looking at it was extraordinary. Dze knew she shouldn't touch its surface, but she wondered at its making. The layers and layers of thin material had been torn, not cut, and looked soft enough to make her reach out, against her training. It felt delicate, as if she touched depths of knowledge behind it.

Communiqués were one of the greatest mysteries in archeology. Their code was rarely cracked, the science or language or information in them locked inside their lines and colors. At nearly every site she had worked, they had found communiqués—sometimes hundreds of them, hung or painted on walls around rooms of otherwise definable splendor— but in most cases, their mysteries were still beyond reach. They spoke the language of sciences which no one understood. Dze's mentor Nge, long ago, had told her that there were a nearly-infinite number of kinds of physics in the Universe. Dze had always dreamed of finding the key to one of them.

Some of the communiqués the archaeologists had found on the many worlds they had visited were simple expressions of wealth or pride; but some, like this one, held such layers of complexity that the scientists at home were convinced they held potent information—if they could only be deciphered.

And yet. . . There was something odd about this one, something terribly vulnerable in the way the edges had been torn. They spoke to her of grief, and of loss. She wondered who had created it, and for the communication of what knowledge, what message? She felt odd looking at it, as if she were seeing something private.

She turned away from the communiqué and went into the dimness. The rooms along there seemed to be storage, however: shelves and stacks of containers and boxes in windowless rooms carved from the rock. They were dull as the landscape outside, mostly white with black markings. Back, then, turning the carpet toward the light.

Beyond the hanging communiqué, the corridor color changed, a warm reddish tone, with swirling, regular designs: a laboratory. It was very beautiful, and Dze skimmed forward eagerly.

The first room was broad and well-lit, with more of the layered communiqués hung around the room. One wall was translucent, with shifting colors behind it, and a brightness. There were several lounges of an unusual symmetrical design: tables and counters holding utensils and vessels of different types. The room had been painted along a different order than the corridor, segmenting the walls into plain-speaking areas of color, with curling invitational tracery around the doorways.

She put her head into the farthest room, which contained a sleeping-couch of some sort, several simple storage units, and shelves—no, a Collection! —of oddly-shaped rocks and artifacts.

So the dweller of this place, the scientist who wrote the missive in torn colors, was also a Collector. Dze shook her head as if to clear it. It was becoming impossible to reconcile this place with the artifacts she had been struggling with for so long.

Dze skimmed closer to inspect her find. There were small bits of melted polymer and a few sparkling crystals from the workings of some dynamic machine. Another image on thin-stuff, this time of two beings with dark complexions, wearing colorful clothes and pulling their mouths back again into that grimace. She wondered if perhaps these beings' faces were made that way.

Below was a shelf of this moon's stones, with square packages of the thin stuff tucked into one end. She picked up a dull grey one and leafed through it. It was ugly throughout, full of diagrams of their machines; but the next one held picture after picture of communiqués, rich in alien beauty, colorful and strange. It made her fingers tingle, brushing the smooth surfaces and looking at the myriad knowledge contained in one small package. She hesitated, then dropped it into the carpet's sac to look at later.

Back in the living area, she glanced around, feeling an old frustration. The knowledge of how these people thought, their science and history was all around her, and as usual she couldn't interpret the language of their forms. As always, it gave her a pang, thinking of all the beings in all the worlds she had visited who had not shared their secrets, whose key she and her colleagues had never found.

She saw now that beyond the translucent wall was a garden—alive and growing. Finding a door, Dze slipped through into warmth and moistness, a dazzling riot of shiny greens and delicate brilliants, open above to what felt remarkably like sky. The dizzying verticals, the wild diagonals of it, the multiplicity and color, disturbed and delighted her senses. To be in nature was to experience beauty as lovely chaos, beyond language, below it and above it at the same time. It was the embodiment of information, not the telling of it.

She longed to touch the ground with her feet. To disturb an ancient laboratory or dwelling was against an archaeologist's training, but to be in a garden required all one's senses—and footsteps could not disturb its growth.

So she stepped onto the leafy soil, drinking in the smells. They were foreign, but not unpleasant, and very alive.

How had this place come to be? Why did the beings work here, disguising his or her (or their) presence? Who were they hiding from— someone on the planet above, or other visitors? What work were they doing? It was possible the person who occupied this space was a genius among dwarfed minds. Perhaps that was it: the person had been exiled for his or her abilities. Yet she knew, even as she thought this, that it was wrong. There was some mystery to the division of inside and outside, beautiful and ugly.

Dze moved on, pushing through the vegetation, feeling the softness of the leaf-pile beneath her feet. The space was fairly large, and fruits hung among the branches; perhaps the person had grown fresh food here to alleviate the long days. A taste of home.

At the back of the space was rock, again, this time irregular and covered with carved designs, of leaves and flowers and the peering faces of creatures she had never seen. Along the upper edge of this was a leaning, chattering, twisting line of figures, some apparently dancing, some in conversation, some simply posing in attitudes of graceful attention. Even their feet, she noticed, looked natural and right. They spoke to her of life, and living, and of being among one's people. They spoke of individuality and collectivity. She could not take her eyes off them.

She followed the line to the far end, where the carving appeared to be unfinished: the figures here were blockier and less defined, hidden behind more layers of growth.

One mound of vegetation seemed to have woven itself around some object there. Dze took out the Eye to Look at it and see what was underneath. It was the former occupant of the laboratory, the soil-creatures long ago having rendered it down to its bones. It sat, rusted tools in hand, where it had sat since it died.

Curious, she touched the tempo dial gently. She wanted to see this being's face, wanted to know who had done all this work. She watched as the bones lingered, then suddenly flesh was rebuilt, then a blurring. *Crooked!* She'd gone too far, and the person was gone. Carefully, she dialed it back, and stopped as the image came clear: a brown face, its aged flesh pleated like a rock formation after eons of rain. The eyes were closed behind thin lids.

It was not so different from her own: two eyes, a mouth. It looked much more aged than she was. She captured an image with the Eye, and then hesitated. Perhaps, if she just dialed back a fraction more. . . ? She had never been face to face with a single one of the occupants of the many worlds she had visited. The thought gave her a tremor. And yet, what harm could it do? The person she would see would be a moment, only. A phantom at the bottom of a well of time.

She touched the dial.

The eyes flew open and, it seemed, stared directly into hers.

Dze was so shaken she nearly dropped the Eye, but when she Looked again, there was the face, staring at her. The contact, the intensity of its eyes, were dizzying. She felt as if they were speaking to her, admonishing her. The beauty of the face was striking, its lines all ones of life and knowledge: a living communiqué, passing its message to her.

Leave me be, the message said. *I have been here for a thousand years. Let me stay a thousand more.*

Dze could feel herself shaking a little, but the gaze on the other side of the Eye was steady.

But what of all the knowledge here? She said back to it. *On the walls, in your carvings? I want to know what they mean, what they say.*

The gaze bored into her. *The things in this house have no message, no information for you. They are what they are, things made for the making only, because I felt the need. I made them, I should know.*

Dze felt staggered. For the making only? She saw the eight-armed image before her, layer upon layer of knowledge. Why, then, had they been placed just so? How was each part chosen? It seemed unthinkable.

How do you mean, she asked. *Do the things have no message? How can that be? All things have meaning.*

The being's face, frozen in time, saw her clearly, in the moment of stillness before death. *These things hold only the stories I told myself as I made them. They are not storehouses of anything but my own self, my art, my life, my culture.*

Art? Dze was confused. The dizziness seemed to threaten to overcome her, and she struggled to make her mind fit around the ideas that flowed in. Art—short for artifice, for the use of aesthetics to muddle information, not the making of something.

The outpourings of my own passions, the being told her. *The meanings that I feel and believe in my time and my place, and nothing more.*

Dze's finger on the dial must have moved at this, for suddenly the eyes had closed again and the intelligence that gleamed from them was gone. Dze lowered the Eye, shaking. All around, in the heat of that place, the living things grew, hiding their secret, living out the cycles of their lives. The being was once again hidden under its blanket of life.

Dze felt as though she were using two brains at once. As if she were seeing one world, one vision, laid over another. In one, the vein of light, of adornment and meaning pulsed its threads through every corner of the sciences, of knowledge. In the other, division: technology in an impossible vacuum, beauty isolated and purified to a degree which terrified her. And yet, the communiqués—the Art—drew her.

Dze wandered slowly back through the place, staring at each communiqué before capturing it in the Eye. *But they're not really communiqués, are they? They are separated from meaning, mere images of passion.* She could not decide whether to be disappointed or frightened.

At the eight-armed woman in the corridor, she paused and touched its soft surface again. The many layers of it confounded her, made her feel extraordinarily vulnerable. Sitting on the edge of her carpet, she stared at it for a long while. *This is what passion looks like,* she thought. *This, and all the others.* She remembered the communiqués she had brought back from Hou7: dark images with light spilling across them like ideas. Perhaps they were that: images of ideas, what ideas themselves could look like if they were physical, if they could be looked at. And there were others, so many others: she longed to go look at them again, to see them as they were meant to be seen.

On the way back to the Dwelling Dze looked up at the poisonous planet above her in the brightening sky and wondered what it had looked like before its inhabitants destroyed themselves. It reminded her of the golden machine, awkward and pretty, with its once-glowing heart.

There were Explorer vessels in the distance, busy with their looting. She hardly saw them; she was too busy rehearsing to herself what she would say to the agent, how she would describe what she had found. *There is something we've been missing,* she would say. *Not all knowledge is aesthetic.* No, not that. *Not all aesthetics are knowledge.* No. Her thinking was all over the place, bouncing from one place to another, separating out beauty from engineering, from biology . . . but that was madness! There was no way to keep aesthetics out of biology. She was leading herself down illogical paths.

Perhaps, although the old person's culture separated what it called Art from science, the division was incomplete. It was very confusing. She looked again at the planet, so lonely in the cold aether.

At the Dwelling, Kke was out. Dze was grateful for this kindness as she took the many-leaved artifact out of her carpet sac and went in through the doorway. She would keep it in her sleeping-chamber; he would never look there. She wanted to keep it to herself, to look at it alone and wonder about it for a while.

She sat on the edge of the lounge and thought again about what she would say to the agent. *I've found a treasure*, she would say. *I need a Freeze order*. She was grateful, too, that the place she'd found was so hidden, so hard to see. No Explorer would find it—it would be safe, until protection arrived.

She got up and stood in the doorway of the communications room for a long time, staring at the equipment. The thought of sharing what she'd found with the sharp-voiced agent made her feel slightly ill.

Still, it was the only way. She must share what she'd found, she couldn't keep it to herself! It could be made into a Museum, with tempovision exhibits. . . Yet she hovered in the doorway, imagining another scenario: the place opened, the things packed and taken away, the plants dying as their atmosphere dispersed. The occupant bundled up to be put in a case and gawked at.

Let me be. The eyes burning into her as the bones were carted away.

She was startled by Kke's voice behind her, coming in through the door to the outside. "There you are," he drawled. "Found something interesting? I've been trying to contact you, but you were deaf."

Dze could hear the carefully-concealed eagerness in his voice, and knew with a certainty that it was he who had called the Explorers, he and Captain Fve. Something hardened inside her, clearing her head. She straightened and almost turned, but his voice stopped her.

"The agent called. It seems they've had word from Captain Fve of how ugly all this junk is. They've given him permission to give the Explorers the go-ahead; I felt sure you wouldn't mind. It means you'll be recalled, of course, but that's hardly horrible, is it? You're lucky to get away from this place. . . . And by the way, I need that work-order before you go Home."

Dze thought of the many-leaved artifact, tucked away in her nest, and of the pictures she had taken, and was grateful all over again for Kke's absence on her arrival.

Turning, she faced him, her expression smooth as the clarity inside her. There was plenty of time, all the time she could need. "You're right," she said, "They can take it. It's all junk, that stuff lying out there. Just garbage; nothing worth saving."

And she went out, into the light of the just-rising sun.

City of Glass
by Christine Lucas

"So this is where the *Dreamcatcher* crashed?" Royo leaned closer to the monitor and planted her index finger on the star system on the screen: an overheating sun and an assortment of planets, mostly gas giants.

Tegan nodded. "Their last emergency transmission puts them in the vicinity of that one." He pointed at a planet with increased volcanic and tectonic activity and an unusually large moon. Not a friendly place: the continents changed within days, rivers of lava burned their way under a constant rain of ash, and new islands appeared in the boiling oceans only to vanish under the waves a few days later. If something lived down there once, it had long perished.

"But they've found something, haven't they?"

"So they've claimed." Tegan shrugged. "But you know Haran. He's always telling tall tales. He always finds *something*. A few huts, a pile of stone artifacts, a temple or two, and he makes announcements about the find of the century. No wonder the Intergalactic Archaeological Society doesn't take him seriously anymore. Do you know how many favors I had to call in to get the permits to come here?"

Royo rubbed her chin. True, her brother was always chasing after the great discovery that never came: the lost wormhole of Proxima 7, the two-dimensional life forms of Orogo 4, the fire-birds of Kanika 6. Always chasing dreams among the stars, with barely a short message to her every now and then: on her birthday, for her graduation, after the landing accident that claimed her husband and child and left her bedridden for months.

Anya. Such a small coffin. So soon.

My fault.

Haran hadn't been there. The Universe always called him further away.

But he was her *brother*. She scanned the star system below; nothing exceptional about it—no ravenous black hole, no legendary gaseous dragon roaming the nebulas close to the rim, not even a raging electromagnetic storm. And Haran had vanished *here*, of all places.

"The inner planets are too unstable for landing." Royo flipped the controls of the scanner and the image of the moon of the third planet appeared on the screen. "Even Haran wouldn't be so crazy to attempt landing there. But this moon seems stable enough."

Tegan leaned over her shoulder. "I don't like it." He scanned the surface. "There's minor tectonic activity there too, although nothing like the planet below. And its axis has a weird spin, probably the echo of a crash with another moon or asteroid in the recent past." He checked the surface temperature, and his frown deepened.

"What?"

"You don't want to be caught on its surface after sunrise. The temperature rises too high. A spacesuit stands no chance." He pointed at the star on the screen. "As long as we keep in the dark side, away from its flares, we should be safe. But the night doesn't last long."

"How long?"

Tegan entered a set of coordinates. "It depends on the landing site, but no more than ten hours. And communications will be affected. Its spin has altered the moon's magnetic field."

"I'll scan the surface for signs of life." Royo entered the full scan interface. After the first readings came in, she frowned. "This is weird."

"What?"

"The storm of solar flares interferes with the data. But if I'm reading this correctly, this moon is hollow."

Tegan looked askance at her. "Sometimes you sound too much like your brother. It can't be hollow."

She scratched her head. "This moon is just weird. Wait." She sat up, her heart racing. "There!" She pointed at a dark spot by a large crater. "Life signs! There!" She flipped the controls. Sure enough, the presence of low energy levels was confirmed.

Tegan took his seat at the navigation control. "I'll bring us around, so we can take a closer look." He glanced at her, his voice kinder now. "If Haran is down there, we'll bring him home."

To be buried alongside the rest of my family.

Alongside Anya.

She managed a thin smile. "Thanks."

Further readings confirmed the first scan: a ship had crashed on the surface of the moon. No other distress signals had been reported in the area, so it was safe to assume they had found the *Dreamcatcher*. The combination of the crater and the moon's tectonic activity made the crash site unsafe for landing, so they chose a plain six clicks away. The space scooter would have no trouble taking her there.

Inside the cargo bay, Royo donned her spacesuit. Tegan secured her helmet's lock and checked the compressed oxygen and water tanks on her back.

"They should last a bit over twelve hours, but you can't stay out that long. The sunrise here is deadly." He glanced at the computer screen by the bay's pressure doors. "The sun comes up in three hours. I expect you back in half that time."

Royo nodded. "The crash site is just behind that hill. Even if I walked there, I'd be back in no time."

Tegan retreated behind the pressure doors. "Stand by for decompression."

The ship's life-support system sucked in the oxygen from the bay area. Her suit's atmosphere scanner detected the drop in oxygen levels and kicked in. Royo gulped, struggling to control her breathing. She'd never gotten used to the taste of stale—dead—oxygen. Even after all her years in exploring, her lungs missed the rich, humid air of her marshy homeworld. She manually adjusted the humidity levels and the burning in her throat lessened.

The hiss of the remnants of oxygen escaping to vacuum signaled the opening of the cargo bay doors. Royo climbed on the scooter. A desert of silver sand stretched as far as she could see. She fingered the com link on her helmet.

"Control, do you read me?"

Tegan's voice echoed strong inside her helmet. "Loud and clear. Good luck, Royo."

"Thanks." She fired up the engine and rode out.

It was an easy ride. Nothing bigger than a pebble littered the fine, grey sand. In the distance, the moon's planet hung low over the horizon. Ashen clouds with streaks of red swirled and parted over patches of dirty brown land and dark blue oceans. A surface sweep had sent back images of bursting volcanoes and rifts spewing magma. The tectonic plates of the small planet danced to the cosmic tide of the combined gravitational fields of its sun and moon. Had anything ever lived there?

Royo reached the crest of the low hill. As the crashed ship came into view, her grip around the scooter's handles tightened. Was Haran down there? Was he dead? She focused on her breathing.

Think of silent green waters under ageless trees. Think of the persistent buzz of countless insects under the light of the twin moons. Don't waste your air. Don't waste your water.

She turned on her com link. "Control, I have located the crash site."

"Approach with caution." After a minute of static, Tegan's voice came through the link again, this time softer. "Don't do anything hasty, Royo."

She smiled. Tegan was a good guy. Her partner in space exploration for more than a decade, she often caught him looking at her *that* way. When he thought she wasn't watching, longing played on his face and furrowed his brow. He had never spoken one word about it or touched her in a non-professional way. He knew her too well for that. She still grieved. She could get another mate any time. But they'd never issue another breeding permit to her. Not at her age, and certainly not after Anya's death.

"I'll be fine." Her voice rang less casual than she had hoped. She steered her scooter downhill. The terrain was rockier here, and she focused on her descent. When she looked back up ahead, at the crashed ship, her jaw clenched.

Most of the hull was still intact, but the observation hatches and the cargo bay doors were blackened. This type of spaceship could survive extreme conditions for a limited time frame. Not for ten straight days. Not with her engine dead.

Not with her captain dead.

Like Anya.

Royo willed the painful thought to the back of her mind and circled around the crashed ship. The emergency hatch hung open.

"Control, I have visual confirmation. It *is* the *Dreamcatcher*. I will check for survivo— Oh, shit!"

"What? What is it?"

Royo pushed the brakes and the scooter came to an abrupt stop. Thin dust swirled around her, quickly settling back down.

"It's—it's a. . ."

All words choked in her suddenly dry throat. Tegan's high-pitched voice dragged her back to reality.

"Royo, talk to me! What is it? What have you found?"

"Haran was right this time." She gulped, trying to keep her voice steady. Her fingers flexed around the scooter's handles. "A building, unlike anything I've ever seen." She dismounted and walked closer.

"A building?" Doubt edged his voice. "The surface scan didn't show any type of structure."

"Because it's a *glass* building. Or, rather, what's left of it." She touched the smooth, translucent wall, blood pounding in her ears. *Who made you?* She retreated a few paces to study the whole structure. Only a corner still rose from the silver sand, its broken edges blunt from the constant exposure to the heat. The northern wall rose three times her height, and there was no telling of how high it had once been. Certainly not a hut made by a primitive people. *Where are they now?* This time, Haran had indeed found something.

Now she had to find *him*.

Tegan was still speaking, his voice distant to her ears and mind.

"...made of glass? This should explain why our scans didn't..."

She cut him off. "I'll check inside the ship. The emergency hatch is open. Perhaps someone made it out alive."

A long silence spoke his doubt. "Just be careful."

Royo used the moon's low gravity to jump up to the hatch with little effort. She turned on her helmet's light and peered inside. Debris littered the cockpit: broken equipment, shattered glass, wiring hanging loose, and a corpse—a blackened corpse face down on the floor.

Haran?

Her throat closed on a scream. She couldn't be smelling the charred flesh—she *shouldn't*, in the vacuum. But she was. She closed her eyes and counted slowly to ten.

Sunset over the Evergreen Marshes. The minnows around your ankles at the beach of your childhood summers. Breathe. Breathe.

Her pulse slowed, but the stench remained.

Anya. He's dead, burned like Anya. So small, so still, so black.

My fault.

The old pain resurfaced. The authorities had cleared her. Malfunctioning landing gear, they said. She should have done more tests. She should have known. All her training useless the one time it mattered. She should be dead instead of her little girl.

It's easy: just lie down on the silver sand of this forgotten moon and await the sunset. Forget Haran. He's dead anyway.

159

No.

She forced her eyes open. She forced her breathing to slow. She forced her body through the hatch's opening. Perhaps it wasn't Haran lying crisp on the cockpit floor. He had a crew, hadn't he?

She flipped the corpse on its back and a deep sigh escaped her throat.

Tegan's voice came through the com link, too loud inside this small space. "What is it?"

"I've found a dead body, but it's not Haran. Her name tag identifies her as his pilot." She looked around. The door to the back seemed jammed, wiring hanging loose from its control panel. "Wasn't there a third crew member?"

"The ship's manifest lists an engineer as well."

She tried the door. It was indeed blocked, and she had neither the means nor the time to force it open. This ship would become an oven come sunrise. "I can't get to the back from here. I'll check outside for another way in. Perhaps I'll have more luck with the cargo bay doors."

"Two hours left, Royo."

"Don't worry. I'll be back before that." She climbed back outside. The starlight reflecting on the glass wall split to a magnificent rainbow and blinded her for a moment. She looked away, blinking until her vision cleared. Only then did she notice a trail of footprints leading away from the crash site. She blinked again. How had she missed that before?

"Footprints! Footprints leading away from here, toward the crater!"

"Easy, Royo." Controlled excitement colored his voice. "Be careful; the crater area is highly unstable."

She didn't reply, only rushed to her scooter, fired up the engine and followed the footprints on the silver sand. A few minutes later, at the edge of the crater, a dark spot on the sand came into view—another body. Or, rather, few blackened bones and suit remnants. The ceramic tag had the engineer's name on it.

"Second body in sight—the engineer. I guess the sunlight caught up with him." She looked around. A lone trail of footprints led further away. "It seems that Haran was still alive at this point. The pattern of the footprints suggests that he sped up from this moment on, running away. But where to?" She looked across the crater and her knees weakened. "Good grief, Tegan! There's a whole glass city out here!"

And Haran is somewhere in it. He must be.

"Fascinating." His dry tone startled her. When he spoke again, concern tightened his words. "A bit over an hour left. Come back *now*. The glass city will still be there at nightfall."

"But Haran might be there! Maybe he found shelter. Maybe he's injured and needs help." Royo stepped closer to the edge of the crater. At the far side, the shapes of translucent domes and towers were barely visible against the stars. But the effect of the glass buildings when the starlight hit them was breathtaking. Countless rainbows colored the grey sand for miles, bringing the wasteland to life in an explosion of blue and green and purple.

Increased static came through the com link when Tegan spoke again. "Sunrise will hit our landing site in an hour. The solar storm is affecting communication already. You need to return for take off *now*."

Her shoulders slumped. Tegan was right. And Haran was probably dead—even if he had found shelter from the heat, his oxygen couldn't have lasted that long. She'd only endanger Tegan chasing a lost cause. *I'm not Haran.*

"Very well. I'm coming back."

Static came through her com link. When Tegan spoke again, relief mellowed his voice. "I will start preparations for take off."

Royo glanced around one last time—at the ruins, at the remnants by her feet, at the lone trail of footprints leading away. *Forgive me.* She fired up her scooter. She had barely turned around when the ground trembled. Her grip tightened, and she managed to keep the scooter upright. The ground shook again, stronger this time, and she cursed herself for having stopped so close to the edge of the crater.

The rock beneath her scooter retreated, and she jumped off just in time. On hands and knees, she scrambled away from the collapsing edge, until she managed to stand upright again. When the ground stopped trembling, she checked her suit and then dared a glimpse over her shoulder.

"Crap!"

"Royo? The scanner reports a quake at your position. Everything okay over there?"

She dared a glimpse over her shoulder. The scooter was gone.

"Royo? Talk to me!"

She approached the edge of the crater and her stomach knotted up. There was no way to get the scooter out of there. Not on her own, and not in time to beat the sunrise.

I'm dead.

161

She clenched her fists. "There has been an . . . incident." She started walking around the crater. Haran's footprints had vanished during the quake and the collapse, but their image survived in her memory.

"What kind of incident?"

"I-I lost the scooter."

No answer—only static.

She tapped her com link. "Tegan?"

Tegan's voice came through the static. Angry. Desperate. "What happened to the scooter?"

"It's at the bottom of the crater. Any chance you could pick me up?"

"Negative. I cannot reach you in time. And the ground there is unstable. The impact from the landing will only lead to further collapse."

Royo's mouth went dry. A faint glow lighted the crest of the hill now.

It's official, then. I'm dead. I'll never find Haran. I'll fry on this stars-forsaken moon.

There was more static now, as sunrise drew closer. ". . .have to take off . . . sorry. . ."

Not as much as I am. She squared her shoulders. "I'm heading toward the ruins. Perhaps I'll find some shelter there."

". . .do that. . .look for you in ten. . ."

"Tegan?"

". . .never told you. . ."

The com link transmitted only static now, and she turned it off.

The overwhelming desire to just sit down and await the sunrise washed over her. She clenched her teeth and picked up her pace. More footprints ahead—and not just Haran's. She trod carefully, inspecting the other footprints. Wider than her own and Haran's, they led toward the glass city. How long had they been there, under the heat? Had they known a time when the sun warmed but didn't scorch? They vanished again after a while, and she pushed on.

She had reached the first ruins now. The city stretched as far as she could see, the remnants of domes and towers spiraling up to the sky, reflecting the starlight a thousandfold. She touched the smooth surface of a glass wall. Nothing marred its crystal surface, no stain, smudge or palm print. Its edges were blunt too, melted down from the sun's scorching heat over the millennia. And yet, it had endured. What kind of creatures had erected such a wondrous city?

She glanced over her shoulder. A thin slice of sun glowed now over the horizon. Soon she'd be scorched to ashes, and would never know of the race who built this. She shuffled the sand with her boot. Were their ashes mingled with this ground too? Was Haran's?

But I'll see my little girl again.

Her vision blurred. She inhaled deeply, willing the tears back. Light reflecting on a glass column blinded her, and she blinked repeatedly. When her eyes cleared, she was not alone.

"Anya?"

It could not be Anya. Had her oxygen levels dropped? Was she hallucinating? Against all reason, the petite form of a girl stood at the distance, waving at her.

"Anya?"

No answer, just a tiny hand beckoning. The monks of Honshun 6 believed that, at the threshold of death, your loved ones came to escort you across dimensions. She shifted her weight from one leg to the other. Was that it?

"Anya? Is it really you?"

A giggle for an answer. The island folk of the Lasho 4 archipelagos claimed that hungry, gaseous entities roamed the frozen void, luring explorers to their deaths by assuming the forms of their beloved dead. And Haran had sworn it was true.

Haran and his tall tales. Anya would never hurt me. She drew in a deep breath and started after the apparition.

The little girl ran off, swirling and giggling amidst glass walls and towers. Sometimes her image appeared distorted through the layers of glass, her wide smile forced, her limbs too long to belong to a child. And sometimes, when Royo looked at her out of the corner of her eye, the smooth pale face turned black, strips of charred flesh peeling off. But she kept on.

Anya would never hurt me. Would she?

The sun had risen higher behind her, its fiery breath at her neck, when the girl stopped by the entrance of a domed building. Royo stopped too, unsure of what to do.

"Anya? Please, speak to me." *Forgive me.*

The girl sat down, cross-legged, and suckled the thumb of her right hand, while she traced spirals on the sand with her left.

Royo walked on, her suit weighing double now. "Anya? Baby?"

With each step, the girl's form lost something of its substance, until it became translucent like the glass ruins around her.

I'm losing her again.

When she reached the dome's entrance, the girl had vanished without looking up once, leaving Royo bereft.

Again.

The apparition had been neither a guide nor a trap—just a merciless reminder of her wasted life.

Is that a hole on the ground over there?

Racing against the sun, Royo hurried inside, sweating heavily inside her suit now. She found only grey sand and broken glass around a deep hole. She shuffled through the sand. If she could cover herself up, she might be able to avoid some of the heat.

Yeah, right.

The ground shook again, more violently than before. Royo lost her balance, flapped her arms sideways, and fell into the hole. Her helmet hit against a broken wall, and her vision blurred.

And then, she kept on falling.

Her back hit the ground hard, her head still buzzing from the first hit. Once her vision and mind had cleared, she looked around. She was in some kind of cave—a cool, dark cave. A flight of stairs led up, to where the hole had been. Relief washed over her. Her oxygen would last for another eight hours—perhaps more if she managed to slow her heart rate. She could outwait the sunlight.

She turned on her headlight and checked her suit. It seemed undamaged by the fall, thanks to the moon's low gravity. She glanced around. This was no cave—someone had built it. She managed to stand up, ignoring her dizziness. She was in a hallway leading to—where?

Haran would be ecstatic. He would have given an arm and leg to see this place.

She checked the ground and adrenaline surged through her bloodstream: footprints on the thin layer of sand. Haran's boots, at the edges of a different trail—the wider, deeper footprints she had seen above, and there were many.

She took out her scanner. There was no indication of radiation or toxins. But there were faint indications of oxygen and nitrogen, fading away fast. She walked away from the hole as the heat increased.

After a long walk in the dark, she reached a door where the trail ended, its surface smooth and without a handle. Made mostly out of lead, it seemed to require some form of energy to operate. There was something like a control panel beside it. Her scanner indicated traces of energy, but nothing sufficient to open it. But Haran, despite all his talents and claims, could not go through solid metal. There *had* to be a way to open it.

The heat increased, and Royo licked her lips. She needed water. She increased the humidity in her breather as much as she dared. There was no telling how long she'd stay here. Her scanner indicated a spike in temperature, as the sunlight had probably hit the glass city on the surface above. Something buzzed at the panel. The controls flashed red and blue. Her heart raced anew. It was solar-powered!

There were only three dials on the panel, and after a few failed attempts the door finally opened. Behind it, a hall stretched on, probably as vast as the city above. Shelves lined its walls carrying cubes. *Stasis units? They look like stasis units.* Royo held her breath. Were the builders of the glass city still alive?

As the heavy doors closed behind her, her helmet's atmosphere scanner buzzed. She checked her hand-held scanner. This hall had breathable atmosphere: seventy-eight percent nitrogen, twenty-one percent oxygen, traces of carbon dioxide and other gasses, but almost no water vapors—too dry and low in oxygen for her needs, but better than the vacuum. Her breather recalibrated, and mixed the external atmosphere with that of her suit's tanks. Relief washed over her. Perhaps she'd make it after all.

The gravity was higher as well. Her steps, slow and cautious, echoed through the darkness as she approached the units. She dusted the glass lid of the first one, only to find its occupant dead. The sterile interior of the unit had maintained the creature's features, so much like her own and yet radically different: a tall, slender biped with two eyes and five-fingered limbs, unlike her four. Dried skin stretched over the angles of a noble face, now darkened. Had it been green like her own skin once? A panel on the unit showed only one heart and two lungs, although larger than her own.

She checked as many as she could, and found them all dead: males, females, their young. Time had caught up with them. But the ship's scanner had registered life signs in the area. Someone had to be alive down here. *Haran.* But where?

She raised her scanner above her head, hoping to enhance its radius. Nothing. She had no choice but to check the units on her own.

A giggle. A whiff of rich, marshy air. A white hand beckoning at the edge of her vision.

165

Christine Lucas

"Anya?"

After one moment of hesitation, she started after the apparition. She lost it after a while, and looked around. This area of the hall housed units with animals, all in pairs. Birds with colorful plumage, four-legged mammals, furry little creatures—all dead. She checked her scanner again. This time it registered faint life signs somewhere to her right. She checked the units one by one, until she reached one with controls flashing red and green. Frantically, she dusted it and found a small creature covered by orange fur. A dial blinked by the glass cover. Her hand moved faster than her mind and she pressed it.

The creature trembled. After a few minutes of agonizing uncertainty, it raised its head and looked right at her, its eyes huge and luminous. It licked its whiskers and spoke just one word.

"Mew?"

Then it closed its eyes and its head fell back down. Royo bit her lower lip.

I killed it! Gods of all the worlds, I killed the poor creature!

The unit's panel flashed and buzzed, and a diagram showed normal chest movements and heart rate. Its breathing slowed, until it stabilized back to stasis levels—at least Royo hoped so, her knuckles white at the edges of the small unit. A different diagram displayed nine bars: eight red and one vibrating green—the last one.

The excitement of her find turned slowly and painfully to despair. The life signs belonged to this alien creature, not Haran. She had failed him.

Just like Anya.

She leaned over the creature's unit, tasting salt. No point of willing back her tears anymore. She was all alone now. Just like this poor creature, left to die under the ruins of a millennia-old glass city.

Through blurry eyes, she caught a glimpse of a reflection on the glass cover of the unit. Something lurked behind her. Had the apparition returned? Had her little girl come to keep her company until the end?

She spun on her heel, her movement too slow in the thick suit and the low gravity. If something had been there, it had vanished.

Wait. That unit over there . . . it works too! And what's that on the ground?

She approached it on weak knees. Brown, crumbled remains littered the floor before the unit. Organic remains, according to her scanner's readings. Familiar amino-acids, but the sequence was unlike any known carbon-based species. So what was in the unit?

Treading carefully, so to not disturb the remains, Royo dared a glimpse inside and almost dropped her scanner. Haran! She placed her palm on the glass cover, tracing the outline of his face from afar, his hooked nose and thin lips, the receding hairline. Her geek brother had figured it out. He slept in silence, among the creatures of his dreams, chasing in stasis his next great discovery. His hand-held scanner lay on the floor a few paces away.

When Tegan returned, they'd bring him home.

Royo picked up Haran's scanner and sat down on the dusty floor, among the furry creature and her brother. She turned it on, and browsed through the database, seeking answers for his adventure. Unknown files were cramped inside its memory card, slowing it down. She had almost given up when one of them opened. Loud music blasted though its speakers. Drums and cymbals, strings and woodwinds, they joined in a glorious swirl, celebrating stars knew what. A holy day, a victorious battle or just *Life*?

Absolution.

Images flashed on the small screen: vast oceans, paintings of smiling females, pyramids and temples of white marble columns. Royo leaned back against the unit. The builders of the glass city had not perished. Thanks to her brother, the memory of their passing survived.

In her own memory, so did Anya.

She closed her eyes, listening to the music of a lost race, and waited for nightfall.

All is Dust and Darkness
by Mark Onspaugh

The Xiin ship *Far Voyager I*, a crystalline structure nearly three meters in height, and shaped roughly like a pyramid, settled into a vast basin on the battered and scarred moon Deemer.

Tyf, being the elder member of the team, was the first to ooze down the ramp. He was not worried about his environmental suit, a miracle of crystal and algae fibers, as these had been tested and perfected on their own satellites since he first joined the program. For a member of the amoeboid Xiin he was quite tall, nearly a meter in height and half a meter in girth when he stood at optimal form. His lumin sacs still bore the scars of an early accident in a crystal farm, but these gave him a rugged and adventurous aspect. Those sacs were still capable of conveying complex and brilliant thoughts, and Tyf was widely regarded as one of the most brilliant of the explorer class. He was a hero among the Xiin, courageous and resourceful. Tyf reached the surface and claimed the satellite Deemer in the name of the Xiin.

Pid, his young colleague, waited anxiously for the signal to come down. Pid was slightly shorter than Tyf, and was so young he hadn't procreated yet. Pid was brilliant and full of youthful vigor though, and they complemented one another.

Tyf summoned him, and Pid fairly rolled down the ramp in his excitement. The gravity here was only half of that on their home world of Na'al, and Pid had to refrain from bouncing like a ball across the Deemerian plain.

Instead, Pid adopted a solemn and respectful stance, keeping his lumin panels dim and respectful. He stared out at the vast plain of gray dust, and marveled at the thought of what might have greeted the Xiin if they had made this journey millions of years ago.

At that time, it was said, Deemer was the satellite of a world that was between Na'al and Kovaan, the bright planet second in from the sun. Now there was only dust, rock and some hunks of crystal to show where that

169

planet had been. The crystals were long-dead probes sent by the Xiin many decades before as they mapped and studied the system.

The journey to Deemer had been a long one, nearly ninety million clephs, and the elder Tyf was not always the best company. Besides being somewhat patronizing, Tyf insisted on using the main spectrum luminescents in conversation. Pid, like many of his generation, had incorporated luminescents all along the visible spectrum, and had also ventured into non-visible waves, using the resulting vibrations or heat to add even more nuance to his language. Time and time again Pid had to rein in his enthusiasm, because Tyf would become stonily dark until Pid returned to the "acceptable" hues to be found from red through violet.

Pid also had grown up reading a lot of science fiction, a genre Tyf found to be silly and irrelevant. If one wanted metaphor, were there not the teachings of Xiinon The First? Pid had studied the teachings of Xiinon, but still he loved speculating about the possibility of life on other worlds, a topic on which Tyf remained skeptical.

When they were halfway out and beyond communication range with the base, Pid again broached the subject.

"I have been studying the work of Doctor Hez," Pid lumined, the integration of infrared betraying his youth and enthusiasm.

"Hez is a fool," Tyf groused. "He was thrown out of the Science Council years ago for pointless speculation."

"Still," Pid lumined, "don't you find his theories of fixed species fascinating?"

Tyf directed an icy display of deep blues and violets at Pid. It was the closest he ever came to cursing.

"The idea of a race of creatures that are not amorphous, who are static and unchanging is not only horrific, but blasphemous."

"But Doctor Tyf, surely a scientist like you can appreciate that, amongst the billions of stars in this galaxy alone. . ."

"Doctor Pid, our world is millions of years old, and yet we have never seen a single example of a fixed creature. If such a thing were possible, don't you think it would have existed at some time in our history, that we would find evidence of these so-called 'skeletal systems' that Hez postulates?"

Pid held his temper. Tyf had utilized a yellow-orange in luming Pid's title, edging ever so close to the shade that would have labeled Pid an impostor, a charlatan. Tyf was old and sometimes forgot that Pid was a colleague, albeit a young one.

"I think such evidence would be difficult to preserve, given the geological upheavals our world experienced eons ago. I'd like to think that life is plentiful and diverse in the universe. How exciting to meet beings different from ourselves! How would they communicate? What would their concept of art and literature be? Great Xiinon, how might such creatures procreate?"

"That's enough, Pid," Tyf lumined wearily. "Go see to the engines."

And with that, the discussion was over.

Now, standing on the surface of Deemer, Pid looked to Tyf for instructions. This was a courtesy, because they had rehearsed the tasks of the mission for many months. It was Pid's way of acknowledging that Tyf was the elder and the commander.

"Let's take some samples near the ship, and then bring out the crawler," Tyf said.

"Sir," Pid lumined, "I know it is not how we practiced, but. . ."

"Then I do not want to entertain any such notions, Pid."

"It's just that, one of us could be assembling the crawler while the other collected samples. It would give us more time for exploration."

Tyf considered this, then luminesced in agreement. "That is well-considered, Pid. Shall I collect the samples?" It was well-known between them that Pid had more dexterity and talent for assembling the complex crystalline components of the crawler.

"If you so direct, Dr. Tyf."

Tyf again lumined agreement, and this time there was a trace of ochre and mauve in his reply, the closest he ever came to a chuckle.

This time, Pid did bounce up the ramp, unable to contain his excitement any longer. All his life he had dreamed of leaving the confines of Na'al, of piloting a ship to the distant stars and establishing contact with distant races. Those that believed as he did were a small minority among the Xiin, and Pid had been careful to contain his imaginings and zeal when he applied to the Academy of Exploration in the capital city of Ba'anduur.

He had studied hard, but had been too young for the first missions to the moons of Na'al. When the first images from the larger satellite Fash had been transmitted, all the Xiin gathered as the public vid-lumins lit up. Na'al had never looked so beautiful, its deep red and ochre plains offset by the blue of its oceans and the green plains of the algae farms. Pid redoubled his efforts, determined to be on the team that went to Deemer, the next closest body to Na'al.

Now he was here.

Oh, he had not been Tyf's first choice. That had been Grif, who had been on missions with Tyf to both Fash and the smaller moon Cyx. But Grif had been killed when a crystal ship he been testing had lost cohesion above the southern pole of Na'al, and all the Xiin had wept as the bright shards had rained down over the crystalline forests of Keebyrrn.

Even with Grif now out of the picture, many considered Pid too young for such a momentous mission. But his fore-self had highly-placed friends in the program, and they had argued that youth might be required on such an arduous journey. The voyage was going to take over a year, and much of that time they would be out of communications range. Surely a young Xiin with top grades and quick reflexes would be a boon to the mission, especially as Pid would have no young mitotes dependent on him waiting back home.

Those Xiin who dreamed of a vast and populous universe considered Pid one of their own, and his image was soon appearing in fan-based group lumins, a fact that did not endear him to the staid Dr. Tyf.

For his part, Tyf liked Pid well enough. If his ideas were outlandish, this was one of the pitfalls of youth. Let him make more journeys to Fash and Cyx. He would soon realize that Na'al was unique in the system, indeed, in the universe.

Life had been given to Na'al by Xiinon in his own image.

Thus, the Xiin were life and the only life would be the Xiin.

Unlike Pid, Tyf wanted to journey to other worlds to help stabilize Na'al. Disturbing readings in the algae farms, in the oceans and in the crystalline forests had shown that imbalances were occurring all over the planet.

The Xiin needed to find what was going wrong and correct it, or their world would become uninhabitable in another hundred years.

Tyf had no illusions that they would find another home world within the system. Kovaan was uninhabitable as was the smaller, scorched world of Preeth. Out beyond Na'al were the gas giants Braal and ringed Edess. The moons of these worlds might be suitable for Xiin, but they would need something more efficient than the current ion drive technology to reach them.

Pid had mentioned building a series of large orbiting colonies, but even he acknowledged that the average Xiin would not willingly choose to live within the sterile confines of those crystal polyhedrons.

As Pid worked on the crawler, Tyf took a sectioned crystal box from one of the storage hatches located on the outside of the ship. He used a harmonic stylus to code the compartments with the date and location of the samples he wanted to collect. Once the coding was done, his pseudopod replaced the stylus in his suit, and he retrieved a collection sack, a small scoop and a pry tool.

Inside the ship, Pid assembled the crawler with speed. Inside the ship's atmosphere he was able to dispense with the somewhat clumsy environmental suit, and that gave him enhanced dexterity and freedom of form. Now that Tyf wasn't leaning over him, Pid used six pseudopods rather than the recommended four. He also configured two of his secondary visual clusters into primitive eyes, and had utilized his lumen panels as additional lighting for the task.

Perhaps Tyf was right, perhaps the Xiin were the only logical and reasonable course for the evolution of sentient life.

But it seemed to Pid that not all life followed logical courses. On Na'al there were small organisms that seemed both animal and plant, and the scientists could only speculate that nature had tried an experiment, one that was successful only in that the species continued; its dual nature seemed to give it no real advantage in the ecosystem.

If that were true, shouldn't there be other "experiments" elsewhere, some beyond what the Xiin would understand or accept as life?

Pid assembled the crawler in less than twenty minutes, which he knew was a record. He also knew that Tyf would not be pleased with the infractions he had committed in achieving such a record. Pid took up extra time double-checking the crawler's programming, power source and cohesion. When he felt enough time had passed, he put on his environmental suit, opened the hatch, oozed up into the crawler and trundled down the ramp.

Tyf was finished collecting samples and stowed the box into its proper receptacle. He lumined a smile as Pid came down the ramp, the crawler coruscating in the sunlight like a vast and impossible jewel.

Tyf oozed up into the crawler and was happy to let Pid take the controls. Their destination had been programmed by the techs back on Na'al; they were to travel to the opposite end of the basin, stopping at five key points to take readings and soil samples.

As the crawler moved smoothly over the Deemerian surface, Pid lumined a song of exploration from his childhood.

It was one of those songs about journeying far across an unknown sea, on a ship of crystal with algae sails, far from home, far from your fore-selves and mitotes.

Pid's luminescence of the song was actually quite beautiful, and Tyf found himself moved by the younger's deft use of complimentary hues and subtle flecks of turquoise and magenta to convey the longing for home and hearth.

Pid looked over at Tyf as if he had forgotten he was not alone. A lumined deep sea green laced with brown showed that he was embarrassed.

"That was beautiful, Pid" Tyf lumined back, "I should think you could have made a good living performing in vids back on Na'al."

"I did win a contest once," Pid lumined, his self-deprecating laughter a small riot of white, pink, gold and umber. "But, like you, I need to explore, to find what is beyond the world we know."

Tyf nodded. He had to admit, sometimes he forgot the simple pleasures of piloting a craft far into the skies over Na'al, going places and seeing things few Xiin ever would.

They stopped twice for samples, Tyf collecting rocks and Pid using the crawler's drill for core samples. So far the soil was largely oxygen, silicon, iron, calcium and aluminum. The rocks were basalt, iron oxides and breccia. It seemed Deemer would hold few surprises and their collecting would conclude without incident.

Near the next-to-last sample site, Pid and Tyf checked the integrity of the location, as they had done previously. The lumins on the crawler display showed the terrain was safe for approximately a cleph in all directions. Neither noticed the crystal facet displaying the lumin had a slight crack, a production defect undetected back on Na'al.

Pid began drilling and Tyf oozed out to collect more rock and surface samples. A brilliant flash to his left drew his attention, and Tyf saw a beautiful rock of a bilious green, quite unlike anything he had seen before.

Tyf oozed toward the specimen, extending a pseudopod with a "grabber" on the end. The device mimicked the grasping of a pseudopod, but did not endanger the integrity of the suit. One tear from a sharp rock and he would be measuring his remaining life in mere seconds.

As Tyf reached for the rock, he felt the surface under him slipping away. There was a nauseating moment of disorientation, and then he felt himself being pulled down under the Deemerian dust. Tyf lumined Pid, but the younger was on the far side of the crawler operating the drill. Forcing himself to remain calm, Tyf tapped a small crystal on his suit. This crystal was harmonically linked to the one on Pid's suit, and both would lumin bright orange if tapped.

Pid was there with surprising speed, lumining alarm when he saw that Tyf was now half buried in the Deemerian soil. However, Pid quickly calmed himself and assessed the situation.

"Stay calm, Tyf, try not to struggle."

"I am quite calm, under the circumstances, Pid."

Pid lumined reassurance and went to the crawler. He cautiously moved the vehicle closer to Tyf and parked. Wrapping one pseudopod around an axle he extended himself and a secondary pseudopod out to Tyf.

"Pid!" Tyf lumined, "You're going to tear your suit."

"Just take my pod," Pid lumined, "before I snap back to optimal and catapult you across the basin!"

Tyf laughed a torrent of purples and silver veined with scarlet and allowed himself to be pulled from the dust pit.

They both lay in the dust gasping for several minutes, and then Pid helped Tyf up. Tyf wrapped a pseudopod three times around Pid's, A Xiin gesture of gratitude and friendship.

Pid responded in kind, and they held each other for a moment, two explorers very far from home.

After they had marked the spot with warning crystals, it was Pid that found the defect in the crystal display. The unit was replaced and tested.

Only then did they take a break and have a quick meal.

"Processed synth-alg in a tube," Pid lumined, "does it get any better than this?"

Tyf lumined a grin and replied, "Voyages always make me yearn for the foods and drink of Na'al," he admitted.

"Braturian algae baked in krill with Crystal Tree Ale," Pid lumined wistfully in purple, cerise and azure.

"Lichen roast stuffed with paramecia and euglena wine," countered Tyf in azure, crimson and emerald.

"Alamoid stew!" They lumined together and laughed in bright flashes of teal, copper and ivory.

That was one of the best moments for Pid, second only to being accepted for the program and the actual launch of *Far Voyager I*.

Tyf checked the readout on his suit display.

"We have enough oxygen for a fifteen minute rest before completing our collecting and returning to the ship."

"I'm too excited to sleep," Pid lumined.

"Nevertheless, we depleted our energy stores during my rescue. If we wish to return to Na'al without incident, we should be in top form."

Pid agreed, and set a crystal to vibrate them awake in fifteen minutes. They each settled into the rear compartment of the trawler, letting their forms flow as freely as the environmental suits would allow.

Part of their training had been in maximizing sleep, for just such periods as these. Each was capable of achieving deep, dream sleep within seconds, the most recuperative state for the Xiin.

Pid, as always, dreamed of piloting his own ship to some far corner of the galaxy, his crew made of his surviving fore-selves and a small army of mitotes. It was a good and restful dream.

Tyf was having a nightmare, the worst he had ever experienced. All around him was blackness, uninterrupted by starlight or his own lumin sacs. Such darkness was intolerable to the Xiin, and he was seized with terror. He turned in every direction, and was met with darkness. He strained and prayed, but his lumin sacs would not give him any release from this oppressive abyss.

Relief came in the vibrating of the time crystal and Pid at once oozed up into work mode. Tyf followed, a little more slowly.

"Sleep well?" Pid lumined.

Tyf, who wondered if the dream might prophecy his end, merely lumined that he had. No use worrying the younger with the ravings of an older.

They reach the final site for collection and double-checked the stability of the surroundings. This spot seemed particularly safe, and they set to their tasks, each anxious to conclude the mission and return home.

Pid set the drill for core samples. It was tedious, because the drill was largely automatic in operation. Although he was thrilled to have been part of the mission to Deemer, he was a bit disappointed. It was a desolate place, unremarkable and colorless. He hoped he might be selected on the future missions to the moons of Braal or Edess, moons which he suspected might be more like Na'al than this barren rock.

He looked around, and noticed an odd depression in the soil about half a cleph from his position.

Pid checked the drill, then moved slowly to the anomaly.

It was lozenge-shaped, and uniformly ridged. Something about it seemed familiar. It was certainly artificial, which meant. . .

Which meant that something other than Xiin had created it.

Pid felt a deep chill, and his entire form tingled as if electrified. He put down a pseudopod in the dust, one suited for movement up an incline or across a slippery surface.

Aside from the uniformity of the other's ridges, the shapes were similar.

Now that he looked, he saw more than a dozen similar depressions in the dust.

Not similar, nearly identical.

Tyf was nearly finished with his task when his alarm panel went orange. Thinking Pid was in danger, he dropped the collection bag and his tools and hurried to the drill on the other side of the crawler.

"I'm all right," Pid lumined, but his panels were a riot of color, unlike anything Tyf had seen before in his conversations with the younger.

Trembling, his lumins erratic, Pid led him to the depressions in the dust.

Tyf stared at them.

"Do you see?" Pid lumined.

Tyf's lumin panels were almost dark; the slightest flush of violet was lost on Pid.

"The shapes are uniform," Pid continued, "and their pattern is similar to a pseudopod set for steep inclines. But no Xiin or amorphous creature would leave such regular, static prints! These are clearly the pod-prints of a fixed. . ."

The pry tool in Tyf's pseudopod had a razor sharp crystalline edge. As if in a dream he saw his pseudopod lash out and cut into Pid's suit, exposing part of his protoplasm to the cold airlessness of Deemer and severing his oxygen line.

Pid only had time to lumin an exclamation of shock and betrayal before he collapsed. It took a full minute before his lumin panels went dark, and in that time Tyf closed down all visual receptors rather than witness Pid's convulsions and riotous display of color.

When he sensed the younger was dead, Tyf went to him. He cradled the younger in two pseudopods and wept.

"Our world is on the brink of disaster, Pid," he said to the dark and silent shape at his feet. "Now is the time for clear thinking if the Xiin are to survive. We cannot afford the panic that knowledge of non-Xiin life would create, especially creatures that are fixed."

Tyf almost expected an answer, but Pid's lumin panels were dark and lifeless.

Tyf erased the vid lumins of the last two hours, and broke the camera. Equipment malfunctions were one of the hazards of space flight.

He used the crawler's cable and wench to haul Pid up into the vehicle, then spent an hour wiping away every one of the anomalous depressions he could find.

When he reached the warning crystals near the sink pit, his oxygen was running low. He drained Pid's tank into his own, giving himself another hour.

He prayed to Xiinon to watch over the younger on his way back to the Great Sea, and to give him an afterlife of joy and discovery. He prayed for forgiveness, and for understanding.

Tyf wenched the younger's body to the ground and rolled him with some effort past the warning crystals. He used the pry tool to push Pid the last bit, and then watched as the dust of Deemer claimed this child of Na'al.

For a moment, he thought Pid's lumin panels lit up, and feared he was burying the younger alive, but this was merely a trick of sunlight on the brightly reflective panels of Pid's suit.

Pid sank below the surface and was gone.

Tyf said another brief prayer, then gathered up the tools and the warning crystals and returned to the ship.

The journey back to Na'al was lonely, and Tyf had time to think of Pid and his imagination, his song, his curiosity.

His report showed that Pid had blundered into a sink pit, the blame a faulty crystal in the crawler's display. Pid was mourned and Tyf received a commendation from both the program and from the ruling council. He made a fortune appearing on vid-lumins and in person. Audiences were kind and understood that, while he would talk about his many journeys off-world, he never wished to discuss the loss of his partner and friend.

Tyf convinced everyone that Deemer was a dead end, not worth another journey. The Xiin should concentrate on cleaning up Na'al and looking for worlds to annex in the moons of Braal and Edess. It took many years, but Na'al reached a balance, and a new colony was established on Ulin, one of the larger moons of Braal. The colony was named Pid-Tyf, in honor of the brave explorers who went to the dead world Deemer.

And Tyf, who lived to be very old, would find Deemer in the night sky and think of the younger buried there, in the dark he thought had been meant for himself. As he got older, he began to believe the story he had told everyone, and mourned the loss of the courageous younger to such an accident.

But when he slept, he dreamed of pushing Pid deep into an abyss, where Pid remained alive but trapped, his lumin panels calling out to Tyf across the thousands of clephs, while somewhere beings of nightmarish fixedness waited. Pid warned him, in a riot of cerulean, scarlet, ultraviolet and x-ray, that such creatures would one day come to Na'al where they would denounce Tyf and destroy his world and all that he loved.

In the Footsteps of Giants
by G. D. Falksen

My name is Ilk-Ayahn. I am a proud son from the third hatching of Madam Yev-Ilk, a law-abiding and respectable woman of no particular social significance. I am an archaeologist on the verge of permanent university employment.

I am a murderer.

I cannot go back to civilization. They would kill me for my crime, certainly, but that is not why I refuse to return; I will die here, in the blackness of space in due time. I cannot go back because of what I have seen, because of the things that I know. I cannot go back because I have been shown that everything we are taught about sanity, order and reason in this universe is a joke, to which civilization is the punch line.

But I am getting ahead of myself, and my time is running short. I should not waste words like this. From the beginning, then, or as near to the beginning as whoever finds this message will care to hear.

I have spent almost one hundred days here, upon this barren piece of rock that circles the dead planet Algus. The purpose of my expedition was to examine the strange markings that crisscross sections of this moon. If you are a person of science, then you doubtless know that these markings come in two forms: long, continuous ditches; and strange ovals set in lines or clusters. Many theories have been postulated regarding these bizarre markings, but the very regularity of them suggests creation by some form of intelligent, organized species. My own theory was that these strange formations were, according to all sensible logic, canals and foundations signifying a complex urban community on what has since become a barren waste. This was the theory that I had ventured to Algus' moon to prove. It was an unpopular theory, and one that I had received much criticism for; but if I could somehow prove so radical an idea it would mean the securing of my career.

I was supported in my endeavor by Aya-Behil, an old friend from my days as a student. Aya-Behil's family was very old and very well off—truthfully, his rather poor attempt at scholarship was largely a formality, for we both knew he would be given an academic position simply because of his name. Indeed, it was his money, drawn from a family allowance, that had funded the entire expedition.

Over the many days of our research, we worked closely together, always enjoying one another's company. In order to cover the vast areas of the moon, we divided up the land into sections for each of us to study and administrate. With an undersized staff, we were forced to do most of the exploration ourselves, but we kept in contact over radio and laughed away the long hours of lonely searching while our small crew struggled to draw something useful from the fragmentary artifacts—or what we hoped were artifacts—that we brought back from the outside world.

Today appeared no different, and as Aya-Behil pulled his skimmer alongside mine in the base camp hanger, he was laughing about what horrors we could expect for what we had arbitrarily taken to calling "the evening meal."

"I predict, my friend, that we'll have stale water, fermented bread, dried berries, and frozen beetles for supper."

I laughed at this. "Apart from the beetles it all sounds pretty awful."

Aya-Behil laughed back, "Does that mean I can have your share?"

"Certainly not!" I replied, as we walked into the airlock.

This banter continued as we waited to be let back into the pressurized interior of the base camp. In the adjoining locker room—which smelled dreadfully of plastic and stale air—we locked away our environment suits and went to freshen up in the dust bathes. Compared to the amenities that people back on-world take for granted, our tiny dust chambers at the base camp would probably seem meager beyond belief. I'll admit they took some getting used to when we first arrived, but after the first dozen days of exhausting work any chance to dust our fur down was welcome.

Aya-Behil took the chamber next to me, and we chatted inconsistently between dust clouds. As was our custom, by this point in the day the conversation began to shift from the various things we missed about home to the more tense subject of our competing theories.

"You know," my friend said, "our time out here's running a bit thin and you still don't have any evidence to support that 'urban civilization' theory of yours."

"What of it?" I asked, flicking my ear a few times to dislodge some bath particles that had oiled up among the fur.

"Well . . . why don't you give up on the stupid thing and join behind my theory."

I snorted at this. "Give up five years of academic struggle and agree with the old dotards that those markings out there are all part of some elaborate worship site? No, I don't think so. Not to offend, Behil, if an archaeologist says something has 'obvious religious significance' it's because he's given up—"

"That's a pretty hard thing to say!" Aya-Behil protested.

"I'm not finished! It's because he's given up, *and* he clearly has no idea what its purpose really was." I stepped out of the dust bath and began to brush myself off. The oily particles tumbled down into the base camp drains, where they were rushed off into a recycling chamber to be re-dried and readied for the next use. "You remember old Professor Thu-Salha's big dig on the Khemmiri Ridge back home. . . ."

Aya-Behil groaned. "We had to spend half a year working there to pass his accursed lecture."

"And you remember those stone basins he found that he insisted were some sort of household shrine—"

"And it turned out the Khemmiri had indoor plumbing," Aya-Behil finished, "and the basins were really toilets." He stepped out of the bath and took the brush that I handed him.

"That's what I mean," I said. "Just because we don't understand it all doesn't mean it has some mystical significance. Why couldn't those markings out there be canals and foundations?"

Aya-Behil twitched his nose at me. "Why? To start, the people who made them would have had to be at most a quarter of our height if not smaller, that's why. Those 'canals' of yours wouldn't be able to push enough water unless the people using them were tiny. And those 'foundations' of yours? Maybe that highway theory of yours is a little palatable, but there's no way anyone is going to believe that this long lost moon civilization actually built houses *that small*."

I was a bit offended at his brusque treatment of my firmly held belief, so I merely made a noise and set about waxing out my whiskers.

"Oh, now don't be all indignant," Aya-Behil chided. "Just because you're clinging on to a stupid idea doesn't mean you're stupid . . . you're just stubborn." He gave me a firm pat on the shoulder to be reassuring. "The sooner you come round, the sooner you'll start getting recognized for all that hard work you do."

"Yes, and the sooner I find myself trapped in some stagnant desk job filing papers for someone who still thinks the Great Star revolves around us. No, thank you." I peered into a nearby mirror and fussed with a brow whisker that refused to curl appropriately. The activity gave me a headache, but I was willing to suffer a little pain to look my best after a hard day of work. "Yes, if I recant I can find myself some meaningless position *somewhere* in the academic bureaucracy, but that's not the kind of life for a scholar. I want to make something of myself, Behil . . . I want to leave a mark . . . I want to change how we look at the universe."

"And you'll do that by ruining your career and becoming the laughingstock of academic society?"

I crossed over to my locker and pulled out a clean red-brown jumpsuit that almost matched the shade of my fur. "You know as well as I do that I don't have a career. If I don't do something revolutionary, I'll be consigned to an insignificant position and I'll eke out my life in obscurity. I'll be a nothing, Behil, just like my father." I buckled the top flap of the jumpsuit closed with great finality. "I won't let that happen, Behil. I won't."

Aya-Behil opened his own locker and began to dress in his jumpsuit of crisp white. "Don't even begin to think about something like that, 'Yahn. You're not a nothing, you're not a failure. But you know, just as I do, that if you don't produce some results, or change your song to one the provosts want to hear, then you're going to be in for it. You can't let these obsessions of grandeur overpower your judgment. Maybe being a university bureaucrat isn't appealing to you, but at least it's better than being destitute."

He was right, of course, but at the time I didn't want to admit it.

"Easy for you to say, Behil," I said, "you're neither. With your family's money, you could be a strung-out nip addict with no job or prospects and you'd still live a comfortable life."

I combed a little frosting powder into the fur around my cheeks and ears to give them the pale, pointed look that is so very fashionable these days. All the while I tried to pretend that I really could use some brilliant new discovery to free myself from the chains of the social order.

My friend peered in over my shoulder and gave me a start. "What are you getting so prettied up for?" he demanded, giving me a playful shove.

I turned around and swatted him, showing my sharpest needle-toothed smile for a moment. "A message arrived from home just before we left this morning. I want to look my best when I watch it and send a reply."

"Who's the message from?" Aya-Behil asked casually. "Your mother?"

He almost choked at my reply:

"Of course not, Behil. My mother's latest won't be arriving for another day. This one's from your sister."

When I say that the very thought of my friend's sister, Aya-Eni, robs me of breath and leaves me light-headed, I mean this with the utmost sincerity. Even now, it is the memory of her and not my present dwindling air supply that makes it so difficult to breathe. If this message somehow makes it into your hands, Eni, know that whatever has happened, I still love you with every part of me that remains.

I realize that if someone is actually listening to this message, it is possible you have never met Aya-Eni. I should like to explain her to you, to describe in rational terms the vigor that the very memory of her sends through my whiskers, or the lightning that sets my toes a-tingling whenever I glimpse her portrait. I realize that I cannot explain such a thing. If you have ever understood love and passion, then you know such sensations better than I could hope to describe them.

Know that she is beautiful: to my eyes, the most beautiful creature ever to be given breath by the stars. Her coat is of the purest pale gray I have ever seen, with tips of white-blue like the snow found upon the highest mountain peaks. Her nose is like a tiny black berry, and her eyes are like a pair of gemstones that twinkle with hope and wisdom even in the most dire of times. Her whiskers are like delicate strings of starlight that wave and dance as she walks. Her tail is long and smooth, and it twitches with such energy when she becomes excited. I'll admit without shame the only reason I ever watched debates in the Lower Senate was in the hopes of seeing her speak.

The video message from Aya-Eni had arrived that "morning" while I was dressing for the day's exploration. I could not in good conscience have held off my work just to go and watch it, but the anticipation of a message from the object of my affections had haunted me throughout the day. I was so nervous and excited as I entered the message chamber that I spent several minutes trying—and failing—to remember my computer passcode; I was very glad the message chamber had been designed for privacy, or else I'm certain the other fellows would have had a good laugh at my expense.

The viewing screen flickered to life and I settled back in the room's marginally comfortable plastic foam chair. Aya-Eni's picture bubbled into clarity before me, and although the poor quality of the image left a bit to be desired, I was able to compensate for its shortcomings with my memories. She had clearly just finished addressing the Senate before making the recording, for she wore the long purple cassock of a junior politician; she must have had a good day of it, for her tail was bouncing back and forth like a thing possessed of life.

"Dearest 'Yahn," she said, unable to keep from smiling as she spoke my name, "I hope this message finds you well. So much has happened since my last message, I don't know where to begin. The Senate is in an uproar today, and I'm certain it's all going to get much more heated by the time you receive this. We've finally got all the old guard backed into a corner and they're about to start eating one another. The Premier's resigned rather than face a vote of no confidence, and right now everything looks possible. We're hoping to rewrite the old tax laws, increase citizenship eligibility for immigrants and refugees . . . there's even talk of giving men the vote!"

She laughed and clapped a hand over her mouth for a moment. "Oh, but I shouldn't go on about work like this. I know how much politics bores you. It's all just so exciting, and I'm so happy to think that the Commonwealth you'll be returning to will be better than the one you left. I can't wait to see you again. To sit down together and talk about the future. Of course, I'll be busy making sure these reforms actually happen, and I just know with all of your revolutionary discoveries, you'll be busy lecturing until your throat goes dry . . . but we'll find time."

She sighed, her tail drooping a little for a few moments. "Mother's being difficult, as usual. She keeps saying that you're not a 'good prospect' because of your family." Aya-Eni's eyes brightened again, and her determination returned to counter the sudden gloom those words cast upon me. "But don't worry, my dearest 'Yahn. Mother just doesn't understand how you academics work. In politics you get where you want because you've got the right family, or the right friends, or the right money, and so Mother assumes that's how everything works. She can't see that it's different for you. With you scholars, even the poorest person can become great just by being clever." She laughed. "At least, that's what you're always telling me. And I know it's true. Once you prove that theory of yours, you'll become the toast of the Capital. It won't matter who your mother was or what your father did. Mother will learn to love you for the person you are, just as I do." Then she added slyly, "Well, not *exactly* the way I do...."

I could hear faint shouting coming from off-screen, which the recorder must have picked up. Aya-Eni's eyes widened with exasperation, and her whiskers bristled in frustration. "I'll be right there!" she shouted to the unseen speaker, before turning back to me. "Ack ... I'm so sorry, my love, they want me back on the floor to give some choice words to the opposition. I'll have to keep this message short, but I promise you I'll send another first thing tomorrow, without even waiting for your reply. Give my love to my brother for me. I don't think I'll have time to send him a message before tomorrow, and you, my guiding star, have the higher priority." She chirped with amusement for a moment. "And tell Behil not to worry so much. He's probably told you a hundred times already, but he keeps insisting that we not become 'too attached' before your success is confirmed. He listens to Mother far too much, and I think he's worried that you'll be devastated if you don't succeed and Mother denies our marriage. He just doesn't understand that you're going to be a success, no matter what, so there's nothing for him to worry about."

With that she gave me a long smile and then leaned forward, gently shaking her head from side to side as if our brow whiskers were touching. Without even thinking, I did the same, and nearly knocked my head into the screen while I was at it.

"Now back to work with you, my dearest," Aya-Eni said. "Only a little longer before we're together again."

It was some time before I could bring myself to leave the message chamber. I must have re-watched Aya-Eni's video half a dozen more times before recording one of my own to send back. It shouldn't have been very hard to do, but I was somehow troubled by her words, and by my earlier conversation with Aya-Behil in the dust baths. The realization that my happiness with Aya-Eni, indeed my entire future, depended upon the success of the expedition troubled me. As Aya-Behil had pointed out earlier, so far I had found nothing to support my theory. In the end, I recorded a brief message wishing my dearest well and leaving her with reassurances that I was on the verge of the major breakthrough that would make my career. It made me feel sick to lie to her like that, but I still held firm to the conviction that my theory was right, and to the hope that I would soon find hard evidence to support it.

In the narrow hallway that connected the various compartments of the base camp, I crossed paths with one of my technicians, a very reliable workingman by the name of Nun-Sorek. He was a sturdy fellow with a ruffled blond coat and a prosthetic in place of his left eye—lost to some terrible machine accident, I was able to gather from our scattered conversations. Nun-Sorek was clearly agitated by something, and he kept glancing at me as we approached one another. His whiskers drooped in a very uncomfortable fashion.

As his superior, it fell to me to initiate conversation. "Nun-Sorek!" I greeted him. "How are you? I hope, well."

"Yes sir, thank you sir."

We stood there awkwardly for a few moments, Nun-Sorek too nervous to speak his mind, and I uncertain of what he was trying to bring up. I coughed a little. "Something on your mind, technician?"

Nun-Sorek wiggled his nose and then spoke. "Yes sir. I . . . there's something you need to see."

"What?" I asked. "Where?"

"It's out . . . well, out *there*," he replied, motioning with his head to indicate the barren vacuum outside the camp. "I found . . . it . . . in Sector 23-7, when I was doing a test run of the radar scanners. Sir, it is very important that you see it."

I laughed, then not understanding his urgency. "That sector's in Aya-Behil's search area. Report to him about it and see if he can look into it."

Nun-Sorek grabbed at my arm, startling me such that I took a step back. "No, sir, *you* have to see it. It—"

He paused and looked down the hallway. I glanced in the same direction and saw Aya-Behil meandering toward us, a spring in his step and smile on his face. He was clearly on his way toward our long-awaited meal of frozen beetles. Nun-Sorek tapped his first to his forehead and began to back away.

"I . . . I . . . must just see to . . . the machines. . ." he mumbled. "But come and see me, sir, after your supper."

I watched Nun-Sorek depart, very confused at the situation. Then, shrugging, I fell into step with Aya-Behil.

"What was that about?" my friend asked.

I flicked my ears in confusion. "I've no idea, actually. Something in Sector 23-7 that I desperately needed to see. I told him to speak to you about it."

Aya-Behil gave a slow nod. "Yes . . . just as well. I wonder what it could be about. There's nothing out in 23-7 but a bunch of rocks."

"He mentioned he was testing the radar scanners. Maybe they picked up something under the ground."

"Maybe." Aya-Behil licked his teeth for a moment and then shrugged. "Well, I'll ask him after supper."

My stomach grumbled loudly. "Yes, speaking of supper. . . ."

Supper proved to be exactly what we had predicted, with the added treat of some high-carbohydrate soup and vitamin paste. We were joined at the round dining table by a couple of other staff members, but while the initial conversations were all-inclusive, things rapidly descended into a debate between myself and Aya-Behil concerning the one topic we could never agree on: theories.

"'Yahn, you're eventually going to have to accept that this theory of yours is a fantasy! Foundations and canals? It's ridiculous!"

I popped a beetle in my mouth and gave it a firm crunch with my back teeth before replying. "Why? Why must it be 'ridiculous'? Because you don't understand it? Because it suggests that there was an advanced civilization in this solar system before we came along? Because it proves there was intelligent life out here?"

Aya-Behil pressed his hands into the fur at the top of his head, his ears wiggling in frustration. "We know there was intelligent life out here. We have the remains of their *religious decorations* to prove it."

"No, no, no, no!" I cried, shaking my head violently. "Those markings out there aren't some sort of elaborate worship system. For one thing, there are too many of them; and for another, they're too widely distributed across the moon!"

"This from the man who expects me to believe that those oval shapes out there are foundations?"

"Yes! Yes, I do expect you to believe that. Remember, we don't have any idea what the people who made them look like. We don't know if they had fur, or were bald; if they were mammalian or reptilian or ichthyoidal—"

"Oh, not your 'fish-man' theory again!" Aya-Behil cried. The other workers slowly nodded their heads in agreement; at one time or another, I suppose I had subjected them all to my discussion of what a fish civilization might look like.

"We don't know!" I repeated. "And most importantly, we don't know what sort of size we're dealing with. We assume everything should be measured based on us, and if we do that then yes the markings seem too small to be foundations. But, what if these people were slightly smaller than we are. Those oval foundations could be supports for a roadway, or a raised passage . . . or even the foundations of skyscrapers."

"But then the people who made them would be almost microscopic!"

I bristled at his trivializing of the point. "They would be extremely small, yes, but that is no reason to dismiss them out of hand. Small animals do exist, Behil, and some of them display signs of intelligence and organization. Why couldn't one of them have evolved to a state similar to us?"

Aya-Behil moaned into his vitamin paste: "Oh why, oh why did the Senate accept evolution? It would be so much easier to deal with you if it was still illegal for you to use that argument!"

"Don't start, Behil!" I warned. "Unless you want to argue that our primitive ancestors built a space ship and flew up here, some other civilization must have been responsible for those markings."

"Yes, of course. They were obviously made by some dead-end, insignificant, abortive attempt at civilization that floundered in barbarism for generations and then finally died in whatever cataclysm robbed this moon of its atmosphere."

"Assuming that it even had an atmosphere."

Aya-Behil planted his hands on the table and leaned forward, neck extending aggressively toward me. "If it didn't have an atmosphere, 'Yahn, then how did a civilization develop to make those blasted markings?"

I refused to be intimidated by his posturing. "I'm beginning to wonder whether those markings were made by people native to this moon at all. I think the civilization came from somewhere else in the solar system, attempted to colonize, built a series of contained environments—"

"Contained environments?"

"—which they then dismantled when they departed, for whatever reason. How else do you explain the complete lack of ruins and artifacts."

"Obviously, any artifacts have either been buried, broken beyond recognition during the cataclysm, or stolen away by the salvagers who first discovered the moon."

"You're grasping at air," I remarked.

"Oh, fine," Aya-Behil snarled. "If you're so clever, where did these 'space men' of yours come from? The irradiated pit of death this moon is circling?"

I scoffed. "Don't be stupid. Of course not! Nothing could survive down there. They probably came from the red world further away from the Great Star. But there's more reason to believe that a species of extremely small . . . well . . . somethings came onto this moon, built buildings, then dismantled them and left, than there is to believe some deluded theory about primitive agrarians digging perfectly regular oval shaped holes with ridges inside of them before dying conveniently when some fanciful event destroyed the atmosphere."

Aya-Behil pounded his fist against the table with such force that our dining companions drew away in fear. "Yahn, will you stop trying to defend this insignificant little species?"

"No! No, I will not! We know nothing about these people, Behil, and until we do, I'm willing to give them the benefit of the doubt. People, ideas, civilizations, they all need to be given a chance to prove themselves. If we just assume they're insignificant out of hand, then we risk overlooking some of the greatest finds in history."

"No! That sort of talk is foolish, idealistic, and even heretical!" Aya-Behil rose to his full height and puffed out his fur to appear as large as possible. "Some people are born to rule, to do great things, to enjoy life . . . and some people are born to work, to live thanklessly, to accept their place in the world. *And it is the same with all things.* Beetles exist for us to eat, birds exist for us to listen to, and we exist to enjoy them. Religion tells us that our people have existed since the beginning of time, and we will continue to exist until the Last Dawn when all things end. If the people who made those markings out there no longer exist, it's because they were an inferior species of no significance, who died when it was expected of them. They've accepted their place in history! Why can't you?"

And with that, he turned from the table and stalked off in fury. There was a long silence, broken intermittently by the slurping of soup and the crunching of beetles. I glanced at the workingmen, but they refused to meet my gaze. I looked back at my bowl and ran one claw through my food for a few minutes, and cursed the stupidity that had driven me to exchange such angry words with my friend.

Some time later, after waiting for hot tempers to cool, I went in search of Aya-Behil. I wanted there to be no bad blood between us, and I was prepared to humble myself for that purpose. However, as I picked my way through the base camp, I could find no sign of him. He was not in his quarters, nor the message chamber, nor the dining areas, the recreation hall, the workshops, the laboratory . . . or anywhere. I was terribly confused, and I searched the complex from end to end with no success. I questioned the scientists and technicians as to Aya-Behil's whereabouts, but they all shook their heads and mumbled that they hadn't seen him. Then, on the fifth pass, I found Nun-Sorek in the workshops, tinkering with the radar scanning equipment that he had been signed on to regulate. When he saw me his eyes widened and he busied himself with his work once again, keeping his face away from my gaze.

I was oblivious to the significance of his action, and greeted him casually. "Technician, have you seen Aya-Behil anywhere?"

Nun-Sorek almost dropped his adjusting tool, and I saw his ears and tail droop. "I . . . I . . . ."

"I've searched the camp from top to bottom," I continued, crossing the room toward the technician's work bench, "but he's nowhere in sight. Do you think he's gone out for another run?"

To my great surprise, Nun-Sorek turned toward me and grabbed my jumpsuit desperately. "I'm sorry, sir! I'm sorry! I . . . I needed the money!"

"The—" I wiggled my nose in confusion. "What money?"

"The money he was giving out, sir. The money he gave me to keep quiet."

"The money *who* gave you? Aya-Behil?"

Nun-Sorek nodded in shame, which only confused me further. "I told him what I'd seen and he paid me not to show you . . . but it was wicked of me to accept, sir. Wicked. You've a right to know, sir."

I placed my hands on Nun-Sorek's shoulders and slowly detached him from jumpsuit. "Technician, please explain yourself. I have no idea what you're talking about. Is this about Sector 23-7?"

"Yes sir." Nun-Sorek took a number of deep breaths and folded his hands to keep them from shaking. "I found *something* out there, sir. Something terrible and unholy. I told Aya-Behil about it and he . . . he paid me to keep it quiet."

"Why would he pay you to keep quiet about something?" I asked. "Just what's out there?"

Nun-Sorek dipped his head and began rocking back and forth in agitation. "I can't tell you, sir. I can't bear to think of it. And you'd never believe me either. But it's out there, sir. It's out there, and Aya-Behil's gone to put an end to it."

Still confused but determined to have an answer, I left Nun-Sorek and made my way to the hangar. As expected, Aya-Behil's customary skiff was gone. Without hesitation, I readied my own vehicle and headed out into the gray waste. Each sector marked off was a sizable area, but fortunately the skiffs were fast and able to fly high enough to bypass most obstacles. They also had a radio beacon installed in them, but for some reason Aya-Behil's had been turned off. I could neither find him on my navigation screen nor raise him on the headset.

Eventually I found him, standing beside a pile of tumbled rocks and dust on the inner slope of one of the moon's many craters. His skiff was resting at the top edge of the crater, and I landed mine beside it. I could not understand what had driven him to abandon his vehicle, or why his radio systems had been turned off. Afraid that some mischief had befallen him, I took a utility stick from my skiff's tool chest and hurried down into the crater.

Aya-Behil was observing the pile of white and gray with folded arms and a frustrated stance. He did not seem to notice my approach at first, and when I tapped him on the shoulder he jerked away in fright. As he turned around to look at me I heard his radio crackle to life; it was the short-range signal used over distances of only a few dozen yards.

"Yahn, what are you doing here?" he demanded.

"Nun-Sorek told me you were out here," I replied, "and when there was no radio signal, I was afraid something had happened to you."

Aya-Behil calmed down slightly and quickly took me by the arm, meaning to lead me back up to the skiffs.

"Sorry, sorry, didn't mean to snap," he said. "You just startled me."

"Are you all right?" I asked.

"Yes, yes, of course I am. I'm just finishing up some work out here."

I hesitated. "But I thought you said the sector was empty?"

"Uh . . . it is. . . ." Aya-Behil pushed me up the crater's side with greater haste. "It's . . . um . . . ."

I broke away from him and turned to face the crater's interior. Something was not at all right. As I stared with growing curiosity at the pile of debris Aya-Behil had been studying, I gradually came to realize that not everything was dust and stone. The main component of the pile was a great mass of white material that I had first taken to be some sort of oddly-shaped moon rock. This had been partially-covered by a cluster of gray objects; some of which were bits of rock and dust, but some of which I slowly recognized as metal. I approached the pile with hesitant steps and ran my gloved hand against the great white shape. As I regarded the things more closely, certain particular aspects of them became horribly clear to me. I stumbled backward, trying very hard not to understand what I was looking at.

You will not believe me when I say this, but the white shape that I had first mistaken for stone was in fact an environment suit of unthinkable proportions. The mass atop it, setting aside the bits of rock and dust that had covered it, was clearly some form of primitive, land-bound cart or buggy. There could be no doubt that what I saw before me were the remains of a dreadful accident. The white suit had been punctured in numerous places, leaving me to wonder whether it was the crash that had killed the occupant, or the dreadful exposure of vacuum.

And the size of the thing. . . . I was in no condition then to try and take measurements, but suit's dead occupant must surely have been a giant, three times my height at least—and let the record show that I am an unusually tall man. I poked at the thing with my utility stick; while the abyssal cold of space had caused some conditional damage to the remains, it had preserved them as well. Some strange thought drove me to examine the giant's boots, and there I saw the distinctive markings that in my supposed "foundations" I had taken to be supports or the remains of plumbing ditches.

"Footprints. . . ." I hissed, suddenly short of breath. "They weren't foundations . . . or canals . . . or religious sites. . . . They were footprints . . . and wheel tracks. . . ."

For a moment I was elated at the prospect of this, a totally unprecedented archaeological find. Then a darkness began to gnaw in my stomach, and I turned toward Aya-Behil in anger.

"You knew!" I shouted, pointing my finger at him accusingly. My fur was bristling. "*You knew!*" I grabbed Aya-Behil by the shoulders and shook him. "This is the find of the century! When were you going to tell me?"

There was a long pause. "I wasn't," Aya-Behil said slowly. He pushed me away violently. "I wasn't."

I was astounded. "I've heard of dying for your cause, Behil, but are you crazy? This is incredible! A race of giants in our solar system . . . that we've never before encountered a trace of. . . . Behil, this will make our careers! We'll be professors without a doubt, provosts by the time our first children are born!" I laughed. "Don't tell me you were going to let all this slip through your fingers? Were you really going to pretend you didn't see this, and let me have all the glory from this find?"

Aya-Behil turned on me with a snarl. "You numbskull!" he shouted. "You fish-brained idiot! Don't you get it? Don't you understand?"

"Understand what?" I asked feebly, drawing back in surprise.

"You're not supposed to get the glory!" he shouted.

"But the expedition—"

"You idiot! This whole expedition was supposed to be a failure! Why do you think I pushed you to do it? Why do you think I paid for the accursed thing? You were supposed to come out here with that *stupid* theory of yours and find *nothing!* Then you'd return home a failure, in disgrace, and be gone!"

The pain of hearing my dear friend, the brother of my beloved, shouting at me in such a manner made me feel sick. I stumbled backward as if to flee from his words—could I have covered my ears with my hands I surely would have.

"But . . . but . . ." I stammered. "Behil, why? I thought we were friends?"

"Friends? *Friends!*" Aya-Behil laughed at the idea. "I could never be friends with a low-born like you. You should have been grateful I even allowed you to be my servant, my helper, the one who told me how to pass my exams! But it wasn't enough for you to flatter me and be thankful for the privilege, was it? No! You had to presume to be of my level! You had to dare to lust after my own *sister!*"

"What?" I cried. "What does this have to do with Eni?"

"Don't you dare speak of her in that familiar manner!" Aya-Behil yelled, taking a step forward. For a moment I was afraid he would strike me. "My sister is a great woman who will go on to do great things. She'll be a senator one day, ready to marry the greatest of men. She has more important things to do than to waste her time loving you!"

"Behi—"

He did not even let me finish speaking his name before the ranting continued. "I wouldn't have cared if it was only you, of course. She's *my* sister, so naturally you'd desire her. You could have pined away all you liked as you toiled away like the low-born worker you are. . . . But that

195

wasn't enough for you. You had to go and make her fall in love with you, too!" He was pacing back and forth now, shaking his hands erratically in anger. "That was the end of it, you know. Our friendship. My tolerance of you. To aspire to be a part of my entourage is one thing . . . to aspire to marry my sister is another! And when you did that, I knew I had to destroy you."

"Destroy me? But why?"

"Because, little Ayahn, you somehow made her love you. Truly love you. She'd give up her prospects to follow you into poverty if she had to. And if you'd become just another faceless bureaucrat, part of the lowest rung of the academic class, then she'd be allowed to. The dividing laws aren't nearly strict enough, you know. A professor's no different from a collegiate secretary where the law's concerned. But if you destroyed your prospects, Ayahn . . . if you threw away your career on one last desperate gamble and then failed, you'd be evicted from academia. You'd be a workingman at best, and the law is very clear about that: no one of my class can legally mix blood with someone so low and foul."

There was a significant point here Aya-Behil was not getting. "But, Behil!" I interrupted. "This discovery's changed all that! This find will make me, I know it will. I'll be a professor on my way to provost in the blinking of an eye. And then I'll be of your class. Then I'll be worthy of Eni."

"Worthy? Worthy? You'll never be worthy of her. Why do people like you never understand these things? People aren't *made* worthy. They don't *become* worthy through talent and hard work. They're *born* worthy . . . or, in your case, they aren't. Your mother was a low-born, Ayahn; your father was a low-born; you're a low-born and you always will be."

I had finally recovered from the shock of his betrayal, and I set my face into a hard scowl. "That's as may be, Behil, but the law's all that matters. I'm going to make a report on this find whether you like it or not, and then just you try and keep Eni and me apart."

"You're not going to make this find," he replied. "I've already decided to destroy the evidence."

"Destroy it?" As an archaeologist I was horrified at the thought that someone would destroy so priceless an artifact out of mere spite.

"Yes, destroy it. I'm still working on how, but I'll find a way. I thought of burning it, but of course there's no oxygen. Maybe acid would work."

"Now you're grabbing at thin air, Behil. Nun-Sorek knows, and I'll tell the rest of the team. They won't let you destroy the evidence, not all of it."

Aya-Behil laughed cruelly. "I've already taken care of the team. I bribed every last one of them this evening, after Nun-Sorek admitted what he'd seen. None of them will back your story up. Even if I can't destroy this bloody thing, they won't let you bring it back on the return trip."

"Then I'll mount another expedition," I cried. "With new men! Loyal men!"

"With what money?" Aya-Behil laughed. "Besides, I'd just bribe your new team before you left anyway. Admit it, you're finished. Your career is over, your life is over, and you'll never have Eni."

I know I should have felt a crushing despair descend upon my heart as I heard those words. Aya-Behil was right, of course. He had the money, the name, the influence. If he was against me, there was nothing I could do to save myself. No matter how right I was, or how hard I tried, I would be a failure. I had gambled, foolishly, and he had ensured I would lose.

But it was not helplessness I felt in that moment; it was anger. I could feel my heart begin to boil at the thought of what was being done to me by a man I had mistaken for a friend. That anger coursed through my limbs like wildfire across the grasslands, and as the heat began to pour through every inch of me, I could feel it move my body.

My grip tightened around the end of the utility stick. My finger pressed the button to release one of the many sharp tools contained within. I felt my feet begin to move, hurtling me forward as slowly as time could imagine. My ears heard Aya-Behil shouting at me over the radio, but my brain could not register a single thing he said. In the last instance, as our helmets almost touched, I fancied I could see him through the tinted faceplate, staring at me in wide-eye horror.

I held him there until he stopped struggling. In spite of my bloody rage, I had taken care to only puncture his suit and not his body. He was whole and well as the vacuum took him. In retrospect it makes me sick to think that I could have done such a thing, but I cannot bring myself to feel guilt for the crime. The injustice he had sought to do against me was, in my addled mind, as cruel a thing to do as what I had done to him.

This brings me to the present. Having left the corpse of my former friend to be found by whatever search party would come after us, I crawled out of the crater. Wracked by violent shivers, I wandered aimlessly for a time until I came here, to this place: a barren patch of ground on a great ball of barren patches of ground. I suppose that I could have found my way back to the skiffs if I really wanted to, but what would be the point? Eventually someone would go searching and find Aya-Behil's body. The cause of his death is all too apparent, and I cannot imagine there would be any doubt to my involvement in the crime.

Perhaps I am a coward for not returning to face justice, but I cannot bear to think of the pain the murder will inflict upon my dearest Aya-Eni. I could face the executioner a thousand times over before I could ever face her. I have made this recording while I wait for my air supply to run out. I suspect it is nearly there. I am light-headed, my eyes are heavy, and my chest hurts beyond describing. I can see strange lights in the sky; lights that are not stars. I wonder, is this what it is like to asphyxiate?

Those lights grow brighter. To me they are Aya-Eni's beautiful smiling eyes, which twinkle when she speaks. As I leave this world, my thoughts are only of her . . . and of the life I wish we could have had.

The Last Traces
by Kate Kelly

Each step felt like flying. It was a strange sensation, drifting above the surface of the moon with every bounding stride. I sucked in dry bottled air between my teeth and grinned, squinting through tinted glass at a horizon that curved more and was closer than I was used to. The mountains were white and smooth against a pure black sky, and above was the planet, a sphere of blue and green whisked through with cloud, hanging suspended amongst the stars.

I pushed off with my booted feet once more and spread my arms as I floated back down. I wondered how long I could make these strides and my heat raced with the thrill of the strange and new. We were the first here.

I glanced round at Pirri, turning my head inside the glass bubble, and he grinned back with a flash of copper teeth, flexing his long fingers beneath the gossamer thin fabric of his nano-suit. His skin pulsed bronze and gold in his excitement.

"This is wonderful," he said, his voice bursting through the intercom and I flinched at the excessive volume. But I couldn't blame him. I felt like shouting too. To be the first to set foot on this moon—this was some honor!

Then Pirri paused and looked down at his wrist console and I saw a light reflected against his helmet; a green light flashing off and on, and when I raised my own arm I saw that mine was the same. I tapped the keypad.

"Metal," said Pirri. "Aluminum, and a small amount of titanium. It's not far from us."

I tapped a few more keys, inspecting the environmental readouts and nodded. "There's enough left on life-support. What do you think it is?"

Pirri shrugged. "There's not much. I doubt it's a natural deposit. Meteorite?"

"Could be, although I'd expect iron. Maybe it's a stony meteorite that contains some of these metals?" My heart pounded. Meteorites were my field of research. To think I might find one here—it would be perfect—

untarnished by the oxidizing atmosphere of the planet below. It could tell us so much about this system.

Pirri led the way, our long shadows rippling over the moon's surface as he moved and I followed, my breath short and sharp as I bit my sharp canines into my lower lip and tried to quell my excitement. It could be nothing. It could be everything.

And then Pirri paused and I could tell from the hunch of his shoulders beneath the fine fabric of his suit that it was not what he expected to see. I knew in that instant that it wasn't a meteorite and my stomach turned to lead. I drew level with him on the rocky rim of a wide valley and looked down; kilometers of fine dust regolith, smooth and undulating, stretching to the humps of the mountains beyond. And then I scowled and looked again, narrowing my eyes against the glare of the sunlight.

"What's that?"

"I'm not sure." Pirri started forwards, a slower pace now, skin pale amber with curiosity, and I followed, tilting my head, trying to work out what we were seeing.

"I think it's artificial," I suggested after a while. "Maybe it's one of the Elder's probes?"

"How would it end up here?"

"Hmm." He had a point. But what else could it be? It was definitely artificial, small and squat and oddly shaped. But the moment that I realized it had wheels was the same moment that I saw the footprints. I stopped dead in my tracks and Pirri, when he saw what I was staring at, stopped too. He let his breath out in a slow hiss and his face turned from amber to a pale grey-blue.

"Footprints," I said and started forwards, skirting around them to leave them intact. I reached out and touched the machine.

Pirri didn't follow at first, but soon bounded over to where I was running my fingers over the surface, sensing the metal through my nano-suit.

"Do you know what this means?" he said and a shiver passed through my skin.

"We're not the first after all."

"The Elders must have landed here when they first came," said Pirri. "But why didn't they say? I thought we were to be the first. I thought they ignored the moon and went straight to the planet." His face deepened to blue with disappointment.

But my heart was racing. This couldn't be.

"Pirri," I said. "Look again. This isn't our technology. These aren't the footprints of our people. Someone was here all right, but not one of us."

I shivered again as I spoke and looked around at the rolling white hills. These footprints looked so fresh they could have been made yesterday. But in the vacuum of space they could have been here for millions of years, with no atmosphere to stir the dust and no wind to winnow them away. And when I looked closer at the metal of the machine I saw the tiny pockmarks from the bombardment of minute particles of space dust on this atmosphere-less world.

These things had indeed been here a very long time, and I let out a slow breath of relief. For a moment I feared whoever had made those footprints might still be here.

"Are you suggesting that we're not the only space-faring people?" Pirri asked and his face was mauve with incredulity, his eyes wide despite the brilliance of the sun, and he flexed his long thin fingers as he spoke. "How come we've never come across them before?"

I shrugged for I had no answer. I pointed towards the footprints. "Bipeds," I said. "And this machine would seem to be some sort of wheeled transport device. There appears to be a seat. This will tell us a fair bit about their size and shape." I scowled. "The technology is pretty basic for interstellar travellers," I murmured.

Pirri wandered away from me, following the footprints. "Look." He stooped and picked it up. "Some sort of plaque covered in what I guess must be a form of writing." He held it up. "And a little figure. Perhaps it's what they look like?"

I scowled at the writing, which was unlike anything I'd seen produced even by the more advanced races our people had encountered. The figure was rudimentary, impressionistic. The machine could tell us more.

"Let's see what else we can find," I said.

Pirri found the next artifact and let out a whoop of excitement; he turned towards me holding up another plaque.

"A map of their world," he said his face pulsing gold.

I bounded over for a closer look. It was indeed a map. I frowned. There was something about that map, the way some of the pieces of continent seemed to fit, although they were closer than they should be.

"What's wrong?" said Pirri, "You're showing lilac."

"I'd quite like to show this to Dil," I said.

Pirri laughed. "What? That lunatic!" Then he frowned orange. "Why?"

"I think it's a map of the planet, before it was mostly covered with ice, before the continents drifted so far apart."

"Maybe it is," said Pirri, the gold flush glowing once more. "Maybe it's what the planet looked like when they came here."

I grinned at him. "Of course, you're right," I said. But in my heart was a strange disquiet.

I paused on the gallery and looked down over the railing at the floor below and the figure hurrying towards the exit. It was Dil, a shawl pulled round his bare shoulders, and his skin pulsed red with defiance. I clasped the railing, cold beneath my fingers and leaned forward for a better look. Where was he going so near to sunset? I still wanted to talk to him, although I knew that to do so would bring down the wrath of the Elders. We were not allowed to mention the artifacts we had found to anybody.

I glanced at my wrist console. The debrief was over for today and was due to resume in the morning, and I was tired. But there was something about Dil's color and the way he walked. And he walked like the Dil I had known of old, before they discredited him.

I swallowed and when I looked down at my hands I saw that my own skin pulsed red as well. I was going to follow and it seemed that my skin knew this even before I admitted it to myself.

Outside the domes I paused, blinking in the last of the light. The distant mountains formed jagged silhouettes against the setting sun and the chill breeze of evening stroked my bare skin. In the distance the fields were quiet, the harvesters stilled for the night and the workers had gone to wherever it was they went at dusk. I shuddered. This wasn't a good time of day to be out here alone.

Dil's red glow was moving along the track towards the trees and I narrowed my eyes. If I didn't move fast I would lose him in the woods, and I set off after him, never taking my eyes off his crimson light, my feet heavy and clumsy after the lightness of space.

Soon the dark canopy closed over my head and the path narrowed to a dusty track. I blinked and squinted into the gloom. Darkness came quickly in the forest, but I could still see Dil's light up ahead. And then I tripped.

I've no idea what it was, a root, a stone? One moment I was striding along and the next I was face down in the dirt with a mouthful of grit. I rolled over and the trees spun above me, dark branches obscuring an indigo sky. A few stars winked at me through the canopy, and when I stood up there was no other light. Dil had vanished and my own glow had faded to the dull grey of fear. I blinked but could see nothing.

I started to creep forwards, feeling the ground with my feet, holding my hands in front of me, testing for obstruction. My eyes strained against the black. Why was I doing this? I should be at home awaiting tomorrow's debrief. I shouldn't be chasing after Dil. Our friendship was over, forgotten. I should leave it that way.

The ground was uneven now and I stumbled. Either the path had gone or I had strayed. I paused. I should go back. But when I turned I had no idea which way 'back' should be. I couldn't see the sky to orientate myself. I gulped down my fear.

And then I heard movement. I wasn't alone.

I froze, hoping they wouldn't know I was here, my eyes struggling to see. These forests were full of wild creatures, some savage and dangerous. But whatever these were, they knew I was here and from the rustle of leaves and occasional snap of a twig I could tell they were coming closer. I shuddered and cursed my foolishness.

Then they were all around me, touching me, testing, and my flesh recoiled in horror at the alien contact.

I blinked and for a moment I could see their eyes, purple with reflected light. There was light on the trunks of the trees as well, and I could see them, their hunched stature and coarse manes of hair—Primitives, and I cowered away from their touch. And then they were gone, a scuffle of leaves, and they vanished into the undergrowth.

I looked around at the source of the light and my glow of green relief mixed with the light from the figure standing between the trees.

"Dil," I gasped.

The figure gave a flash of pink surprise at the sound of my voice.

"You?" The pink merged into red. "What are you doing out here? It's dangerous."

"I saw you leaving the domes. I was wondering. . ."

"I hear you've been on the moon," Dil said.

I faltered. "Yes, yes I have."

"So why did you follow me?" There was an edge of bitterness to his voice. I swallowed.

"I'm sorry Dil, I'm sorry about everything that happened."

"And?"

"And there's something I need to talk to you about."

The red tinge to his skin ebbed to orange. "Something about the moon?"

"Yes." My voice was barely a whisper.

"And of course the Elders don't know you're here?"

"No."

Dil smiled and his orange hue pulsed to amber. "You'd better follow me."

He led the way between the trees, and now the forest was full of sounds, insects chirping in the night and small creatures scurrying away as we passed, but they no longer threatened. When I glanced up I saw that the canopy had thinned and the sky had lightened with the moonrise. Occasional bats darted between the branches—fleeting silhouettes. With Dil beside me my earlier fears evaporated. He walked with confidence, without fear. He knew this place.

In time we came to the edge of the forest and looked out across a broad beach; sand silver in the moonlight, and the waves breaking on the shore gave off a faint phosphorescent glow.

It was the fire that drew my eye, and I stepped back into the shelter of the trees. Flames blazed and sparks rose into the sky to vanish in the night. Yet it was the creatures around it that made my flesh crawl; one of the higher forms native to this world, but animals none the less.

"Dil!" I hissed, but Dil just laughed.

"Come on." He started forward but stopped and turned when I did not follow.

"They've got a fire!" I hissed.

Dil grinned and his skin turned yellow. "That's right."

"But how?"

"They made it. Come on. They won't hurt us." He turned towards the fire.

This time I followed, trying to walk in silence, every instinct screaming at me to leave. I didn't want to go anywhere near these creatures, a species that I had only ever seen from a distance. They were of no use to us, but were harmless. Not like the others that we used to work the land, or the creatures I had just encountered that I would rather forget.

Dil walked straight up to them. They stopped what they were doing and turned to stare, their eyes turning to me, scanning me up and down. My skin squirmed beneath their gaze, yellow eyes above broad muzzles.

One of them moved aside to make a space on the log upon which it was squatting, balancing itself with its broad tail and Dil sat down, running his hand over the smooth fur of its head. It half closed its eyes and a soft growl rumbled in its throat.

I stood on the edge of the firelight, stretching my long fingers. The night chill had settled on the forest and I yearned for the warmth of that fire, yet I dared go no closer. Dil turned and beckoned me over, but when I shook my head he turned away, and the creatures turned away as well when I stood and watched, bemused.

One of their number was crouching on its haunches by the fire, waving its arms in rhythm with the strange guttural sounds it was uttering. The others sat in silence, watching it, eyes fixed, enthralled.

And Dil watched, too.

After a few minutes I started to creep closer. The creatures didn't seem to notice, and there was something hypnotic about the rhythm of the speaker's voice. The fire spat, drowning out its grunts, and sparks jetted into the air. The others leaned forward as if trying better to hear.

I joined Dil on his log, lowering myself to sit beside him. He turned to me and smiled.

"What are they doing?" I hissed.

"Listening." He was still stroking the creature beside him and it half opened its eyes to look at me, then closed them again.

"Listening?" I asked. "To what?"

"It's an ancient legend."

"What?" I turned to look at the creature by the fire, the rapt expressions on the onlooker's faces, and then back to Dil. "Can you understand them?" I asked.

Dil nodded.

"What are they saying?"

"It's an ancient legend." Dil's voice was barely a whisper. "I've heard it told before, but this one tells it particularly well. It tells of a time when there was only one moon in the sky—a constant moon that did not change, a moon with a face that never changed. But then the second moon came and sang a song of the first moon's love for the sun, and the first moon was ashamed for she had been hiding her feelings for so long. So now she runs before the sun and hides her face from him, and only when she is alone in the sky will she shine in her glory, before running to hide once more."

I stared at him and then at the orator who was still speaking, oblivious to Dil's whispering.

"He speaks of us?" I turned back to Dil and Dil nodded.

"He does indeed. The second moon is quite clearly the ship that brought the Elders here, two hundred years ago and still up there. To these creatures it would appear as a second moon."

"But that's amazing. That they should remember!"

Dil smiled. "This species is evolving fast. They have fire and language and the more time I spend with them the more I realize that they have a very complex social structure. They also have this strong oral tradition."

"Is that why you're here? Are you studying their legends?"

Dil smiled. "I think there might be some substance to their tales, so, yes."

"And you think they might support your theories."

For a moment Dil's color faltered and the creature beside him opened its eyes to stare at me.

"You know me better than I know myself," said Dil. But I was staring at the creature beside him, for there was something in its eyes that was more than just a pet being stroked. I saw that it was female and it had feelings too—feelings that before that moment I had never thought animals such as these could have. And I wondered if Dil could see it too.

Dil and his theories—he'd been discredited—couldn't he see that? His ideas were quite plainly wrong. But I looked at the speaker beside the fire and the female purring at Dil's touch and I wondered.

The speaker finished his tale and some of the creatures moved off into the sea to dance in the phosphorescent waves and Dil's female went with them. We sat together on the log and I watched the firelight playing through the embers.

"So why did you come?" Dil asked after a while, and suddenly it was as if we were friends again and nothing had ever happened. And maybe I could mend what I had done, for it was I who had caused his downfall.

"We found something on the moon," I said. "I wanted to show you."

For a moment Dil's skin pulsed faster. "Did you?"

"Look." I held out my arm and tapped my wrist console with my fingers to project the holographic image into the space before us. One of the creatures whimpered and crept away at the sight and the others still around the fire watched in silence with curious eyes.

"This is the transport device we found," I said as the first image hovered in the air.

Dil blinked. "Look at those footprints - maybe one, maybe two individuals. That transport device looks rather primitive."

I smiled. "Yes, I know. But that's not what the Elders are saying."

"Oh?"

"And this is the figure we found, and the first plaque."

Dil leaned forwards for a better look. "A curious script."

"Have you ever seen anything like that?"

"No, never." Dil scratched his arm and his skin assumed a puzzled orange.

"And this is the second plaque."

"Ah," Dil reached forward as if to touch the image, but remembered and withdrew his hand at the last moment. He turned to me and his eyes were bright, his skin golden once more. "More of that script," he said. "And a map."

I nodded.

"So what do the Elders want you to say?"

I smiled, same old Dil, always the rebel, always looking for a conspiracy. But this time he was right.

"At first they wanted to say that it must have been our ancestors who visited the moon after all, despite all the records which tell that they passed it by as a barren rock and came straight to the planet."

"But it's pretty obvious it isn't," said Dil. I switched off the console and lowered my arm.

"Then they decided that it must be another space-faring race that visited that moon in the distant past. After all, those relics and those footprints could have been there for millions of years."

"That much is true," said Dil. "But the species that built that machine didn't have the technology for interstellar travel."

"They say that the map shows the world from which they came."

Dil snorted. "And what do you say?"

I smiled. So Dil could see it too. "Well if you imagine those continents a little farther apart, and then cover most of the northern and southern hemispheres with ice then, well, it's this world the map is showing. This world as it must have been millions of years ago, before the ice came."

I was almost breathless as I finished, looking up at Dil as I had back then, the pupil staring at the teacher, yearning for approval. Dil nodded and the glow of his skin showed that I was right.

"So it proves that your theories are correct?"

Dil shrugged. "Perhaps." The embers reflected in his eyes as the creatures that had been romping in the waves returned to the fire to groom and dry their fur in the warmth. Dil looked across at them.

"Incredible aren't they," he said. "They've evolved so far so fast, language, fire, folklore. The more I study their language and their society the more I admire them. This world is ready for a higher species, a greater intelligence than that which it possesses now."

"But you can't mean—not them."

Dil laughed. "No, of course not. This is a new species, recently evolved. But maybe in a few million years they might advance enough to develop space flight."

"But you still think that whatever made those footprints and left those artifacts must have come from this world and not another."

"The technology they have could only have permitted travel within this solar system. None of the other planets contains life, so the only solution is they came from this one."

I straightened up and grinned, my whole body pulsing with delight. So I was right. I knew it.

"So do you have any evidence for this?" I asked.

But Dil shook his head. "Perhaps there was once, but if there was a civilization on this world all traces of it have been scraped away by the ice."

I sighed. "And they became extinct when their world changed. Such is the fate we see so often, for those species that never made it to the stars."

"Perhaps they became extinct, perhaps not."

I turned and stared at Dil, biting back the urge to laugh. He was serious.

"What other species on this world could possibly have been to the moon. They are all just animals."

"Try the Primitives."

I shuddered and my skin turned icy blue at the thought, those animals in the forest, crowding round me, touching, sharp teeth and ragged manes of hair. I pulled a face.

"They are just animals."

"They are now. And soon they will vanish into oblivion for our friends here," and he nodded towards the creatures by the fire, "are about to supersede them. Yet for now they cling on."

I stared at the creatures by the fire. The female smoothed her whiskers and looked up at Dil. Then she moved across to join us once more.

"The Elders won't accept this," I said in a whisper. "The Primitives are vermin, to be treated as such. To suggest they may have once been civilized will be unthinkable. They're not going to like it when I tell them."

"I know that," said Dil.

I looked across at him, the golden glow of his skin reassuring. He belonged here, with these creatures. And he didn't mind what I had done, all those years ago.

"That's all of them," said Pirri as he tossed the last of the space debris into the lunar transport. He pulsed with the multicolors of satisfaction and flashed his copper teeth in a grin. I glanced up at the planet, blue and serene, then back down at the footprints, traces aeons old where once the Primitives' ancestors had walked across this empty landscape, their first faltering steps into space, steps that had gone no further.

I tightened my grip on the brush, then swept it across the fine regolith as were my orders, obliterating those footprints for all time.

No one now would ever know.

Colony Earth Redux
by Louise Herring-Jones

*T*he *surface of the blue planet appeared pristine from the air. It was only when the explorers landed that they found the foundations of great cities, crumbling under the overgrowth of millennia.*

Commander H4H Dagma stood on the briefing room dais. Although the exploration station was built on the side that always faced the planet, he pointed to a two-dimensional view of the opposite side of the orbiting natural satellite.

"Although no debris was found on this moon's far side, the mission was costly. Let us expend a milliglot of silence in memory of S7C Agros and C7C Bartus, who sacrificed their shells to that endeavor."

All but one of the crew bowed their heads and closed their lesser and greater eye-lids. A6C Telos wondered if anyone else sensed the irony of the situation. Agros had been a shameful Soil-Combustible cross. His male progenitor was landed gentry who had toyed with a female from the most servile bottom-rung of the base populace. Bartus had been bred from doubled Combustible breeding stock. It was well known that the Service viewed Combustibles of any breeding variation completely expendable to their assigned missions.

He glanced around the briefing room. All the other crew members were immersed in humble, shut-eyed contemplation. He looked to the dais. Commander Dagma stared down at him across his ridged proboscis. Closing his eyes quickly, Telos mimicked the appearance of his fellows, if not their respect for the fallen workers who had toiled too far into the hit zone to merit survival. Telos swore that he would never trade productivity for safety in a losing bet with his life as the stakes.

At least the planet-side is not as likely to be struck by meteorites. As only an artist could, he pictured Agros and Bartus smashed into broken shells and gore by a huge rock. A soft chime sounded. The milliglot ended and the two heroes were forgotten as if they had never lived at all.

211

Louise Herring-Jones

The Commander changed the screen display to a grid overlaying the satellite's planet-side. "We've already purified the planet, now ready for scheduled mutation. Only this satellite remains to be surveyed prior to mobilization of the settlement."

He set his pointer against his protruding abdomen, leaning at an oblique angle toward his audience. "It's a big job, but we can do it. Together, we can turn this rock into a proper docking station."

"Agreed, H4H," the crew voiced together, using the numerical honorific of their commander. Hydra double-bred officers were as rare as alarium on clarifying missions. To serve under a dual thinker was an honor not many of them would repeat again in this hatching. It underscored the importance of the mobilization.

"Check your monitors for partner reassignment." Dagma tapped a monitor, fixed inside a generic helmet visor. *As if he ever worked outside*, Telos thought as he pulled down his visor, a snug fit against his trunk. He hoped that his own Atmosphere-Combustible mix favoring creativity preferred him in the new match-up. Not many crew with Combustible breeding could record the accomplishments of a mission, both in written form, bordering on the poetic, and in images.

The cacophony of groans and sighs informed him as certainly as a morale-mem that only half the workers were happy with their new pairings. The marine reek of oiled hides crowded into the hall signaled their discontent. Telos read his monitor and grimaced. By some unlucky stroke, he had drawn H6C Bekra as his new partner. A female worker who had been reassigned from hatcheries, Bekra had been denied promotion in spite of her Hydra upper standing. She had a reputation for discord and crucial, sometimes fatal, mistakes. Telos wondered if her fallen partners had chosen oblivion rather than another day spent with Bekra.

He could seek transfer, but that was a futile and vain pursuit. Since Bekra's propensity to shorten the life span of her partners became common knowledge, a persistent rumor had spread. Assignment with her was said to signal that the Service found her co-worker either undesirable or especially capable. This could be a test for promotion, but Telos had the niggling sensation that Dagma wanted him gone, permanently. He should never have approached the Commander's Hydra assistant, at least not while she was under her superior's command. Even though their eggs would be raised anonymously in the common nursery, the time-honored custom of their species, a mating contract with a Hydra female would improve his status.

Telos looked over at Bekra. The female was looking over her own monitor with her trunk coiled in a knot. Perhaps his own A6C rating was what disturbed her? Bekra also was a technical worker. He'd heard that she was superb at mapping despite her other flaws. But her topside breeding was Hydra, H6C, a thinker combined with a Combustible. Like the water and fire each represented, hers was a volatile mix, a Hydra thinker male joined with a Combustible fiery female. And from all that was rumored about Bekra, the combination had proved to be a disaster.

The audacious female was on the move, headed straight for him. Telos wasn't ready, but he straightened his brawny male shell and held in his abdomen, gone to flab from lack of strenuous missions and not enough dedication to the training module. He would be sure this female knew who was in charge.

"Telos, I presume," Bekra said as she approached. She did not raise her forelimb in greeting, a sleight that might have caused a duel here on this off-planet mission where discipline was not as firmly entrenched as on the home world. "I've looked up your rating. On the downside, we're both Combustible-bred. On the top-end, I'm Hydra while you're Atmosphere. I'm in charge. Follow my lead. We're going to Central for orders."

"But I have five more years of service than you. Clearly, I'm the senior and should dominate our partnership."

"Take it up with Command," Bekra said with a wry grin.

She knows, Telos thought. He knew he would lose any close issue raised with Dagma after his unsuccessful bid to mate with the Commander's assistant. His friends had warned him, but Laira had been so delectable, so irresistible, so willing. His career would be forfeited if her superior learned of their premature dalliance prior to his proposal.

Bekra returned to the base center. Telos caught up with her hurried waddling.

"Bekra, think we'll find any life forms on this rock?"

"Not likely," she said. "None besides our own."

"Who would live here?"

"Someone like us." She gestured to a view port where the image of a blue and green planet hung suspended in a dark sky pinpricked with starlight. "Someone who wanted that planet for expansion."

"Yes," Telos said. "I understand, but I can't agree. Why did they kill all intelligent life?"

"There's no life here, that's sure," she said, changing the subject, her reputation for subtlety proving itself.

"Let's bet on it. A bottle of pap-blend wine to the winner?"

"You're on," Bekra replied. "What do you say we make it two bottles?"

"Done," Telos held his forelimb out and Bekra slapped it with her own, her claws curled inward. "I'll be looking forward to that drink."

Telos chuckled at how quickly Bekra had taken the fly in her yap. Maybe gambling was her weakness? A recollected rumor to that effect flashed in the back of his head like a fire bug blinking in the darkness.

"Don't you two have a mission to fulfill?" Varkof, their H5C junior officer stood with forelimbs on torso, standing in the branch tunnel that led to the equipment lockers.

Bekra frowned as she saluted, but answered, "Affirmative, Officer."

Telos repeated a standard, claws-out salute, his trunk neatly tucked against his chin. Perhaps he and his new partner had more in common than he had imagined possible.

They were assigned initially to collect rubbish from the elevated highlands of the satellite. Although the new colony planet with its delectable blue oceans was temptingly visible, he had seen about all the rock and dust tolerable to a water-loving creature. Telos grumbled, inaudible from the confines of his enviro-bubble with his comm-unit adjusted to low volume.

The bubbles encapsulated their bodies and shells plus the elements needed for respiratory function, roughly equivalent to the atmosphere and temperature of the equatorial zones on the recovered planet visible in the sky beyond them. Trapped within the warm sphere, Telos struggled not to gag on the concentrated, held-in stench of his own bodily humors. Although the bubble and his work visor doubly protected his eyes, his translucent inner eyelids were closed, an involuntary reaction to the appearance of the barren surface

"Haven't we looked enough?" he asked Bekra, turning up the bubble's comm-system.

"Almost done," she said. "Want to be sure we've scanned this last sector." She looked up at him, her drawn inner eyelids hazy beneath her visor. She turned and pointed at the final ridge on their assigned exploration grid. "What's that?"

Telos stared in the direction of her gaze. Two large objects, their angles at disparity with the smooth lunar surface, rested against jagged boulders. He followed Bekra as her bubble glided onward.

The objects' exteriors were damaged by the ultraviolet rays of the nearest star. The tallest one, supported by four jointed legs, had the remains of a sheath of metal foil on its surface, now flaking and gray. The other larger object, a vehicle with four circular wheels, was also gray, and was grazed by the dust that coated the surface in a light film. There were smaller objects on the surrounding ground.

"Great, just great," Telos said, kicking at one of the rectangular cases that littered the surface. "We're only survey crew, but they should have sent purifiers instead. Best get all this contraband together for quick destruction. Command won't want anyone infected by alien ways."

Bekra said nothing. She donned multi-jointed pick-up tongs and walked around the site slowly, staring first at the four-legged construction and then at the wheeled vehicle, whispering into her work visor at decibels Telos could not hear.

She stopped by the vehicle. "This must have been a transport of some type," she said. "They were shorter than we are, but not by much." She stepped over the side and sat down in an angled pocket. Her shell rested awkwardly on tattered webbing as she gripped an apparent guidance device wheel through the protective shield of her atmosphere bubble. "What do you think, Telos?"

"I think we could get in a lot of trouble, fooling around with this stuff, but thanks for asking my opinion." He slipped on a set of jointed work-tongs.

"Too bad it doesn't run anymore," Bekra said, climbing out.

"Let's get the smaller objects together. We can use that vehicle as a collection point." Telos placed an enclosed case into the chassis, then leaned over and popped open the restraints with his tongs. Inspecting its contents, he leaned back and extended his tongs to maximum length to snap the case shut.

"Telos, come look. They left more than their junk behind."

"I know, frozen feces," he said, pointing to the case.

"No, something else."

"What do you see?" Telos asked.

"Depressions in the dust, lots of them."

Telos peered over the vehicle at the marks in the sand. The prints were small, not even as long as the width of the path that the enviro-bubbles caused as Bekra and he moved over the surface.

Telos sighed. The wake left by the bubbles shifted the dust into smooth swathes which would soon erase the prints left by their predecessor explorers entirely. The prints would be obliterated, no matter how long the marks left by the early explorers had survived the slight occasional dusting on this atmosphere-free moon. Neither Bekra nor he moved, avoiding the ancient prints in an involuntary milliglot of respect.

"Too bad they'll be ruined," Bekra said. She walked around the prints toward one of the relics left behind. She picked up the object and slid over the prints toward the vehicle, adding her load to the case that Telos had gathered. The pair criss-crossed the area of heaviest prints, gathering up the artifacts for the demolition team that would follow. After a span of steady work, they scanned the site for any missed detritus.

"Over there, something is still on the surface." Telos pointed to a thin protrusion from the dust just beyond where the heaviest concentration of tracks had been.

"I'll get it," Bekra said. She walked over to the last bit of trash, erasing another series of prints with her passing bubble. She reached for the object with her tongs set at the closest caliper-width.

"What is it?" Telos asked.

"It's small, only a corner isn't covered." Bekra pulled at the protruding edge. A flat object, encased in a thin covering of translucent material, rested in her pincers. She brought the object toward her face, her glistening eyes focused with both lids retracted.

"What is it?" Telos repeated, striding toward her when she did not answer immediately.

"A depiction of some sort," Bekra said, shaking the thin envelope and extending it to Telos as he reached her. "It's faded, but the dust seems to have protected it from the worst of the radiation."

Telos looked at the picture. Four aliens stared back at him. They had no trunks, only stubby nostrils above open mouths showing teeth.

"Hideous," he said, unable to hide his revulsion.

"No, not hideous at all," Bekra said, taking the picture out of his grip. "Don't you see? There are two large aliens and two small ones, progenitors posed with their hatchlings."

"That's ridiculous. No one knows which hatchlings are theirs."

"These creatures did. Not only did they know who they were, they

216

associated with them. See how the grown ones shield the young from whatever might approach from behind them." Bekra pointed at the faint blur above the taller aliens' heads.

"Adults, shielding hatchlings, protecting them? Surely, that's the job of assigned workers. This must be a hatchery record." Telos grunted.

"No. I worked in the hatchery for many spans. No records like this were made of workers and young shells." Bekra studied the picture, looked up at Telos, and smiled. "I'm sure of it. These are the hatchlings' progenitors."

"Barbaric. Wouldn't they be in danger of clinging to their young? What if a hatchling succumbed to disease, or had an accident?" He made a sweeping motion with his tongs opened wide. "I'm sure you've heard of hatchery workers whose productivity has fallen after a young one in her charge died."

Bekra looked away, toward the planet. She spoke in a soft voice, not looking at Telos. "I was one of them."

"What?" he asked. "But you're here."

"But I *was* a hatchery worker. Three small shells in my care became ill and died. The medical attendant could not save them."

"But you're here now, working and productive."

"Only because I was forced out of hatcheries. They said I was too attached."

Telos grunted. "Not you, Bekra. I've heard you're tough, hard. Didn't you lose two partners and keep working?"

"Yes, but I had quit caring about others' welfare after the hatchlings died." Bekra shook more dust off the picture's cover. "This image proves that other species raise their own young. We could raise some of our new shells in small groups like these, just the progenitors and their offspring?"

"Our offspring number in the hundreds. That's why they're culled at birth so that only the very best survive. Otherwise, there would be far too many unskilled workers." Telos grabbed the picture from Bekra's hold. "You must forget this."

She yanked the picture back almost puncturing his bubble with her extended pincers. "I don't think so," she said. Bekra turned toward base, propelling her bubble at a speed Telos could not match with his heavy masculine shell encumbering him.

"Difficult, small-shelled females," he mumbled. "Who needs them?"

*   *   *

By the time Telos reached the station, copies of the picture Bekra had found were displayed on view screens along the passages of the base. As he walked toward his living quarters, every message screen he passed carried the aliens' image with slogans printed across the truncated faces. "Raise our own." "Hatchlings are our future."

Telos terminated his enviro-bubble before entering his personal area for a welcome interval of rest. He'd had enough discord, thanks to his new partner and her disrespect for tradition. And he still had to pair with her until the new work cycle began.

On their next assignment to a valley surrounded by hills, Telos made a point to hurry to any alien objects first. His plan was to conceal anything that might inflame Bekra's vivid imagination.

He hid two troublesome objects inside the foil remnants clinging to one of the larger structures. A rigid sheet was marked with lines of emblems that might have been a communications code. He pushed the sheet so far down into the foil he was afraid more of the remnants would loosen and reveal it to Bekra.

He had an easier job covering a small, three-dimensional metal image of what appeared to be an alien explorer. Instead of a bubble for protection, the alien statuette wore a close-fitting suit with no carapace protruding. It was easy to cloak the object within the layer of foil.

Telos was relieved by this paucity of identifiable images of the alien creatures. And there seemed to be no more pictures of small shells and possible progenitors left on the moon.

Bekra, for her part, avoided him as he did the bulk of the work at the grids to which they were assigned. She spent her days on her com-unit, talking with someone at the base. From time to time, her trunk would twitch and she would turn away. This made it that much easier to hunt for objects that might offend Command's purification directive.

In spite of his diligence, Telos found nothing more exciting than similar structures amid the tracks and additional cases. Since the containers were very much like the one containing alien excrement, he made no attempt to open any more of them.

Telos checked his visor for messages after returning from duty ten spans later, his tour with Bekra thankfully over.

"Meet me in an hour at the recreation module." The message was anonymous, but Telos believed it must be from Laira. He had not seen her since his proposal had been rebuffed by Dagma's intervention. How he longed to balance shells with her again. He rushed into his cleansing room to scrape off his smelly hide and brush his shell with wax.

When Telos arrived at the module, Laira greeted him with an energetically raised forelimb. As she closed with him, he felt a discreet tickle of her trunk against his. He tickled her back, sending chills along the dorsal nerve beneath his shell.

A podium stood on a raised dais at one end of the room with the alien picture magnified and forming an over-sized backdrop. Other crew entered the large auditorium, some alone, but many in matched pairs, males entwining forelimbs with females. Telos could sense the hormones raised by his own excitement as Laira leaned against his shell.

Telos was not surprised when Bekra mounted the stand in front of the aliens' picture, and behind the podium, but he was startled to see that Varkof stood just beneath her. He had not known that Bekra could muster an officer in support of her ideas. Just then, Laira squeezed his forelimb. He looked down at her radiant, petite shell. Thinking of Bekra's comely trunk, he realized that he was not the only male on this moon to be overcome by thoughts of breeding contracts. Officers, like their all too vulnerable crew, were not immune from amorous alliances with attractive females.

Bekra trumpeted for the crowd to attend her words. "Officers," she began, looking down at Varkof with her trunk twitching, "and crewmen. I've gathered you here to tell you of the momentous discovery A6C Telos and I made and what it means for all of our futures."

Telos felt the hairs on his trunk grow rigid at the mention of his name as part of Bekra's schemes. But then he felt the tip of Laira's claw slip beneath the side of his shell and scratch the delicate skin protected by his carapace. His doubts faded as he basked in her attentions, almost too intimate a touch to be committed in this open space. Perhaps this was a day for change?

Bekra pointed to the alien image magnified behind her. "This representation is proof that other intelligent species raise their own young in small units with their progenitors. The sentients that once visited this satellite left behind wheeled vehicles—" here she flashed an image on the overhead screens of the alien transport before they had filled it with debris "—and the base of an even greater achievement, an intra-system travel pod."

Bekra changed the screen displays to an image of the tall structure with jointed legs.

Telos thought it presumptuous to believe this was part of a travel pod, but Bekra was Hydra-bred topside, her status lending credibility to her opinions. It was true enough that the creatures who had left their tracks could not have survived for long on this barren moon. They must have lived on the planet or even arrived from somewhere farther away. Normally, the advance purification teams would assure that no trace of an alien culture would infect the honored patterns that governed the lives of the shells. Given the purifiers' failure to destroy these proofs of other successful lifeways before Bekra disseminated them throughout the base, perhaps her Hydra-bred guesses were correct. Were her thinker's abilities good for something other than fomenting dissent? Certainly that was what she was doing now.

"Yes, we can raise our own young. And without the hatcheries taking over for us," Bekra cried. Paired workers listening to her speech broke into cheers. Varkof was the first to tootle his trunk in support. Telos heard Laira's sweet fluting as she joined the acclaim. He trumpeted with all his breath as his mate gripped his forelimb.

"Urgent message to High Command. Commander H4H Dagma transmitting." Dagma waited patiently as the tele-crew member repeated his introduction.

"Sunspots." Dagma beat his fist against the side of his shell. What was he to do with the growing tension? The "raise-your-own-young-only" movement was infecting not only the crew, but his officers as well.

Rallies were held daily now in favor of "R-YOYO," as the alien-based thesis was nicknamed. Prospective progenitors spoke in favor of raising some of their own hatchlings. Sedition-control had been lax on the satellite—who had time for disobedience with so much work to be done—but after that incredible picture had been found, everyone talked about the possibility of pairing with a mate and raising their little shells together.

Even his assistant had embraced the new ideas. Laira had sent a private message to him just before locking herself in the quarters of that Atmosphere-bred artist Telos. She would have young soon and he was the progenitor with her. They planned to join the colony and raise their young as a unit, totally apart from the hatchery system. Almost the entire populace at the base had turned against the hatcheries which had maintained their species, controlled growth, and trained new workers for generations beyond memory.

"Send the message again," he ordered as the tech worked the signaler. The Commander tapped his visor and waited as the bright bleep sounded receipt from High Command. No response followed. He returned to his quarters, instructing his staff to summon him as soon as a reply arrived, but under no circumstances was High Command's message to be further relayed without direct orders from him.

Four spans later, a response scrolled across the monitor and staff summoned the commander. Dagma rushed to the main signaler to learn his orders in the face of this crisis:

"Do nothing to deter this experiment, but do not allow any infected shells to return to the home world. All on the satellite will join the new colony on-planet. This includes all Command Personnel. This specifically includes you, Commander Dagma. For your colossal negligence in allowing these alien notions to spread, you are exiled from the home planet for the remainder of your life."

Dagma pounded his chest for a centiglot.

"How do you think it feels to hold a small shell?" he asked his signaler. He left the room before the tech could answer.

Dagma was long past breeding years. But he thought Laira and Telos would forgive him and might even allow him to visit their new hatchlings.

In a few hundred spans of time, the workers purged the moon of relics. They also built a pod transfer station for colony landings.

Bekra and her new mate Varkof stood at a viewing port. The new mag-lift would launch their pod to the planet. When their crew finished construction of temporary habitats, other colonists would join them. Almost all the new settlers had adopted the life-way of the alien picture.

Telos and Laira, soon to eject her eggs, stood beside them, admiring the beautiful blue seas of their new home. Laira's shell sparkled, reflecting her maternal joy. They would join their Commander and others who had volunteered to colonize the planet. Telos had agreed that Dagma, with his superior double-Hydra breeding, would act as grand-progenitor to their hatchlings even though any physical relationship between him and the little shells was unknown.

*   *   *

221

They took their new culture to the colony. As Dagma had learned from High Command's reply to his anxious report, the Service restricted to this one planet the alien practice of paired reproductive units raising their young. Otherwise, the home world did not interfere with the social experiment that the alien image had set in motion, only sending learned elders to study and record the phenomenon.

In time, the new pattern was adopted across the colony with the new reproductive units known as R-YOYO's forming into separate settlements.

The hatchlings toddled over to Grand-Pro Dagma as soon as he cleared the threshold of their habitat. They searched around the edges of his shell for the treats he always brought them, bits of sugar-cane, shiny stones, pine cones, and sometimes soft, gray moss for their pillows. The oldest male trumpeted through his trunk in a shrieking parody of adult applause as he admired a translucent piece of quartz with scarred pockets and inclusions that resembled scampering herbivores.

"Welcome, Dagma," Laira said, carrying a tray of split coconuts brimming with milk. Telos followed her, the small shells leaping to show off their prizes. He laughed deeply in his throat.

"Does anyone want to go swimming with me today?" Dagma asked.

A chorus of "me, me" answered him as the small shells bugled their excitement.

As the governor of the colony, Dagma formed alliances among settlements. He did all that he could to promote the exchange of foodstuffs, building materials, and other resources which the planet offered in abundance.

New hatchlings flourished and prospered in the care of their progenitors. In spite of stern warnings from the elders sent by the home planet, no young were culled. Their progenitors wanted all of their offspring to survive them.

Dagma became old and passed into the next life, long before his species expanded across the entire planet.

Many, many more shells were born and stayed on the planet. The Supreme Command did not interfere with the colony's extraordinary growth. After all, this was the only place in the universe where their species were allowed to raise their own young as their proboscides, and the alien picture, led them.

Time passed, cities grew, and the planet became crowded with the shelled species of sentient beings. When the oldest city needed more nutrition than its own land could produce, disagreements arose and grew into war. When much of the colony's resources were destroyed, even the home world was invaded. The conflict spread from planet to planet, until more shells were killed than could be replaced, even in the traditional hatcheries that the colonists had eschewed.

Telos sat in aged reverence at the memorial service for the last of the hatchlings Laira and he had borne together. He often wished that fate had spared him his artist's viewpoint. Their great dream had come to naught, the last of their young dying here on this distant planet or in conflict on other worlds. Telos was only glad that his beloved had not survived to learn the fate of their young shells. They had always been a long-lived species, but cluster bombs, land mines, and torpedoes had no respect for longevity.

The surface of the blue planet appeared pristine from the air. It was only when the explorers landed that they found the foundations of great cities, crumbling under the overgrowth of millennia.

Ghosts
by A.D. Guzman

Captain Rarck was many things, but of all his varied and colorful attributes, ambition was the most prominent. It was a quality that bled over into his other traits. He was taller, stronger and in his opinion, smarter than his fellow Latians and now he was about to prove it to the entire galaxy.

He typed the last few words of his speech into the data pad, then stood, cleared his throat and began to read in his finest, booming voice:

"Greetings to all on this historic occasion! And an especially warm greeting to my fellow competitors, who braved the same rigors and trials of the Igalacth's two hundred-million-kilometer stretch of the harshest and most desolate reaches of space as I did, and have come through as better individuals for it. I can only encourage you to continue in your efforts and perhaps next year you will be able to emulate my success. (Pause to smile at crowd and wink.) If I don't decide to compete again myself, that is."

Rarck quickly punched in a line of notes for himself. (Pause for laughter.) Then continued.

"And perhaps a moment of silence to honor the memory of those entrants who were not so fortunate. (Pause for silence.)

"The Igalacth's prestigious history spans back thousands upon thousands of years, long before space travel was a gleam in my grandcestor's eye. I know the Latians are a relatively new species to emerge on the galactic scene, and I can only express my humblest pride at being the first to make the planet Lati a name known in households throughout the galaxy.

"And not just because of my victory in the Igalacth, but because I, Rarck, had the foresight to embrace the new technologies showered upon us by our neighbors. Not to create appliances that can sing, dance and do practically everything but what they've been originally designed to do, but to adapt these technologies for serious commercial endeavors. A venture that has been met with some modest success for me and my little *Hammer*."

Rarck stopped again and jotted another note to himself. (Smile modestly and acknowledge knowing chuckles from audience.) As if there were a single doubt as to the superiority of his famous trio of long-distance haulers—*Hammer*, *Scythe* and *Anvil*. The largest of the three, *Hammer*, was the real feather in his cap, his personal pride and joy, his preferred method of giving his engorged ego a masturbatory fondling.

He shook himself to get his thoughts back on track and began to pace as he read. "What more fitting way for me to embark on my mission as captain than with victory in the Igalacth." He conveniently omitted the fact that this was his tenth (and still uncompleted) attempt. "But the real reward is not the substantial cash purse, but the prestige and honor that come from having my name added to that list of elite pilots and achieve an eternal legacy."

The Latian captain was so caught up in his speech that he didn't hear the timid throat-clearing of his first lieutenant until the poor fellow had nearly coughed up a lung. Rarck tucked the data pad under his arm and sank regally into his chair. He let the young bull stew for a few seconds, just for the sadistic pleasure of it.

"Yes, Grom, what is it?" Rarck finally asked and swiveled around in his cushioned captain's chair to face the lieutenant. He gave the soft, black leather an appreciative caress. That had been one of his innovations on the alien technology. Well, that and the swivel. It couldn't really be the captain's chair if it didn't swivel and smell obscenely expensive.

Grom shuffled in place, scuffing the recently polished deck with his hooves. If it weren't for that unnatural timidity, the bull might have been a threat. His horns were nearly as big as Rarck's and he hadn't even finished his final growth spurt. The fur on his broad face was a pleasing shade of brown—a color Rarck would have chosen over his own roan hair if he could—and the young bull's musk could nearly overwhelm Rarck's. Yes, if the bull ever came into a set of balls, he'd be a real threat. Good thing Rarck had made him his second-in-command—the better to break him.

"Well, Lieutenant, what is so urgent that you interrupted one of the best speeches I've ever written? Unless you can tell me we've finally found the Twins' trail, I don't want to see so much as a hair of your mangy hide."

Grom lifted his head and stopped shuffling. He was smiling in a way Rarck didn't like—full of pride. "We've done better than that, sir! We've found them, though it took some doing. The Twins are crafty. They are, in fact, within hailing range. If you wish, I could—"

"Hail them immediately," Rarck snapped, swiveling back to face the screen that occupied the entire wall in front of him. "Filthy smugglers. I want to see the look on their faces when they find the *Hammer* coming down on them. I, Captain Rarck, have discovered their secret route and am about to seal my victory with it."

"Yes, sir!"

Grom trotted over to the communications desk and rapped the sleeping corporal across the horns. "Captain wants the Twins' ship hailed. Now! And put it on screen. Captain wants to enjoy his victory."

"Yes, sir!"

Captain Rarck leaned forward in his chair and planted both hooves on the ground. Finally, he had those slippery siblings. Erisian scum, that's what they were. He would never forgive them for stealing second place right out from under him last year. Despite complaining to the Igalacth marshals that the Erisian's secretive stance on their technology violated the spirit if not the letter of the race's laws, the authorities had ultimately disagreed and dismissed his dispute, allowing the Twins to keep their second place standing.

This year he would make sure that didn't happen again.

"I have their ship on screen now, sir," the communications corporal announced.

Rarck leaned back, forcing himself to relax and focus as the lithe Erisian cruiser appeared on the screen in front of him like a silver fish in a vast black ocean. He'd never seen inside an Erisian ship, so he would need to keep his eyes open for secrets that might be revealed during this brief glimpse.

Much like a small fish wary of the approach of a much larger predator, the Twins' vessel flitted to the left and right, not quite running from the *Hammer*, but not staying still long enough to present an easy target either. Rarck frowned and stroked the hair on his chin thoughtfully. How was it possible for a machine, a hunk of metal and wires, to react with the agility of a living creature? A type of hydraulics unique to the Erisians perhaps?

Rarck was so intent on watching the other ship's movements that he nearly fell out of his chair in surprise when a set of large, lidless black eyes protruding from a heart-shaped face popped on screen. Its skin was a pale blue color and as smooth and hairless as a newborn.

He hid a shudder of disgust by sliding his bulk back into the leather of his chair as if he had merely been stretching his legs. Instead of horns, the

Erisian had a darker blue mane of what looked like thick tentacles floating in the air around its head, almost as if it were long hair drifting in water. It had no snout or even much of a nose above its smirk of a mouth.

There was no way to tell which of the siblings this was, the female Saelf, or the male Zaelf. The image on screen was only shown from the waist up, but a wider view wouldn't have helped. Most Erisians looked too much alike to tell apart and the two being twins made it that much harder.

Instead of giving himself a headache trying, Rarck focused on the background. Saelf (or Zaelf) sat in what he assumed was the captain's chair surrounded by what looked like an adolescent's dream room. He recognized an interactive game unit that cost nearly as much as one of his ship's engines (a fact he'd discovered when he'd had to buy one for his son) and an equally costly collection of gadgets whose sole purpose was diversion.

It was no secret the Twins actively engaged in piracy, which would account for the virtual fortune he could see lying around, but this was ridiculous. Where was the crew? Who ran the ship while they tinkered with video games?

As if in answer to his question, another Erisian walked into view and bent down to whisper something in her (or his) ear—well, where an ear should have been. Whichever twin it was nodded and dismissed the other with a gesture from its webbed hand. Near transparent lids flashed across the bulbous black eyes and its head tilted to the right.

"Ahhh, Captain Rarck, what a pleasant surprise," the Erisian said in a cheerful, lilting voice.

Rarck dipped his horns and returned the pleasantry. "The pleasure is mine, Saelf." He knew for sure it was Saelf now by the higher pitch to her voice. "Forgive me if I think you far too good a captain for this to be a surprise, though."

Saelf rocked for a second, as if engaged in a soundless laugh. "I believe my preparedness stems more from an awareness of your character than my navigational skills, Captain. Your reputation precedes, follows, and very much encumbers you."

Rarck beamed. "Why, thank you!"

Another crewmember, he could tell by the different uniform, marched up to Saelf and whispered a report. As soon as they were gone another, and then a third, did the same.

That made four, plus the two siblings, for a total of six.

"Is this a bad time? Your crew seems rather . . . preoccupied."

Saelf made a dismissive wave with her hand. "No, not at all. We were simply in the middle of an important game of Weightball, and I'm afraid my team isn't doing so well without me to serve. Was there something in particular you needed?"

Captain Rarck hid a start. Weightball required at least ten people per team, putting their numbers at twenty. Probably more since someone had to fly the ship while the others were busy. If he wished to carry out his plan, he would have to be a bit more subtle. A direct attack would be useless against a crew that outnumbered his.

"No, I simply wanted to get a feel for my competition in the area. You know, I don't believe any of the other competitors knows about this little system. One of your smuggling runs, perhaps? And a convenient shortcut for the Igalacth."

He wished he could read Erisian facial expressions, because he knew having their short cut found out by the competition would infuriate them.

Saelf only shrugged and replied, "It is . . . convenient. I take it, then, that I have no need to warn you about the upcoming asteroid field. I'm sure a ship as fine as yours could navigate it on autopilot. Practice makes perfect, no?"

Rarck beamed again, oblivious to the veiled insult. Leave it to a female to give away a valuable tidbit like that by accident. Now that he knew it was coming he'd have no trouble getting through the asteroids.

"Well, good luck to you, Saelf."

"The same to you, Captain."

The screen went blank. Rarck rocked back in his chair and let out a bellowing laugh. Grom clopped hesitantly to his side. "Captain?"

"Plot a course through the asteroids, Grom."

"Asteroids?"

"Yes, they're ahead on our way out of this ugly little system. And, Grom, make sure to leave a thank you gift for the Twins." Captain Rarck was happy enough to sing as his ship purred to life and sailed away from the little cruiser. "It is a secret route, after all. And we want to make sure it stays that way."

Saelf sagged in weary relief as the screen went blank. That had been a close one. Even across the emptiness of space between them, she could feel the malice that Captain Rarck projected like the business end of a spear, or in his case, a great, big, brutish club. Last year, it was rumored that he'd been responsible for the two Atrian ships that went missing, crew and all, from the distant G15 system. And though it couldn't be proved conclusively, there was enough circumstantial evidence to suggest he'd crippled five of the six ships that had dropped out with various mechanical failures.

She could only hope he wouldn't turn the *Hammer* around and decide to call her bluff. The asteroids should keep him busy enough for them to slip by. Hopefully. She and her brother wouldn't stand a chance in combat against a full crew. She bent and unclipped the weighted boots from her feet, then kicked up away from the floor to swim in the synthesized *ghilepf* atmosphere as she massaged the webbing between her toes.

She hated walking as much as she hated being on land, but secrecy was the protection of the peace-loving Erisians and she could not put her entire species in danger to avoid a few moments of discomfort. Pacifists with rare talents tended to end up as slaves, and while she and Zaelf didn't always hold to the nonviolent creed of their fellow Erisians, they did believe that the best conflict was the one avoided. Saelf tugged the crew uniform over her head and shoved it back into a storage compartment with the other three.

Saelf, Sister, what are you up to now?

Identical to his sister in every way except for being a few centimeters taller and broader in the shoulders, Zaelf swam into the room and surveyed the mess Saelf had created to mislead Rarck's scrutiny. Her entire being lit up and she projected an overflow of warmth and love to her brother as she moved to meet him. Zaelf returned the sentiment and pressed the palm of his left hand against hers affectionately. As empaths, their species had moved well beyond the limits of facial and physical expressions, though few, even among empaths, were as close as the twins.

How was your Cycle, Brother? You look rested.

You've nearly spent yourself. We do not have the luxury of wasting precious energy until this race is won. Zaelf projected a stern frown. *The honor of our home planet is riding on our victory this year. There has never been an Erisian champion throughout the Igalacth's history, and there has never been as fine a pilot as you or I in all the known universe. Our names deserve to be added to the winner's list.*

And the money certainly wouldn't sully our honor either, Saelf added with a smirk.

Zaelf ignored her remark, but let the matter drop. *What* have *you been doing?*

Nothing I couldn't handle, Saelf assured him and projected the memory of the encounter with Rarck into Zaelf's mind.

A flash of snarling fury bled into Saelf's thoughts until her brother reined in his emotions. *Rarck the Latian! How did that dullard find us? And why did he not attack? He would kill his own mother in her sleep if it would win him the Igalacth. This year will be his tenth attempt.*

And tenth failure, Saelf added. *We are fortunate he is such a stupid bull and your sister is so clever.*

Could he not tell it was you changing clothes the entire time?

Saelf shrugged. *To Latians all Erisians look alike, but we were indeed fortunate to have encountered such a foolish member of their species.*

And you didn't send him into the asteroids? Zaelf's thoughts were colored with wry humor—a vaguely red and purple emotion.

Dearest Brother, I would never violate the Igalacth's rules and directly sabotage a rival. I specifically warned him of their danger. It is not my fault if he does not heed my words.

Zaelf's smile flooded her mind. *You have done well, Sister. Now you must get to your cabin for Cycle. We have a tough run ahead of us if we wish to slip past that brute and solidify our lead. He is foolish and proud, but not nearly so stupid as he seems.*

Saelf readily agreed. It had taken a good deal of her energy to sustain the ship's defensive maneuvers and engage Rarck directly. The hologram of herself in the chair wasn't difficult, but maintaining the illusion required precision, which in turn required more of her already depleted reserves. In plain terms, she was exhausted to the point of collapse and couldn't wait for a chance to renew herself in Cycle.

She relinquished control of the ship to Zaelf and let the artificial *ghilepf's* circulating current carry her to the galley, savoring the coolness that flowed over the fringes of her gills as she took slow, deep, relaxing breaths.

After a hearty meal that left her almost uncomfortably full, Saelf swam into her cabin—more of a tiny cave than a room—but it held all her navigational charts, books, clothes and what few possessions she'd brought with her when she and Zaelf had left Eris to seek their fortune in the universe. It was as cluttered as the rest of the ship, but it was home. Saelf had scarcely settled onto her bunk before she fell into the deep renewing sleep of her Cycle.

* * *

Alarms were never meant to be a pleasing sound, and for good reason. A monotonously soothing chime or even a rollicking melody simply isn't capable of rousing one from a deep sleep strengthened by enjoyable dreams the way a harsh, grating whine can.

Saelf stirred reluctantly, snatching at the remaining motes of her dream even as the ship's intrusion pounded them into irretrievable dust that slid from her grasp like fine grains of sand. Without checking the time, she knew she had only been into her Cycle for two of the required eighteen hours—not nearly enough to be renewed. What little energy she'd recouped was already being siphoned by the ship's emergency response drive, a failsafe that should only be utilized as a last resort during a catastrophic emergency. Like getting snared in the gravitational field of a sun or caught in the pull of a black hole.

And by her last calculations, they were more than a safe distance from the sun of the A14 system—somewhere in the vicinity of the asteroid belt that formed a barrier between the first three or four planets and the rest. And even this desolate section of the galaxy had been studied sufficiently to know that, though uninhabited, there were no black holes near enough to cause their ship trouble.

Her first panicked thought was that Rarck had changed his mind and decided to attack them outright, but even if he had, Zaelf would have fled and there was no ship in the galaxy that could match theirs at a sprint. She sat up and glanced at the status panel on the wall just inside the door of her cabin. Aside from the alarm, all seemed well enough. The artificial atmosphere maintained an ideal balance of the *lefp* and *ghi* needed for them to breathe, and the pressure readings were stable, so the hull couldn't have been breached.

But the ship *was* drawing energy from her as an emergency reserve. She tempered fear with cautious rationalization. It must have been a malfunction in one of the ship's sensors—an easy theory to test. Saelf opened herself to the ship just enough to scan the systems. Even that simple task was wearying, though, in her weakened state. Not to mention unpleasant. Her consciousness flowed into the ship as easily as her hand into a glove, but it was a glove she had been wearing for twenty hours straight already and the mental equivalent of blisters made even the slightest effort painful.

She grimaced. Zaelf should be the one doing this, not her. It was her brother's turn at the helm, as he well knew. Endurance was Zaelf's strength. Her own talents lay with the finer, detailed work, which was why she acted as navigator.

Saelf's fear mounted into terror as her inspection continued. Engines had failed, and the holding tank, a massive battery that collected the unused residual energy and stored it for hyperspace jumps and emergencies, had gone offline completely. The failsafe that had awakened her from Cycle was now all that kept the deadly emptiness of space at bay. Where was Zaelf?

As if in answer to her unprojected question, her brother's thoughts darted into her mind like minnows, erratic and frantic, and his pain and fear tore into her in their wake.

Leffy! Sister . . . Sister, are you well?

He hadn't called her Leffy since they were children on Eris who had yet to lose their tails! Saelf reared back, nearly striking her head on the metal paneling behind her, and had to fight to keep from casting him out of her head in a blind panic. The ship lurched and shuddered violently, buffeting her inside the tiny cabin. Saelf, still connected to the systems, convulsed along with the ship's death throes, unable even to shield her body from the bone-jarring impacts with the walls.

Zaelf, Brother, I'm here, she projected back at him, partly as a vent for her own terror and partly in hopes of allaying his. It worked. His fear subsided, or at least he managed not to project it at her, and she regained enough rational thought to extricate herself from the ship's network. It was like being plunged from hot, dry air into cool *ghilepf*, the relief instant.

There was no time to enjoy it, though. The careening of the ship had grown worse. It was all Saelf could do to keep a grip on her bunk. Her charts, notes and books churned around her like waves driven before a hurricane. Something struck her side, then a thunderous boom rippled through the ship as if it had just slammed into a solid object. Instead of glancing off and spiraling on into space, the ship continued to shudder and emit a low, growling sound. The lights went out as the ship ground to a slow halt.

The silence that followed was eerie, the calm before a storm. Saelf held her breath and stared into the utter darkness as she waited for the next impact, or for the entire ship to implode on itself. A cloud of blood, faintly blue and luminescent in the utter darkness, drifted through the *ghilepf* liquid in an alarming amount. She touched her hand to her side and stirred up a greater cloud of glowing gore. Gingerly, her fingers explored the feathery fringe of her gills. A nasty cut ran diagonally across the delicate flesh, making it painful to breathe, but the injury was relatively minor—gill injuries always bled copiously.

233

Nothing had happened for seconds, and now minutes of nothing crawled past on their way to becoming hours. She had to assume it was over, find Zaelf and start getting the ship's network back online. Saelf felt her way along the wall of her cabin to the smooth, rectangular glass of the status panel. She pressed her palm against the screen until even the webbing between her fingers lay flush with its surface. It was easier to access the ship via direct interface.

Careful not to become too entangled with the ship's network, Saelf activated the panel and accessed the environmental systems. Zaelf, somewhere on the bridge according to the environmental scan, didn't have much left in his reserves and Saelf hadn't had the full eighteen hours to recoup her own, so she didn't risk activating more than the emergency lights and life-support until they had both had a chance for a full Cycle.

It wasn't much, but at least she could see now. The manual operation lever for her door had been hidden away in an unobtrusive cabinet beneath the status panel. She accessed it and pulled. The locks holding the door shut released with an audible clank. Saelf shouldered the heavy door open just enough for her slender form to slip through and shot like a bullet into the dimly lit corridor. Ignoring the superficial damage, she swam as fast as she could to the bridge.

Zaelf floated just below the ceiling in a growing cloud of luminous gore. He stirred faintly as if he sensed her presence, but said nothing. Saelf dragged him down to the floor and made him as comfortable as she could, using one of the uniforms that had been tossed free from storage during the crash as a pillow. She smoothed the tentacles on his head and discovered a wide gash above his eyes that continued to stain the *ghilepf* blue. The cut on his leg was more serious. Bone protruded from the skin of his shin at a sickening angle. She squeezed her brother's hand and projected all the soothing happiness and peace she could muster to counteract the pain.

I'll be right back, Brother. I need to get the medical supplies.

Despite the burning in her injured gills, Saelf swam as fast as she could to the infirmary and rummaged supplies from the mess. The cabinets had been knocked over and many vials of medicine had broken and been lost, but the bandages were still good and she finally found a strong painkiller. She cursed Rarck the whole way back to the bridge, certain he had been the cause of this. *Just like those ships last year.*

Zaelf hadn't moved and his blue skin had grown gray from blood loss. Saelf's fingers trembled so much it took twice as long to get the bandages unwrapped and on his cuts. When she'd staunched most of the bleeding, it was time to set the bone and splint his leg. Even though he was unconscious, Saelf restrained his leg before pushing the bone back into place.

There were some disadvantages to sharing so much with someone else. Raw pain woke Zaelf and his screams ripped through Saelf like knives. She clutched her own leg and howled with sympathetic agony. It took five minutes before either sibling could form a coherent thought, and even then they sat in silence until Saelf forced the pain medicine down him.

Finally, when the drugs seemed to be taking the edge off his pain, Saelf asked, *What happened?*

There was no need for him to project a name into her thoughts; the venomous hatred that seethed out of him was enough to confirm her suspicions. *How?*

Zaelf hissed and eased himself into a seated position. Saelf helped him adjust his leg and waited for an answer.

A trap! That stupid bull laid a leech trap for us about a hundred fifty kilometers outside the asteroid field. By the time I realized it, the Hammer *came out of hiding and blindsided us with a blast from a laser cannon. The shields held, and I fled through the asteroids to escape from him, but by then his leech had worked its way into the engines, draining power more quickly than I could supply it. We lost the reserve tank. I don't know if it was the blast or if he simply bled it. I tried to keep the ship from tapping into you for as long as I could, but when I passed out. . .*

Saelf blinked. *He didn't just try to take us out of the race. He tried to kill us. That bastard tried to murder us!*

Zaelf's hand against her face surprised Saelf. He caressed her cheek and said, *I'm so sorry, Sister. I should have been more alert. Rarck's ambition and ruthlessness are legendary. I should have expected as much after your encounter.*

His hand moved down to her gills. *You're bleeding. Were you injured badly?*

Saelf put her hand over his. *Nothing I can't handle, Brother. It's times like these, though, when I think it would be nice to have an external energy source.*

Zaelf's chuckle tickled inside her head. *You run an electrical current through* ghilepf *and you'd kill us. It would be easier to breed ourselves to live on land.*

Your levity cheers me, Brother. Cycle and renew. I'm going to see about getting our reserve tank back online before the ship drains us completely.

Saelf busied herself in the back until the drugs had rendered her brother unconscious. As soon as he was out, she shimmied into a spacesuit and ventured outside to inspect the damage. It was cramped, awkward and the cycled *ghilepf* had a stale, musty smell to it, but Saelf never tired of space walks. There was an awe-inspiring freedom to the idea of having nothing but a sealed and pressurized suit between her and the crushing entirety of the universe. And for an empath with as strong a gift for telepathy as hers, these were the only times when she felt the utter peace and tranquility of solitude.

It was a sobering experience also. To look out at the myriads of stars, galaxies and nebulas—the infinite landscape of space—and know that only a mind-bendingly miniscule portion of it supported life at all. Saelf took a deep, pain-laced breath and tore her gaze away from the stars.

Having never ventured past the asteroid belt when using this little-known place for smuggling, it took a minute for her to take in all that she was seeing. Their ship had crashed on a moon of some sort. The landscape was bone dry and her scans indicated there wasn't an atmosphere to support even a land-dwelling creature. She took a cautious step onto the dusty soil and noted the limited gravity that slowed and exaggerated each movement. The dust was a curious gray color that seemed to reflect light more than any soil she'd encountered before. Then again, she didn't spend much time on too many moons—at least not on their surfaces anyway. Near Lati there was a moon near Lati with a bar she and Zaelf liked to frequent, but it was all safely sealed inside an artificial environment dome.

Just above the horizon was the moon's blue-green planet, a welcome sight against the vast emptiness. Saelf stared at it a moment. It resembled her own home planet Eris except for the masses of green and brown, which she assumed were land. Eris was a *ghilepf* world, with less than one-tenth of its surface being dry land. It could have been the stress from the crash playing tricks with her mind, but the planet almost looked hospitable to life. Perhaps, once they finished the Igalacth and added their names to the history books, she and Zaelf should come back and run some scans.

Enough gawking at the scenery, she reminded herself and began the awkward hike to the far side of her ship. The shields seemed to have done their job; there was relatively little external damage from the attack or the crash. Nothing that couldn't be repaired anyway. It must have been the leech, then, that sent them down. That was good news, though. It meant that once they removed the leech, repaired the ship and restored their energy, they would probably be able to take off. If she could only get the reserve tank online, it would be all that much quicker.

Unfortunately, once she reached the far side of the ship and stripped the leech, Saelf discovered the reserve tank wasn't offline, it was missing. She cursed Rarck again and checked her energy levels. The suit didn't drain her much, but it, the ship's life-support and the exertion combined had taken their toll. She had maybe an hour or two left before she would need to Cycle.

She glanced out across the lunar surface. The crash site extended for about a kilometer. If the tank had landed intact, somewhere along that trail, she could bring it back and repair the ship. If she ran, she could search the entire kilometer in less than an hour. Saelf stifled a whine. She hated running more than she hated walking, but they really needed that tank.

After a half-hour of searching, Saelf noticed the prints. At first she mistook them for her own boot prints, but they didn't always go in the direction she had been traveling, and soon she noticed them in places she hadn't stepped yet. A chill ran up her spine that had nothing to do with exhaustion. She glanced over her shoulder at the blue planet.

Could it be inhabited? Not by rudimentary life forms, but by an intelligent, space-going race? *Again, not the time to be curious*, Saelf reminded herself, and returned to her search. Five minutes later she noticed something like a crumpled piece of metal a short distance away. It didn't look like anything that might have fallen from her ship, so she assumed it had been something on the surface that had been disturbed in the crash. Curious and desperate now, she made her way over, on the off chance the tank might be somewhere near it.

Upon closer examination she saw it was an ancient spacecraft, though it seemed more like a child's toy when compared to her sleek ship. There was no way something like that could have traveled from anything farther away than the blue planet, and even that was doubtful. Weary, Saelf looked once more at the ancient thing before turning back toward the ship.

If whatever lived there had made it this far, what had stopped them from further explorations? Being this far out from the civilized places of the universe, they'd probably gotten discouraged and assumed they were alone. How sad to spend lifetimes believing nothing else was out there.

Suddenly a fierce surge of emotion jolted through her so hard she dropped to her knees. Red and white stripes filled her vision along with a sense of triumph and joy so profound she could taste it. Strange words in a tongue she had never heard poured through her mind like a recording cycled through an intercom.

Saelf crawled forward, trying to free her mind from the unexpected assault. As abruptly as it came, the impression vanished, leaving her alone with her thoughts. Trembling, Saelf regained her feet on the third try. Behind her were another set of prints, half-ruined by her own, but still visible in the fine dust. She extended a hand toward the prints and jerked it back when the emotions threatened to return.

It took a good deal of mental and emotional energy to leave a ghost, or imprint, an emotional hotspot so to speak, on a place. Something had definitely been here, something intelligent and unlike anything she'd ever encountered before for it to leave a ghost as strong and enduring as this.

Zaelf was awake when Saelf returned, ripped from Cycle by a crushing tide of emotions fed into him through his bond with his sister. The brief rest and painkillers had benefited him, though. Some of the color had returned to his skin, and though the bandage had turned blue, the bleeding had clearly slowed. As his sister swam through the door, he projected a wave of disapproval at her unassisted space walk. She should have waited for him to wake.

She let him sense her contrition by way of apology and projected the memory of her excursion to him as she changed the used bandage for a fresh one.

What was that? he demanded, knowing Saelf would know which 'that' he meant.

A ghost. Saelf shuddered. *A really strong ghost.*

Zaelf started. *Impossible. This system is uninhabited.*

The reserve tank is missing. I couldn't find it in the debris field, so it must have fallen off before we crashed. Saelf had quickly changed the subject, but she couldn't mask how his words had stung her.

And the ship?

Some damage, but not irreparable, Saelf reported. *If we take turns, even on a half Cycle we should be able to make the repairs and finish the race.* Giving up was not an acceptable option for them. Obstacles like this were simply normal in the Igalacth. *But we should activate the distress beacon just in case. If we don't report at the next checkpoint, they're bound to send a search team.*

Zaelf tried to rein in his frustration so that it wouldn't overwhelm Saelf. *Repairs could take weeks that way. And no one but Rarck knows our position. Do you think he'd report us down after what he did? We need our holding tank, Sister.*

Their situation was grave. Saelf stared at him, her skin pale and her tentacles limp from the stress; and though she bravely tried to hide it, he caught her holding her side, nursing the wound to her gills. His own leg throbbed as if it would burst open at any moment and would need proper medical treatment sooner rather than later if he wanted it to heal properly. No, they couldn't wait around for help to find them. They needed that tank. Perhaps it had been caught in the gravitational pull of the planet Saelf had shown him.

Sister, give the ship over to me, he demanded suddenly. Saelf blinked and jerked her hand away from her gills, feigning vigor.

No! Your reserves are too low and you're injured. I can hold out a while longer yet. Cycle and renew. I will call you when I cannot continue.

Zaelf shook his head and projected an image of what he wanted her to do into her thoughts. Her already pallid skin took on a sicklier hue.

I can't go to the planet. Please, Brother, let's wait for help.

It takes less energy to operate the shuttle than the ship. I would go myself if it weren't for my leg. He could almost taste the fear that radiated from Saelf, something out of character for his often over-confident sister. He projected cool, soothing emotions at her. *I'm right here with you, Saelf. You won't be alone, not for a second.*

That is not my fear, Brother. I'm afraid I might not *be alone.*

He almost laughed. *The planet is uninhabited. We are obviously not the first to have come—someone left a ghost to scare you, Sister—but there is nothing to fear from an empty planet.*

Okay, okay . . . I'll go, she agreed, but a gray reluctance enshrouded her like a cloud.

Zaelf repeated his reassurance to her as she slid her slender form back into a pressurized suit, and again as she boarded the shuttle, and then throughout the shuttle's journey through the surprisingly thick atmosphere. That and the distance made it a bit more difficult to communicate with her, but he was determined to make good on his promise. She would not be alone down there.

Saelf's nervous death grip on his consciousness eased as she reached the planet's surface and began the scans. At first she projected the data facts back at him, pressure and temperature readings and the molecular make-up of the atmosphere.

Then suddenly a wild torrent of images rushed over him, so quickly he could barely process them all. Saelf's excited thoughts tumbled over one another in her rush to share her experience.

Beautiful. A paradise. It's as if every environment of every planet has been transplanted in some form to this one, where they don't just exist, but flourish.

Magnificent green forests scaled impossibly tall peaks, which gave way to rolling plains as flat as anything on Lati. Sparkling rivers of a substance like *ghilepf* danced across the land to join great seas that so resembled the *ghilepf* oceans of Eris. It was pristine, untouched and unspoiled by any hand or tool.

Moments later he received an image of their holding tank lying at the bottom of a blast crater, battered and charred from its trip to the surface, but otherwise unscathed. Saelf's laughter poured into him, pure unadulterated joy.

It's a paradise, Zaelf. If only you were here with me! I'm going out to retrieve the tank, and once we're renewed and we repair the ship, we'll explore this planet together.

Zaelf shared in her laughter. *We need to get you and the tank back to the ship first. Don't forget that your reserves are almost empty.*

Another giggle reached him through their bond, then she opened the hatch, stepped onto the surface and slid down into the crater. She hefted the tank over one shoulder and scrambled back up the slope, projecting a jaunty working tune into Zaelf's head as she went. Saelf slid the tank into the shuttle, hopped in after and turned to shut the door.

That's when the screaming began—a cry of pure terror so raw and painful it threatened to freeze the blood in Zaelf's veins. On instinct he reached out to Saelf, prepared to suffuse her with his comfort and reassurance. Instead he came upon silence. A raw, gaping emptiness where Saelf's consciousness touched his own. It was as if some clawed fiend had grasped both his and Saelf's souls and torn them apart.

Faint with terror and confusion, Zaelf couldn't remember acting, but somehow he got the shuttle back and docked with their ship. He dragged himself to the shuttle bay and forced the doors open as soon as the joint had sealed.

Saelf sat near the back, her knees tucked under her chin, and rocked back and forth. Her usually bright, clever eyes were nothing but empty black orbs that didn't seem to see anything. The reserve tank lay in the corner, but Zaelf never saw it. He dragged himself over to his sister and cupped her face with his hands.

Saelf? What happened? Zaelf projected fearfully. This maddened creature couldn't be his sister, could it?

Saelf made no response, no attempt to alleviate his worry or share her own with him.

"Saelf? Sister? Answer me, please. What happened?" His physical voice sounded strange, and he realized that he and Saelf had never spoken to one another in this way before.

That got her attention. Her face swung in his general direction, but her gaze slid past him like water over stone. She rocked wildly and babbled, "So many. There are so many. So strong. So determined. Not lost. Not forgot."

Alone for the first time, and frightened beyond measure, Zaelf pulled Saelf to his chest, held her tight and waited—for death, for help, for any kind of an end to this nightmare.

Captain Rarck looked good. His fur had been brushed until it shone, his horns and hooves polished until he could see himself in them, and he'd dressed in his best uniform. His stride deepened to a swagger as he recalled how the Latian cows—and a few females from other species—had all swung their heads to look at him as he ascended the podium to accept his prize.

The money was a substantial boost to his already healthy bank accounts, but what he most enjoyed was seeing his name etched into the great record stone alongside names of the universe's most elite pilots. He met his lieutenant Grom at the entrance to the *Hammer* and handed him the token trophy that had been presented to him during the ceremony.

Grom whistled. "That's a beauty, Captain. The bulls will be glad to see that displayed in the *Hammer's* helm. Igalacth champions. It hardly seems possible that after ten tries we finally won it."

Rarck snarled at his underling, reluctant to be reminded that it'd taken so much effort on his part to receive what should have been his ten times over by now. "Just get in the ship, Grom, and get us out of here. There are a couple loose ends we need to make sure stay that way."

"There's no way the Twins are still alive, sir. It's been a month, and we saw their ship go down."

"Shut up, fool!" Rarck snapped and shoved the younger bull physically into the ship, then shut the door. "Do you want everyone to know how we got that trophy? Now do as I said. Take us back to that little system. I want to make sure the Twins stay missing, just like the Atrians."

Grom ran as fast as his hooves would carry him for the bridge, leaving Rarck alone in the hold.

A cold, low voice slithered out of the darkness behind him. "Well, well, it's good to see you've been so concerned for our wellbeing, Captain."

Rarck whirled so fast his hooves nearly slipped on the slick floor. Black bulbous eyes and a thin blue face emerged from the shadows. The dark blue tentacles hung limp around the familiar face, nearly concealing a thick scar across the forehead. Taller and more muscular in person than she'd appeared on screen, the Erisian limped into the light on an injured leg that had been crudely splinted.

"Saelf!" he exclaimed with a surprised hiss.

"Guess again, Rarck."

"Zaelf," he amended.

Another figure emerged from the shadows, drawn by the hand like a small child. Saelf, clearly smaller than her brother now that Rarck could see them side by side, rocked back and forth on her heels, muttering an eerily nonsensical mantra. As he'd spoken her brother's name, she looked at him, but those black orbs didn't seem to see him.

Rarck shuddered and focused on Zaelf. The Erisian glared back at him with an almost tangible hatred.

"Captain Rarck, you violated the sacred rules of the Igalacth and made a mockery of its honor and tradition. You sabotaged our ship, causing us to crash in an uninhabited star system and left us to die from our injuries and exposure. And now you plot to desecrate what you assumed was our final resting place and keep our fate secret from our friends and family."

Rarck sneered. "I see you are tougher to be rid of than a cold. How kind of you, however, to save me the trouble of seeking you out. And even if you do escape me this night, it will be your word against mine, Erisian. You can prove nothing."

Saelf laughed loudly, nearly doubling over from the force of it, and shouted, "Nine! Eleven!" The sheer volume was enough to make both Zaelf and Rarck jump, and the crazed randomness of it made Rarck shiver.

He watched Zaelf calm his sister and asked, "What in the world is wrong with her!"

Saelf's laughter finally faded to giggles, then hiccups. Her large eyes settled on Rarck and didn't move. He shifted to the left, and they followed. "Tell her to stop staring at me. Stop it!"

"That planet, the one near the moon where you crashed us—" Zaelf said, ignoring Rarck's concerns.

Without warning, an image of a great, blue-green sphere hovering above a barren, silvery landscape filled Rarck's vision. He waved his hands in front of his face, then squeezed his eyes shut. "What kind of hologram is this? How are you doing that?"

Oh, it is no hologram, Rarck. The Latian pressed his hands over his ears, but Zaelf's voice rang clear inside his head. *Have you ever encountered a ghost, Captain? A mental or emotional imprint left by an intelligent being on a place or object? Some are faint. Barely rumors of whispers, and others are more like hot spots, a spark of energy that will give you a little shock if you brush up against it.*

Rarck opened his eyes when Zaelf's voice fell silent. Saelf was standing in front of him now, her face centimeters from his. Zaelf stood at her side, his left hand clasped in her right. They stretched to touch his temples with their free hands. He shrank back, but there was a wall behind him.

"That's the big Erisian secret," he exclaimed as the realization dawned on him. "You're a telepathic species. Well, you better stay the hell out of my mind, or I'll lead an invasion of your sorry little planet! Kill every last one of you!"

"That planet, the one near the moon where you crashed us," Zaelf said aloud, ignoring Rarck's threats, "was home to an ancient civilization. One nearly as advanced as our own, that has been gone for so long that the planet itself has erased and forgotten their presence. But they did leave something behind, Rarck. Ghosts. Strong ghosts. An entire race of ghosts who were so determined not to be lost and forgotten that they invaded the first being to stumble across them who was receptive enough to hear them—Saelf."

That explained the madness at least. Rarck tried to lift his head out of their reach, a little afraid that insanity might be contagious. "How could I have known what was on that planet? Besides, Saelf will probably recover in a year or two. It's just a case of shock. Better her than you, right?"

Saelf giggled quietly, her fingertips close enough to brush the fur of his face. Zaelf shook his head. "Not even a few centuries would cure her, Latian. There's an entire civilization trying to preserve its memory in her head."

Zaelf and Saelf touched their fingers to Rarck's head in unison, completing the circuit between the three of them. Their skin was hot and oddly moist, dampening the fur of his face.

243

"And now my sister and I would like to introduce you."
That was when the screaming began.

The twins stood over Rarck's prone form. The giant Latian lay on his side, curled into a fetal ball. His eyes were glazed and unseeing as he rocked back and forth, muttering under his breath.

Zaelf squeezed Saelf's hand. She squeezed back and glanced at him. The spark of sanity had returned to her eyes. *Are you certain you are okay with leaving him like this, Sister? I believe he deserves far worse, but my conscience is not so tender as yours.*

Saelf's gaze swept over Rarck and shudders of revulsion passed through her body and into Zaelf through their bond as she echoed the Latian's earlier sentiments, *Better him than me, right?*

Zaelf rejoiced in sharing his laughter with his sister once more. The ache from the past month's separation was still there, but it had begun to fade. *I believe I have more sympathy for the ghosts. I imagine he is not a pleasant host.*

He started toward the hatch at a swift limp. *We should leave before we are discovered. I'm sure they will eventually notice his absence. What are you doing now?*

Saelf was bent over Rarck's body. When she straightened, she held a wad of money and fanned it for him to see. *We have repairs to finish and his ship no longer has a captain's salary to pay. Waste not, want not.*

I've never heard that saying before.

They could write books with all the things you haven't heard, Brother. She glanced meaningfully at Rarck before taking her brother by the arm and helping him out of the ship. *Perhaps someday I will tell you about them.*

. . .that I carried you
by Erin Cashier

"But I already have a research mission—"

Jorg shook his head so hard I could almost hear his jowls flap through the viewscreen—"

"Dump it Siddi. Put a beacon on it and jettison it out the back."

"You use military codes to shut my ship down, yank me out of the Intestines, and tell me to turf my research?" I'd spent too long excavating and finding nothing to trust the few things I had found to the vagaries of the galactic tide and Jorg's promise of a retrieval ship. "What's more important than Owner artifacts? Maybe even bones?"

"Let me send you the data. Please." Jorg leaned closer, putting both his hands on either side of the screen we distantly shared. I could see his clean clipped nails through it, and I couldn't remember the last time I'd had or needed a nail trimmer—scrabbling through digs claimed most of mine.

I crossed my arms. "Why don't you just hack my AI again?"

"We want you on board, Siddi. I want you on board." Jorg's hips twitched nervously as he balanced himself, his lab coat slipping out of place without a proper tail to fold around. He'd cut his tail off when he'd joined Scicom, all the labbies did—none of them wanted to show any external emotion, their joys were inward, or so they claimed. I pointed my tail between the struts of my captain's chair in quiet defiance.

Jorg leaned in so close that his jowls practically touched the screen. "It's the pawprints of the Owners, Siddi. Not bones. But their original pawprints. For once we can put the question to rest—who were they more like? Felina, or Rex? Centuries of animosity, just a few coordinates away! Please Siddi—"

"Pawprints?" I cut him off. The things I'd found in my searches—replicants of replicates of replicas—were just the top part of the inverted pyramid that led down to the Owners at the small sharp base. An actual Owner artifact? Created by an actual owner, not one of their genemodded progeny?

Heavy brows lifted, wrinkling the Scicom director's forehead. "Pawprints. Actual pawprints."

I subtly nodded, and my ship's AI, Fidelis, gulped Jorg's waiting data down. "Why me?"

"The place is 13,000 Bounds away from us, but you're already in the old systems. And you're science, not military—the truce says they can't touch you, not where matters of the Owners are concerned—"

"Wait—I won't be alone?"

Jorg licked a mottled black tongue across his bottom lip. "It's Felia intel. They've sent a military scout ship. If you're going to make it there in time, you have to turn around and leave now."

"No way Jorg. This is a science ship, not a freighter and—"

Jorg cut me off. "I know, I fund you, remember? If the worst comes to pass, just hang back and take pictures. They have to allow that, at least." He bared his teeth in hope. "You're in, right?"

Pawprints. Actual pawprints. My fears played tug-of-war with my archaeological instincts. Skirmishes had just broken out along the Felia/Rex border on a shared moon. But I'd spent decades of searching for Owner artifacts, fruitlessly. Even the things in my hold right now I couldn't guarantee were original. I knew they were close, but—I looked back up to the screen. "I'm in."

Jorg sighed with relief and dropped his hands to the floor. Lab coat and dignity forgotten, his tail end danced with delight. "What are you waiting for? Go—go!"

I turned the comlink off and looked up to my ship. "Put a beacon on the cargo in hold three, then jettison it out."

"Sir?"

"Then turn us around and get us back into the Intestine and follow the coordinates you just received."

"Yes sir."

The ship spun around and I watched the product of three years labor float off behind me on a viewscreen.

"Data sniffed sir. Anus opening in three, two, one—"

"Good boy." I buckled myself into my seat again. The pink entrance to the Intestines flared open and my ship launched itself inside.

Our truce with the Felina was more like a stalemate. Once upon a time, we'd raced them through the Owner-made Intestines around the galaxy on a quest to find as many water-soaked worlds to colonize as we could. But not all the other alien worlds were unoccupied—and both of our races had had our paws slapped on our journeys, sometimes with nitronium bombs. Litter-ships were lost. Whole colonies. And then entire worlds. Our ability to survive our enmity with each other, and with the strange things that assaulted us, was based on our ability to utilize the Intestine technology to block foreign access to the Anuses we possessed. It was then that the tenets of the truce were written, that we should help each other discover new Owner technology and share it equally, based on the age old premise that the enemy you knew was better than the one you didn't.

After the news of recent violence between our people, and our longstanding feuds, I wasn't so sure I agreed.

"Beginning deceleration," Fidelis announced, distracting me from my thoughts. "Re-entry in a quarter Bound."

I went to my gear closet and zipped up the suit I'd wear on-planet below. Regardless of its missing atmosphere, I'd want my full synesthetic array, taste, smell, everything, available to me. I grabbed my helmet and went back to my seat, preparing for another bumpy ride.

According to Fidelis' database, the location Jorg sent me to was a dead end in the Intestines. No one knew what was on the other side.

"Re-entry in three, two, one."

I braced as my ship matched the space-time outside and the Anus ahead of us dilated. Outside, chunks of rock blocked our path, and my ship wheeled down and to the right, before I could even tell it to evade. Plates of jagged metal glittered under Fidelis' exterior lights.

"Those asteroids—natural? Or not?"

"They're from local materials. I cannot be sure as to their original placement."

It would be an overt trick, even for the Felina. And how would they intend to get back to the Anus themselves? My ship continued to make small adjustments through the detritus, till a grey moon was visible below.

"There's a cloud of frothane up ahead, Captain. Definitely artificial."

"A trap?"

"Its dispersal ratio makes that seem unlikely. Also, Captain, the Felina scoutship is on the horizon."

My viewscreens showed me the world below. Monotonous grey rolled by, pockmarked with crater sites. A shattered crystalline dome had held atmosphere, once upon a time, but now it was empty, with the exception of one Felina lifesign. The planet this moon orbited was

247

quickly scanned, and found dead as dead can be. Fidelis received an incoming ping.

"Hi! I can't believe you beat me here!" I said, reaching behind my head to tie back my ears. "I knew you all were fast, but—"

The Felina captain's face occupied my viewscreen, whiskers and ears cramped inside her helmet. "You have some long tail coming here—"

"I'm Siddi. I was on a mission on Betal-3, and I got these coordinates off of an old glyph. I figured since I was in the area, I'd check them out on my way home!" True, true, and untrue. "You're looking for the pawprints, right? The glyph said they'd be here! I shared the data I found per the tenants of the truce, section 8-delta-B, but I didn't think I'd find anyone here so quickly!" I made myself sound as chipper as possible. They should have declared this find before sending a scout. And who was to say if this Felina operative knew where her original data had come from? It was a good enough excuse for being here and she technically couldn't tell me to go.

The Felina captain's slitted pupils narrowed at me, but she remained silent. "I'll jump down, okay? See you soon!" I blinked, and the connection closed. "All right Fidelis, you're on your own."

"Good luck, sir,"

"Thank you." I patted my armrest companionably and made for the rear airlock.

The tetherline gave me the forward momentum I needed to leave the ship. It zinged me down on its pulley towards the moon's surface. I disconnected at the end and dropped onto all fours gently, while my ship retrieved its line. An arrow on my helmet's viewscreen guided me in.

I was inside the perimeter of the broken crystal shell. Buildings loomed up on either side of what had once been a pavilion. Windows as dark as the sky above stared down like empty eyes. I'd been in ghost colonies before, but this one gave me chills.

"Captain, the Felina's scoutship has its armaments trained on you."

"Of course," I said, but vowed to continue on with my cheerful persona. The Felina tended to be a serious lot, and anything I could do to irritate them—

The Felina soldier waited for me, standing outside a metal structure, shiny as the day it was made. Extruded? Excreted? I scanned the structure for clues while bouncing in, as the soles of my shoes tasted/felt/smelled the ground they briefly touched.

"Hello!" I said, reaching out a hand. "I'm Siddi Star—"

"I heard," she said, cutting me off. Her hands remained crossed. "I'm Lieutenant Mause." She looked me up and down, and if my suit had had dark-gaze or hatred-sensors, I'm sure they would have lit. "Well what now, scientist?"

I turned around. The building she'd chosen to stand by was the largest and most important looking of the lot. The other buildings seemed gathered around it by comparison. If there was something as monumental as a pawprint here, surely it would be enshrined inside.

"We go in," I said.

Her bifurcated upperlip frowned. "After you?" she said, gesturing grandly.

"Don't mind if I do," I said cheerfully, and stepped inside, wondering if I'd made a mistake in showing her my back.

"Welcome!" said a voice around us. Spots of heat flashed on my viewscreen as automated things found power and began ancient programming runs. I didn't understand the words they said, but Fidelis captured everything phonetically. Was this the language of the owners? My tail thumped hard against the inside of my suit. "Welcome to the Moon Pavilion! Welcome to the place where Mankind First Set Foot on the Moon! Welcome to Hotel Luna!"

My fears of a Felina double-cross and quick execution ended as Lieutenant Mause came alongside me. "What is this place? Can you tell what they're saying?"

"I don't know, and no." The voice continued as lights flickered on, and viewscreens much like our own began flashing symbols down at us.

"If you're looking for history, you've found it. See the place where Armstrong's foot first met the Moon! Appreciate art? View the lovely crystalograms being woven by our artists in 3D. Take one home with you! Need relaxation? Come bathe in a moonmud spa and wash your earthly troubles away!"

"There are colors you can't differentiate here, Captain," Fidelis informed me.

"Warning signs?"

"Nothing I recognize as such."

"Keep me posted."

After being in a dig on a quiet unoccupied planet for three years, this felt overwhelming. "Whatever this place is, I don't like it," Mause said. I nodded.

"But it is a once-in-a-lifetime chance—" I said. All of this data—we'd have to come back with a whole team. A find like this would take a lifetime to sift through. It would make or break careers, it would move our knowledge of the Owners, if this was indeed their doing, forward by megaleaps. I shook my head in amazement, and looked over at Lieutenant Mause.

She was looking askance at me through the side of her helmet. "Let's split up?"

It didn't sound like a good idea. But I didn't want to cling to her tail, and I could collect data more quickly and discreetly by myself. "Sure."

"Meet you here in an hour. And then we can share our findings." She finally held her hand out to me. "For the good of all."

The last line of the truce. "For the good of all," I replied, shook her hand, and took off on my own.

My entire life had been spent trying to get into the Owner's minds, one dig at a time. Who they were, how they'd lived, why they'd left us—these were the burning questions of our time, or that occupied my time, at least. More important than the recent fights we'd suffered with Felina. Figuring out *how* the Owners had terraformed half the galaxy was much more significant than arguing over the scraps they'd left behind.

How could they have been so brilliant, only to disappear? Were they wiped out by one of the other alien races that looked for us in the Intestines, even now? I grabbed hold of a beam set halfway up the wall and used it to propel myself along.

"Cellulose components," Fidelis informed me, analyzing the contact I'd made.

I wound through the corridors, a leap at a time. I found rooms for making waste with broken vacuums and shattered mirrors: rooms full of broad bolted-down tables and chairs with straps, and machinery that would take people up and down from level to level, despite the fact that with the low gravity, jumping upwards was not very hard.

I bounded up to the next level and opened the first door.

Inside was a room with what looked like a sleeping mat attached to the wall. It was too big for a Rex or Felina, but too small to hold a litter. I walked over towards it with reverence. Had an Owner, at some impossibly distant time, laid their head down here to rest? I touched the pillow, wondering if anything would be left behind.

"Cellulose fibers," Fidelis said, and I released the breath I hadn't known I was holding.

A warren of beds comprised the rest of the floor. Throughout my journey, I couldn't shake the feeling that I was being followed. Watched. It would be just like a Felina to say they were going one way, and then follow me, hoping to glean something from my archeological talents. I cursed myself for lingering over the pillow and made sure to not talk to myself or stare at any one thing too long—I could go over my data later, in the safety of my ship, without giving the Felina anything worthwhile. Still—above and beyond my wariness and reverence, this place felt like it was strange. Like it was missing something. All the places for living were here, but none of life's tools. A Rex could not live on pillows alone, and neither could the Owners.

At the end of the corridor I reached a room with a sealed lock. More symbols played over the door, and Fidelis recorded them faithfully.

Mobile

Unit

New-type

Kitchen

Employees

I traced them in midair. And then I pressed the glowing button to the right.

The room inside the lock was chaotic. My entering set up a cloud of colored strings and metal shards from the floor. Things that I recognized as the hallmarks of civilization, clothing, tools, jewelry—even if I couldn't tell which was which, it was all here, all of it. The destruction that the rest of this place belied, that the shattered dome had promised—here was where it made its nest.

"Breathable air present, sir," Fidelis said, but I was inclined to keep my helmet on. In just the way that you didn't want to sit down on certain people's couches, I knew I didn't want to breathe this air. My helmet hampered my view—but it probably kept me alive.

A robot leapt out of a pile of debris. Limbs telescoped out from it and braced it against three of the room's walls, while its fourth and fifth limbs, bashed clubs towards my head. Inside my helmet, my viewscreen stuttered, and then relayed damage reports.

"Clear screen, now!" I yelled, and curled myself into a ball. "Exit strategy?"

"There's a door ahead of you—" Fidelis replied, and an arrow appeared. I scrambled for footing and swam through the low-grav instead.

More limbs extended from the creature braced above. It grasped me with a pincher, hefted me up, and began dragging me, without any actual drag, along.

"Shall I retrieve you, Captain?" Fidelis asked, concerned.

"No! Just keep getting data!"

We went from room to room, the creature and I, each room a treasure cave of unknown and heretofore unseen delights. While the thought of Fidelis rescuing me was comforting—even a science ship could use well aimed flares and towropes—it would come at the cost of destroying this place. I'd just found the heart of the Owners; I wasn't about to let anything happen to it. "Data, just data!" I implored, and Fidelis, through the mechanisms of my synesthetic suit, complied.

We felt the carpets we were bumped into, named each chemical we saw by molecular name; we tasted the titanium claws that dug into my back. A small packet hovered in reachable range—I grabbed it and shoved it into my pocket, without thinking. At the end of our too fast journey, the thing chained me to a table in a mostly empty room. I hovered alongside it, while other creatures like the first came in. Over each of their heads, those five symbols - MUNKE - were written on the metal, in black.

"What are they?"

Fidelis answered. "They're cyborgs. Barely. They don't have much organic material left."

"And where are we?"

"At the end of the pressurized hall. Shall I come get you now, sir?"

"No. Project my voice." I addressed the creatures. "Hello—"

More of the MUNKEs entered the room, and these other ones had additional tools.

"Sir!" Fidelis said, circling an area on my viewscreen. The Felina's face, through a duct above. I saw her eyes narrow, and she disappeared.

"Hello—I come in peace," I tried again, as the nearest MUNKE telescoped its limbs for leverage against a blow to come.

Three shots were fired, and Fidelis diligently recorded the vaporized molecular samples the Felina lasergun provided. I looked up, and the Felina peeked out of the duct again, pulled her body through, and drifted down.

One by one, she released my pawcuffs. "That—that was excellent shooting."

Lieutenant Mause shrugged. "I'm military, not science."

"All the same—thanks." I caught one of the drifting bodies, and winced as I felt/smelled/tasted its burned organometallic flesh.

"You owe me," she said, plain and simple.

I released the creature. "I suppose I do." I didn't want to give the rumors I'd heard regarding Felina dietary preferences credence. All the same, I also didn't have a first-born pup to trade her, nor would I, had I one.

She looked me up and down again and frowned, again. Or maybe not. Reading Felina expressions was a touch-and-go affair. "You can pay me in frothane. I hit an asteroid on the way in, lost a fuel tank."

My shoulders slumped with relief and she laughed. "Did you think I was going to ask you for your first-born from your next litter?"

I pulled my lips up inside my helmet and showed my teeth. "I think my people suffer from translational difficulties. But it's a deal. For the frothane, of course." I looked around the austere room we were in. "Did you see any of those things on your way in?" I asked her.

"Nope."

"Then let's take your way back out."

We hopped up to the duct, and scrambled inside.

Making our way along on the inside of a small metal tube was much easier than flailing about openly in the halls.

"I was looking for a fuel depot here. I thought I found one, but I couldn't make it work," she said, as I followed her through the tunnel. "Then I saw the lights go on in that window, and investigated."

"You know you could have just asked for the fuel, when you met me."

She paused and looked indelicately back between her legs at me. "Ask for help? Me, Lieutenant Mause?" She sneezed. Or laughed. I wasn't sure. "And you think *your* people suffer from translational difficulties."

We emerged through another lock onto the top of the building with the destroyed dome directly above us.

"That's the fuel depot," she said, pointing to a place in a clearing below.

The entire building we were on appeared to circle around and hug that one spot. I slowly spun, keeping my feet on the ground, and saw how the entire layout of the buildings once protected by the dome all seemed to converge here.

"No it's not," I said. "See how this place is protecting it? Sheltering it?"

"I was down there, there were fueling teats," Mause sniffed.

"Maybe they just looked like teats." I smiled to myself inside my helmet. Why would you put a pawprint indoors, when you could keep it outdoors, where it belonged? "Think we can jump that far?" I asked.

"Felina always land on their feet," she answered, and leapt.

I could understand why Mause had thought this was a fueling station. Decorative objects had been placed around it, and to the unimaginative or uninitiated, they could indeed look like the connections we had from fuel tankers to ships. But I saw them for what they were, graceful metal barriers that protected the object equidistant between all of them. I slid easily through the curved metal tubes and went towards the center of the forlorn circle.

In the exact center was an overturned metal dome, mirroring the one that ought to have been in the sky above.

"Is it under there?" Mause asked. I nodded, and reached for it, my paw shaking in my suit.

"Sir! The cyborgs!" Fidelis alerted me. Mause's ship must have done the same—I looked up and saw her attention was on the walls of the building behind us.

"They're coming—" From all the windows behind us, MUNKEs welled out like a relentless wave.

"May I retrieve you now, sir?" Fidelis asked.

"Yes!" I told it. "Mause—my ship is on its way—"

"Mine too—" She looked up. "But there's only room for one ship to maneuver above us. I can shatter the rest of the dome—"

"No! You'll only make things worse! Call your ship off!"

She looked at me.

"I owe you, remember? Please. I'm a scientist. This is a fragile area, those creatures have already done enough damage. The Owners—"

Her link to me flickered, and when it reopened, she said, "Done. Your ship it is."

We watched the MUNKEs together. They seemed hesitant to individually leave the security and leverage that a limb against the wall provided, but sooner or later they'd figure out how to work together, and when they did, the metal cage we were in would be small protection.

"Should we look now?" she asked, pointing at the protective dome we stood near.

I wanted to. Oh how I wanted to. But now was not the time to think with my tail—the Scicom labbies had had that right. "Leave it how it is. It's safer now like this. We can come back later. We will come back, later."

Lieutenant Mause nodded, then added. "Only if your ship hurries up."

Fidelis approached, and lowered its tether. I stood on the small dome, feeling strange about stepping on an artifact from the Owners, and strapped the tether to my suit's pulleys, and took the Felina's paw. "I'll hold you, okay?"

This time, as her tongue touched the base of her nose, I knew I'd witnessed her disgusted face. I wanted to think it wasn't at me, but at the ungainly situation we were stuck in. "Fine." She stepped onto the dome and let me take her in my arms. My suit tasted the cool polycarbonate outside of the Felina's suit, and smelled where somewhere on her travels, she'd busted an external seam.

"Look, sir," Fidelis said, as he began hauling us up. The MUNKEs had indeed overcome their shyness with one another, and were forming themselves into a row with telescoping limbs, the front ones stretching ever forwards as new ones pressed them from behind. When they reached the solidity of the metal gate, they began a new project of the same sort, reaching after us with graspers.

"Faster Fidelis, faster!"

"Scientist—" Mause said, half in concern and half in warning.

"Mause, long-hair, or short-hair?"

"Long—why?"

"Forgive me!" My gloved fingers found the flaw in her suit, and ripped it open fractionally. Pressurized air shot out, giving us just enough of a burst to get above the MUNKEs paws, and Fidelis swallowed us into its waiting hold.

I stripped her out of her suit and put her into a warming blanket in my cabin. "Now how am I going to get to my ship?" Lieutenant Mause was just a bit shorter than I was, with a not-unappetizing tabby coloration, and an exceedingly long tail.

"Trouble ahead, sir," Fidelis announced to both of us. A viewscreen opened in the room. We'd risen to the level of the asteroids blocking the entrance to the Anus, and MUNKEs swarmed here, too. Were they the ones that'd put the space junk in the sky, just waiting to cannibalize anything that came through? Like they'd cannibalized the remnants of the Owners below? They were pulling a net up between the hovering stones, to block our way.

"I'm going to shoot them now." Mause said.

"By all means."

Her ship flew in, spending the last of its fuel in delicate maneuvers around the rocks, charring MUNKEs right and left. She found the other seat in my cabin and stroked her whiskers with satisfaction until it was done. Then she turned to regard me.

"I thought your being a scientist was a ruse, and if it is, this is the saddest military ship I've ever seen." She shook her head, and then continued, "So tell me, as a scientist. Why couldn't the Owners leave us more to go on? Why did they have to be so difficult, so silent? How hard is it to explain yourself?"

I held up empty paws. "I ask myself that every day, and I still don't have the answers. Maybe they thought we'd be more like them?"

"That *we'd* be like them, you mean," Mause said, showing bright pinpricks of teeth beneath her amused upper lip.

"We'll go back there, with a team. With the right equipment, the right people, and enough time, maybe we'll—or you'll—finally know." I curved up a lip in mirth myself. "Bring your ship alongside, and we'll refuel you."

"But I can't walk over to it without my suit."

I looked from her, to where I'd cast off my suit, and back again. "You can wear mine."

"It won't fit—"

"Not perfectly. But it'll get you over there." I picked up my synesthetic suit off the floor and held it up while she fit her paws inside. It was too big for her, but it'd get her across the divide between our ships. Fastening her in, I felt the small object I'd managed to grab while being dragged by the MUNKE still stuck in my pocket and pulled it out. There was a waxy coating on the outside.

Mause looked down, my helmet still flipped back. "What is that?"

"I'm not sure. A tribute? Money? A prayer?" I shook it. It sounded fragile, and if it was from the Owners, it was worth more than my ship and Mause's ship, combined.

"Open it," Mause said.

"We shouldn't—" I began, but my claw found the edge, and tore. A small flat image fell out, and I dropped to all fours to see it.

"Emulsion covered paper," Fidelis announced. But we didn't care about what it was, so much as what was on it. A perfect outline, grey on black.

"The Owner's pawprint," I murmured aloud.

"But that doesn't solve anything," Mause knelt beside me. "It's the Owner's bootprint. Not even the outline of a paw! We'll never know who they were more like, Scientist. Never."

But I looked over at her, inside my own suit, which didn't fit her perfectly, but fit her closely enough. I smiled. "Maybe, Lieutenant, that's the point."

The Hunt
by Gerri Leen

A bright sun illuminates the footprints that lead to nowhere. The hunter kneels and assesses them, knowing they do not belong to the prey he seeks, but learning all he can about them anyway.

His mate, Zanar, would have found them fascinating. So old, so deeply grooved. The steps saying so much without words. Just as she did.

She hunted at his side for half his life. She has been dead just as long. He should not still miss her.

"What's so fascinating about a bunch of old tracks?" his client asks. "The people who made them aren't going to help you hunt."

"If you do not see the beauty of such things, I cannot help you."

"You're not exactly excelling in this hunt. I'm telling you she went there." The client, bulky in his rented spacesuit, points toward the blue and white orb that hangs so beautifully in the sky—Zanar would have loved that, too. Would have taken a snap of it, adding it to her collection of beautiful things. The hunter still has that collection, in an airtight box in a storage locker he has prepaid for his lifetime.

The hunter ignores his client's assertions. The man has told him three times where his woman went and three times he has been wrong. This is why he is not the hunter.

He turns back to the footprints. "These are full of stories. They tell of lives gone and people unremembered." Who will remember Zanar when the hunter is gone? Who will remember him?

"Do they tell you where Lirrell has gone? Because I'm not paying you to be nostalgic about a bunch of strangers."

The hunter is regretting taking this man as a client. Unfortunately, his honor is in his perseverance. No matter how boorish his client becomes, he will do what he has been contracted to do: he will hunt.

He pushes himself up, the low gravity giving him greater lift than he has on his home world. His hunting suit moves like a second skin as he bounces, following alongside the footprints. He and Zanar loved worlds like this. It made them feel young again to bounce and race and laugh. It has been a long time since he laughed; he is not sure he even knows how anymore. He tries a smile, feels the muscles of his face protesting, like the lid of a container that will not budge.

He bounces higher, landing lightly, a small puff of dust blowing from the impact. The footprints run out and he turns to go back to his client.

"This is a waste of my time and money." The man is following awkwardly behind him, and the hunter fears for the integrity of the footprints. "We're going to the planet next, aren't we?"

"She is not there." The hunter holds up his hand when the other man would argue. "I am the hunter. I say she is not there."

"This is not going the way I'd planned."

"You do not plan the hunt." The hunt is, in fact, a living thing. No one plans it, not even the hunter. He follows it, learns from it, *is* it. But he does not control it.

The client throws his hands up in what looks like disgust, but it is hard to tell with a suit so cumbersome. He says nothing, just stomps back to the hunter's ship and closes the hatch.

The hunter imagines the client trying to start the engines. They are keyed to his own biometrics. "Do what he says," he murmurs, then whistles a series of tones and the engines roar into life.

The hunter's headset rings with static. "She's there, I tell you. And I'm going to prove it. Then we'll see who the real hunter is."

The ship's beacon goes off; it is protesting the command to lift off without him aboard. The hunter feels a surge of satisfaction; this is a good ship. He and Zanar built in all these fail-safes. Once she was gone, the ship kept waiting for her to board, and first it made the hunter angry and later just sad. It took him years to finally reprogram the ship and remove Zanar from its protocols. It felt like a betrayal of her. He has since learned to live with it.

Another sequence of whistles lets the ship take off. Let his client search the planet he is so sure houses his woman. He has brought his fate on himself. If it is his time to go, nothing can save him. If not, nothing will take him.

The hunter sits down by the footprints, watching as his ship disappears, swallowed up by the poisoned planet that rests so beautifully in the blackness of space. The orb swirls with blues and whites. The planet where Zanar died was blue and gold, but the cloud patterns swirled the same way. She was brought down in a fight, by prey who did not want to return to the prison from where they had escaped. They were murderers, and they destroyed his life when they killed his mate.

The hunter ripped them apart, lost in a berserker rage he never knew before that moment and has never felt since. Even now, sitting alone on this dust ball with only alien footprints for company, he feels no panic, no dread. If he dies today, then he will join his mate in the afterlife, and they will hunt together forever.

That would be pleasant, so he is relatively sure it will not happen.

He holds his hand next to the footprint; the walker's foot was two hands long. Or perhaps not, perhaps the walker wore thick boots like his client does, adding length to the print that was not due to flesh.

There are no settlements on this moon, but there are buildings—long deserted now—on the red planet. The hunter thinks that's where the woman has gone. Did she think there would be people there to help her? She has piloted her stolen ship well, this Lirrell who his client will risk all to have. She has shown great flexibility of thinking, nothing like a hunter, but still more than his fool of a client has displayed.

His headset rings, another klaxon sent by his ship. A distress call this time. He whistles the tone that will bring it back to him. He does not know if his client will be on the ship, and he does not care. He did not tell his client to leave him here—most probably to die—and by doing so, the man has lost his right to any courtesy.

The hunter sees the ship coming; the blue and white sphere seems to spit it out. The ship appears undamaged and his assessment does not change as it comes in slowly. He whistles for it to ease down in a place far from the footprints.

He rises and walks to his ship, striding around it, evaluating it. There are some marks on the door, not blaster residue, not projectile shots. They look more like the scratches of primitive weapons. He opens the hatch and sees no sign of his client.

"Visual," he says.

The ship's cameras, placed to capture all angles, display their take on the main viewscreen. They show him his client opening the door, calling out for Lirrell as if she will come after having led them so far for so long. His client stands there, hands on hips, turning his whole body so he can see to his side in his impractically clumsy suit.

Suddenly he slumps, and the hunter sees an axe lodged in the middle of his chest. Something hairy and mottled with sores pulls him out of the ship. His client screams once, then goes silent. But the scene is not quiet, there is the sound of flesh being hacked off, of . . . a feast.

The hunter feels sick. He is glad when he sees the hatch slam shut, and the cameras switch to external, and what is left of his client is lost to view as a mass of creatures storm the ship.

The hunter closes the hatch and flies back to the surface of the planet. From the air, it looks beautiful, but he can see by his readings that the soil is full of poison, the water too. Radiation and other contaminants fill the planet, and the ship's computers tell him not to stay on the surface, even in his skinsuit, for more than ten minutes. He does not intend to linger for even five.

He follows the flight path charted by his client and as he passes over the landing spot, he sees the man. Or parts of him anyway. One boot remains. And what looks like an arm.

He lands near the remains, sends out a hail of blaster fire to cut down anyone within range. A nearby bush catches on fire, but he does not do anything to put it out. Let this place burn if that is fate's wish. He opens the hatch and jumps out, retrieving the pieces he can find and slamming the hatch back down as the creatures rush the ship.

From the external camera, he can see their faces. They look like beasts, mad things, and it is hard to believe that they are probably the descendents of a people capable of making footprints on this world's barren moon. He sends out another blast of fire, catching most of them up in it. Some scream and run, trying to put out the flames, and others just fall and die. The hunter lifts off, flies too fast out of the atmosphere but doesn't slow until he is well clear. Then he puts the ship on auto and stores what's left of his client in an airtight box so it will not start to smell.

His duty to his client is over, but his hunt resumes—it will not end until he finds his prey. He flies away, onward to the red planet, and the woman who has proven so elusive.

The red planet is deserted; no infrared readings light up his sensors, but the woman could be hiding under a thermal blanket. The hunter knows she is here because he has found her ship under a camo net that is half frayed. He knows she must be aware he is here; his ship came in loud, and he wanted it that way. Sometimes the hunt is for the stealthy, but this is the end of a long chase, and there is no honor in guile. His prey should know he is here, should lie quaking under whatever is giving her cover.

The planet is nowhere near as beautiful as the toxic pit he just left, but he thinks it is related. A colony of some sort was here, and it is clear this settlement did not go peacefully when the end came. Blaster fire riddles the buildings and the vehicles scatted around. But there are no bodies. He wonders if there was a war between the blue and white world and this one, if the colonists here were captured and forced back to the home world. Are their children the things he just saw—or were they meals for those creatures?

It takes him a long time to find the woman. Much longer than he expects. She is at the edge of the settlement, lying huddled under several thermal blankets, and her air is dangerously low. Through her faceplate he can see she is beautiful. No wonder his client wanted her back.

"The hunt is over," he says, and his voice is gentler than he means it to be.

"Let me go."

"I cannot."

She does not plead, does not wheedle or cajole, or offer him her body as so many others—both men and women—have done. Neither does she curl into a ball, cringing at his feet and soiling herself. This one stands up with great effort, staring at him the entire time, her breath rapid as she holds her ground.

"The hunt is over," he says again. It must be said three times if the prey will not surrender.

"I can't go back to him."

She pulls a utility tool from her suit's belt. He tenses, ready to knock it from her hand, but she does not lunge at him. Instead she holds it to her air hose.

"I suggest you do not do that."

"I *won't* go back to him. Life is not worth living if it's with him."

His next move is prescribed. She will not surrender, so he must say again that the hunt is over and then he must kill her. He opens his mouth but instead of the ritual words, he says, "There is not much of him to go back to."

She seems startled by his words, but no more than he is.

He forces himself to stand tall, to ignore how her eyes gleam the same way Zanar's would have as the sun hits her faceplate. He is the hunter; he has an obligation. He will not falter, no matter what. "The hunt is—"

"I surrender to my fate. I surrender to the hunt. I surrender to you." She understands his rituals, says the words of surrender perfectly. It is unexpected.

He holds out his hand, ready to jerk it back if she is lying and tries to cut his skinsuit, but she puts the tool in her belt and holds up her hands. Her steps are heavy with defeat as she walks next to him to his ship, and she lets him fit her with cuffs that he clips to a ring in the back of his ship.

"You know the words of the hunt?" he asks as he tests her bonds.

"My brother is a hunter."

Once the hatch is closed, he eases off her helmet, letting her breathe more easily, and she gulps in air as if her supply was gone, not just low. Unmasked, she looks nothing like Zanar, but still there is something in her amber eyes.

The hunter leaves her and takes the controls, piloting them back to the moon and landing near the footprints again.

"What are you going to do?" Even if she were not related to a hunter, she would have heard horror stories about his kind. It is often said that hunts end in death, but that is not true. All hunts end with him catching his prey. Whether they are caught dead or alive is up to them and to their fate. His honor demands he try to catch them alive, to bring them back to whatever client has called for them.

"You know the ritual, don't you? Or did you not pay attention to your brother's stories after he had caught his prey?"

She does not answer, and her eyes seem to shine like the cold sun of this world. He looks away, taking the container of what is left of his client, and putting it between him and the woman.

"What is lost is now found. All things are returned to him who has retained me. The hunter hunts, the prey is captured. I give you Lirrell. Our contract is at an end."

He bows his head, holds out the keys to the cuffs, waits, as is the custom, for the client to take them. He hears the woman shifting, as if she's trying to see what's in the box.

"Where is he?" she asks, and fear makes her voice shake.

The hunter remains silent, and after the proper time has passed, he unlocks the woman's cuffs and puts them and the key away. "It would seem he does not want you after all."

She rubs at her wrists, even though the cuffs could not have hurt her over the spacesuit. "I don't understand."

The hunter points at the box. "Open it."

She does. "Oh." She slams the lid down, the hiss of the seals fill the small space, and he thinks she might throw up, but she controls herself.

"It is right that you face the man who wanted you. The hunt has come full circle." He nods toward the hatch. "I am going out. Do you wish to see this place?"

"My suit's almost out of air."

He takes that as a yes and refills her tanks from the ship's stores. Then he takes the box and carries it to the hatch, bouncing out onto the unrelieved gray and white of the moon's surface.

"Are you going to bury him?"

"No. His people will want to bury what is left of him."

"They'll be happy he's gone. He was not a nice man."

The hunter agrees with her, but says nothing. Instead, he puts the box down and opens it. Pulling out his client's boot, he walks to the footprints and lets the boot hang over one of them. They are the same size.

"Did he leave those prints?" she asks.

"No. The people who lived on that planet left these." He points to where the horrible world sits.

"It's beautiful."

"It's not. But I think it was once." He puts the boot back, sealing up the case, then walks back to the footprints, studying them for the last time. He will not return unless a hunt brings him, and so far, this is the only one that has brought him here.

"What are you doing?" she asks, and the hunter thinks her voice is lovely, even behind the hiss of the air in her suit. "What do you see?"

"I see hope. I see optimism. See how this edge is lighter. Whoever left this was happy. Excited. But also not used to this gravity. The side here, a little more pressure right here. As if the walker was getting used to this place."

"You can see all that in a footprint?"

He nods and continues his study.

The woman walks away, to where the hunter has left a footprint just as deep. "I don't see the same things here."

"No, you do not." He learned to walk in this low gravity decades ago. And he has not known hope or optimism or anything but the obligations of the hunt since Zanar died. He is one of the best hunters; that has had to serve as his entire life for a very long time.

"What will you do with me?"

"I have a feeling my client would wish me to take you down to the planet and let you die at the hands of the things that killed him."

She says nothing.

"Or I could return you to his family."

"They know nothing of me. My disagreement with him was personal."

The hunter knows this. His client insisted on meeting in darkened bars.

The hunter checked up on the prey as he always does. Lirrell was the man's mistress, tired of his abusive nature. The client did not want his wife or family to know.

"I have a question," the hunter says, leaning in to see her face. "If you're brother is a hunter, why did you not send him after your lover? He hurt you, did he not, this man who contracted me? Beat you?"

"And worse." She turns away. "I am not like him. I don't want to be like him. I just wanted to get away."

"You thought my client would be merciful?"

"He did not spend his money lightly and a hunter is expensive. I underestimated how much he would want me back." She stands taller, takes a deep breath that resonates through the speakers in her suit. "Are you going to kill me? Because if it's all the same to you, I think I'd rather you just left me here, next to these happy footsteps you find so intriguing. I'd like the last thing I see to be that planet you say is not lovely."

Her answer is unexpected. It is full of honor and a sensitivity he does not expect. He can imagine that Zanar, if she was not a hunter, was instead chased across five star systems, would have said the same thing.

"What do you see when you look at those footprints?" he asks her.

"I see loneliness." She points to the footprints he has made. "I see it there, too."

"I hunt alone."

"Have you always?"

"That is not your concern."

"Since you may kill me, I believe I can ask."

He stares down at the tracks in the gray dust. "I have not always hunted alone."

"I'm sorry." And she does sound as if it is so. "I would rather not die, hunter. Just so there's no ambiguity. Sitting here waiting for my air to run out is a distant second choice to life."

"Yes. I know." He turns to go, leaving the footprints behind. Leaving her behind.

She does not try to follow him and when he turns back, she is staring at the planet.

"I am under no obligation at this time," he says. "I have hunted and I have found my prey. The lost has been rejoined with he who was left. The hunt is over." It is now up to him how this ends. With his client dead, she is his. He can free her or he can kill her.

She turns slowly and he realizes she does not know this part of the ritual. Perhaps her brother is a hunter who likes only to kill, who never shows the mercy they can, at times, display.

"What is your name?" she asks.

"I am the hunter."

"You must have another name."

They stare at each other across the footprints. In his heart, his name beats against the walls he has erected since his mate died; she was the last to call him by his true name. In his soul, his spirit wishes to fly again. He could push his heart and spirit back; they are accustomed to losing to his intellect, his will—to the hunter.

But . . . he does not want to push them back. He whispers, "My name is Jadresh."

"It is a fine name."

"It is just a name. Nothing noble or elegant about it." But his heart is beating it out as if his name is life itself. Ja-dresh, Ja-dresh, Ja-dresh.

"It does not have to be noble or elegant. Just yours."

"I had a mate," he says softly. "She died on a hunt."

"That must be hard for you. I imagine every time you hunt, you see her."

"I have learned to live without her." He can tell she does not know what to say to that. He wonders if she had someone she loved, someone before his client, who left a hole in her heart that time refused to fill.

"What now?" she finally asks.

"There is a world full of footprints like these, only mammoth. I was there a long time ago and still remember the marvel I felt upon seeing them." Zanar said it was the most wondrous thing she had ever seen. "I think I will go back there before I agree to another hunt."

"I . . . I should like to see such footprints. If you want company, that is." She is not moving, not edging toward him, not reaching out. She waits, and he loves her in that moment for her quiet courage and her wavering voice.

"I should like to have company, Lirrell." He holds out his hand to her. "I must return this man to his family. Honor will prevent me from divulging the nature of the hunt he contracted, since he made it clear he did not want them to know."

"Convenient."

"Sometimes, yes."

"And then?"

"And then we will go." The two of them, on his ship. She, no longer prey, but a willing passenger. Maybe someday something more?

She moves then, hurrying as if she is afraid he will change his mind.

She should know better. He is the hunter. Once he has chosen his course, nothing will deter him.

Relics of Interesting Times
by Nathaniel Williams

She spent her vacation on the other side of the world, where her brother kept the Moon. Freden, her only sibling, worked there, preserving relics of the solar system's previous inhabitants. When he invited her to help celebrate the completion of some major undertaking related to this project, she didn't hide her reluctance. Freden typically only wanted company when he had some great *Statement* to make. Cridenta wasn't sure how much grandstanding artist sophistry she could handle, especially given her recent circumstances.

When he transmitted his message, however, he had seemed genuinely enthused about his latest project. He appeared so . . . frustratingly satisfied. Not second-guessing his motivation seemed easy in comparison to not resenting him. The whole thing simply reminded her that his craft lent itself to such revelries. Lucky boy. Each job had a clearly defined beginning and end. Nothing like her life in politics.

She became much more determined to announce her news while she was with him. Not that she wanted to one-up him, or detract from his celebration. That was more like something Freden would do to her. No, she simply wanted to share her decision with him. They would both have something to celebrate.

As her light-shuttle deposited her at the coordinates Freden had provided, Cridenta found herself mildly surprised by the landscape. True, she didn't anticipate bustling avenues and towers, all the frenetic joys of metropolitan life. Freden would have none of that. On some level, however, she had expected Freden's workplace to be filled with churning excavation machines, covered in dust and debris. Instead, his Archive stretched into the horizon along the virgin landscape, an enormous white rhombus that dwarfed the tall, yellow trees and vacant fields surrounding it. Glass windows reflected sunlight back into her eyes, just as the entire location reflected Freden's personality, each girder and slab exuding his work ethic and his pride. Insects hummed in Cridenta's ears, the closest nature came to silence. Rustic nightmare, she thought.

Freden stepped outside to greet her. His features hadn't changed, but he'd bulked up in his midsection, just below his foremost legs. A fellow adult, she thought hopefully. He saluted her with his thick upper arms while he wrapped his lower arms around her shoulders. On his right, lower arm, he wore an adornment, an antique band of crystal that had been treasured by a young anemone from a planet circling a distant star. As she embraced her brother, the band emanated a profound sense of well-being, residual feelings of water-warmth and the child's giddy self-confidence. She realized he'd worn it especially for her.

"Wonderful to see you," she said.

Freden grinned. "How are things?"

"About to fall apart," she said. "As usual."

He nodded and led her toward the entrance. "What now?"

"You've heard about the disbanding of the Territorial Committee? Even out here, that must be news."

"I guess I've heard some rumors," Freden said, in a tone that meant he'd listened and analyzed every report even as he resented their unavoidability.

"All that work falls on my shoulders now," she said. "I suppose you didn't make that connection."

Freden understood Cridenta's difficult work on the World Committee, had sent her a lukewarm congratulatory message seventeen cycles ago when she received the position. Beyond that, he typically made a point of undermining the importance of her job.

"Surely you have some help," he said.

"I have a mass of whining imbeciles who begin undoing each other's social repairs as soon as they're undertaken. The World Committee will disband before this cycle is over."

In the front room, a serving tray and pitcher of hot milk awaited. The arched ceiling towered over them, and natural light filled the room. Freden's workshop had some comforts.

"Anything else?" Freden asked.

"Communities on Continents Six, Seven and Eight have grown together. It's not a mere alliance; they're interbreeding and identifying as a single race. In a few generations, we'll be at their mercy."

"Terrifying," Freden said with a smirk.

His sarcasm made her wish he were an aide or public employee. Unfortunately, brothers couldn't be fired or demoted or transferred to some distant department when they smarted off. Soon, Cridenta realized, she wouldn't have such power over anyone. She decided that moment would do as well as any to make her announcement. She summoned her courage and spoke.

"I'm retiring," she said.

"I know," Freden replied. "Eldro told me."

Her assistant. Oddly enough, she hadn't made the announcement to Eldro, although she'd imprinted it in her personal notes several times. Spying again, Cridenta thought.

Freden approached the serving tray and raised the shiny, metal lid. Inside it sat a ceremonial pastry from Continent Three, no doubt baked by one of their famous chefs.

"I thought we'd celebrate early," he said. "You've made a brave choice."

She waited a moment to see that he wasn't just mocking her. Sometimes Freden said "brave" when he meant "stupid."

"I'm spent," she told him. "I joined World Committee because I believed we could reconnect to the collaborative spirit of our ancestors. Create a long range plan that would benefit everyone. Instead, I've wasted cycle after cycle preventing World Committee from devouring itself and leaving each Continent to defile the ruins. I've brought forward eight different proposals to unite the Continents in one executive body. Each one failed."

Freden gulped down a slice of pastry. "You know, as I've worked with Human culture, I've learned some things."

Of course, she thought. Freden had ignored her vulnerable comments and went right into discussing *his* big project. Shouldn't have expected otherwise.

"The Humans had a saying," he continued. "It's difficult to translate. It went . . . 'May you live in interesting times.' A curse of sorts. 'Interesting' could have good or bad connotations, but nearly always precluded some kind of turmoil. And they universally seemed to dislike chaos. In that sense," he said, "you'd have made a splendid Human, Cridenta."

She ignored his flippancy and continued. "If I'd been appointed centuries ago, I could've done something . . . guided better decisions to prevent us from reaching this point. But now I feel anarchy breathing down our collective necks. If I can't prevent wars and hoarding, what good can I do?"

"Truly," Freden said, "these are interesting times."

Cridenta detected no sarcasm this time. Freden's unexpected sincerity caught her off guard, and she nearly choked on her sip of milk.

"I told you I'd show you the Moon," he said with his mouth half full of cake. "It's back this way, behind that door."

Their solar system held other moons, of course. The red planet near them had two; the large gas giant past that had over sixty. Still, the former satellite tended by Freden earned the distinction to be called "the" Moon because it was the one circling the planet at the most inhabitable orbit, the one called Earth that their ancestors used as a stage to build the world after they arrived in the solar system.

Their ancestors had built the world around the pre-arranged schema used in every other solar system they established. The world circled the sun. It held many continents, each one with enough land to grow food for it's own citizens, each one with at least one natural resource that it could trade with other Continents, each one joined to the other by land bridges spanning bountiful oceans. Allegedly, this social architecture flourished on other worlds her race had founded. Individuals hoping to undermine the system, however, frequently claimed that other worlds intentionally overstated their citizen's level of contentment when they met with Cridenta's people, that their harmonious existence was only a veneer meant to mask their own social troubles in order to save face among fellow worlds. Such accusations were to be expected from the rabble rousers Cridenta opposed. She had little doubt that her world was indeed the lone exception, falling short of its ancient founders' goals. On her unfortunate world, the system designed to foster cooperation had instead devolved into the competitive nightmare she faced daily.

No longer needed for tides or light, the Moon was dismantled, its most resonant pieces sent to archivists like Freden. It made for dull work. Perfect for Freden.

Freden, like every preservationist Cridenta had ever met, cultivated an air of refinement. He'd been a know-it-all child, and had grown into a similar adult. He loathed practicality. He admired dramatists who conceived of performances that lasted cycles, or the talented psychometrists who could imprint an object with a single, vivid, empathic moment instead of a string of events. Freden viewed himself as an artist who used past civilizations as his canvas.

"How many visit this facility of yours?" she asked.

"We're not open yet. I *told* you that when we last spoke," he said.

She noted her brother's familiar exasperation. He thought, no doubt, that she had little better to do than remember every tidbit of his schedule.

"So how many do you expect?" she said.

"Many billions, once the general public learns what we have here. I had to perfect something first. It took some intense labor."

Here comes the delicate artiste's tale of success despite adversity, Cridenta thought. Surprisingly, he didn't continue speaking, but quietly guided her down a cramped corridor into a foyer that led into an enormous workroom. Artifacts of Human culture sat scattered throughout the room, suspended from the ceiling or sorted into a grid-like pattern of open cabinets, in the early stages of organization.

"This also requires some work on your part," he said. "You'll need to wear protection, obviously. And you need to see at least a few things first. They'll give you a perspective once we get to the Moon."

Once in the workspace, where the many relics sat, Freden became more animated. He scuttled from display to display. Freden gave Cridenta a long robe made of synthetic fiber, along with a headpiece of charged gauze to shield the objects from her. It felt like wearing a heavy blanket wrapped around her head, and each time she turned or nodded it threatened fall off and take her body down with it. All in the name of safety. For the artifacts, not for her. Individuals, particularly those as strong-willed and assertive as Cridenta, couldn't be near these objects without imprinting them with some of their temporal existence. Anyone encountering the object after her would sense as much of her, the events in her world immediately preceding and following the moment she engaged with the object, as any other moment associated with the object. Perhaps more.

Freden reached his two topmost arms into a reconfiguring device. He adjusted the controls with his lower digits. When he withdrew them, his arms had become slender, jointed posts. His extremities branched out into tiny, stick-like appendages. Archivists thrived on such transformations. It made up a large portion of their professional pride, knowing that their jobs entailed physically mimicking the races whose abandoned worlds they encountered.

Such tiny, fragile arms! Freden waved them, his sense of showmanship still intact, but Cridenta found herself slightly repulsed. She almost pitied her brother for having to work with such meager appendages. She'd seen and sensed images of Humans many times, but when their form was brought into direct contrast with Freden's own stout, powerful body, they seemed even more slight and frail than she'd realized.

He picked up one artifact, clumsily held it in the two Human extremities rather than balanced in all four palms. Years of training and temporary body reconfiguration enabled him to touch the object without imprinting on it. He caressed its side, then waved it toward Cridenta. She took it in visually first, gauging its narrowness and its flattened, outstretched end. As Freden brought it closer, she focused and began to sense the object itself.

Press. Drag. Press. Drag. She walked forward on two legs, digging the object into the dirt, breaking it up, creating furrows where seeds would grow. Heat on her neck. Aching hands. Repetition. Waves of Old Earth days and years, rising and falling, like the motion of her slender and meager arms. As the sun crossed the sky, weariness grew. Urgency in each drag of the . . . the hoe, staving off an oppressive season of cold that came each year. Winter. Hands. Harvest. Pride, then fear. The unceasing rhythm of desperation.

Cridenta moved away from the object. So *many* individuals had touched and used the object that she felt no precision, no single temporal moment or emotion to focus upon, but an overall sense of its use.

"Their diurnal pattern takes some getting used to," Freden said. "They didn't have constant sunlight, so they scheduled sleep patterns around the sun's presence or absence in their sky."

Cridenta nodded. "So the Humans used this object to grow food?"

"In their early world. It's a primitive instrument. It seems to have been preserved at some point, enclosed from exposure that made it more resonant."

"A short-lived people," she said.

"Back then, yes. Several generations utilized this very tool. The equivalent of one hundred cycles. An Old Earth *Century*, measured in revolutions of the planet around the sun."

Freden moved to another object. He picked up two skinny, matching pieces of tapered, ivory-colored wood.

"These will give you a better idea of their culture."

Cridenta leaned toward the objects and sensed them.

Weakness. Pain in her midsection. Scents made her feel even weaker. Craving. She felt hands moving the objects frantically, hand to mouth, curling long tendrils of food around them and devouring them. The pain subsided. Again, repetition. Again, waiting. The sticks stood between her and death, and yet through all the hands that used them, something changed.

Faces smiling. Rows of people eating. The hunger lessened, and the pain between each time they used the sticks grew less acute.

Cridenta felt the world around the objects. Floods and famines. Roads repaired. Humans moving. Humans building.

An accidental fire consumed a hut. Flames leapt up as smoke stung her eyes and throat. An old woman burned to death. Her family sobbed beside her corpse. The home fell into charred remains and was raised again.

Work carried on. Hard toil rewarded with payment. Work done indoors, shaded from the sun. Individuals conversed over their meals. Ideas, too numerous to process. Ideas about governance, religion, arts. A ritual of eating without the gnawing hunger.

"At least they weren't starving any longer," she said.

"Yes," said Freden. "By the time Humans stopped imprinting on these particular utensils, they'd become accustomed to regular meals. You felt that transition." He smiled slyly. "Guess how long a time span you experienced?"

"Another century?" Cridenta replied.

"Correct!" Freden said. "Like any other culture, Humans produced more and more artifacts as their basic needs were met. Did you sense the fire?"

"Yes. Very vivid."

"I worked hard to retain that, was able to augment it a bit. Many of the Humans who touched those sticks remembered it. Some of it gets lost."

Freden prided himself on his ability to sense—and even amplify—the temporal and emotional resonances of objects. Like many outside the archival field, Cridenta joked that archivists enjoyed dead races more than their own. Freden certainly fit the bill, caustic and unconcerned about his own culture's events while relishing his ability to evoke life of a past world.

"As their world changed, they became more and more aware of events around them, along a wider scale. Even if a relatively few Humans touched an object, the events imprinted could span a greater period of time or location. That's just how it works. Things get jumbled the more advanced a culture becomes, and it makes my job harder."

"How much further?" she asked.

"Let's take a shortcut," Freden said. He escorted her to a small, red elevator that raised them toward the roof of the building, then opened on the opposite side, revealing an enormous vault of Moon.

Each piece of the Moon seemed larger than the next, as Freden led her past vast expanses of chalky terrain that flanked them. They had left the elevator behind and now walked along the elevated pathway with a breathtaking view. In the distance, a large, beautiful crater sat preserved under a translucent, etheric shield. Cridenta wondered how immense a section of the Moon Freden would show her. Would it be larger than the crater? Would she actually be allowed to walk on it or sense it without wearing Freden's unwieldy apparatus? There seemed to be Moon in abundance. Surely not all of it needed preservation. Surely some of it could be sensed raw and unfiltered.

Freden's shortcut wasn't one. They walked until all four of her legs ached. Freden stopped at a section of walkway that lowered them toward a nearly empty area. They descended several stories toward the one object below them. Inside a small, ebony sphere, behind thick, etheric coating that protected it even from Freden, sat a round chunk of the Moon.

"This is it," he said.

"That? So small!" Compared to the other sections they'd passed, this part of the Moon seemed insignificant.

"Take a look. It'll be worth it."

As she stopped in front of it, Cridenta glanced into the sphere at the Moon surface. Granules of soil made up the small expanse of monochromatic terrain. A strange series of tracks punctuated the topography. They formed an unmistakable, alternating pattern. With a little imagination, Cridenta could envision the Human on two legs, leaving these artifacts behind it as it moved. The tiny remaining traces of a tiny being.

"Footprints," she said. "Human footprints."

"Yes."

"That's what you've been working on for these cycles?"

"Oh yes!" Freden said. "When our ancestors found it, it was covered in a material that prevented anyone from touching it or getting too close to it. Original scholars thought it was perhaps a dangerous weapon, until later when we learned the Humans weren't like us. According to our histories, they had no temporal sense, no psychometry. They could sense with their skin, and know things around them through odor and a limited range of light spectrum, similar to ourselves. But they suffered from immediacy. They couldn't sense time and emotion with any precision. You felt that somewhat when you held the hoe."

Freden walked to an array of brightly colored lights, hidden behind a pillar. He began to manipulate the controls using his two, non-Human arms.

"I'm going to open it up," he said. "You're protected. Lean in and really get a good read of it."

The spherical seal around the Moon-slab hissed and bubbled. Freden's arrangement lit the Moon starkly against the black casing around it. Cridenta saw the glare of white reflected on the front of her protective robe as she inched forward. She followed the contours of each foot, analyzed the rectangular lines that divided it, the odd blend of natural curvature and precise geometry. She opened her senses. There. She shuddered.

Death around every turn. Fed and healthy and sane people still felt crazed. Bodies trampled bodies, marching against . . . so many things she couldn't tell. Anger grew. Watching soldiers die, becoming carrion to be fed upon by vultures.

First the trials, then more death. Repeated pleas of guilty as thousands shouted in the streets. Great men had died, and now their assassins bargained and oozed self-pity. Names swarmed through her mind. King. Kennedy. Sirhan. Ray.

Numbers and facts. Humans hurled information at each other like sharpened stones. Groups formed and disassembled, all planning to destroy something. Plots against bodies. Plots against plots.

Even laughter seemed like anger. Comedians mocked leaders. Censors coerced owners to pull them off the air. Smothered speech.

Police beat the men who loved other men until the bricks began to fly. Authority exploded, became a weapon. No one trusted anyone.

Somewhere amid the chaos, she felt weightlessness and power, the descent from the craft and the pressure of the lunar terrain. The crunch of soil beneath a tentative foot. She was each footprint, freed from the chaos around it. Supreme confidence. Supreme risk. Sudden attempts at levity. The Moon's vacant expanse surrounded her. A million eyes watched, enthralled. Years surrounded her, the history of the race leading up to one moment. Satisfaction. A promise made.

Then she fell back into the tumult. A leader visited the place where the killings happened and accomplished nothing. More soldiers died. More people marched. More despair. A pregnant woman lay stabbed to death. Who could do such a thing? Words written in blood on the wall. Crazy words from the music.

Songs pervaded the chaos, filling streets with traffic and naked bodies, invoking deities. Love and the Devil. Chanted choruses over vibrating electric sounds. Refrain upon refrain. Heat stroke summer in a place called New York. Noise collided with new perceptions, as if they wanted to experience more than their meager, five senses allowed. Triumph. Exhaustion. Music in a coliseum where vehicles sped in circles. Another murder. Loss.

No escape. The wildness spread. Somehow, under it all, she still felt the nearly weightless beauty of the moment when the foot touched the Moon.

Cridenta stepped away from the sphere that held the footprints. Freden stood behind her, as if prepared for her to collapse.

"Overwhelming," she said. Let Freden decide if that's a compliment or a criticism, she thought, steadying herself on her hind legs and reestablishing her poise.

"I work with what the object gives me," Freden said.

"And you say they *disliked* chaos?"

"Abhorred it, as far as we can discern," Freden said. Usually when Freden was proud of an accomplishment, he couldn't stop talking about it. Surely, life away from society hadn't transformed him *that* much. He was being obtuse, withholding something. Cridenta probed for more information.

"How long did you work on this?"

"Several cycles."

"You enhanced it . . . how exactly?"

"That can wait. What did you think? Describe it."

She used Freden's word. "It seemed like an *interesting* century."

Freden leapt at this. He began babbling. She realized she'd hit on what he wanted. "That's just it!" he said. "The object captures a moment. What you felt wasn't an Old Earth Century. It wasn't even a decade. It was simply the six *months* preceding and following the moment the footprint was made, the temporal resonance of *only one* Old Earth year."

"Their entire planet was devolving when these happened?" she asked.

"Wrong again!" Freden shouted, his voice taking a sing-song lilt. "That was only the temporal consciousness of the *single area* most associated with the footprint. I molded the object's temporal core geographically. You experienced merely a few months in the history of *a single part of one of many continents.*"

"How did you. . . ?" she began.

"The object lends itself to such handling. It's a rare find. Something uniquely of a moment without the imprinting of many additional consciousnesses on top of it."

No wonder he'd invited her. She understood now why Freden would devote so much time to such an unlikely end. She also realized just how much prestige Freden must hold among his fellow archivists to be granted permission to work on this object. Pride for her brother swelled inside Cridenta.

"You didn't have to remove layers of Human thought?" she asked.

"No," he said. "*They* preserved this! Something so pristine. Understand, only one Human touched this piece of ground. And they valued it so much they prevented it from ever being touched again. Can you see why?"

Cridenta considered this. "They were going mad," she said. "And yet, facing all that, they ventured into space and reached their closest satellite."

"Exactly!"

Awe swept over her. It only took a moment to realize that this emotion had been Freden's real purpose. He hadn't been just showing off. She knew now why he'd invited her there. He'd planned this. Up to his old tricks again.

"Even as things fell to pieces around them, they moved outward," he said. "*They* kept their enthusiasm. *They* never gave up."

Manipulative little brat. Talented, brilliant, but manipulative. Comparing her unfavorably to Humans. Mocking her frustration at the World Committee. And yet, this backhanded encouragement was the closest her brother had ever come to really showing concern about her work. On some level, he valued what *she* did and genuinely wanted her to continue. Cridenta recovered from her wave of emotion and scowled at him.

"All right, Freden, you have me. I suppose I learned precisely the lesson you intended for me to learn. You and your Humans. But tell me this . . . did it work? Did they ever succeed?"

"We don't know," he said with a dramatic wave of his slender, Human arms. "Was that the pinnacle of their civilization? Or simply one of the last times something reached that level of purity? Other items we've discovered indicate they had an extended existence, but there are so many emotions attached to each of them, and the items are so long-lived, it's difficult to tell."

Freden stepped aboard the powered walkway and beckoned her to join him. The walkway shuddered and lifted.

Pieces of the Moon shone up at her. Disoriented, perhaps by the walkway's rapid ascent or perhaps by uncertainty, Cridenta considered her own future. Back home, a committee needed to be staffed, a snooping aide needed to be chastised, a world—despite itself—needed to be preserved. She wondered how the Committee would take her ninth proposal for unification. Bathed in moonlight from below, Cridenta smiled.

The Moment
by Lawrence M. Schoen

Four tiny, cerulean lozenges winked in and out of phase for a moment, twinkling like silvery fish, sardines really, as they shimmied into position and formed the corners of a tetrahedron above the lunar surface. On cue, Cwaliheema—the highest rated archaeocaster across seventeen star clusters—flared into existence at the center of the pyramid, a lifeform that to human senses would have registered as a ball of golden light, a sense of longing for one's first love, and the memory of comfort food gone bad. Cwaliheema rotated upon first one axis then another, and locked onto the object of her intention by whatever perceptual system her kind possessed.

Despite her appearance, when she addressed her audience the archaeocaster spoke in English. "Friends and lovers, this is an exclusive quantacast! I'm coming to you live via timeslow, and using authentic, reconstructed linguistic systems because this is a rare moment, my darlings. Mere pico-seconds have passed since my producer Gilly sacrificed his own consciousness to jury-rig the lockout mechanism to get me here. My location has been kept under interdict by forces that refused to acknowledge our queries, let alone be interviewed. Even stretching this instant as we are, there isn't much time before those selfsame curmudgeons break through what remains of Gilly's potential memories and bounce me, so pay attention while you can. I'm hovering mere *sklues*—pardon the slip, I meant to say "inches"—above the only surviving Mark! Yes, you know what I'm talking about, and why I'm doing so in a language whose speakers are long gone. How better to honor them? Below me is the sole remaining artifact of a once proud people who cast their entertainments into space for the benefit of us all. Burn and then freeze this image into your receptors, you'll likely never get another chance. This is all we have, the last remnant of any of the Marks, and even this has been denied our experiencing until now. Experts disagree, speculation runs rampant, but it is this reporter's opinion that we are experiencing Groucho. Note the depth of the indentations, the comical pattern of their relief. Night and Day, Opera and Races, this is not the work of Gummo. I know, I know, the silent vacuum of the locale begs the question for many, blatantly insisting that this Mark is Harpo, but I'm here and they're not, and I'm telling you that I'm glocklerizing an undeniable sense of Groucho here."

One of the sardine-like corners blackened, shriveled, and slurred. Another followed suit, and then a third. The blur of Cwaliheema lost cohesion and flickered out of existence as the curmudgeons in question shattered the last bits of unrealized recollections and secured the site once again, annihilating the archaeocaster in the process.

The generation ship of Krenn frantically dumped velocity as it splooched from the fuel-efficient but mind-numbing slowness of intramolecular phasetransit back into the normal time-space continuum, less than a cubit above the moon. The ship crashed into the middle of the heelprint. Its immaculate hull that had withstood the flailings of phasetransit for a quarter million years without so much as a ding, shattered itself against the unyielding bulk of a grain of lunar dust. Of the six thousand seventeen Krenn onboard at the time, a scant several hundred survived the crash. Nearly all of these recovered from their injuries and disembarked over the next month.

None of the first generation of Krenn had lived long enough to reach the site, though none had expected to. The very first Krenn had conceived of this journey in the distant past, dedicating his life and his posterity to the pilgrimage with an ever-recycling population of clones. Like their clone-father, each was an optimized collection of smart matter no bigger than a speck. Hundreds of generations of Krenn had lived and died during the voyage, their remains enshrined into niches in the very walls of the vessel that now lay shattered at its destination.

The survivors flooded out upon the steppes of the heel, rejoicing despite the crushing weight that gravity forced upon them. They settled in, constructing mansions of haze and shadow, and waited for enlightenment to come. The mission and purpose of the first Krenn remained with each of them. This place had been the site of the greatest triumph of the greatest archaeocaster in all of history. Before the beginning of the quest, Krenn—the original Krenn—had felt drawn to it. He had cultivated the tales, sifted myth from coincidence, mastered the lost language of the interview-eschewing, spatial curmudgeons of the ancient dark times, and recreated the route through dimensional puzzles to this theoretical location. The odds of success had been so absurd not a single entelechy of Krenn's crèche dared invest time or expense in the project. And yet, here they were, nearly three hundred unique individuals sharing the template of Krenn.

They waited. Enlightenment did not come. The Krenn diverged from one another, much more so than they had upon the voyage here. No longer held together by the dream of basking in the dead essence of a nigh mystical archaeocaster, they found little in common despite their shared Krenness. Over time, they disagreed. As the years passed, the disagreements became arguments. Soon after, arguments begat fights. Fights acquired weight and number and expanded into battles. By the time the Krenn population doubled—for the cloning had continued after landfall—their homesteads had spread beyond the heel and across the sole. Some few hearty adventurers had dared to venture beyond the cliff heights at the toes' edge, but none had returned with any tales of what lay beyond. Nor would they.

The battles turned into war, a vast conflagration of violence, Krenn against Krenn, that defied all sense, and did not end until every last speck had been slaughtered. In its final moment, perhaps the last of the Krenn found an ironic enlightenment in the situation. Perhaps not.

After the better part of another half million years, Seela, heir apparent to the Vegetable Worlds that were all that remained of the folly of short-lived, meat-based intelligence in that part of space, came to the moon and the end of another sort of quest. He—using a very loose definition of the gender—resembled a ten-meter stalk of articulated broccoli. After a moment's glance, he ignored the imprint before him. It did not occur to him to wonder how it had survived for so long when the rest of the barren surface lay pitted and random. Nor did he know anything of the pilgrimage of the Krenn, save that the minuscule and sentient specks had indeed ended their existence upon this barren worldlet, the last spheroid that species had settled. Ages earlier, several of Seela's closest florets had confirmed the details. They had rummaged through that race's long dead worlds, part scavenger hunt part morbid feast, as they had cracked open every last reliquary and steamed random memories from the shriveled remains of trillions of specks. After consuming their fill, they had flash-frozen themselves and returned to the royal court. Once they had thawed and quickened, still bloated on alien thoughts, they stumbled before their prince.

Seela had delighted in their accounts, and then snipped their stems and sucked up the disturbing memories secondhand. Cannibalism, though infrequent, was a tradition among the royal lines of the Vegetable Worlds, and one must suppose that the hangers-on that orbited Seela, fawning upon his buds and proclaiming his fractals, had to have known the risks. After draining the last of his stunned nearest and dearest, he found himself still cognitively peckish. No matter. The morsels he'd consumed provided the knowledge to track down the tiny lost colonies that had quit their world of origin and never looked back.

Seela sought them, the relatively large and the disappointingly small. None of the colonies still survived, but the dreams and imaginings of their tiny lives lingered in the desiccated flesh of each speck. One by one, Seela sucked them dry, gorging palate and mind, and in this way, he arrived at the moon, and the last of the lostlings. He gathered up some from the dusty surface, while others had to be carefully peeled out of tombs built into the walls of a quaint vessel scarcely the size of a mote. He steamed them open, restoring their nigh microscopic minds to the fullness of episodic memory, then slurped their petty feuds and pointless arguments. Despite the tastiness of their thoughts, Seela failed to comprehend the lingering history of purpose that had brought them hither.

The ingestion of dead thoughts from this last remnant of the species disagreed with Seela. He experienced an allergic reaction to the concentration of Krenn. The resulting indigestion proved terminal. With barely a realization of his own demise, Seela wilted and passed from this plane of existence, ending his family's line, and indirectly dooming the Vegetable Worlds that would have been his domain. In the years that followed, without the guidance of an undisputed ruler, they fell into anarchy brought about by revolutionary molds and rebel fungi, and passed into history.

A peer review chorus from the *Trindle Journal of Medical Profundities* convened to hold forth on a particularly truculent cantata by a novice gastroforensiologist. In itself this failed to impress—truculence being a common feature of digestive music, particularly among the newly initiated—but this specific alimentarian had sung the ironies of the scion of vegetable royalty succumbing to a fatal ingestion of long dead mnemonic ephemerals during a period of obscure history. The combination of extremes, while the very heartbeat of irony, required investigation. It wouldn't be the first time some junior coloratura tried to pull a fast one in pursuit of a publication in the most prestigious journal to which a Trind could aspire.

The remains of the royal victim had presumably long since been retrieved by its vegetable kin, succumbed to the passage of time, or otherwise vanished from this place, but that was as the review choir expected. And yet they'd been drawn to the scene, seeking a lingering vibration of the original atopic syndrome, as the novice gastroforensiologist had evoked in his article and composition.

The choir gathered in loose formation around the footprint. Though they failed to recognize what it was, they intuited some significance to the location in relation to the cantata, the vegetable prince, and the primitive dots of memory it had consumed. They communed, allowing both the music and the medical narrative to take shape among them. Astonishingly, the combination sustained the gastroforensiologist's arguments. The irony rang out, cruel in its finality, leaving a diagnosis that suggested an expensive course of treatment, one which would prove pointless but might lead to future papers, promotion, and even grants in support of pure research. With one voice, the choir burst into a spontaneous motet of adoration, acknowledging their privilege to have reviewed such artistry, and sending a unanimous approval of the article to the editor of the journal.

Having discharged their duty, the chorus abandoned its unity, retreating to the anonymity of the disparate identity of its membership of Trindle physicians, medical researchers, and choral directors. After they vanished, a few lingering notes of the novice's composition clung to the edges of the footprint, like blue photons enmeshed in the syrup of a solar wind, but only for an instant, and then these too faded.

A library protocol, the sort of officious and untiring bit of code that kept the great machine at the heart of the galaxy from winding down, had been seeking the mysterious and inspiring mark referenced in a footnote from a member of the peer review that had signed off on the piece of antigen consequence art that sparked a revolution among aesthetes for several million years. Like most algorithms, this particular library protocol had eschewed heuristics that might have allowed it to eliminate ninety percent of the false loci reported as containing the desired mark, preferring to investigate each one, chugging along strings of folded vacuum, exhausting sufficient conceptual fuel to power the dreaming of at least three medium stars. Library protocols are dogmatically thorough that way.

It had reassembled the academic lineage of each member of the review chorus and evaluated their descendants' genetic dispositions, musical tendencies, and medical proclivities. Beginning at the galactic core, it had proceeded through its list of loci in an ever-widening spiral, rejecting locus after locus, until at last arriving at a cold and airless moon orbiting a lifeless world. Here it found some seventy-seven points of corroboration, fifty-three more than the next best locus. It immediately sent a signal back to the great machine with a single message glyph: Success!

After each of its previous stops the library protocol had been free to move on, squirting a glyph core-ward to update the great machine of its status. Now, having achieved its goal, it had no choice but to settle in and wait. In time the great machine would respond with new directives. Perhaps, now that the lost locus had been found, a renaissance of research would result and scholars and music lovers would swarm to this obscure place. Perhaps an academic institute would be established in the name of the Trind artist, though a quick review of library systems revealed not a single citation of that worthy in the past six hundred thousand years. In fact, even among historical synthesists, interest in antigen consequence art had faded from academic interest since the protocol had begun its quest. Barely a terabyte of new journal articles had been generated on even tangential topics.

Caught up in the frenzy of its quest, the library protocol had failed to keep current with the relevant literature. Only now, as it waited amidst the dust, did it begin to explore—via judicious use of quantum-level info-squirts—the new directions of information that had entered the galaxy's libraries in lieu of the field that had defined its purpose.

Many regimes of servitors of the great machine had come and gone in the time the library protocol had been about its business. Organic, inorganic, phantasmal, even conceptual support staff had cycled from probation through retirement, caring for the vast records complex of the great machine. It was unlikely any individual among them had the slightest awareness of the trillions of library protocols that had been released on their specific missions throughout the galaxy, let alone this one in particular. It was only when a protocol accomplished its task and reported in that anyone might become aware, and be dazzled at the outcome and the influx of long-sought knowledge. Or not.

A terse two-glyph message, "budget exceeded," was the only reply from the great machine. To even a simple creation as the library protocol it spoke volumes. There would be no renaissance, no institute. The entire area of research had long since been discredited and forgotten. New budget priorities dictated new agenda, and these did not include the expense of revamping a far-off protocol. The reply, witnessed in passing by some unknown servitor of the great machine, decommissioned the library protocol and snuffed out its algorithms, leaving only a momentary flicker of recursive data that had once been self-aware.

A paradigm shift of planetary consciousnesses brought on a terrible backlash of fiduciary compliance inquiries that not even the galaxy's most gargantuan—let alone those that were merely great—machines could survive unscathed. Cometary particulates were harvested, imbued with low animal cunning and accounting skills, and unleashed upon the trails of flagrant misuse of data funds. The process was slow, even by civil service standards.

By the time the auditing particulates reached Luna, the galaxy had lost any recollection of any record of any individual that had ever known that the former great machine of the galaxy had permitted an investigation. The trail itself would have been lost to even the most ardent of temporal sniffers, had the obscurity of its location not caused it to stand out, the only data point flagged for possible fraud or abuse in a dully average arm of the galaxy.

Like most audits, this one took far longer than required, yielded nothing of interest, and had been completely unnecessary. And yet . . . the particulates remained. They attempted to resurrect the pathetic strands of pseudo consciousness that had been a wastefully expensive library protocol, but failed. That caused no surprise, though there were signs that the thing had lingered, maintaining some fragment of existence far beyond its specifications, though how or why could not be discerned.

This portion of the galactic audit completed, these particulates should have discorporated, per standard procedure. Instead they rejoined their brethren, the tale of their mundane audit becoming a bit of lore among their kind that perseverated as a regulatory fable passed from generation to generation, unremarkable yet nonetheless somehow compelling.

A coterie of proto-godlings transitioned into reality at the site, their manifestations as ephemeral as ghosts, constantly shifting through the archetypal forms of past sapients of the galaxy. A tutor accompanied them, a docent to service their yearning for insight and understanding to better guide them in their impending deocracy. She took a form of an ever-cycling rain of liquid hydrogen, speaking to her pupils in a language that used the position and speed and orientation and shape of droplets as you might use sound and pitch and the shape of your lips to form words. Her very existence was an unending discussion conveying many simultaneous topics, all interwoven in complexities of time and meaning beyond human understanding but well within the grasp of the young beings in her charge.

"What do you sense here?" she rained, a portion of herself beginning a new line of conversation. "Tell me why I have brought you to this place."

Though each could ignite stars or bring entire eco-systems into existence, the proto-godlings had long since learned not to answer in haste. After a decade, one of the younger and most precocious said, "Something happened here."

The cascade of hydrogen contracted, casting the equivalent of a withering gaze upon her students. "Something is always happening, everywhere, at every instant. If nothing is happening, that very absence is significant, and thus may be considered as happening."

"No, no, that's not what I meant," said the proto-godling, its appearance flickering at greater speed through a range of lifeforms, each more distraught than the one before it. "Something happened here that made a difference—I know, everything makes a difference, somehow, to something—but this mattered to the galaxy. This was a Moment."

"Good. We have studied Moments. What can you tell me of this one?"

"It is like the Face of Netteya," said a second student. "Though it has long since been destroyed, its locus fills all who occupy that place with a sense of peace. All sapience is drawn to it, and those who encounter it go to war to claim it."

"It is nothing like that," said the precocious one. "It's ... different?"

"Are you asking me or telling me?"

"I ... I'm telling you. It's not like the other Moments you've shown us. The significance of this locus is unlabeled and not apparent. But it impinges upon the mind even so."

"Exactly," said the tutor. As one the proto-godlings sighed with relief. "Unlabeled Moments are rare, and this is one of the oldest of them. Intelligent beings find themselves pulled here. The fabric of the galaxy causes this to happen, but does not explain itself. Not knowing the real reason, they look around and latch onto whatever explanation seems plausible. They routinely err in their theories, reifying their mistakes, and leaving them for others to build upon. Open your perceptions to this place, sort through the stories and confusions. Who can tell me when this Moment really began, and why?"

A century passed, and then another. The proto-godlings conferred, and as a group thrust their youngest member forward with an answer.

"The mark on the surface," he said. "A physical being stood there, long ago."

"That's right," said their tutor. "And the galaxy has chosen to preserve that imprint. But why? Of all the races that have grown to sapience and entered space, why is this one significant?"

The proto-godlings conferred again. They allocated resources among themselves, exploring the intervening ages an instant at a time. Such was their power that they relived the communications, the delusions, the misperceptions of every sapient mind that had occupied this locus back to the very beginning of the Moment. They concluded nothing and once again pushed the youngest forward.

"I don't know," he said, trembling in anticipation of the tutor's wrath.

"And you cannot inherit this galaxy until you do," she said. "Now pay close attention.

"When the galaxy was young, an intelligent species evolved on one of this solar system's planets. They developed the means to leave their world. This standing place that you have identified, is where they paused. Who they were, whatever else they accomplished is lost to us."

The youngest, the most precocious of them, manifested an image that might have been a child of the species that had first stood here. "Tutor, I do not understand. There are other lost species. Many others left their worlds before another species came to them first. What is so special about this one that it caused a Moment to occur?"

"They believed themselves alone in the universe, and yet set forth to prove themselves wrong," she said. "They turned away from everything they knew, to experience what they could not know. This Moment is not because they stood here."

"What then?"

"When one takes a step, it is possible to step back. In fact, it is a common occurrence." She paused to draw their attention. "That's not what happened here."

The proto-godlings peered at the footprint, tunneling past the perceptions and experiences of all the other beings that the Moment had drawn to this locus.

"I still do not understand, Tutor. Why then is this a Moment?"

With a sprinkling of light rain the tutor gathered her charges around her, smiling through the hydrogen of her words.

"This is where they jumped off."

Lightning Source UK Ltd.
Milton Keynes UK
15 August 2009

142730UK00001B/27/P